Alan Dunn was born and bred ~~on the~~
fringes of the Lake Dis~~trict.~~ ~~He won the~~
Ian St James Award-~~winning~~ ~~and has~~
been anthologized tw~~ice and widely~~
published. He has be~~en a~~ ~~folk~~
administrator, insurance ~~clerk, folk~~
musician and teacher ~~but now he~~ enjoys
running, cycling and colle~~cting toy babies.~~

Die-Cast

Alan Dunn

PIATKUS

Copyright © 2000 by Alan Dunn

First published in Great Britain in 2000 by
Judy Piatkus (Publishers) Ltd of
5 Windmill Street, London W1T 2JA
email:info@piatkus.co.uk

This edition published 2001

The moral right of the author has been asserted

A catalogue record for this book is available from the British Library

ISBN 0 7499 3254 6

Set in Times by
Action Publishing Technology Ltd, Gloucester

Printed and bound in Great Britain by
Cox & Wyman Ltd, Reading, Berkshire

This book is dedicated to my father Norman, the only singing Trade Union Officer to compere a TV variety series. With a dad like that . . .

Thanks, as usual, to Jan for everything; to Diana Tyler for her endless energy on my behalf; to my sons, Michael and Peter, for making me laugh; to the poetic Wild Women; and to the Caldew Boys – James, Phil, Lee, Chris, Bob and Dougal Mac – who insisted they be mentioned.

Beforehand

Beneath the fraying, light-fringed blanket of midsummer night, in the still heat and quiet with an hour before dawn, it's cool near the river. Darkness hides from streetlamps reflected in oily grey water. Curved waves slap, lazy and sensual, on timbers bulwarked deep in the riverbed.

On cloudy nights the sky never loses its haemorrhage of pink, the stigma of the city beneath. But tonight the sky is clear. To the north there's a stain of blue, it fades overhead to a sullen southern blackness where only the brightest stars are visible, those able to outshine the haze of smoke and fumes.

Throughout the city bodies turn and sweat, throw sheets to the floor; windows left open admit no breeze. Old people, faces lined and tannined, gasp and long for winter. The heatwave is in its third week.

High above the river rise the bridges. One is a green steel arch supported by towers of pale concrete; another moves the rapid transit system from bank to bank in a sweeping catenary; a third is built on stone pillars islanded in the river, it has two decks, the lower for road, the upper for rail. It grumbles beneath the early morning express whose seats lie empty or sleeping.

The river's north bank once held wharves and shipping offices, customs houses and sailors' pubs, brothels and dark alleys and warehouses. Then the world discovered Polish coal, Indian cotton, Korean ships, American chemicals; and the tall, steep-roofed Georgian buildings were abandoned, left to grow senile. Damp and rot invaded, pigeons clattered through broken windows, rats crawled into crumbling sewers. Starlings found companionship and winter warmth on ledges, jackdaws nested in chimney pots with no fear of fire below. Weeds grew between loose-limed bricks.

The picturesque decay was banished by the property boom. Offices and apartments grew within the genteel shells of the old foursquare buildings fronting the river. Dockside became fashionable, the river once again became the centre of the city. New restaurants served stylishly

3

small portions to the newly wealthy. A new theatre performed for the newly literate. And in the basement of an old flour warehouse, the thick-sleepered floors above held aloft by strong iron pillars, a nightclub opened.

Its name, *Ladders*, was chosen carefully; from a basement the only direction is up, and the implication – that climbing (both business and social) was welcome, important even – wasn't lost on its clientele. A high entry charge did little to deter those intent on spending money on loud music, alcohol and discreetly purveyed drugs. Frequent – though subtle – changes in decor, a complete annual refit and an acknowledgement that money could buy anything kept the club fashionable. Those who went there regularly were pleased to be recognised and ushered into private lounges; those who saved and then queued for the privilege of mingling with their betters appreciated a different, improved, exclusive world.

Ladders now occupies three storeys. It comprises two dance areas, four bars, a casino, two restaurants and several rooms whose privacy is never breached and whose bed linen is always clean. Above are two floors of offices whose occupants control the nightclub and many other leisure interests throughout the city and beyond. All are legitimate. The casinos and betting shops are clean in all senses of the word. The cinemas and nightclubs, the bingo halls and video shops, franchised fast food restaurants, amusement arcades, all are subject to regular inspection by local and national authorities. All pass every test. Even the sex shops are considered, so far as is possible, wholesome. All income and expenditure is clearly annotated, the auditors (a respectable national company) agree that the accounting systems are both accurate and well-maintained.

On the fourth floor – the sixth storey, allowing for the basement and sub-basement – the illegitimate businesses are controlled. Prostitution, drugs, protection rackets, car ringing, receiving stolen goods, computer hacking, the provision of guns and those willing to use them, all are

4

organised by men and women looking no different from those in the two floors below. There's no connection between the different layers of this organisation; they operate independently. But those who know (and others who think they know but have no proof) acknowledge that they're linked by one man.

In semi-darkness he stalks the room. He's naked in the cool, conditioned air, his skin a piebald of whites – moon and snow, down and ice, cloud and milk – stretched tight over hard muscles and strong bones. He has no hair on his body save that framing his genitals, and that the same grey-white as the pony-tailed hair on his head. If those strands were dark he'd look thirty instead of forty-five. Only his eyes tell the truth, they're too weary for middle age, their rings and circles add fifteen years.

He crosses the room with the grace of a dancer, the elegance of a fighter. He switches on the light at a wide, polished desk. He presses a button on a piece of machinery in front of him, a mixing desk with sliding controls and small dials. Lights flicker red and green. He sits down on a leather chair draped with a towel.

Ahead of him, at eye level, a bank of four television screens arranged in the shape of a squat capital 'T' come to life, crazed with black and white lightning.

'Let's review tonight's performance,' he says to himself. He reaches to his right and touches a switch to usher in the dissonance of experimental jazz; his fingers tap a rhythm which ignores the music. The television screens cease their madness. Each of the top three shows a different view of the same object, a large bed decked in a clean, white unruffled sheet. The fourth screen is for the master edit.

A ripple of light across all the screens shows they're running tape at fast-forward, but this is halted as a man moves jerkily on to the bed in all of the televisions. He's dressed in a white towelling gown, his grey-white hair is tied in a pony tail. He leans back and glances briefly at each of the cameras (an emotionless acknowledgement of

- their presence) then decorates his face with a smile and looks away. His fingers move like a centipede's legs against the sheets. On screen he's the actor. Watching himself, he's the editor.

'I need more cameras,' he says regretfully, 'I seem to remember her dancing was rather seductive, even if it was prompted by alcohol. A pity not to have it on tape.'

Once again the movements of the actor quicken. A button touched brings back normal time. The actor gestures; to the editor the invitation seems out of place, it's a lure, too gaudy, too sweet. But it serves its purpose. From a pool of darkness beyond the actor's back steps the body of a woman, only her torso and legs can be seen. She sways from side to side. The hair between her legs is rich and dark, a faint line of it runs up to her navel.

'Slightly wider angles might also help,' he says, switching the views from the upper screens to the master screen and finding none to his liking. But he's patient. He has a good memory. He knows what will come.

The actor, with a laziness born of confidence and practised ease, leans back on the bed. He pulls at the neatly tied towelling belt with one hand and his gown falls aside to reveal his erection.

'Oh, Priapus,' the editor whispers. He watches the screens intently. The actor slides backwards, removing his gown as he does so. He's followed by the woman, crawling after him on all fours. Her dark hair hides her face, but by skilful use of different camera angles the editor manages to capture the sway of her breasts as she moves hungrily up the bed, the curve of her long back, the roundness of her backside as she lowers her head greedily to the actor's erection.

The telephone rings. On screen the actor is reaching down to turn the woman, aware of the three camera positions. He presses her flank and she turns on to her side, his erection still in her mouth. He touches the inside of her thigh and her legs open, he touches again and they open wider. The camera devours her.

6

The editor picks up the telephone, still watching the twisting, turning bodies in front of him.

'Yes? No, you didn't wake me.' His voice is even, measured, as if the words are being produced automatically while his mind is working elsewhere.

'What am I doing? Did you ring just to ask what I'm doing?'

He jams the receiver between his shoulder and the side of his head, uses his fingers to manipulate angles, views, movements.

'Well, if you must know, I've just started watching a video. No, it's not a sexy video.' He glances briefly down at his penis, small between his legs. 'In fact it's not arousing at all.'

The actor moves, detaches himself from his partner, then enters her from behind. Her face is buried in a pillow but his hands reach beneath her to pull at her nipples and she moves enthusiastically.

'I'd go as far as saying that it's quite boring. Now perhaps you'll tell me what you really want?'

He presses a button. On all four screens the motion ceases.

'He's rung you tonight? Woke you up? My heart bleeds. And why did he do that?'

He turns down the volume of the music to leave the redundant whisper of the loudspeakers; a distant car horn; the hum of electricity in the mixing desk; a fluting of song as a blackbird greets the dawn too early; and the shrill, small, Martian chattering of the telephone.

'I'm not surprised he's worried, it would be unusual if he wasn't worried. But we can deal with it.' He glances at the screens, impatient, eager to continue with his task. 'I know someone who can do the job the way we want it done. Do you have a pen? Good, write this down . . .'

He gives his instructions then puts the phone down. His life continues as it always has done. He rewards – four months ago the pub manager who recognised a drunk in his

7

bar as a city councillor and, instead of throwing him out, paid for a taxi to take him home, received a thousand pound bonus; he manipulates – a month later the same councillor convinced his colleagues that they should approve planning permission for demolishing a listed building; he persuades – his suggestion last month that a local builder offer a substantial discount to prevent 'unpleasantness.' was accepted; and he punishes – the squatter, still in the building even as demolition work began, was encouraged to leave until his red woollen hat was matched by the blood seeping from his mouth, nose and ears.

He's oblivious to time, to weather and to seasons, to darkness and to light. But he turns his head slightly as the blackbird, ridiculously adventurous, a refugee from the shrubbery lining the river walkway on the south bank, perches briefly on his windowsill and begins to sing again. He sees the beginnings of daylight outside his window. He ignores the birdsong and the day and returns to his work. On all four screens the woman is approaching her first orgasm.

And the river flows down to the sea.

Tuesday

Chapter One

Every morning when I come into the office I open my brief-case, take out a pen and roll it across the desk. I leave it where it lies. It would be a simple act to straighten it, to place it in the centre of the blotting paper, parallel to either the long or the short sides of the desk. But I force myself to leave it alone. For the past week it's remained exactly where I left it, from nine in the morning until five thirty in the evening. I consider this an achievement.

I try to keep busy. It's best when I'm busy, but I've had no work for a week. That's why the pen's an achievement.

Yesterday I had a phone call. The woman made an appointment to see me, here in the office. She's late, I'm beginning to think she won't appear, and that makes me nervous. My pen is making sweet, urgent 'touch me' noises.

To keep my mind from my pen I'm playing a computer game. The computer bleats, an aggravating, childish note. I'd like a soundboard but can't afford one. I'm manipulating a figure on the screen, it's walking up to a castle. Against the castle walls are four ladders of different sizes allowing access to windows in the walls. There's a gate guarded by a portcullis, but the drawbridge leading to it has been destroyed. Billy (the figure on the screen is emphatically, empathically me) can climb the ladders or take them down, use them to cross the moat and enter through the

-portcullis. If I hadn't discarded the rope two turns earlier I could have tied two ladders together and gained access to a higher window, avoiding travelling through the dangerous lower rooms of the castle.

The aim, according to the instructions, is to rescue the princess. But in a week of playing I haven't even seen her. The castle is guarded by dragons controlled by the snake-king, and I've been eaten or poisoned every time I've played.

I make my decision. I select the second tallest ladder and begin to climb, but I'm interrupted by a knock on the door. I close down quickly and switch off.

'It's open,' I shout, 'come in.' The pad on my desk is headed 'Caroline Ratcliffe'. Her voice on the telephone was warm, friendly, she answered my questions easily and clearly. And her accent? East London, I decided, but she hadn't lived there for a long time. There was a touch of mid-Atlantic in her pronunciation, though not in her vocabulary. Age? More difficult. She sounded younger than me, in her early thirties. But it's difficult to tell anything from women's voices, they hide rather than reveal information. As the door swings towards me I realise I misjudged her age. She must be in her mid-forties, a decade older than me; but she hides it well. Her make-up is subtle. She smiles. I return the smile, step around the desk and offer my hand.

'Mrs Ratcliffe?'

'You must be Mr Oliphant. Pleased to meet you.'

We shake hands. Her fingers are slim, her nails long and painted red, her hand smooth and warm. Her wedding ring is wide and thick, her engagement ring studded with diamonds. She's wearing tight jeans and a baggy white T-shirt, loafers, sunglasses on her forehead. She's tanned, but not to excess. She's carrying a brown leather shoulderbag. Her eyes are curious. She's paying as much attention to me and my surroundings as I am to her.

'Would you like a glass of cold lemonade?' I ask. 'I've some cans in the washroom, lying in a basin full of cold water. It's the coolest place in the building.

'That would be nice.'

'No sooner said. If you'll excuse me . . .' I work my way round the desk and pass behind her, go out into the corridor. We – the tenants on this floor – asked the landlord for permission to install a vending machine. Nothing happened. It's the way things don't go around here, improvements of any sort are frowned upon. Still, the rent's low and the leases are long, though I'm not sure which is cause and which effect.

I find two cans and go back in.

'Would you like a glass?' I ask.

'The can will do.' She pulls back the ring, drinks deeply, unselfconsciously. 'I didn't realise how thirsty I was. It's too hot.'

There's nothing I can do to help in that direction, the windows are open but there's no breeze. I nod and sip at my own can, put it down to signal the end of our small talk.

'I'd like to go over what you told me yesterday,' I say, 'then you can let me know a few more details.'

'Sure. Go ahead.' There *is* something American in her voice.

'Okay.' I examine my pad. 'You own a small double-glazing firm . . .'

'Not own. I'm a director of Winner Profile Systems, the company was bought recently by Ratcliffe Holdings, that's my husband's family business. I was sent in, oh, just over a month ago, to liven WPS up, get it running more efficiently. But I don't actually own any shares in WPS.'

I write it down. 'You mentioned you're suffering from vandalism and you want me to look at your security systems. Give you some advice. Quote for carrying out some work.'

'Yes.'

'I hope you don't mind me asking, but how did you find me? It helps me prioritise my advertising.' Any lie will do, I can't afford to advertise.

'You were recommended. I asked the police to come round, the crime prevention officer said he wasn't allowed

- to promote any individual firm, he said to get a selection from yellow pages. Then he scribbled your name and number down on a piece of paper.'

'The CPO? Can you remember his name?'

'No. My factory manager spoke to him.'

'Probably Tommy Wardell. He said he'd get me some leads. He's a good lad.' I take another drink. From outside the open window comes a machine-gun clatter of pigeons' wings.

'I charge £200 a day for my time,' I say, quickly. I don't like talking money. 'The survey should take half a day, allowing for a site visit and subsequent pricing. I can call round just after twelve and have a quotation with you by five. Then it's up to you.'

'That sounds fair.' She doesn't seem put off by the price, I should have asked for more.

'You'd better give me the address then. And your phone number at WPS.'

She pulls out a sheet of headed paper from her shoulderbag, hands it to me.

'It's all on there,' she says, 'we're down by the river on the south side . . .'

'I'll find it.' I rise to my feet and hold out my hand. 'You'll be there when I do the survey, won't you? I may need a decision on options which could affect the price.'

'I'll be there.'

She shakes my hand again, turns to leave. The interview – that's what it was, both of us seeking information – seems to have terminated abruptly. People have told me I'm like that, I cut them off, don't have time for niceties. Or it could be that I'm naturally rude. But I'm professional, I know what the job needs. I can smile and ingratiate myself when I need to.

'Oh, Mrs Ratcliffe?'

'Yes?'

'Your name, it seems familiar and I think I've remembered why. I read that a firm called Ratcliffe was taking

14

over sponsoring the London marathon. Or was it one of those televised fund-raising events? Anyway, there was a photograph of the chairman, Charles Ratcliffe. That wouldn't be your husband, would it?'

'No, Mr Oliphant, it wouldn't. My husband's uncle is chair of Ratcliffe Holdings and his first name is Alfred.'

'So your husband isn't a Charles either?'

'James, Mr Oliphant. Jimmy to his friends.'

'Oh. I'll have to check it out. When I find out who it was I'll let you know.'

'Thank you, Mr Oliphant.'

'You're welcome, Mrs Ratcliffe.'

I watch her leave, close the door behind her and deposit her can in the wastepaper bin. I open the top drawer of the filing cabinet and take out a duster and a spraycan of cleaner, fire it at the barely discernible marks the can has left on the desk. I polish until the desk top gleams from all angles. Only then do I put the cleaner and the polish away. I pick up the phone and dial.

'Hello, Norm? Billy here ... Not so bad, thanks ... Listen, I've a job for you. I need a car and a driver for the afternoon, if it works out I might need you for the whole of the week. Can you do it? Good. Yeah, get here soon as you can. Ten minutes? See you then.'

I dial again. This time there's a long delay, I press the button marked 'hands free' and put the receiver down. The ringing tone bleeps insistently about the room. I wait.

'Who is it?' says a woman's voice.

'You took your time, Rak. It's me, Billy Oliphant.'

'I'm workin', Billy. What d'you want?'

'Information.'

'So what's new? It'll cost you this time.'

'You still owe me.'

'That's what you always bleedin' say! I've paid you back a dozen bleedin' times.'

'Once more, Rak, just once. Next time it'll be proper business, you can invoice me.'

15

'I prefer cash.'

'Cash then.'

'So what d'you want?'

'All you can find on Winner Profile Systems Limited, sometimes known as WPS.' I read out the information from the letter heading. 'Company registration number 2346721. Managing Director Mrs Caroline Ratcliffe. The address is Riverside Park, phone 8893431, fax 8873726. No e-mail.'

'Everythin' I can find? I could be on for days . . .'

'I need it by this afternoon. Four o'clock.'

'Fuck off, Billy!'

I'm good at ignoring her. 'Accounts if you can get them. Names of other directors. County court judgements, mentions in the local press, anything at all.'

'D'you want me to part the Red Sea while I'm on?'

'No. But you can also find out about Ratcliffe Holdings, I've nothing else but the name, chairman is Alfred Ratcliffe, one of the directors is James Ratcliffe. WPS was recently acquired by Ratcliffe. That's less urgent, tomorrow morning'll do.'

'Thanks.'

'If I'm not in you can fax the information through.'

'Yeah.'

'Listen, Rak. I wouldn't ask you to do it if I didn't think you were the best.'

'Yeah, I bet you say that to all the librarians you know. Look, Billy, I'll do what I can, I'm not promisin' anythin'. They get suspicious if I spend too much time on the net. Oh shit, Manny's comin' right now! I'll 'ave to go. Bye.'

'Bye,' I say to a phone already cut off. I take my briefcase from the filing cabinet and put my pen inside, snap the lid closed. I turn my chair to face the door. As I move round the desk I reposition the chair Carrie Ratcliffe vacated only moments before, turn it so it faces my own, at right angles to the desk. Like I said, I consider the pen a triumph; but leaving the seat out of place can wait for less trying times.

16

Chapter Two

The car's a Volvo, very old, shaped like a turtle shell, all curves and leather. It's in the process of being overhauled, some of the paintwork has been rubbed down and the chrome strips and badges have been removed. Its original cream colour is mixed with patches of bare metal, primer and undercoat. All the windows are open.

''Lo boss,' says Norm. He's leaning against the car, dressed in shorts and a garish shirt which can't hide his paunch. His feet are in sandals and his socks are grey, he's wearing a straw hat.

'Nice day again, boss. Says on the news it'll keep this way for at least a week.'

'That's good.' I climb into the back of the car.

'You should get yourself a hat like mine.' He pads round to the driver's door, increases the volume of his speech to make sure I hear every word. 'Keeps the sun off you. People like you'n'me, slapheads, they should watch out. Sunstroke.'

'I'll bear that in mind.'

Norm slips into the car and starts the engine. It catches first time and runs smoothly. His talents as a driver and mechanic make up for his lack of dress sense.

'Now it just so happens a friend of mine's got a large supply of straw hats just like this and he can let me have them cheap. I can get you one or two, but if you order more

17

– you might want to sell them on yourself – you get a good discount.' He pulls out into the traffic. 'By the way, where we going?'

'Riverside Park.'

'South side? You got it! Now then, as I was saying, why not buy them by the gross? I can even get someone to sell them for you, got a stall on Sundays, he could do them on commission . . .'

I listen without hearing, scribble a list of what I might need for the Ratcliffe job, the people I might need to hire, the length of time it might take to carry out the installation. Then I look out of the car, narrow my eyes against the brightness. Offices are disgorging lunchtime workers into the noon's heat. Pubs have set up tables and umbrellas. Shop doors are open wide; music pours into the streets.

'Hats isn't all that's going well at the moment, boss, there's these little fans, the battery-powered ones, now I can do them for . . .'

We twist through cobbled lanes and steep streets, curling back over our route in an attempt to beat the one-way system. Norm never seems to accelerate or brake wildly, but our motion proves efficient, relentless even. He's always in the right lane at the right time, never flustered. I can taste a faint sea breeze as we cross the river, but it's chased away by a shimmer of heat-haze and the odour of hot tarmac. Then we're southside. I can feel the sweat pooling under my arms, running down my back. I check my case, I've another shirt and a change of socks and briefs inside.

'Riverside Park's quite a size, boss. Anywhere in particular?'

'Winner Profile Systems, WPS, they make plastic windows . . .'

'Yeah? I read about them, they've just got a couple of contracts from the council to replace all the windows and doors on the Bentley Estate.'

Norm sees my puzzlement in the mirror.

18

'Bentley, boss, remember? The riots three years ago?' Ram-raiding? It's a hell of a size, must be near on a thousand houses plus four tower blocks. What's it cost to put new windows in a house? Four thousand? That's four million quid straight off. Then there's the blocks, how they'll manage those I've no idea but it must be another half a million each, perhaps more. Say six, seven million altogether. They having problems?'

'Problems? I don't know, Norm, that's why I'm going to look round.' I should read more, then I wouldn't be so worried about why Caroline Ratcliffe didn't mention that WPS had just won a contract worth seven million pounds. I don't have to make a note to ask her about it, my curiosity has a short half-life, it degenerates rapidly into suspicion. And I'm suspicious.

We're in Riverside. I look out on the low, squat concrete buildings of a sixties industrial estate. Some have no roofs, their forecourts are sprinkled with weeds, their windows broken. Others have been divided into smaller lots, let to scrap merchants and waste-paper collectors, back street garages awash with oil, one-man joiner's shops with unpainted plywood shutters. Once it must have been busy, thriving, a place of optimism. Now it's dishevelled, dusty, slowly dissolving. There are few people on the streets, few cars parked or driving. A pack of mongrels is watching two of its members mate enthusiastically.

Norm turns the car through two gates in a tall mesh fence topped with barbed wire. A dozen cars are baking in front of a two-storey building. At its side, where corrugated steel fascia meets functional grey walls, are three doors; two are small, people-sized, while the third is large and open. A large truck could enter easily. Close to the building are two tall silos, stainless steel the colour of the blue-white sky. Pipes lead from them through the wall of the factory.

The rest of the compound is strewn with bleached weeds and dying thistles, spines of grass, all brown as the dusty soil beneath.

19

'I was hoping there'd be a tree, somewhere with a bit of shade,' says Norm. 'I'm gonna cook sitting here waiting for you.' He pulls the Volvo to a halt, opens the door immediately and reaches into the rear to open the back door as well. I take my dictaphone from my case, check the battery level then motion to Norm to ensure his silence.

'Winner Profile Systems, tape one, side one, property profile. Site approximately 200 metres by 250 metres, chain-link perimeter fence, access through double chain gates, padlock fitted but not in use at time of survey.' I climb out of the car, squint against the sunlight. Sweat beads on my forehead. I stroll towards the fence.

'Fence in poor condition, breaks visible from fifteen metres. Average height two metres, topped with two horizontal strands of barbed wire.' I walk towards the nearest corner.

'Side one, containing gates, heading clockwise one – no, two – stanchions corroded, soil excavated from two concrete stanchion bases. Soil dug away from base of fence fifty metres from gate.'

I continue my monologue as I walk the perimeter. It takes almost fifteen minutes. I stop frequently to push against the fence or examine the metal links. I spend a further few minutes examining the gates. Then I return to the car. Norm has reclined the passenger seat and covered it with a towel, he's stretched out on it, his face covered with his straw hat. The radio is on, set low to a local news programme. The commentator is talking, inevitably, about the weather.

'Got everything you need, boss?'

'Yes.'

'Know how long you'll be inside?'

'As long as it takes.'

'Yeah, thought you'd say that.'

'I'll tell them you're here, waiting. I'll ask them to send out a drink, you could ask if anyone else has been round to measure up for a quotation.'

Norm's hat nods, I hope he'll remember. I feel dirty, sweaty, I check but can see no marks or stains on my shirt. It might be hotter still inside the offices, inside the factory, there's no point in changing yet. That morning I chose the lightest slacks I own, now I feel their material clinging to me as I head across the car-park. All the office windows are gaping wide, the entrance door's wedged open. Inside, though, it's mercifully shady, comparatively cool. A vague remembrance of a breeze blows through the reception area.

'Hello sir, can I help you?'

The man approaching is young, despite the heat he's wearing a tie neatly knotted and his shirt sleeves buttoned down. His hair is well cut, his smile broad and bright. He's a salesman, cast from a standard mould and polished, brilliant, uncirculated. If he can sell double glazing in a heatwave like this he'll be worth his commission. I'm tempted to pretend to be a potential customer to see how good he is, but the heat and lack of time conspire against me.

'I've an appointment to see Mrs Ratcliffe,' I say. If the salesman is disappointed then he's well trained enough not to show it.

'I'll tell her you're here, sir. What name is it, please?'

'Oliphant. Billy Oliphant.'

'Thank you, Mr Oliphant.' He gestures to a sofa. 'Please take a seat. There's some coffee brewing, or I can get you something cooler.'

'Later, perhaps. But I've a driver outside, he'd probably welcome a drink.'

The salesman enters the nearest office, leaving the door open. 'I've a Mr Oliphant to see Carrie.' I notice the use of the familiar name. 'Could one of you take his driver some lemonade?'

I pick up a brochure showing the company's products. I also manage to slip a copy of the price-list from the salesman's desk into my jacket pocket. I like to know about my potential customers.

21

The salesman reappears. 'I'll show you to Mrs Ratcliffe's office, Mr Oliphant. Follow me please.' The journey isn't far. A short corridor, two or three doors to either side. The wall on the left is block-built, that on the right is made largely of glass in PVC frames, doors spaced at regular intervals. In the offices thus formed the occupants are working hard, no one looks up. At the end of the corridor there's a flight of stairs, the salesman bounds up them. I follow at a more leisurely pace. There's a small landing at the top from which leads another corridor, directly above that on the ground floor, but ahead is a wooden door, ajar. I can see Carrie Ratcliffe behind the desk, head bent over a computer print-out, talking urgently into a telephone. She's wearing glasses.

'Go straight in, Mr Oliphant,' says the salesman. He turns and leaves before I can mumble my thanks.

'Mr Oliphant, how nice to see you.' Carrie Ratcliffe's phone call is finished, she's out of her seat, her glasses and pen laid to one side. We shake hands and I allow myself to be guided to a seat.

'Something to drink? I've lemonade, cola, fresh orange juice? Or if you'd prefer something stronger . . .'

'Just water, please. With ice, if possible.'

'Perrier?'

'I prefer tap.'

'Brave man. Tap water it is, with ice. You don't mind if I have a whisky?'

'Not at all.'

My host heads for one of the two doors in the wall behind me. She doesn't close it, I can see into a small galley kitchen. The other door, I presume, hides the executive washroom. Like the rest of the building, the office is clean, freshly painted, functional rather than decorative. It's at the corner of the building. To my right the windows opening onto the car-park are almost hidden by vertical blinds; the wall behind Carrie Ratcliffe's desk is plain, three large photographs of conservatories are displayed

22

together with a WPS logo, red intertwined letters; and to the left is another bank of blinds. Within the room there are two desks, a table with eight seats around it and, in the corner behind me, to the left of the door, a long, low, fat sofa and a coffee table holding three or four trade magazines. It's all standard issue middle-executive furniture. And nothing personal, no photographs.

'I saw you looking at the fence,' says Carrie Ratcliffe from the kitchen, emptying ice from a tray.

'Yes,' I reply, more for something to say than as part of the conversation.

'And?'

'And what, Mrs Ratcliffe?'

'What did you think? About the fence? And please, don't call me Mrs Ratcliffe. Everyone here calls me Carrie, I'd appreciate it if you would too. Since it's possible we're going to work together.' She hands me a glass, takes her own and sits down behind the desk. She looks more tired than she did only a few hours before. She almost looks her age.

'The fence is a token gesture, Mrs Ratcliffe . . .' I don't want to upset her by continuing to use her surname, but there are some ground rules I won't break. I'm not being unfriendly, I just need to keep some distance between me and my clients. My potential clients. So she'll have to get used to me calling her 'Mrs Ratcliffe'.

'The fence is nothing more than a gesture at security, as a deterrent to anyone who wants to get into the grounds it's useless.'

If she's upset by my need for formality she doesn't show it.

'Would it be expensive to repair? To get up to standard?'

'Why bother? Yes, you could repair it. But people would still be able to get through.'

'But Billy – you don't mind if I call you Billy? – how do we keep the vandals out?'

I do mind being called Billy. My employees call me

23

boss. My parents called me William. My clients call me Mr Oliphant; regular clients might be allowed to call me Bill. Only close friends get to call me Billy, and Carrie Ratcliffe isn't one of those. Nor is WPS a client, not yet. But I've a feeling that however I pitch my price, whatever work I suggest doing, I'll get this job. It is only a feeling, one which I could test by standing up and leaving, refusing to tender for the work. But I won't do that, I need the money. Still, it unsettles me enough for me not to suggest that Carrie Ratcliffe uses my surname. And I have to work hard to remember what I was talking about.

'How do we keep the vandals out? Well, Mrs Ratcliffe, first of all you answer some questions, about your company, about the damage being caused. We see what the problems are. Then we find the solutions.'

'But the vandals . . .'

'Not just vandals, Mrs Ratcliffe, regular attacks like this are more than vandalism. The attacks are symptoms; I want to find the cause. Okay?'

'I suppose so.'

'Good. I need to look round, of course. But first . . .' I take out my pocket recorder and set it on the desk. 'You don't mind, do you? It's easier than writing everything down.'

'No, not at all. Be my guest.'

I switch the machine on. 'Interview with Mrs Ratcliffe of Winner Profile Systems. Now then, you told me WPS was recently acquired by Ratcliffe Holdings, a family company of which your husband is director.'

'That's right.'

'Why did Ratcliffe Holdings buy WPS?'

'Pardon?'

'Why did they buy the company? It's not a major national manufacturer. Not even in the local big league. So why?'

'It has a good reputation. Good balance sheet, good profits.'

24

'Is that all?'

'Mr Oliphant, I don't see . . .'

Stress alters the way people think, the way they talk. Carrie Ratcliffe returns to addressing me by my surname, and I start wondering why my question made her anxious.

'The question is relevant, I assure you.'

Carrie Ratcliffe swallows, sips her whisky but says nothing.

'Insider information, perhaps?' I continue. 'Friends in local government? Someone who let slip that WPS were about to land a very big contract?'

She's still silent. She looks at the tape machine, then at me. I press the stop button.

'Thank you, Billy. I can see you've done some homework, you seem to know a little about WPS. But you're wrong about insider knowledge. Someone in Ratcliffe was sharp, that's all, did their homework, guessed that WPS was going to be awarded a contract. A large contract, over five million pounds . . .'

'Is that all? Surely it's nearer seven or eight.' I add a million to Norm's estimate. Carrie Ratcliffe's anxiety shows in her face, my guesses must be reasonably accurate.

'Eight and a half,' she says, 'to the nearest half million.' She leans forward and lowers her voice; I copy her movement.

'Let me explain,' she says. 'The local council knew what they were doing with this, the specification for the contract was very strict. The requirements for the profile were stringent, triple chamber and 2.5 mill thick extrusions from ICI polymer. They wanted steel and aluminium reinforcements, internal beading, co-extruded gaskets, they wanted company ISO 9002 and they wanted supplier ISO 9002. Do you know what that means?'

I shake my head. 'I haven't understood a word you've said.'

Carrie smiles her sympathy. 'I felt the same way until a few weeks ago, but I learned quickly. Basically, the council drew up a damn good, watertight specification for top quality windows and doors complying with all relevant British and European Standards. Normally that means one of the major profile manufacturers gets the work, either directly or through one of their client firms. But not this time.'

'Why WPS, then?'

'Okay, let's go from the beginning. Windows and doors are made from lengths of hollow uPVC profile ...' She notices my raised eyebrows. 'uPVC? It stands for unplasticised Poly-Vinyl-Chloride, let's call it plastic for short. In its raw form it comes in grains or powder. The polymer is heated and pushed through stainless steel dies to make lengths of profile, the profile's made into windows and doors. Okay?'

I nod like a guilty schoolboy.

'Good. WPS used to extrude their own profile, but they'd been tinkering with the designs and had just ordered a complete set of new extrusion dies from Evans Steel, a foundry owned by Ratcliffe. Someone at WPS got talking to someone at Evans about the quality of the new profiles they'd be able to produce, that person talked to Ratcliffe, enquiries were made. Ratcliffe has friends in many places, including the consultants who helped draw up the council's specification. Ratcliffe knew the newly designed profiles would meet the specification before WPS did. They bought in, they bought cheaply. Now they stand to make a fortune.'

I whistle. 'No wonder you wanted the tape switching off.'

'Nothing I've mentioned is illegal. WPS still had to tender for the work. They still had to get the price right.'

'But the specification was so tightly drawn that none of the other window firms could do it.'

'That's one way of looking at it. They could re-tool. Or they could buy in expensive profile from abroad. But that costs money.'

'So your price could be high. Clever stuff. But some of those other firms, some of your competitors, they've got muscles.'

'You think they might be behind the attacks? No, they can't do anything, they've their reputations to think about.'

'Local firms, then? Smaller firms?'

'Perhaps.'

I switch on the recorder again. I've decided to move in a different direction.

'Mrs Ratcliffe, you've been here a month?'

'Five weeks. Though I first came up about three months ago, with my husband, just after the acquisition. There was a team of accountants, they looked at the books. He brought me along because I'd never been here before.'

'And when did the attacks start?'

'There's always been a problem with vandalism, over the whole estate. But the first threats came about four weeks ago. And the attacks seem concentrated on us.'

'So it got worse just after you arrived?'

'Yes.'

'What's your position in Ratcliffe Holdings, Mrs Ratcliffe?'

'I told you, I don't work for Ratcliffe. I work for WPS.'

'So how did you get the job? Do you have experience in this type of work?'

'In the widest sense, yes. I've a degree in business studies, I've worked in multinationals – that's how I met my husband – I studied in my spare time for my MBA. I'm qualified for the job, Billy, you can be certain of that.'

I nod to register that I accept the statement, but I heard the emphasis of Carrie's reply. She felt I was implying she shouldn't be doing the job.

'I'm trying to determine, Mrs Ratcliffe, whether the threats might come from someone jealous of your appointment. Someone sacked at takeover? A bitter former employee?'

She shakes her head. 'No one was sacked. We took on

27

extra staff, we're still doing so. And as for me taking someone else's job, the Chairman and previous MD were both happy to resign, their payoffs were very generous and we pay them retainers to act as consultants. I don't think that's the answer. I don't think it's someone who worked here.'

'Okay. Perhaps we could have a look around now.?'

'You mean the interrogation's over?'

I drain my glass. The ice has almost melted, but the water's still cool, refreshing.

'For the moment,' I say, not commenting on her choice of words, 'but I may have some more questions later. You see, Mrs Ratcliffe, any security operation is designed to prevent damage, or intrusion, occurring. But the best prevention is to find the source of your problems. I can set you up with a security system which no one can get through, but it would take a lot of time and a lot of money. If I have some idea *why* you're being targeted, then the measures I suggest can be designed specifically to suit your needs. That's why I need to ask questions.'

'Oh, I understand that, Billy.' She drains her whisky and rises to her feet, walks over to the internal wall and draws aside the blinds.

'It's just the way you ask questions that's a little offputting.' She motions to me, an invitation to join her. Below us is the factory floor.

'You sound just like a policeman, and that makes me feel ... Well, it makes me feel as if I've done something wrong. It makes me feel guilty.'

'I'm surprised Tommy Wardell didn't mention it to you when he recommended me.' I join her, gaze down at the workers and machines below.

'Mention what, Billy?'

'That I used to be a policeman.'

28

Chapter Three

The factory's divided into three parts. The first, the earliest in the production sequence, is where plastic granules from the hoppers outside are extruded into lengths of uPVC. These extruders, eight different machines in almost constant use, are kept separate from the rest of the factory by a partition wall. The extrusions, different cross-sections for different parts of the windows and doors, are then cut to six metre lengths and stored. The extrusion shop is peopled by men and women wearing white coats and carrying clipboards. They cut small sections of profile and take them away for testing. They behave like scientists.

There are no scientists in the manufacturing section, only workmen. They wear jeans and T-shirts, they sing along to the radio's pop tunes, they talk and joke. Here, following the instructions given on computer-produced labels, the lengths of plastic are cut to size and reinforced with metal, formed into rectangles of frames and vents, fitted with hinges and handles, gaskets and draught strips, beads and wedges. There are drills and saws, routers and welders and polishers, all competing for attention in the buzz and hiss of the workshop floor.

Finished items are stored in racks, married up to their glass before being taken away to be fitted into houses. But for the council job the racks are wheeled into metal containers, the type stacked twenty high on ships, except these have wheels. When a container is full it can be pushed or towed outside by a forklift to await collection, secure before, during and after transportation. Clearly I don't have to worry about the finished windows, locked inside these metal safes.

The tour of the factory takes almost an hour. I make notes in my tape recorder, ask questions, talk to workers and managers. Then I examine the outside of the building, request a ladder to look at the roof. Carrie Ratcliffe accompanies me (though she declines my offer to see the roof firsthand) and it's mid-afternoon before we're back in her office, hot, sweating.

'We work on the principle of having everything ready just in time, keeping stock to a minimum,' she explains as she fetches drinks. 'We work backwards from when finished products are needed. Install on a Friday? The glass is delivered on Thursday just as the windows are finished. That means production starts, depending on the size of the order, on the Tuesday, say, so the profile has to be ready on the Monday. It's all very precise.'

'One slip and the whole thing falls down?'

'That's about it.'

'And have things started slipping yet?'

'Slipping and falling. That's why you're here.'

'Are you under pressure?'

'The council understand. But if it continues they won't be quite so easy to deal with. After all, it's just the pilot we're installing at present.'

'The pilot? You mean you haven't started the main contract?'

'No. I thought I'd told you. One street, about fifty houses, that's what we get to start with. After we finish that, they survey it, check everything's okay. Make sure we can meet the standards on quality and time. Then we get to start on the big one.'

I'm thinking, fingers drumming the desk, unaware I'm making any noise until I catch Carrie Ratcliffe looking at me. I stop, drain my glass. I feel hot and uncomfortable. I need a shower and a clean shirt.

'What about installation?' I ask. 'Have there been any problems there?'

'No, the council's doing other work at the same time, modernising bathrooms and toilets. The tenants have been moved out, the street's like a fortress, uniformed guards at night, passes to get in. We use sub-contractors, they're good. There's no problem there.'

'Okay.' I've got my information. Now I have to use it. 'What I need to do now is cost some options, consider the best way of doing things. I'll do that as soon as I get back, I can have a price with you by tomorrow morning.'

'I'll be working late tonight, Billy, you can always contact me here. If everything's okay I can give the go-ahead on the phone. On that assumption, the price and specification being right, could you start quickly? Like tomorrow?'

Carrie Ratcliffe is letting me know the pressure she's under by applying some of it to me. She's assured me she has the qualifications to do this job, but she's behaving as if someone else is in control. I could ask her directly why she's in such a hurry, but the answer would be straightforward; the schedules demand speed, urgency. I could counter by suggesting she ought to have taken action soon after she arrived. No doubt a plausible answer could be found; she was too involved in learning the business, vandalism on a small scale had happened before, a combination of those and any other points she cares to mention. Speedy work of the type she appears to be demanding comes at a premium. Price, however, doesn't seem to be a deciding factor.

'I suppose I can put people off, get started on it first thing tomorrow if everything else is okay.' Why should I tell her I've nothing else on?

She stands up and offers me her hand. I can see dark

31

stains of sweat under her arms, around her neck, down her back. Cotton's not good in weather like this.

'I'll be waiting for your call tonight,' she replies. That's my cue to leave.

Chapter Four

The journey back to the office catches the beginning of the rush-hour. Norm – after finding out from the woman supplying him with lemonade that no one else has inspected the factory – was able to find a shaded patch of grass and sleep while I was inside the factory. Thus refreshed his driving commentary is surreally song-like.

'You see, boss, it's a combination of the heat, the traffic and the roads ... down into third, uphill bend coming up, watch out for the Mondeo, a rep if I ever saw one ... makes everyone frustrated, bad tempered. Let's face it, the roads weren't designed for this amount of traffic ... brake lights at the underpass, jam coming up, check the mirror, inside lane clear, sneak across ... silly bastard, fart and give us a clue! ... up the slip road on to the roundabout, that's better ... so you get road rage and all that. Too many cars, too many lorries. I mean, I'm a professional, I make a living from them, but you ask me and I say they should be restricted in some way ...'

There are many targets for the tuneful slings and arrows of Norm's outrage. Back in the seventies the city centre was torn apart by a knot of new roads, dual carriageways and motorways both. All they did was, initially, speed traffic from one jam to the next. Now they're a source of jams in themselves and no one can live or work near them because of the noise and the air pollution. The city seems to have evolved (and it's evolution by design) for use by cars. Though I share Norm's concerns I try to ignore him, to concentrate on the task ahead. Designing and pricing a security system for WPS won't be difficult. Ignore the fence and the gate, look at the building itself. The PVC hoppers, they're a weak point, they need to be protected; build a fence round them? Bright lights as a deterrent on the main building? Or infra-red and video cameras? Any suggestions I make have to fit the needs of the business, an expanding business working twenty-four hours a day. Another thought comes to me, I flick on the tape recorder, hoping that the noise of traffic blowing through the open windows won't render my voice inaudible.

'Memo, WPS, check personnel records for previous employers, see if any of the new staff have worked for WPS's competitors. Also check old employees for bad debts. Get Rak to run them through the county court register?'

I suck my bottom lip into my mouth. All I've been asked to do is provide WPS with a security system, not to investigate the reasons for the firm being targeted for vandalism. There's no need for me to consider motivation, no reason to feel any obligation to identify those carrying out the crimes. The fact that I feel there are specific individuals to be caught is itself worrying. Vandalism is easy to deal with, but an organised criminal act is more difficult. It's something I thought I'd left behind.

'Here we are, boss. Want me to wait for you?' Norm's double parked, almost blocking the road, smiling happily at the cars waiting to pass him.

'No, just let me out. I might need you later, though.'

'No problem, boss. Give me a bell if you need me.'

'Okay.'

'Good luck with the pricing. Let me know how you get on. I could do with the work.'

He doesn't need to work at all. He sold his garage business, Ford franchise included, when he was fifty-five. He moved to Spain with his wife, came back a year later

34

when she died. He wanted something to do, started servicing friends' cars, doing resprays and so on. He helps me out as a favour, enjoys the diversion. He always has a stock of vehicles he's improving, he was helpful in the past, providing cars which wouldn't be recognised as police-owned.

'Norm, what vans have you got at the moment?'

'Vans? I can lay hands on a long wheel base Transit or a Renault Trafic. Trafic's smaller but it goes better.'

'How much?'

'For your pricing? Twenty a day including insurance. Plus petrol and driver if you need one.'

'I might need you to drive the van *and* to get me about.'

'Forty for me, twenty for each vehicle?'

'Right. Thanks, Norm.'

I unglue myself from the seat and enter the shade of the building. A breeze blows through the corridor, dispersing the smell of carbolic and old newspapers, of rubbish bags waiting to be laid out for the binmen. As the lift cranks its way down to ground level I check my watch. Four. Rak should be in touch soon. I close my eyes and lean against the cold metal of the lift's walls. The graffiti were painted out two weeks before, the building's for sale and the owner wants to create a good impression. I don't know why he bothered, whoever buys it'll want to demolish it, build a new block, luxury offices.

The third floor has three offices unoccupied. I rent a fourth. The fifth has a dusty nameplate informing visitors that Wolff, Artman and Silverstein, solicitors, may still operate from behind the locked door. I've only ever seen Mr Wolff, a tremulous old man with a suit fashionable in the late fifties. He was at the tenants' meeting to discuss the proposed sale, advocating that we should start looking for alternative premises straightaway, accept the landlord's offer to buy us out. When I pointed out that, as sitting tenants, most of us with long, cheap leases, we'd be better waiting for a purchaser to buy us out, he made harrumphing noises, sat down and said nothing else. I don't think I endeared myself to him.

Further along the corridor, beyond a fire door normally wedged open, is the entertainment agency. Further still, beside the draughty fire escape, is an office where a young girl works, always typing, always in the office before me, always leaving after me. If I hadn't, from curiosity, gone along to introduce myself, I would have assumed that the clicking of fingers on keyboard was a recording, so regular, so monotonous was its soft clamour.

There are two toilets. I ignore the office, head for the door bearing the unskirted figure. I bolt the door and turn on the cracked washbasin's single tap (cold water only, no plug) remove my shirt and drape it over the metal hanger jangling from the doorhook; the rest of my clothes follow. Above the washbasin is a mirror, black at the edges. The man I see there has a hairy body. His forearms, face and head are the frailest of browns, the yellow-orange of early Autumn rather than the tobacco darkness of deep October.

I put the small handtowel on the floor, take the soap and scrub my hands and arms methodically, I pay particular attention to my armpits. I move onto my face and neck, as much of my back as I can reach. I lather the soap at my genitals, scrub between my legs and down to my feet. Then I put down the soap and use my cupped hands to pour water over my body, rinse it clean. The towel beneath my feet absorbs what it can, but the floor is soon drizzled with moisture. I rub my body again with cold watered hands, then lower my head into the washbasin. I turn off the tap then wait for the warm air to dry me, I tense and relax the muscles in my legs, then my arms, neck, shoulders. Soon I can feel only a mist of moisture on my back and arms. I dress again, slowly, put on the clean shirt and underpants from my briefcase. The clothes deemed too dirty to wear again are folded and placed in a plastic bag within the brief-case. My task is finished only when the towel has been hung over the rail beside the washbasin and the floor dried with wedges of toilet paper. Refreshed, clean again, I return to my office.

There are no faxes waiting for me, no messages. I switch on my computer and write down what I'll need to carry out the WPS job. I play back my tape, check catalogues and magazines, enter prices onto my list. When the information isn't at hand I use the phone, always asking for an individual by name, always speaking courteously, never overfamiliar. Normally I enjoy pricing. There's a pleasing logic to the pursuit of information, the preparation of specifications. The goal is always in sight. But this time there's something wrong. There's no element of competition. If Norm's informant is to be believed, no one else has been invited to price the WPS job. That shouldn't happen in a well-run business. It's like my pen on the desk, not straight, not right. Except I can move my pen if I want to.

At six o'clock (I check the time) the phone rings. I pick up the receiver.

'Rak?'

'Shit, boss, how d'you know it was me?'

'I was expecting you. Chief librarian goes home at six, I thought you'd want to wait before ringing. What have you got?'

'I'm very well, thank you, had a hard day slavin' over bleedin' computers, pretendin' to be cataloguin' when I've been runnin' up huge bills gettin' data for you. Why don't you get on the net, boss, it's not that expensive. You've got a 486, all you need is a modem, you can get BT Online, Compuserve, that'll give you what you need. Infocheck gives you credit ratin's and finance, it's amazin' what you can get from teledirectories.'

'But it would spoil your fun, Rak, you love every minute of it. I know you.'

My suggestion seems to upset her. 'You know me? You mean you think you know me. Is it possible to really know anyone? After all, how well do you know yourself?'

'Come on, Rak, have you been seeing a psychologist or something?'

'No, boss. I'm just feelin' a bit undervalued.'

'Well I know what you're worth. I just can't afford to pay you. Now come on, you wouldn't be holding back unless you had what I wanted. Do I get to hear?'

There's silence on the phone, silence which resolves into a heavy, asthmatic rasping. I'm confident. Rak hasn't let me down in the past.

'Okay. You got a pen handy?'

'And paper. Off you go.'

'Winner Profile Systems Limited has two directors, MD Mrs Caroline Ratcliffe, Company Secretary Charles Harkness. Two thousand fully paid up shares of a pound, all owned by Ratcliffe Plastics Ltd.'

'Ratcliffe Plastics?'

'A wholly owned subsidiary of Ratcliffe Holdings, but more of them later. WPS has been operating for about twenty years, always traded at a profit, though figures were way down in the recession. From what I can gather they started out makin' wooden windows, mostly softwood for people who bought their council houses in the early days of Thatcherism. Moved onto double glazin', aluminium, hardwood, PVC. Then they started makin' their own PVC windows, buyin' in profiles. MD at the time, Donald Harrison, thought he'd go further down the production line, bought a few extruders, began to make his own profiles. Still didn't do much, occasional small contracts, mostly domestic. Till two months ago.'

'And they got the council job?'

'With a vengeance. New profile design, apparently, don't know where it came from. Must be good though.'

'Okay. Anything in the accounts?'

'Not much. Under-capitalised I'd say, everythin' done on a shoestring. Had to lay people off back in '92. Cashflow problems, a few county court judgements. Advertisin' budget went down. But they kept their heads above water.

38

I'd guess they operated a few cash payments to avoid VAT, nothin' much to talk about, everyone's done it at some time. That's about it.'

'Can you get me copies of their accounts?'

'Been there, done that. I'll post them, they're a bit bulky . . .'

'Can you bring them round?'

'No. You can collect them.'

'From the library?'

'From home, I'm leavin' soon as I put the phone down.'

The stalemate's easily reached. Rak's flat isn't too far distant, but it'll take time to get there.

'I'll think whether I need them. What about Ratcliffe?'

'Far more interestin', boss, if you're takin' them on as clients you're touchin' real class for a change.'

'That good?'

'Better. They're a privately owned company. That means access to information about them is limited. They don't have to publish their accounts, just lodge them with the Registrar of Companies. They do this, on time. They make large profits from subsidiary companies based abroad for tax reasons. Because there's so little financial information available I've dredged the News Digests. Ratcliffe have been acquisitive recently, but mostly on a far larger scale than WPS. They buy worldwide. Montana Oil for 50 million, Fischer-Argent Pharma, a French company, for 35, Indo-Hotels for 20. Those are just examples.'

'Where do they get the money?'

'No one knows. They guess, but they don't know. I'd say profits and bank loans – they probably own a few banks – plus asset stripping. Keeping a profitable core industry and site, selling off everything else.'

'Why don't you know for certain?'

'Like I said, they're a private holding company, subsidiaries in places like the Cayman Islands. The only way to find out what subsidiaries Ratcliffe actually owns is to look for the subsidiaries themselves. If you're lucky you read about them when they're taken over. But starting from scratch is like being told to look for all the needles in the old haystack, but without being told how many there are. How d'you do it?'

'Burn the haystack down?'

'Sounds a bit radical to me.'

I put down my pen and tap my fingers on the desk, then stop when I realise what I'm doing. I've enough bad habits without developing more. I'm finding it difficult to evaluate this information because it was sought without any specific purpose. It was meant to provide some kind of background but seems to do nothing but raise further questions.

'What about Ratcliffe's directors?'

'Not named. But they have to come out of hiding sometimes, and you told me about Alfred and James, that gave me some leads. Alfred's the chairman, in his seventies, he's got two brothers, Charles and Benjamin, 65 and 69. Their sons are on the board, that makes eight, plus two grandsons. I've listed them for you. You asked about James Ratcliffe. He's the youngest son of Benjamin, 45 years old. Alfred and Charles live in the US, though they started the company in Britain. Benjamin stayed here. James is an accountant, degree in Business Studies. I can probably find out more about him if you want me to.'

'Yes, I think I'd like you to do that.'

'But I'd have to charge you.'

'I thought you'd say that. Yes, go ahead ... No. No, wait to hear from me. There's no point doing anything until I know I've got the job. I'll let you know.'

'When?'

'Soon.'

Once again Rak's rasping breath rattles the telephone.

'So you'll be round later for the WPS figures?'

'Yes ... By the way, what were the profits for the last few years?'

I can hear papers being shuffled.

'Net profit before tax in '95 was 30 thou on a turnover of

one and a half million. '94, 28 on one and a quarter. '93, 16 on just over a million. '92, the recession, remember, six, on eight hundred thousand, about the same in '91.'

'Not exactly impressive.'

'They survived, didn't they?' Rak's voice holds a certain disgruntled pride, as if in researching the information she's assumed a sheen of proprietorial defensiveness.

'Yes, they survived. Thanks, Rak, thanks for everything. I need to think now. Well done.'

I put the phone down and lean back in my seat, my attention on the computer screen. Rak's information is interesting enough to be a distraction.

Chapter Five

An hour later I'm almost ready. I've decided what I need in the way of equipment. I know what tools and machinery I need to hire, the length of time I'll need them. All of these provide straightforward costs. I've calculated the time the job will take to complete, the number of men I'll need, their cost as subcontractors. I know my own costs. My overheads are small and can be assigned as a percentage on-cost basis or in proportion to the time I intend spending on the job; both results provide similar answers. Now all I need do is add my profit. I consider the figure on the screen and add twenty per cent. The new total is just over seventeen thousand pounds, more than half WPS's profits in the previous year. I pick up the phone and dial.

'I'd like to speak to Mrs Ratcliffe,' I say, 'my name's . . .'

'Billy? You've worked out a price?' It's Carrie Ratcliffe herself. Does she use my first name deliberately to annoy me?

'Yes. Are you sitting down?'

'That expensive?'

'I prefer to call it value for money, Mrs Ratcliffe. And I'd like to start by telling you what you'll be getting for that money.' I wait. She must initiate the responses herself. She must be put into the position of wanting something from me.

'Go on.'

'Okay. First of all, forget the existing fence, it's too fragile. Leave it as a deterrent for little boys. But you do need to enclose your external PVC hoppers, so I've allowed for a double chain link fence with razor wire spiralled at the top, it's more effective than stranded wire. Does that meet with your approval?'

'Yes.'

Get the potential customer used to saying yes, the only part of active selling I can remember. 'I've deliberately kept away from floodlights on the buildings.' I'm kept waiting, it's too long. Carrie Ratcliffe is thinking before speaking.

'Isn't that the type of thing we need,' she says, 'to keep the vandals away?'

'They aren't vandals, Mrs Ratcliffe. They aren't opportunists out for kicks. You've been targeted for some reason, and floodlights won't keep people like that away. So I'd suggest infra-red cameras instead, two at each corner of the building. Then we can see who's hurting you.'

'Won't it take a long time to set up?'

It's not the question I'm expecting. I thought she might be worried about costs, but money hasn't been mentioned.

'I can have it set up in a day,' I counter. 'Start tomorrow, it'll be in use by midday the day after. You'll need someone to watch the screens, of course. But the beauty of this system is that those trying to cause damage won't know they're being watched. That way it's easier to catch them. Find out why they're targeting you. Find out who's behind them.'

'You're sure it'll do all that?'

'It'll do that. You might need help from the police to arrest them, but the system will warn you, identify the villains.'

The silences are more interesting than Carrie Ratcliffe's questions. Each time I stop speaking I find myself underestimating the time it'll take her to answer me or offer some comment. I can see her sitting in her office, scribbling

43

details on a notepad as I speak, thinking of questions, objections. I'm trying to anticipate these as I talk, I'm trying to fence them in, keep them in order, under control. And she's playing her part too. When she's ready to speak, she stops herself, because she feels it'll unsettle me. But it doesn't. The tactic is familiar. I copy her silence.

'How much will this cost, Mr Oliphant?'

At last. Money. Now's the testing time. 'Let me ask you first, Mrs Ratcliffe, if the system I've described is what you want.'

'It sounds about right. Yes, it sounds ideal.'

'Good. But there'll be more. It'll be backed up with changes of locks on all windows and doors. Sensors as well, an alarm system. Movement detectors in all rooms.'

'You make it sound like a prison.'

'No, not a prison, Mrs Ratcliffe. A fortress. You and your factory, your products, your staff, they'll all be protected. That is what you want, isn't it?'

'Yes, of course . . .'

'And you did ask me to devise a system to solve your problems?'

'Yes . . .'

'Good. I'm pleased I've been able to do as you requested.'

'How much, Mr Oliphant?'

That's the second time she's forgotten to call me Billy. I look at the figures on the screen. Seventeen thousand, one hundred and seventeen pounds. That would allow me a profit far in excess of what I normally earn. There's room to negotiate, to lose a thousand, and I'll still make money. But I still feel there's something wrong. I don't know what it is, a suspicion, nothing more. Not one individual problem, but the whole situation. Carrie Ratcliffe, WPS, Ratcliffe Holdings, the contract, the attacks. They add up to more or less than they ought to, but I can't figure out why.

'Hello? Billy, are you still there?' She's back on first name terms. She's regained her confidence.

'Just looking through my paperwork,' I say, 'making

44

sure the price is right. Hold on just a second.' I lay down the phone and look at my watch. The afternoon's dead, it's moved on to the lost evening hours when people should be at home with their families, mowing summer lawns, going out for walks in neat, well-trimmed parks. But I'm at work, Carrie Ratcliffe's at work. We should both know better.

'Mrs Ratcliffe?'

'I'm still here, Billy.'

'The price for the work I've just described – I'll fax the specification and confirmation of the price through to you – will be twenty-seven thousand pounds.' I speak the words slowly, surprised at how calm I feel as I pronounce the total. Give the price then stay quiet. If you talk, you lose. Then I remember I'm talking to the head of a double-glazing firm. I'm trying selling techniques developed in that very industry, used by commission-earning salesmen throughout the world. Perhaps Carrie Ratcliffe has been taught the same disciplines, perhaps she's waiting for me to speak even as I wait for her. I begin to reconsider. I'm not sure why I inflated the price so much, it's not too late to claim an error, to drop the price by a significant amount. I certainly need the money. I need the work. Does it show? Should I have held off, played a little harder to get? My fingers begin to tap the desk again. Still there's silence. I could put the phone back onto its cradle, pretend we've been cut off. That would give me time to think, to reconsider my price. She won't, can't accept twenty-seven thousand, it's outlandish, completely out of the question. WPS can't have that much money to spare. I pick up the receiver, hold it close to my ear, striving to hear the sound of breathing, anything to show that Carrie Ratcliffe is still there.

'I think we have a deal, Billy,' her voice booms, I have to hold the receiver away. 'If it does everything you say, if you can start tomorrow, if the specification is right, we have a deal.'

I hope my amazement doesn't show in my voice.

'I'll need a deposit of a half,' I say, 'the balance on completion.'

'Okay. I'll have the first cheque for thirteen and a half thousand waiting for you tomorrow morning. Or would you prefer a banker's draft?'

'A cheque will do, as long as it doesn't bounce.'

'Billy, don't you trust me?'

'Of course,' I lie. I don't trust Carrie Ratcliffe because I know she's not telling me everything I ought to know. Or perhaps she's telling me everything *she* feels I need to know to do the job. Something's wrong, I *know* something's wrong. I've just had a ridiculous quote accepted without question, without argument, without negotiation. Something is definitely wrong.

'What time tomorrow?' Carrie Ratcliffe asks.

'Eight,' I reply. 'I'll have someone starting at eight. If that's all right with you?'

'Eight it is, then. I'll be waiting.' She puts the phone down without saying goodbye; my receiver follows it slowly.

From along the corridor I can hear rock music filtered by the thin walls of the theatrical agent's office, he's just started work and I ought to be going home. I've been sweating, but I don't have another clean shirt. I stand up, take off the shirt and hang it from the bottom of the open window sash. It dances in the faint breeze. I amend the price on the quotation, print it out ready to fax to Carrie Ratcliffe.

'Take the money and run,' I tell myself, 'what does it matter if you've got suspicions? You're a suspicious person, it comes with the job. Do what you've said you'd do and get out.'

While I'm waiting for the printer to complete its march across the pages (perhaps I'll buy a combined laser fax and printer, a modem) I punch a number on the phone.

'Norm? Billy Oliphant here, I need you for the rest of the week, and your van. Can you pick me up tomorrow at seven? Good, see you then. Bye.'

The next number is also dialled from memory, but I'm not pleased to be greeted by a recorded voice. I speak as courteously as I can.

'This is Billy Oliphant at 7.30 pm leaving a message for Sly Rogers. I need you for a job, probably lasting the rest of the week. Good rates, long hours. If you're not interested let me know, otherwise I'll expect to see you at 7.30 am at the factory of Winner Profile Systems, on Parkside. Bring your tools and ladders. Hope you can manage it.'

The printer disgorges its letter and I insert the paper into my fax machine, punch the eager buttons. The fax bleeps its acceptance of my instructions. I file the papers and shrug myself into my shirt without enthusiasm. I exit through several screens on the computer and switch off, move the chairs to retain the office's symmetry. Then I pick up the phone again, begin to dial a number, then stop.

'No,' I say, pleased with the excuse I've invented, 'call to see Rak first.'

Chapter Six

I walk up the hill towards the city centre. I pass from steep
streets of cheap offices to an elegant Georgian crescent
where banks and insurance companies shelter behind
tapered colonnades and multi-paned windows. I keep in the
shade, admiring those brave enough to step into patches of
still potent sunlight. The evening brings no cool relief. All
day the buildings and pavements have been absorbing the
heat, now's their chance to return the favour. I can feel the
warmth beneath my feet, my hands can touch radiant sand-
stone. There's a chemical smell in the air, a choking
miasma of petrol fumes and melting tarmac. Yet in the
paved squares (no trees give shade on these streets) white
plastic tables, transfixed by coloured mushrooms of para-
sols, are surrounded by laughing drinkers. They all seem
young, intent on enjoying themselves. They drape themselves over each other, caring little for the fragility of their
seats. They kiss and giggle, touch bare tanned flesh to cele-
brate their bacchanalia.

I hurry past, down the steps beside the war monument
and into the Metro. It should be cool underground but it
isn't, not until a hurricane of wind announces the imminent
arrival of the train.

Rak owns a large three-floored terraced house two miles
north of the centre, lives on the ground floor and lets the
remaining rooms to students. The walk from the station to

Rak's house isn't unpleasant, I stop beside a small park and watch creaking, white-clad pensioners play cut-throat bowls, competitive as cannons. Rak's house faces east, the front in welcome shadow. I lean against the cool polished stone of the door surround. I'm tired. I haven't eaten much, I've drunk too little, and I'm worried. I ring the doorbell.

It takes at least two minutes for a response and the girl who comes to the door isn't Rak. She's young and slim, almost the same height as me, dark-skinned with black hair. She's wearing a long sleeveless T-shirt and, as far as I can tell, little else.

'I've come to see Rak,' I say. The girl's obviously one of her boarders.

'Are you Mr Oliphant?'

I nod in reply. The girl holds the door open.

'Rak said you'd be coming. She's in the back garden, come on through.'

Rak lives in what used to be the house's front parlour and dining room. Double doors lead from the latter straight out on to a small flagstoned area, sheltered and shaded on one side by the kitchen, on the other by a tall fence. Beyond is a lawn and flower beds, shrubs, a laburnum tree, all saturated in evening sunshine. The girl's route, however, leads through the kitchen. The sink is full of unmatched, unwashed plates, stained dishes and blackened pans. The cooker's greasy, there's a smell of burned fat. The walls are painted dark purple, pieces of woodchip have been pulled away to reveal old floral paper beneath. The ceiling was once white.

'Rak's up there,' the girl says as she steps out into the garden, points back to the shaded flagstones. She walks across the lawn to rejoin her friends, lounging on a wide coloured blanket, drinking wine from the bottle.

'Come on, boss,' calls Rak's gruff voice, 'the bleedin' ice's meltin'!'

It's pleasantly, refreshingly cool in the shade. There are two chairs, old rattan, both decked with cushions. I lower myself gratefully into one and accept a pint glass filled with iced orange juice.

'Thanks, Rak. A lifesaver.'

Rak's filling the other chair. She's shorter than me, about five foot, but wide. She's wearing a grubby T-shirt and a skirt made of sackcloth which covers most of her legs. Her ankles are swollen, the flesh mottled. Her head is flat nosed, like a pug, eyes small in a fat face. Her hair is thin and sparse, unstyled, washed but uncombed. She looks deliberately unkempt.

'You want to look at the figures now?' she asks, reaches down to her side for a large envelope. I take it from her and put it in my case, lean back in the chair, close my eyes. I can hear swifts screeching a race-track round the house.

'I'll look at them later, on the way home.'

'You look tired, boss. Burnin' the candle at both ends?'

'And in the middle.'

Rak's laugh is an exhalation of sound somewhere between a cough and a sneeze. She picks up her can of beer from the table beside her, drains it, then pulls another from the coolbox at her side.

'Weather don't help,' she says. 'I was thinkin' 'bout it this morning, alters your mind, weather like this. I mean, look at them lot.'

She gestures down the garden. I can count six, no, seven people. Four are girls, two of them topless, the three boys are in shorts or trunks. They seem happy in their familiarity, laughing, talking, drinking.

'The girls live here. Two are post-grads; Jenny, the one who answered the door, she's a medic. Normally they wouldn't flash their tits like that. On holiday, perhaps, in Ibiza, where there's only their mates to see them. But not here. It's definitely the weather.'

'You could be right,' I say.

'You should stick around, boss. I'll introduce you to them, it'll even up the numbers. They're a good crowd, you might enjoy yourself. Wind down a bit.'

'Do I look as if I need to wind down? Do I look that bad?' I glance again at the students, considering whether Rak's suggestion could be anything more than flippancy. I decide to play safe. 'No, they're too young. I'm old enough to be their father. And anyway, I've someone else to see. But thanks for the offer.'

We sit quietly for a while, hearing unconnected words from disparate conversations. There's a background noise of high, distant aircraft engines. In another garden a blackbird churrs a warning of cats.

'I can remember,' I say, 'when I was younger, lying on a grassy bank with my dad in weather a bit like this. I don't know where it was. I'm not sure how old I was. But it was peaceful, quiet. There was no need for either of us to say anything. Then the old man nudged me, pointed to his ear then up at the sky. It was an aeroplane. It sounded far away, it was droning like a bee. I looked for it but I couldn't see it. The noise of the engines came and went in a regular pattern and it was reassuring because of that, because of its smoothness. It wasn't urgent, like the birds singing, it was lazy like perfume. It was just there. All my childhood in that single sound.' I sip my drink. 'You don't get sounds like that any more.'

'You don't get times like that any more,' Rak agrees, 'the world's too busy for parents to sit down with their kids and do nothing.'

I nod again. It would be easy to relax, take up Rak's offer. But I can't relax, my mind won't let me. 'Library busy at the moment?' I ask.

'What you after?'

I can't hide my surprise. 'Am I that transparent?'

''Course you are. You're a man aren't you? Never yet met one who was interested in more than himself. You don't really want to know about the library, do you?'

'No. No, I don't suppose I do.'

'In that case I'll tell you all about it. First of all, it's too bloody hot, even with all the windows open. I've got a boss

51

who's a bastard, he thinks I'm a cow, he *calls* me a cow to my face. He hates me 'cos I'm better at the job than him, and he can't cope with me being the way I am.'

'The way you are?'

'Fat, ugly, queer and intelligent. It could be because he's thin, likes to think he's handsome, straight and thick.'

'And you've told him that?'

'I've told him he's thick. I didn't bother with the rest 'cos I didn't think he'd realise I was insulting him.'

'You know how to make friends and influence people.'

'Yeah, that's why *you* love me so much. Anyway, he wants rid of me, but I'm too good at the job. No one knows their way round the net like me, no one knows the software, the hardware. Christ, I may be a nerd but I'm a bloody good one!'

The students on the lawn seem to have come to a decision on their future actions. They stand, make their way up the garden. The dark girl, Jenny, heads for our shade.

'We're going to the Crown for a pint or two, Rak, you want to come?' She smiles at me. 'You're welcome to come as well, Mr Oliphant.'

I shake my head. 'Thanks for the invitation, but I've other business. Another time, perhaps.' I turn to face Rak. 'I have to go now, don't let me stop you going out.'

Rak nods to herself. 'Yeah, Jenny, I'd like that.'

'We'll be another ten minutes,' the girl says, 'we just need to get dressed.' She smiled me a goodbye and sashays away. I feel young and old at the same time.

'Sure you won't change your mind, boss?'

'I'm sure.' The truth is, I'm not sure.

'So what is it you're wanting me to do tomorrow? You *were* going to ask me to do something, weren't you?'

'Yes, I was. Information. And I'll pay this time. I want you to find out what you can on Carrie Ratcliffe and her husband. Business stuff if you can get it, but personal as well. By the way, who runs the library?'

'Who runs it? You mean who's in charge?'

'No, who provides the money. The county council?'

'Yes.'

'Pity. Housing contracts are awarded by district councils. They own the housing stock.'

'Yeah. But I've got friends on most of the district councils. What do you need?'

'This contract, the one WPS have been awarded, I want to know who else was tendering. I need to know the tender prices, I need to know who was second ...'

'Hold on, boss, hold on. I'm almost certain that information's secret. It would be a criminal act for anyone to provide it. You're asking me to do something illegal.'

'So?'

'So illegality costs more. I might have to grease a palm or two.'

'Do it.'

'Anything else?'

'That's all for the moment.'

'Good. It should make my day more entertaining.'

'That, Rak, is the main purpose of my life.' I stand, pick up my case. 'Thanks for the juice. Enjoy your drink with the kindergarten set.'

'I will.' Rak doesn't attempt to rise, the effort is too great. 'Give my love to Kirsty.'

Once again my surprise is obvious. 'How did you know ...?'

'I know, boss, I know. Still hurtin'?'

'Yeah.'

'If you need somewhere, just to talk to her, somewhere to be with her, come round. And I'd like to see her again.'

'I'll tell her that. Thanks.'

I brush my lips against Rak's cheek.

'Thanks, Anna,' I say softly, then leave.

Chapter Seven

It's cooler now, with a slight breeze. It takes me almost an hour to complete my journey, two bus rides. I sit on the top deck, concentrating on WPS, on Carrie Ratcliffe. She was too eager to employ me, and I want to know why. I'd been recommended, but there are others around as good as me, probably better, who know crime prevention officers. She could have tried them, I suppose, and I was the only one available at short notice. Even so, I would have expected her to get at least one more price for comparison. Another possibility is that anyone *couldn't* have got the job, it was me who was important. I can't believe I'm that good, so if the deciding factor is me, there's a reason behind it. But what reason? It could be that Carrie Ratcliffe is inept. But she behaves like a professional, and Ratcliffe Holdings is certainly a professional company. Perhaps, unknown to the lemonade lady, one of my competitors *did* quote but made a mistake, quoted even higher than me. The possibility that another firm might have made a mistake in its calculations prompts me to dig into my briefcase and check my own figures. There are no errors.

The walk from the bus stop is short. I'm in the middle of a modern housing estate, one of many stretching for miles to the north of the city. There were once green fields here, communities built on farming and mining. Now there are houses. Children are playing, whooping and chasing, rolling down grassy slopes. Cars are being washed, lawns mowed. I pass a man walking his dog, an old woman walking her husband. There's a smell of barbecues, burning meat and charcoal; palls of hot shimmering smoke rise from behind neatly stained fences and clipped Leylandii.

It's nine thirty. I stop in front of a semi-detached house only slightly different to the others in the small cul-de-sac. The lawn is well-clipped, the borders weeded and blooming. I walk up the path and ring the bell, wait patiently. There's no answer. I try again. Still nothing. I step back then walk to one side to peer through the large front window. There's no one there, the television screen is a dull grey. The doors leading from the room are closed, the room itself is tidy.

'I should have rung first,' I admonish myself, though I have an aversion to telephoning this house, find excuses not to do so. I sit down on the doorstep without looking round, aware that my visit will be reported by unseen neighbours. I take a sheet of paper and an envelope from my case, write the name 'Kirsty' on the envelope and put it to one side. Then I begin the note itself.

'Dear Kirsty, I called round to say hello, see how things are, and to tell you I've had a little luck on the job front. I've some work . . .'

My writing's interrupted by the door behind me flying open. I almost fall into the hallway, but my outflung hands catch the frame and pull me back to a sitting position. I twist round, climb to my feet.

The girl standing before me is wrapped in a bath-towel, a smaller towel encases her hair.

'Kirsty! I thought you were out, I was just writing a note . . .' I hold out the pen as evidence.

'Dad! What are you doing here? I was in the bath.'

'Like I said, I was writing . . .'

'Yes, but . . . You know what Mum's like, you know what she'd say!'

'Yes, I know, I wanted to talk to her – and you, of

55

course – to tell her I'd got a job, a good job, well paid. She's worried about the mortgage, I can let her have some cash in a couple of days' time.'

'She's not in. She's at aerobics. You should have rung.' She's unhappy at having to talk to me like this, she doesn't want the responsibility of that role. She raises her hands to her cheeks, covers her mouth as if frightened that unwanted words might escape.

'I would have phoned, love, but your mum and I always seem to argue. I thought if I came round …' I shrug to signify that my intentions are well meant. 'Anyway, how are you?'

'All right.' She smiles. 'A bit wet.'

'Yes, so I can see. How's school?'

'Okay. Look, Dad, I feel an idiot standing here, why not come in, I'll get dried, I'll be down in a minute or two.'

'Come in?' Calling round is one thing, actually going into the house would be sacrilege. I look across the road; a curtain twitches shut. 'I don't think I'd better,' I say, 'your mum, she's bound to find out.'

'I know she'll find out, Dad, I'll tell her. *I* don't hide anything from her.' The emphasis, intentional or not, hurts me.

'Look,' Kirsty continues, dripping on the doormat, 'you come in if you want, make a cup of tea, you know where everything is. Or stay there, I don't mind. But *I'm* going back upstairs to get dried and dressed, okay?'

I nod my approval and watch my daughter bound up the stairs; then I step warily into the house. Little has changed. I go down the hall into the kitchen, fill the kettle with water and switch it on. The teapot and mugs are where they ought to be, I stand them ready. The draining board contains plates, knives and forks, a casserole dish and a pan. I take a dishcloth and wipe them down, put them away. The tray in the cutlery drawer is in confusion, the compartment for knives has forks in it as well, that for spoons contains serving spoons, tea spoons, soup spoons, every possible breed of spoon. I sort them out, rearrange them neatly. Then I go back out, sit once again on the doorstep where I feel safe. I try to soothe away the tension in my shoulders, rotate them forwards and backwards, individually and together. It doesn't help. I put my hands behind me and lean back, let the muscles in my neck relax.

Kirsty comes rhythmically back down the stairs, she's wearing black track-suit bottoms and a white T-shirt, her hair still towel wrapped. She seems older than she ought to be.

'The kettle should have boiled,' I tell her, 'the pot's out, teabags inside, mugs ready. Can you do the rest?'

'I think I can manage. Still milk and no sugar?' She's talking as she's walking away.

'Yeah. You still taking three sugars?'

'Two, it was always two!'

'You'll get fat.'

Kirsty returns, the tea brewing in the pot.

'Fat?' she says. 'Me, fat? Don't be silly, Dad, look.' She lifts up her T-shirt to show a stomach flat and trim, skin healthily tanned. 'I don't get fat. Mum says I'm ectomorphic. Do you want a biscuit?'

'No,' I say, 'because I'm endomorphic. Just tea please.'

Kirsty goes back into the kitchen, reappears with a mug in each hand and two biscuits sandwiched between her teeth. She gives me one mug and removes the biscuits from her mouth.

'It's hot, mind,' she says.

I put the mug down on the ground beside my feet. Kirsty puts hers on the bottom step of the stairs.

'Want your hair drying?' I ask. My daughter's eyebrows rise in surprise. She looks horrifically, beautifully like her mother.

'With the towel?' she asks.

'If you want.'

'Oh, yes please. Just a minute.' She dashes into the living room, comes back with a cushion which she places on the ground between my legs.

57

'Make room!' she says, nudging me to one side. She pushes my knees apart and sits at my feet, pulls the towel from her hair and lets it drop into my lap. I rub my daughter's long, blonde hair. It's six months since I left home, six months since I was last able to do this for her.

'Can you rub just a bit harder on my scalp. Mm, yes, that's wonderful.'

I continue drying her hair, rubbing first her scalp then moving the towel down to dry the furthest lengths of each strand. Neither of us says anything. After five minutes I have to speak, but even then the subject is mundane.

'Got a brush, love?'

'I'll get it.' Kirsty rises lightly to her feet, hurries into the house.

'Would you rather I gave Mum a message,' she shouts, 'or is it important that you speak to her?'

I wait for her to return, to sit down again in front of me. I pull the brush gently through her hair.

'It would probably be best if I spoke to her myself, if I leave a note or a message she might think I came round deliberately when she was out.'

'But you didn't know she was going to be out.'

'When you get older, love, you'll find that logic and your mother don't always go well together.' I check my watch; it's almost ten. 'Anyway, where did you say she was? Aerobics? I didn't know she was that interested in exercise.'

'It's her and some of the girls from the surgery. I think she goes for the company as well as the exercise, but it's doing her some good. She's lost nearly a stone, looks far better for it. And John . . .'

'Is he from the surgery as well?'

'No, you know who John is. Mum's boyfriend.'

I stop brushing. Kirsty turns her head slowly, her hands on my knee. She looks straight at me. I shrug, raise my eyebrows.

'I thought you knew,' she whispers, 'I thought Mum told you.'

I shake my head.

'He's all right,' she reassures me, 'though I don't know him that well. They've been going out for about two months now. He's a joiner, least that's what his van says on the side.'

I shouldn't ask, but I do. 'Does he stay nights?'

Kirsty nods. 'Sometimes. At weekends. But Dad, that's Mum's business now, really it is. You've been gone for half a year. You can't expect ... I mean, she's young, she's not bad looking. And you ...'

She stands abruptly, snatches the hairbrush from my hand.

'I can't help it, Dad. I can't help what you and Mum do with your lives! I've got no say in the matter, nobody asks what *I* want! I'm just your bloody daughter!'

She pushes past me and rushes upstairs; I hear a door slam. I feel suddenly weary, weary but concerned. I don't want to go back into the house, it's part of the agreement I have with Sara. But I can't leave Kirsty like this, particularly when I've been the cause of it.

'Kirsty,' I call up the stairs. 'Kirsty, I'm sorry. Please come down, I didn't mean to ... that is, I know – I think I know – how you feel, and I want to do anything I can to help, but ...' I listen carefully but there's no reply. I make my way up the stairs. All of the doors on the landing are closed, but I assume Kirsty still occupies the same bedroom. I listen outside the door, hear the sound of crying within. I knock gently.

'Just go away, Dad. I know you want to help but there's nothing you can do, you just make it worse. Please, go away.'

'Kirsty love, I can't do that. I didn't mean to hurt you in anything I said or did. But I can't help reacting the way I do, I can't help feeling the way I do. I can't hide the way I feel. And your mum hadn't told me about John. It just ... well, it came as a shock, that's all. I don't blame her, I'm not trying to run her life for her. But it came as a shock. I'm sorry.'

I listen again. The crying has stopped, it's replaced by a snuffling, whimpering sound.

'I think I'd better go now, love. Tell your mum I've got some work, I should be able to get some money to her in a few days, as soon as the cheque clears. Tell her I called, you'd better say you got a bit upset. Tell her ...' The door's thrown open. I can see inside, briefly, the impression is of more posters than I remember, more clutter of clothes and magazines on the floor. Then Kirsty's in front of me, her eyes red, her arms around me. She's almost as tall as me.

'I love you, Dad,' she mumbles into my neck.

'I love you too, Boston strangler.'

Chapter Eight

It's wrong to say I'm happy when I leave the house. I'm happier than I was; Kirsty's calmed down, we've managed to talk a little. But I'm less happy than I ought to be. My thoughts are, unwillingly, of my wife. My estranged wife, I tell myself. We've separated. We haven't lived together for six months, we've agreed to divorce. But that doesn't help. I picture her making love, not to me, but to a stranger, to John. I don't know what John looks like, but I know Sara. I know the feel of her body, the noises she makes, the way she moves, the way she reacts when she's being touched. I can picture too easily the look on her face when she's close to orgasm, the need, the urgency. Sometimes the tears. All these things I can imagine, all these things occupy my mind as my legs take me unbidden along familiar pavements.

'Billy! What the hell are you doing here?'

Sara's voice is strident, it hauls me back to reality. I didn't recognise her car, wasn't paying attention to traffic anyway. But it's definitely Sara. She makes no attempt to get out, but the window's down and her face is angry.

'Have you been home? Have you been to see Kirsty? I hope you haven't upset her, she gets upset when she sees you, you know that. You're due to take her out at the weekend, couldn't you wait until then?'

I walk across the road, crouch down beside the open

window. Sara's changed her hairstyle, it's much shorter, its natural yellow streaked with a deeper gold. Her face is colourful, healthy, though she's still found time to apply a patina of make-up. She's changed from her aerobics kit into a skirt and blouse, I don't recognise them.

'Hello, how did the aerobics go?'

'You have been home! I've told you not to go there when I'm out, I don't want Kirsty . . .'

'I didn't know you'd be out. It was you I wanted to see, not Kirsty.'

'Why?' The question's launched, not out of curiosity, but from a determination that the conversation should be as short as possible. The manner of asking demands brevity, facts, information. I answer accordingly.

'You said, last time we spoke, you were short of cash. I wanted you to know I've got a contract, good pay, a big deposit up front. I can get some money to you as soon as the cheque clears the bank, say three days' time.'

'How much?'

'How much can I give you? A thousand to start with. There'll be more when the job's finished.'

'A thousand? From a deposit? Must be a good job.'

Her face relaxes slightly. The lines in her forehead seem shallower, but her voice retains the same querulous tone.

'What type of job is it, Billy? You don't get money like that from security work. You've not been gambling again, have you, you said you wouldn't . . .'

'It's for installing a security system in a double glazing firm's factory, that's all. Winner Profile Systems, they're called, WPS.' I try to keep my voice calm, friendly. I've been accused of condescension in the past and I don't want to make Sara angrier than she is. 'It needed doing urgently, I quoted today, I start the job tomorrow. That's why the price is good.'

Sara relaxes a little.

'I knew you were worried about the money side of things,' I continue, 'that's why I came round. I don't like

62

telephoning, we always argue. I didn't know you were going out.'

'All right, Billy, all right. I'm sorry I was angry.' Sara curls her lips into an almost-smile. It's the nearest she can get to a proper apology, the words not quite telling the truth. My legs are stiff with crouching, I stand up, shake them loosely.

'You've lost weight,' says Sara. 'Are you eating properly?'

'Yes,' I reply, unable to remember when I last cooked a meal that wasn't from a packet. 'Kirsty says you've lost weight as well.'

'Yes. Some of it's the exercise, plus I'm working extra hours at the surgery. Stops me nibbling. But I'll have to go, I've a pile of ironing to do. And please ring next time, even if it's just to say you want to come round.'

I bend down again.

'Sara,' I ask, 'who's John? Kirsty mentioned you were seeing someone called John.'

The softening of Sara's manner ceases. She stares straight ahead of her, her hands grip the steering wheel.

'I don't see that it's any of your business,' she says firmly, 'now if you'll get out of the way I'd like to go home.'

'It is my business, Kirsty said he was staying over some nights . . .'

'So what? So I'm sleeping with him! Jesus Christ, Billy, I'm not a nun, who I sleep with has got nothing to do with you!'

'It has Sara, because having him in the house can affect Kirsty, and she's my daughter as well. I'd like to know what type of person this John is. Kirsty says he's a joiner. Has he been married before? Does he have any kids of his own? She didn't say much and I didn't want to press her, but . . .'

'Billy!' Sara's voice is a scream. 'Shut up!' She quietens her tone but manages to keep within it a slowly rising pitch

63

of venomous anger. 'Any man I take to my bed is *my* business. And it just so happens that John loves me, he makes me feel good, which is more than *you* ever did in the last five years of marriage. And making me feel good, making me *happy*, also makes Kirsty happy. She gets on well with John, they don't know each other well yet, but they will. You're her father, Billy, I'm not trying to take her away from you, she'll always need you and want to see you, if you treat her right. But your life and my life are two entirely separate things now. I don't ask who shares your bed. I don't want you asking me that question either. Now I'm going.'

She starts the engine and crunches the car into first gear. I stand back as she sweeps round the corner. It's beginning to get dark. I head for the bus-stop amazed at the rare talent I have for hurting those close to me. I can smell the scent from the flowers in one of the gardens, a deep, cloying, summer scent. It's similar to the perfume Carrie Ratcliffe wears.

Chapter Nine

When I left Sara – when Sara asked me to leave – Rak offered me a room at her place. I didn't want to owe her anything, I didn't want to be dependent on her or burden her with my problems, so I found a place to stay in the East End. It's only a single room, but it's large, it has a shower and an electric hob, a bed, a wardrobe, a table, some chairs. I had a telephone installed, my one luxury. I don't spend much time there. The building smells of boiled cabbage and the other occupants don't seem to work. Televisions and radios play loud during the day, and a lone guitarist practises at night, badly.

It took me a weekend to clean it when I moved in, a weekend of scrubbing and polishing, dusting, vacuuming. Despite that there's little of me in it; a pile of books beside the bed (poetry, anthologies mostly; biographies; SF comic books), everything sorted by size. A photograph in a frame.

It's almost eleven when I get back. I fill a glass with water and pick up the phone, its cordless, allows me to exercise as I talk. I walk the room as I dial.

'Hello? Sly? Billy here, Billy Oliphant. Did you get my message? And can you do the job? Great! I don't suppose you've still got that scaffolding tower? Two? Mobile? Sly, I love you! See you tomorrow, then.'

Sly Rogers doesn't talk a lot, that's one of the reasons I enjoy working with him. The others are that he's good at his job, strong, and seems to have no fear. Now he's agreed to join me there's little I need do until the next day. I strip off my clothes and consign them to the washing bag (which is growing too full, too quickly), take a shower and lie on the bed.

There's a streetlight outside my window, even the thickest curtains (and mine are woefully thin) can't mask its brightness. But tonight it's reassuring, I can concentrate on it, it helps me forget my worries until I fall asleep.

Wednesday

Chapter Ten

A sparrow nests behind the gutter above my window. It wakes me every morning at about six. Usually I curse it, but this morning it earns my thanks as it drags me from my nightmares. Carrie Ratcliffe, serpent-tailed and cobra-fanged, pursues me to Sara's house. I can't get in, but Kirsty lowers a ladder from her bedroom window. As I'm climbing, Sara appears, she pushes the ladder away from the wall and I fall into Carrie's clutches. That's when the sparrow wakes me, sweating, the sheets tangled around me like a snake.

I decide to go for a run, pull on red shorts and my new shoes. I take a vest but don't wear it, the day's already hot. I head into the Park, then north under the new road and into the Valley. It's cool there, shady, green. There's no one else about.

My new shoes feel comfortable. I haven't been running long, I'm not a natural, I'm too short, I've a poor style. But it keeps me fit and stops me thinking. When I run, tunes rise unbidden to the surface of my mind and repeat themselves in time to my feet striking the pavement. Today it's Manfred Mann's 'Pretty Flamingo', it's the melody, I decide, which inspired Oasis' 'Don't Look Back in Anger'. Plagiarism is the best form of flattery.

I double back in front of the Free Hospital and down the long straight stretch to home. By the time Norm arrives at seven thirty I've showered and dressed (jeans and T-shirt today, manual labour's called for) and Norm's itinerary's planned. He's in a blue Transit van, its panels dented and rusting, but the engine's running smooth and the gear change is slick.

'What's on today, then?' he asks as we set off.

'You drop me at WPS, then you go shopping. The orders are made out, all at places where my credit's good, the prices are quoted. Then you get back, unload and act as electrician's mate.'

'Long as it's not labouring. I'm a skilled mechanic, I am. Last time I helped you out you had me labouring.'

I can recall the occasion, that's why I've upgraded the role to electrician's mate. By the time Norm realises it's the same job, it'll be over. His protests weren't serious anyway – he just needs something to complain about.

'I brought you a present,' he says, reaching behind him, 'cos of the weather. Here.' He hands me a straw hat. By some miracle it's the right size.

'Very kind of you, Norm,' I say. His proposals for setting up stalls to sell the things wash over me as we head for work.

The Wall is a snaking curve of flats, designed to shelter more traditional houses from a motorway that was never built. It's on our left as we drive into the city centre, sheltering boarded-up shops, bookmakers' and amusement arcades, video stores, an occasional small cheap supermarket, a newsagent, a bakery. Life's lethargic here, slow to wake and rise.

We head for the bridges by the river route. Norm's chatter has been replaced by a strange mumbling noise, it takes me a while to realise he's singing; the good weather has a lot to answer for. We cross the river by the small bridge, then head up on to the Southside Highway, another monument to the worship of road transport. Its high level carriageways pass feet from tower blocks rendered unusable by the noise and dirt. Norm's starting singing again.

'Little Boxes'. I don't have it in me to ask him to stop. Instead, I try to concentrate on the work ahead, but a night's sleep hasn't diminished my concern at the ease with which I won the job. I should be thinking of the installation, but I'm going over the conversations I had with Carrie Ratcliffe. I don't like that, I ought to have one thing on my mind, and that's the security system at WPS. That's when I decide what to do. I'll ask her why she chose me to do the job. I'll ask her if she had any other quotes. I'll ask her why the speed, why the urgency.

We aren't the first to arrive at the WPS factory. There are as many cars as there were the day before, and Sly Rogers' van. Norm pulls up beside it and Sly climbs out. He's dressed in immaculate blue dungarees, a blue bandana tied round his forehead. He's a foot taller than me, his chest is like a barrel, his arms look as if they could tear me in two.

'You didn't tell me that black bastard would be on the job!' Norm says loudly.

'Did you say some'at, Cockney arsehole,' comes the reply. Sly's skin may be black but his accent is pure Yorkshire. Norm steps up to him.

'I did, shithead. What you gonna do 'bout it?'

'This!' says Sly. He pins Norm's arms to his side and picks him up, stares at him and plants a large, wet kiss on his forehead.

'Put me down, put me down,' whinges Norm, 'it's worse than having a bloody labrador lick you!' Sly does as he's asked. I climb out of my seat and join them.

'Together again, Mr Oliphant,' says Sly. We shake hands.

'Together again, Sly. A nice job, too. Easy to do, get in, get out, get on our way.'

'Sounds like sex,' offers Norm.

'Sounds like you're not doin' it right,' says Sly.

'Nah, don't believe in all this foreplay, all this fiddlin' about. And as for talking afterwards, bloody hell, I can talk

71

all I want down the pub. *And* there's draught bitter and darts.'

'You're a misogynist, Norm,' I say.

'Thanks boss. Now where's those orders?'

I hand him the paperwork, tell him to make sure he hurries without breaking any speed limits, then send him on his way. He still finds time to present Sly with a straw hat 'to protect him from the sun.' As he drives out, Carrie Ratcliffe strolls across to join us.

'Hello Billy,' she says. 'And this is . . .?'

'Sly Rogers. You'll be seeing a lot of him for a day or two, he's a good electrician.'

She's dressed for a business meeting, red skirt and high heels to show off her legs, red jacket, white blouse. She pulls her sunglasses down to look at Sly.

'I look forward to seeing a lot of both of you,' she says, smiles and walks away. Sly looks after her.

'Did she really say that?' he asks.

'I don't think she meant it to be quite so . . . suggestive,' I say, 'and anyway, she's the boss of the firm we're working for. Her husband's a big cheese in the firm owning *this* firm. Hands off, I'm afraid.'

'Mr Oliphant, as if I would! I'm a happily married man. And Paula's expecting again.'

'Again? How many's that?'

'This'll be the fourth.'

'So that's what you do in your spare time.'

He's already unloaded a pile of scaffolding, it's resting against a corner of the building. 'You're ahead of me, Sly, as usual. You want to get that up to roof level? There's a couple of things I need to sort out with madam inside.'

I head straight for Carrie Ratcliffe's office; she's waiting for me.

'Coffee?' she asks. The machine's bubbling in the corner.

'No thanks.' I enjoy good coffee, strong coffee, but it doesn't like me; too strong a diuretic.

72

'Did you read my specification? I faxed it through last night.'

'Yes, I read it. It seems okay.'

'And the contract?'

'That too. I assume you've brought one along with you for me to sign. I've asked our company secretary to prepare a cheque for the deposit, he normally gets in about eight thirty. You don't mind waiting . . .?'

'Not at all.' I sit down opposite her, open my case and bring out the contract. I hand it to her, we both sign, I give her the top copy and retain the second.

'There are still some things I need to know,' I say. She puts her elbows on the desk and her chin in her hands.

'Ask away, Billy.'

'The video system we're putting in, where do you want the monitors? I can put them wherever you want. In reception?'

She stands up and moves to the internal window, pulls on the drawstring to tug the blinds aside. I can see that the factory's busy.

'We're keeping up with demand,' she says. 'Just. No problems last night.'

'Good.'

She steps back a pace. 'How about here?'

'For the monitors? But . . .'

'But it's the MD's office? True, but it won't be for much longer. I'm having some alterations done, Billy, and this room will become three or four smaller rooms. Whoever's in charge of security can watch the screens and the factory floor at the same time. Any problems with installing here?'

'No, none at all. There'll be a lot of noise while we're working, you won't be able . . .'

'Oh, I'll be very interested to watch, Billy.'

Not only does she insist on calling me Billy, but she won't let me finish my sentences. Small things like that aggravate me.

'Why did you give me this job, Mrs Ratcliffe?'

If I'd hoped to provoke her into a confused confession – which was, I'll admit, my intention – then I'm doomed to failure.

'Why did I give you the job, Billy?' She turns the question over in her mind, in her mouth, like a wine taster. It becomes a statement. 'Why did I give you the job. Because I like you. Because I like your price.'

'It wasn't a cheap quote, Mrs Ratcliffe. Did you contact anyone else, for a comparison?'

She laughs, a loud laugh, the type used to express forced amusement. Then she comes back to her desk.

'I'm interested in semantics, Billy, the meaning of words, the way words change their meanings. Like two words we've both used before, "price" and "quote". What did I say? I think I said "I like your price," and you replied that "it wasn't a cheap quote". I chose my words carefully. Did you?'

The way she wears her superiority is beginning to grate on me. I don't mind if she's better than me. For every person who's better than me at something, and there must be a hell of a lot of them, there's one who isn't as good. At football, for example, I'm hopeless; I think I'm good at designing security systems. But I don't go round telling everyone how good I am. And I don't have this suffocating air of superiority which Carrie Ratcliffe owns.

'"Price" and "quote" can mean the same thing in different contexts,' she says, 'or different things in the same context. Are we speaking in the same contexts, Billy? That appears to be the main question.'

'No, Mrs Ratcliffe, I disagree. The main question is why you gave me a contract to do work at a greatly inflated price when you could have had the same job done more cheaply by virtually any other company in the area, local, national or international?'

She stands up again. The coffee machine has stopped bubbling and hissing, the aroma is captivating. She saunters over to it.

'Sure I can't tempt you?'

'No thank you. You still haven't answered my question.'

'I admire persistence, Billy. And I admire you, though I don't think you feel the same way about me.' She waits for me to protest to the contrary and I feel perversely pleased not to do so.

'Admiration isn't enough to let you pay ten thousand over the odds.'

'That much? Your needs must be great, Billy. Or your greed. Which is it?'

'Neither. I guessed you'd ask me to do the job. It was a way of testing you, testing me, perhaps. To see if I was right.'

'Like gambling, you mean?'

'No. No, not like gambling at all. There was no gamble in it. If you'd said no, the price was too high, I would have lowered it. I could have found a mistake. But you didn't say no. So why did I get the job?'

Carrie Ratcliffe's suit is made of silk. Not cheap silk, not the kind you buy in C&A or Marks and Spencer. It's tailor made for a start, cut to fit her, and it gleams as she walks back to her seat. But high under her right arm, where it fits tight, there's a spot of darkness where the material has absorbed a little sweat. Perhaps my questions are getting through.

'Do you want out, Billy? Do you feel it's too much for you? I can find someone else.'

She can't, not if it's me specifically she needs. But I'm not sure I want to take that much of a risk. Sara needs the money, damn it, I need the money. Why won't she tell me? If it's something innocent she could say so; if it's not, then I want the option not to be involved.

'I can do the job,' I say, 'but I know how much profit WPS has been making in the past few years, I've seen the company's accounts. Can it afford to pay me?'

She looks at me with a little more respect. Or perhaps her expression doesn't change and it's wish-fulfilment on my part.

75

'I'm surprised you have time for homework, Billy. But . . .' She stands up again, walks behind me and closes the door.

'What I'm going to say to you is confidential, Billy. No one else must know.'

'I'll say nothing. As long as it's legal, that is.'

'It's legal, Billy, entirely legal.' She moves back to her seat as if she was on a catwalk. 'The truth is, Billy, that WPS won't be paying you. Oh, the cheque will be a WPS cheque and it'll be honoured, there's no problem with that. But the account it's drawn on won't be the company's trading account. And there's a good reason for that. You see, WPS has a cash-flow problem. It'll make a profit, a considerable profit, on this contract. But we won't actually get any cash for at least another two months. If you've seen the accounts you'll know we're under-capitalised, we have no reserves. So we're being bank-rolled by Ratcliffe Plastics whose funds are controlled by Ratcliffe Holdings.'

'So the money comes from Ratcliffe rather than WPS. It still has to be repaid.'

'That's the beauty of it, Billy. It doesn't. You see, Ratcliffe Plastics needs to make a loss to be carried into Ratcliffe Holdings accounts for tax relief. So the cost of this work doesn't really matter, a few thousand pounds here and there are nothing. That's one reason the price doesn't matter. But there's another.' She stops, gulps at her coffee. Then she sucks her bottom lip into her mouth and inhales, as if summoning the nerve to tell me something I ought not to know.

'I need to make a success of this, Billy. It's the first real job I've ever had.'

'The first? But you told me . . .'

'My qualifications? They're true. And I did work for Ratcliffe, a long time ago. That's how I met my husband. But he didn't want me to work. At first I was occupied with the kids so it didn't really matter. But I studied in my spare time. Last year the youngest, Ben, went off to university. I

76

told James I wanted to start working again and he was . . .
well, he was amused. He thought I meant a part-time job,
or voluntary work. When he came up here to look at WPS
he said he'd need to appoint someone as MD. I told him I'd
do it. He said no but I was persistent, I nagged him, I even
went over his head to his father. Eventually they agreed I
could give it a shot. But I'm on trial. Any mistakes and I'm
out. I need to get this contract through safely, we're
depending on it. But although I'm MD here, I feel like a
puppet and my husband's pulling the strings. He has access
to all production information. He knows about staff
turnover. He knows about the vandalism. I've had to plead
with him to help out. It was my suggestion that a loss could
help the tax position.'

'So now you're vindicated. What's the problem?'

'Billy, James doesn't want me to succeed in this. I might
just prove I'm capable of something apart from mothering
his children. *He* would have done what you suggested,
drawn up a specification, asked for a few quotes. But I
think we need action now, quickly. You're good, Billy, you
can do the job quickly and on time. I'm depending on you.
That's why I'm willing to pay you a premium.'

'And the fact that your husband's company foots the
bill?'

'That is, I'll admit, an added attraction. Can you understand, Billy? Can you see what's motivating me?'

I think I can. She wants to win in a race against her
competitors, against those (whoever they are) causing
damage to her property, and against her husband.

'I can understand your need to come out on top, Mrs
Ratcliffe.'

'It's more than that, Billy. Winning isn't enough. I want
to obliterate every bastard who's ever tried to hold me
back. I want them dead by the side of the road.'

I hope she doesn't mean it literally. And I hope she
doesn't consider I'm trying to hold her back.

'So that's the whole story, Billy. Are you with me?'

The implication is that if I'm not with her then I'm against her. The word 'neutrality' isn't in her dictionary. Before I can answer there's a knock on the door. She raises one red-tipped finger to her lips and stares at me. 'Come in.'

The man who stalks into the room is tall and thin, his arms, legs and body barely able to support the weight of his well-pressed suit. His shoes are a brightly burnished black, his thinning hair pure white. His skin is smooth, as if it's been polished.

'Morning, Charlie. Coffee?'

'No thank you, Caroline.' He doesn't wait to be offered a seat, he pulls a chair to the side of the desk and folds himself into it.

'Billy Oliphant, this is Charlie Harkness, company secretary. Charlie, meet Billy, he's seeing to our new security system.'

He nods at me, too distant to shake hands without standing again. He decides I'm not worth the effort.

'Have you brought the cheque book?' Carrie Ratcliffe asks.

'Of course.'

'Good. Just sign a cheque and leave the book there, will you? I'll fill in the amount on the stub.'

'But Caroline, I really do think . . .'

'Don't fuss, Charlie.' She turns to me and explains. 'Charlie's a Ratcliffe man, Billy, been with the company since before he was born and he'll be here long after he dies. Is that right, Charlie?'

Charlie nods and I feel a swell of sympathy for him. I'm sure he prefers being called Charles, and I suspect he detests the offhand way Carrie Ratcliffe talks to him and treats him. His discomfort could be reaching the point of physical pain, so grim is his face. He manages to summon enough energy to take a pen from his inside pocket and sign a blank cheque.

'Charlie specialises in putting right the financial and

78

administrative inadequacies of new acquisitions, so he's got his work cut out here.' She reaches across and slaps him on the knee, takes the cheque book from his hand. 'But I don't want to keep you from your ledgers, Charlie, you can slip back now. I don't think we'll need you any more.'

He stands to leave and seems surprised when I too rise to my feet. His head moves slightly, backwards and forwards, he's like a mantis about to pounce.

'Thank you very much Mr Harkness,' I say, holding out my hand. He takes it in a soft, papery grip. 'It's been nice meeting you.'

'You too, Mr Oliphant,' he replies as he leaves. When he closes the door it's with a soft, gentlemanly, self-satisfied click.

'He's a smug bastard. Everything I say and do gets back to my husband through him. Well, almost everything.' She writes out a cheque and hands it to me. It's a sign for my dismissal. I put the cheque in my wallet, slide it into my back pocket and head for the door wondering exactly what she meant by that last comment.

Chapter Eleven

The installation's straightforward. The building's rectangular, so there's a double camera on each corner. This allows two views of each side of the building. The cameras are under the eaves, but dummies are also fixed on the corners themselves, bright yellow boxes with red lights. Anyone wanting to damage the system will, hopefully, attack the boxes rather than the real cameras.

While Sly and I are fixing the cameras, Norm's bolting plastic ramps to the entrance road. It's hot, we're all wearing Norm's straw hats. Sitting on top of the scaffold tower, dust and dirt sticking to the sweat on my body, I wonder whether his idea of setting up a stall to sell the hats isn't such a bad idea.

By midday the cameras are in position, but all the cable ducts have to be inside the building. We need electricity to power the cameras and their motors, plus the cables linking them to the monitors. It's too hot for me, up at the junction where walls and ceiling meet. Sly's showing no signs of distress, so I leave him, go outside to supervise Norm. The ramps are in place so we begin fixing the ground supports for the poles which will hold the fence protecting the PVC hoppers. For once Norm doesn't say much. The poles lock into hollow steel tubes which have to be drilled into the earth. The job's noisy and the ground's hard. There's a constant mist of dust, it crawls up our noses, fogs up our goggles, grates in our eyes. The girls from the office bring us out a bottle of water every thirty minutes; half is drunk, we pour the rest over us. I wish I'd worn shorts.

We break at about one when Carrie Ratcliffe brings us sandwiches and cans of iced coke, lemonade and fruit juice. Sly's van has a rear door hinged at the top, it provides us with some protection from the sun. Our hostess insists on staying while we eat. She doesn't seem to notice that the conversation is stilted, that Norm keeps looking at her legs, that Sly says little at all. It takes ten minutes to devour everything she's brought, then I rise to my feet. Sly and Norm do the same, they can see we'll need to work well into the night to achieve anything.

'The Victorian work ethic still exists, I see,' says Carrie Ratcliffe. 'Or is it more like the cooperative movement, everyone pulling together. I'm pleased to see you so involved with your work, Billy.'

'I like to keep an eye on things,' I reply.

'Do you know when you'll be finished?'

'We'll have the fence up this afternoon, the cameras by late evening, the monitors in position as well.'

'But the cameras won't be connected up tonight?'

'Well, they'll be capable of working. But the internal wiring, the monitors ... I don't think so. Tomorrow we'll be fixing internally, connecting up the window and door alarms, setting up the control desk so anyone can use it. We'll be finished by tomorrow night.'

'Good. I'd like to know myself how everything works, I'm starting a night security man in two days' time, I'll want to show him the ropes.'

'I can do that. I've allowed for it in the spec.'

'I know, Billy, but I too like to be involved in all aspects of my business. Look, I'd like to stay and watch but I've a meeting this afternoon. Just get into my office when you need to. I'll be back about seven. Do you prefer Chinese or Indian food?'

The question is unflagged, and I'm sure I sound rude in my one word response.

'Why?'

'I'll bring a take-away back, for you and the boys. Or do you want me to decide for you?'

'Thank you,' I say, not used to my employers looking after me quite so well. 'I'm not sure what Sly and Norm would like. If you just make a decision . . .'

'I'll surprise you, then,' she says, walking away, 'I'm good at surprises.'

Chapter Twelve

When Sly's drill decides it's had enough punishment I have to send Norm for another. This means we get behind with the fence. Then we find one pack of conduits is the wrong size, so Norm has to make another journey to replace it. Sly helps me with the fence, we finish it as Norm returns. It's cause for celebration, the completion of the outside work.

'I'm fuckin' knackered,' says Norm, 'you're a bloody slave driver, you are.'

'He's just too proud to admit he can't work as fast as me,' says Sly. We're carrying monitors and stands into the building as the office staff are leaving.

'Yeah, you're half my bloody age and twice my bloody size!' complains Norm. 'And to think, I gave you a hat. What do I get in return? Insults.'

'You're both working hard,' I say, not sure this time whether my companions are really arguing, 'and if we finish on time there'll be a bonus for both of you. Not to mention a free meal when Mrs Ratcliffe gets back at seven.'

'A free meal?' says Norm, 'I don't know if I'll have enough strength to lift a knife and fork, let alone chew food.'

'I've know you turn down anything free in the past,' says Sly.

'In fact,' continues Norm, 'if that Mrs Ratcliffe came in wearing nothing but whipped cream on her nipples, I wouldn't have the strength to lick it off.'

As we head for Carrie Ratcliffe's office Charlie Harkness slippers towards us. His head is bowed, he's carrying a file of computer print-outs large enough to curve his spine. He raises his eyebrows as he sees me, lets Sly and Norm past, then blocks my way.

'Mr Oliphant.'

'Mr Harkness. Is there a problem?'

'No, switchboard says there's a telephone call for you.' He looks up and down the corridor then gestures to a door behind me. 'Perhaps you'd like to take it in my office? Then could we have a word? I won't keep you too long.'

'That's okay.' I motion to Norm and Sly to show I'll catch up, allow the accountant to open the door and switch the light on. The office is small. There's no natural light, only the dull glare of the fluorescent tube above my head. There are tables against two of the walls, all covered with papers, but there's logic and neatness in the piles. The remaining space is taken up by a desk and two chairs, a safe so small Sly could lift it.

'Just pick up the phone and press the flashing button,' says Charlie Harkness. He goes back out into the corridor, closes the door behind him.

'Hello?' I say, expecting it to be Rak. She's the only one who knows where I am, the only one who needs ring me. But it's not her.

'Mr Oliphant?' It's a woman's voice, a voice I don't recognise.

'Yes. Who is that?'

'You're an *elusive* man, Mr Oliphant. I've had a *terrible* time tracking you down. I've left *three* messages on your ansaphone today, you really *should* call into your office more often.' She stresses key words in her sentences, like a teacher prompting her class.

'Look, who is this?'

The voice ignores me. 'The only other point of contact we have is your *home* number, though your file says "gone away". Still, I tried it. Your *wife* told me where I could find you.'

'I don't care how you found me, unless you tell me who you are, unless you tell me why you're ringing, I'll put the phone down. You have three seconds. One, two . . .'

'I didn't tell you who I am? I'm so *sorry*, Mr Oliphant, how *remiss* of me. Allow me to put matters right. My name is Alice Palmer. *Mrs* Alice Palmer. And I'm the head of Finance and Recovery Services for Kingfisher Leisure.'

The woman's name means nothing, but the obfuscation of her job title can't hide the work she does. And I certainly know Kingfisher Leisure.

'You rang my home? You spoke to my wife? I just hope you didn't tell her who you are, I hope you didn't say why you were ringing, because if you did, I'll descend on you like a ton of bricks! What the hell do you want anyway? I'm not due to make another payment until next week.'

'Mr Oliphant, please! I dislike threats. I try *very hard* not to use them myself, and I appreciate clients who offer me the same courtesy. Of *course* I didn't tell your wife why I was ringing. I could have done, I'm not bound by any agreement not to do so. But I didn't. I told her I wished to seek a *quotation* from you. And she was *most* helpful. She said you'd told her where you were working, a *double-glazing* firm, she couldn't remember the details but she was good enough to look through Yellow Pages until she recognised it. And so I'm ringing you. How *are* you Mr Oliphant?'

'Busy, Mrs Palmer. And on schedule to make another payment next week, as promised. So if you'll excuse me . . .'

'One moment, Mr Oliphant. That's the reason I'm *ringing*. You see, your scheduled payment has been *rescheduled*. To *tomorrow*. And the *other* monthly payments, they've become *fortnightly*. With *immediate* effect.'

'Tomorrow? That's ridiculous!' I remember that Charlie Harkness is outside the door, I try to calm myself down. 'Now look here, Mrs Palmer, I don't know exactly where you come in the hierarchy of Kingfisher Leisure, but I have an agreement . . .'

'Had, Mr Oliphant. Past tense. And I'm *afraid* I'm top of the pile. The *pinnacle*. The *zenith*. I answer *only* to the directors. I'm really sorry about this,' she says unctuously, falsely, 'but we feel your debt repayments need a *little* more zip, they need a touch of adrenaline. Intravenously, of course, delivered by someone experienced in the art. That's me. That's what I'm doing now. Administering the dose. So I'll look forward to seeing you . . .'

'And if I don't have the money?'

'Ah. Yes. The perennial difficulty. *Remind* me, Mr Oliphant, what is the extent of your debt?'

She has the figures at hand, she's a professional working for a professional company. But I humour her, I won't give her the satisfaction of making me lose my temper again, I won't aggravate her. If she does have the authority she claims, then annoying her might make matters worse.

'I owe you just under twenty thousand, interest being charged at the ridiculous rate of about forty per cent. I have – thought I had – an agreement to pay it off at a thousand a month.'

'That's accurate enough, Mr Oliphant. But the trouble is, that will take *too long*. So I really *do* need something from you tomorrow. Say five thousand?'

'Five? But I've been paying a thousand . . .'

'Cash-flow, Mr Oliphant, blame it on cash-flow. You're working, aren't you? A good job? Your wife *said* it was a good job, *surely* you ask for a deposit. I'm *certain* you'll be able to sort *something* out.'

Carrie Ratcliffe's cheque's still in my wallet, hot, urgent. I can divert some of that to Palmer, give myself a little time.

'I'll see what I can do,' I say, reluctantly.

'*Good*, Mr Oliphant! I *do* like optimism. And please, if you see your wife, pass on my regards. She seems *most* charming.'

'We've separated. I don't live with her any more.'

'But you just *happened* to tell her about this *project* you're involved with at the moment. Ah well, it's not for me to pry.'

I think she's going to ring off, but a new note enters her voice.

'Do you have a *daughter*, Mr Oliphant?'

'Why?'

'Oh come, you have a *daughter*. I *heard* her in the background, I spoke to your *wife* about her, innocently of course. How *old* is she? Early teens?'

'Fifteen.'

'Pretty?'

'Yes, I like to think so. Why are you asking?'

'Oh, no reason. Call it general interest. Call it an aid to *focusing*, Mr Oliphant. You decide. I'll see you tomorrow. Personally.'

The phone clicks. I'm cold, for the first time in three weeks. I slide into a chair, I can see nothing but Kirsty's face, feel nothing but her arms around me. Then there's a knock on the door and Charlie Harkness's nervous grin slips into the room.

'All done?'

I place my thumb and forefinger either side of the soft flesh at the base of my thumb, pinch hard. The pain restores my voice and my concentration. 'Yes, thank you.'

'Not bad news, I hope?'

'No, quite the opposite. A potential customer.'

'Oh. I thought I heard voices raised . . .'

'Negotiations, Mr Harkness, tough negotiations.'

'I see.' He slides into his seat past the monitor I've placed on the floor, past the crush of paperwork.

'I'm sorry for the rather cramped conditions, Mr Oliphant, as an extra member of staff at a very busy time

87

this is the only accommodation which could be found for me. You see, I need privacy, I can't work if I'm subject to interruptions.'

I'm not normally brash and rude with people I don't know, but my telephone conversation has left my patience abraded. So I vent my frustration at the first person available.

'Don't you mean, Mr Harkness, that Mrs Ratcliffe put you in here out of spite? You could have been in one of the offices downstairs, but you're in here because she doesn't like you. I'm sure it's nothing personal,' I continue, softening my voice. I don't need to affront this man, I hardly know him. Friends, allies, acquaintances are *always* helpful. 'I'm sure you've done nothing to offend her. But she doesn't want you here, that's why she makes life difficult for you.'

He's not as good as Carrie Ratcliffe at hiding his emotions, he's surprised to hear what I've just said. But he pulls himself together quickly.

'You're right, of course. Mrs Ratcliffe doesn't like me being here. But you're wrong when you say I do nothing to offend her, though I do try to be as pleasant as I can in her company. However, I sense that my very presence offends her. I'm too staid, too set in my ways. You see, I believe that management is a science which can be applied to any set of circumstances. Given *A*, then *B* will follow, which will lead to *C*. That's the way I learned and it's always served me well. But Mrs Ratcliffe feels that management is an art. She thinks it needs flair and talent, she thinks companies are run by inspiration rather than a dogged, methodical approach.'

He has my sympathy. It's difficult forming a relationship with someone whose mind works in a different way entirely, whose sense of direction isn't necessarily wrong, just working with a different set of bearings.

'I can see you have your problems, Mr Harkness, but why . . .?'

'Have you cashed your cheque yet, Mr Oliphant?'

'No, I've had no time . . .'

'I would advise you to make time, first thing tomorrow. Did Mrs Ratcliffe explain that the cheque isn't drawn on the company's current account?'

'Yes. She told me why as well, because of problems with cash-flow. She said her husband had agreed to fund the shortfall through a special account, and that it didn't matter how much was spent because the loss would be . . .'

'. . . offset against tax? Mr Oliphant, it would be nothing of the sort. Mr Ratcliffe's instructions were that this account was to be used for normal business transactions as and when required. The decision as to when funds were to be transferred was to be a joint one, taken by Mrs Ratcliffe on my advice. The payment to you does not satisfy that decision.'

'So why are you telling me to cash the cheque tomorrow?'

'Not just cash it, Mr Oliphant. Ask your bank to present it for payment immediately. It will cost you a small fee, but the funds will be transferred electronically as you wait. At approximately ten thirty tomorrow Mr Ratcliffe will be returning from a short holiday, I've left word for him to contact me. I shall advise him of Mrs Ratcliffe's profligacy. He may attempt to stop the cheque. I shall certainly advise him to do so.'

I've suffered rubber cheques in the past, but the prospect of this one bouncing is more than I feel able to cope with. 'Hold on, Mr Harkness, hold on. You've lost me. You're telling me you're going to stop my cheque?'

'Yes. But I'm also advising you to cash it before I have the opportunity to stop it.'

'I don't understand.'

'Then I shall explain. I already have grounds for stopping the cheque. I've seen a copy of the contract, I know the amount involved. You're making a lot of money from this job, Mr Oliphant, I've asked around, I know what a fair price would be.'

89

'I've a signed contract,' I protest.

'I'd be willing to argue it with you, through the courts. Ratcliffe is a wealthy company, Mr Oliphant, we could tie you and the cash up for some time.'

'So why tell me in advance? Why warn me to cash the cheque?'

'Because I want it to be cashed. It gives me more leverage. I can say to Mr Ratcliffe "I warned you, but we were too late." There will have been a large and specific loss entirely attributable to Mrs Ratcliffe. It may be enough to have her removed. Then I can get on with running this company as it ought to be run, without her interference.'

The matter of Charlie Harkness's definition of interference doesn't concern me as much as being paid. I've already promised some money to Sara, I have my suppliers to pay, Norm and Sly, Rak. And there's the matter of the cash for Alice Palmer.

'And what about the balance? That cheque was for half the contract value, it barely covers my costs. The profits were all in the second cheque. What about that?'

'Mm, yes, I can see that might cause you a problem.'

'It might cause you a problem too. I might just decide to tell Mrs Ratcliffe what you've told me. I don't think your closeness to her husband will be any good when she comes after you with a carving knife.'

He blanches, quite difficult for a man whose pallor is already that of a corpse.

'We can solve this problem quite easily,' he says, 'without any need for telling tales. Or violence. But it requires honesty, Mr Oliphant. Now I've been honest with you, I need you to be honest with me. What is a fair price for the work you're doing now?'

I know my calculations by heart, my original figure was just over seventeen thousand.

'I'll remind you, Mr Oliphant, that I've done a little investigative work today. I've had access to your specification. I've had other companies "tender" for the work. And,

90

in case you have any misplaced loyalties to Mrs Ratcliffe, let me further remind you that your contract is not with her as an individual but with WPS. Any additional cheques she issues will, I guarantee, be dishonoured. Now then, a fair price.'

I dislike being cornered. I even dislike people feeling they've cornered me, particularly when they haven't. And for two people to pressurise me within ten minutes makes me very angry. That anger could easily be directed against Charlie Harkness. With difficulty, I force myself to the conclusion that he, at least, is concerned for his company, that there's a small amount of morality in his proposition. So I concern myself with my price. My specification is top heavy, I know what the national firms will charge. And I suspect that Charlie Harkness will only have contacted national firms. He's that type of person, the pens on his desk are all top of the range Parker.

'Twenty-two,' I say, grudgingly.

'Too much,' he smiles back at me, 'twenty is more than enough.'

'I've dropped other work to carry out this job, there's a premium for that. No one else could do it this quickly. Twenty-one.'

He arches his fingers. He appears to enjoy the touch, the pattern, the symmetry. He stares at me through his hands before realising how silly he looks.

'Done,' he says, 'I'll let you have the balance on completion.'

'Now,' I say, 'I want to bank it straightaway. Just in case Mrs Ratcliffe finds out and murders you.'

He grins at me with sour sarcasm, but he's already reaching for the safe behind him. He unlocks it, takes out a cheque book and begins to write. But he stops before signing it.

'There's just one more thing, Mr Oliphant.'

'What's that, Mr Harkness?'

'A favour. I took the opportunity a few days ago to

purchase a small machine which can be attached to Mrs Ratcliffe's telephone. It can, so I was told, record all conversations and the telephone numbers of those calling her. The trouble is, I'm not very good at things mechanical, things electrical. I need to have the listening part fitted to her phone, while the recording part – I have it all here, in my drawer – remains here, in this office. Obviously, I have no wish for her to know about this. Would you mind doing this for me, while you and your men are working in Mrs Ratcliffe's office? While she isn't here. As soon as you get into the office, let us say.'

His pen hovers above the blank space on the cheque. I nod. He signs with a flourish, hands the cheque to me and follows it with a plastic bag taken from his desk drawer.

'So pleasant doing business with you, Mr Oliphant.'

'And you, Mr Harkness.' As I leave I notice the pens on his desk. I've arranged them, while we were talking, in neat ranks parallel to the desk sides. I know I'm under pressure.

Chapter Thirteen

Carrie Ratcliffe returns just before seven. She unpacks two plastic bags on to the coffee table in her office, takes out plates, knives and forks from the cupboards in the kitchen. She's changed out of her suit, looks more at home in jeans and T-shirt (undoubtedly not the same ones – she's the type to wash clothes after holding them up in the morning to see if she'll wear them). She's friendly, almost motherly in her attitude, chiding us when we don't drop tools as soon as she announces the food is ready. She serves us king prawn chop-suey, chicken foo-yung, char-sue and beansprouts, sweet and sour chicken, yung-chow fried rice and prawn crackers. There's far too much, even allowing for Sly's appetite and Norm's hoarding the leftovers. She's even brought a bottle of wine; I stick to water.

When we return to work she washes the dishes. Then she watches us.

Sly's busy drilling holes in the wall to allow cables to pass through. Norm's helping me wire up the control desk, then running to hand Sly tools, cables and wires. That's when Carrie Ratcliffe decides to help. At first she looks over my shoulder and gets in Norm's way, then she stands too close to Sly and gets covered in dust. Then she moves over behind me.

'You'd get on more quickly if Norm helps Sly and I help you.'

I look at her hands. The fingernails are long, painted red. She catches my glance, wiggles her fingers.

'Divinely decadent,' she says, 'but also false. If they break, they break. I can have new ones fitted any time.'

'It really does require a little knowledge,' I say, 'it's not just handing me tools.'

'Billy, even with long nails my hands are smaller than yours. I can thread wires through to you, I do know a little about electrics, and I'm not as stupid as you think.'

'I haven't said you were stupid,' I defend myself.

'Non-verbal communication,' she replies. 'Off you go, Norm, give Sly a hand.'

Norm shrugs, does as he's told. Annoyingly, we do get on faster working as two teams. And Carrie Ratcliffe is useful. Once she's been shown what to do she doesn't need telling again. Just after nine Sly and Norm start tidying up; within ten minutes the floor's been vacuumed, equipment and machinery stacked, and they're standing like expectant puppies waiting for their reward.

'All done?' I ask.

'Ready for launch, boss,' Sly says.

'And ahead of schedule,' adds Norm, 'I reckon your new apprentice deserves thanks for that. It's far easier workin' on just one job, 'stead of tryin' to do two at once.'

Carrie Ratcliffe's lying under the control desk, connecting leads. On hearing Norm's words she slides out. Her T-shirt is dirty, her jeans dusty and her hair's in knots.

'I consider that a compliment, coming from an expert like you, Norm,' she says. Even to my cynical ear she sounds sincere.

'Thank you,' I add, then turn to Norm and Sly. 'Okay, you can go. Back tomorrow at eight, we don't leave until we finish. And thanks.'

Sly nods, shoulders his bag and heads for the door.

'Don't you want a lift, boss?' asks Norm.

'No,' I say, 'we've got on faster than I thought. Another hour or two and I'll have the screens working, I think I'll stay and get that done. I'll get a taxi home.'

Carrie Ratcliffe sits up. 'You're that far on? Great, I'll stay, then,' she says, 'help out.'

'It's okay, I can manage by myself. It's mostly fine-tuning.'

Norm too is on his way out, there's still valuable drinking time if he hurries home.

'If it's going to take longer than half an hour I'll have to stay anyway. Late shift finishes at ten, there's no one else to lock up.'

'What about the night shift?'

'There's no night shift tonight or tomorrow, it's shift swap-over time. There's no permanent night shift, it's a rota that alters every fortnight.'

'So there's an empty factory and no security guard. Not quite the best way of running things.'

'But there's the deterrent of cameras on the outside walls, Billy, and locked doors. And we have the internal lights on time-switches, so it looks as if someone's in. I don't think it's that much of a problem.'

I seem to find it easy to offend Carrie Ratcliffe, and once I do so there's no easy way to retreat. She goes on. 'Can I suggest we – or you, if you insist I can't do anything – get on with things? I *do* have a home to go to.'

She's still helpful, even with the more complicated tasks I'm carrying out. At ten the shift manager reports in, Carrie asks him to pull her car into the factory and lock the building's myriad doors before he leaves.

'I'd rather have the car inside,' she explains, 'the local kids throw stones at the Merc in the daytime, God knows what they might do to it when it's dark.'

We keep working. At eleven I have the first monitor active; by eleven thirty all four are on and the random switching gear is showing the view from each camera in turn. There's still a jumble of wiring hanging from the control desk, few of the controls are connected, but the system is, as far as I'm concerned, largely complete. Carrie goes over to the bar, pours herself what appears to be a very large whisky.

'Don't you think you'd better stop now?' she says. 'You look tired. I can give you a lift home.'

'Just a little longer,' I reply. 'There are one or two things to tidy up. If you need to go you can always leave me to lock up.'

'It's okay. I've nothing pressing. But first, a toast to hard work.' She lifts her glass. 'Can I tempt you with a Perrier?'

'Tap water would be fine.' She hands me a glass and I raise it to her. That's when my worries return. During the previous four, almost five hours, I've been so involved in my various tasks I've been unable to concentrate on anything but them. Now the problems fill my mind again. Charlie Harkness and his cheques, Alice Palmer's demands, the veiled threats against Kirsty and Sara. Then there are the new worries. I've bugged Carrie's phone and I feel I've betrayed her. She's been helping me, without her the installation wouldn't be as far advanced as it is, and I reward her by deceiving her. The combination of all these obviously has some affect on me, on the way I look.

'Billy? What's the matter? You've gone very pale, are you okay?'

'Just tired,' I say, 'it's been a long, hot day.'

She trundles a chair across to me, commands me to sit down. I do so, there seems little point in arguing. She holds out her hands in front of me. 'You were right about the nails,' she says. They're chipped and broken, the red varnish flaking away. 'But there are advantages to having short nails.' She moves behind me and I feel the pressure of her thumbs on my shoulders, the trace of her fingers at the bottom of my neck. Across the room the monitor screens merge into a blur of blue light.

She's good. Perhaps the labours of the day and my general tiredness are conspiring against me, but I don't believe I've ever enjoyed a massage quite so much as that one. If one of the blessings of life is that pain can never be remembered – an individual can recollect being in pain, but never the pain itself – then the same must be true about pleasure. And striving to regain remembered pleasure is the motivation for so many things we do. Look at a typical human courtship ritual, for example. The formalities both parties usually adhere to are driven by a need for sex; to be specific, a need for orgasm. If we could remember the feelings one orgasm brings there'd be no need to search for another. The pleasure Carrie's fingers are giving isn't orgasmic, but it's equally transient. As she lifts each fibre of muscle, rotates it over the bone beneath, the dull ache in my neck and shoulders disappear in a warm haze of luxurious tranquillity. My eyes close, my whole body relaxes.

'You missed your vocation,' I say.

'I couldn't do this for a living,' she replies, 'not on demand, not for payment. There has to be an element of choice in it. My choice.'

Her fingers rise to my neck, circle my ears then squeeze the bridge of my nose. Her thumbs are pressing at the outer corners of my eyes. She pulls her fingers back over my scalp, over the top of my head and down again onto my shoulders. I shiver at the sensation.

'Cold?' she asks.

'No,' I reply, snigger at the thought. The windows are still open, there's dust in the air and it's going to be a hot night again. I can feel the blood rising to the surface of my body; though I'm sitting still I'm beginning to sweat.

'It's no good,' she says, 'the seat's too high, I can't get any purchase. Go and sit on the sofa.'

I'm incapable of disagreeing with her. It takes an age for me to climb to my feet, to persuade my legs to carry me across the room.

'Do you want these things switching off?' asks Carrie, pointing to the monitors.

'Just leave them, they're not properly wired up, I don't want you to electrocute yourself. I'll do it in a minute.'

The sofa is an off-cream colour. I look at my dirty jeans, my sweat-stained T-shirt.

'Do you have a towel, something I can sit on? I don't want to get the sofa dirty.'

Carrie smiles, walks over. I realise I've been thinking of her as Carrie and not as Mrs Ratcliffe, yet I can't remember when the transition occurred nor what prompted it. It's a sign of my tiredness.

'The covers are removable,' she says, 'washable. Don't worry about it. Sit.'

The cushions are wide and deep, when I'm leaning back my feet barely touch the ground. Carrie settles herself behind me, I think she's kneeling down, and she's concentrating again on my head. Her fingertips graze my eyelids, press hard at my temples, move round my ears and my jaw.

'That's really good,' I say after a few minutes. 'but I really should finish off, it's getting late. There's only the video recorder to wire up, then that's it for the night.'

Her fingers cease their motion. I'm still wearing my smile, the one that indicates a state of soporific trance. It's the one I wear when Kirsty scratches my back or when I visit the hairdresser and the washer rubs my scalp to bring up a lather of shampoo foam. Carrie moves round, I feel the cushion depress and open my eyes to see her kneeling beside me. She puts her head on one side, looks me in the eyes.

'That's the first proper smile I've seen on your face.'

Eye contact is dangerous. I try to avoid it, it gives too much away. Witches believe it's the time a person is most vulnerable, it's the time when souls can most easily be stolen. It's as if a shield has been removed, looking straight into someone's eyes, it allows direct access to the mind within. I can see into Carrie's eyes. I can see she wants to kiss me. I know she can see a reflection of her own feelings in my eyes.

Her mouth is hot, her tongue wet, both still retain the bitter taste of the whisky she's drunk. As she leans over me her hands cup my face, as gentle as her kiss. But then she takes my tongue between her teeth and at the same time rakes her fingers down the stubble on my cheeks. My eyes fly open to see the excitement on her face, but it's a brief glimpse, she throws a leg over my thighs to straddle me and we kiss again.

Sara and I didn't make love for two months before I left. Since then my only sexual encounters have been in my dreams, embarrassing confrontations leaving me to wake alone, sticky and frustrated. Now I can feel myself awkwardly constricted within my jeans as Carrie pushes against me, a fight of friction, denim against denim. In an effort to relieve the battering I pull her T-shirt from her waistband, reach for her breasts. The fabric of her bra is thin and satiny, her nipples already erect. I roll them gently under my palms.

'Harder,' she hisses into my neck, her fingers now behind me, digging into my back. I do as she says, pull at her breasts. It isn't enough.

'Harder,' she says again, 'do it harder! Take the fucking thing off!'

The urgency of her request isn't lost on me, I don't bother with the strap, simply pull the cups down over her breasts. Her T-shirt is under her chin, she pushes one nipple into my mouth as I knead the other with my left hand. My right is behind her, groping at her rear, sliding between her legs.

'Fucking jeans are almost as good as chastity belts,' she says as she rolls off me to my right. Then our tongues are in each other's mouths again, but this time our hands find the work easier. She pulls at the leather of my belt then tugs hard to release it; our buttons and zips fall easily beneath combined assaults, then her hand's hot inside my briefs, my fingers are gliding beneath damp cotton, negotiating wiry hairs.

'Christ,' she murmurs, spreading her legs further. I can't say anything, my mouth is attached limpet like to one breast while both hands explore her.

'Oh, Billy, that's good, that's so fucking good!' I hear her say. Then her words are replaced by moans. The excitement she feels is indicated by a more than proportionate increase in the noise she's making. One of her hands pumps more vigorously at me, the other's cracked, sharp nails dig into my back.

'Slow down,' I whisper, but either she doesn't hear me or she chooses to ignore me. I can feel the warmth building deep inside, I move my own fingers faster in the hope that Carrie's own pleasure will slow her down, but she just moves faster and louder. The noise is coming from both of us now, as if we're trying to outdo each other.

'You bastard!' I hear myself say as I ejaculate, 'you fucking bastard!' And then I'm incapable of voluntary motion, I sink back into the seat. The sofa will definitely need cleaning, as will Carrie's T-shirt and jeans. She too subsides, breathing heavily.

'I'm sorry,' I say, hoping she'll understand I'm apologising not for the mess but for my untimely detumescence.

'Has it been a long time?' she asks, her hand still holding me.

'A long time,' I echo.

She takes a deep breath and stands up. She pulls her T-shirt over her head and discards it as she hooks her shoes off. With one hand she undoes the clip on her bra and lets it fall to the floor. Then she wriggles out of her jeans. Her briefs, white cotton, do little to hide her sex. Black hair creeps out at the top and sides.

She's well preserved for, what, forty plus years? Her breasts and buttocks are still firm, her stomach is almost flat. As I watch she begins to move, a little dance. One hand is submerged in her briefs, the other pulls at her nipples. Her eyes are glazed.

'You'll soon be fit again,' she says, and I can already feel the truth of her words. She moves towards me, hips swaying, until she's close in front of me. I can smell her excitement. She pulls down her briefs, and as she bends I glimpse behind her a flicker of movement on one of the monitors. She kicks the final item of clothing away from her, stands naked before me, but I'm already trying to see round her.

'I wanted you the first time I saw you,' she says, then notices my attention is elsewhere. I struggle to my feet, fastening my jeans as I do so. I run across to the monitor table.

'It might just be a stray dog,' I say, 'but it could also be ... Yes!'

'What is it Billy?'

'Three men, baseball bats, east side.'

'Shit!'

I can hear her behind me fumbling for her clothes.

'And petrol. They've got cans, I think. I'll get a close up. Yes, definitely cans.' I look around. Carrie's found her T-shirt and briefs, her jeans are inside-out and she's fighting with them.

'Leave those, get on the phone to the police. Tell them it's suspected arson. Tell them ... No, wait.' I scribble a number on a piece of paper. 'Ring that, ask for the duty officer, it's quicker than 999.'

She does as she's told as I search the room, desperate to find something I can use as a weapon. There's nothing. I hear her ask for the duty officer, I take the phone from her.

'Who's that?' I say.

'Inspector Bryden,' comes the reply, a female voice, 'can I ask who you are?'

I feel my shoulders tense. I would have preferred any officer to Kim Bryden. But choice is something I lack at the moment.

'Kim, it's Billy Oliphant here. I'm at Winner Profile Systems on Parkside, I'm installing ...'

'Billy Oliphant? What the hell are you doing ringing this number, you know ...'

'For Christ's sake, Kim, shut up and listen! I'm installing a security system at WPS, we've caught some

101

villains on the screen, equipped for burglary, and they've got petrol cans. If you shift your arse you might just stop them burning the place down. I'd recommend a fire tender as well. Got all that?'

'Two units and a tender on their way, plus ambulance alerted, Parkside Estate. And I want a word with you, Billy.'

Carrie's bent over the desk watching the screen, her shirt halfway up her back, her backside bare.

'They're pouring out the petrol,' she says.

'Damn! Sorry, Kim, I'll talk to you later. I've got to go. Here, have a word with Carrie.'

I hand the receiver to Carrie, at least she'll legitimise my call.

'Quick, where are your keys?'

She points at her jeans on the floor, I fish a set of keys from her pocket.

'Which one's for the front door?'

'Red tag.'

I run out, down the stairs and along the corridor to the reception area. There's a fire extinguisher on the wall there, I pick it up, remember another in the general office and dive in to collect that. It seems to take an age to open the door, but then the lock clicks. I kick the door ajar and head into the night. I still don't know what I'm going to do when I round the corner. Three against one, the odds are favourable. I slow down, listen carefully and hear whispered voices.

'No,' one says, 'we'll do as *I* say. You go round to the left, Fatman, Zag here'll go to the right. Empty your cans then come back to the corner, signal, and we'll set them off together.'

'But we'll get a better blaze if we do it all here,' says a second voice.

'Aye, it's quicker as well,' adds the third.

'Shit, Fatman, we could've had the fucking thing burning if you two hadn't decided to have a fucking debate on it. Just do as you're fucking told!'

102

There's a chorus of grumbles, then the sound of footsteps. I shrink back, put one of the extinguishers down, hold the other above my head. A figure appears at the corner. I bring the extinguisher down hard on his head, I'm rewarded with a metallic ring as he crumples to the ground.

'Zag, did you hear that?' asks the first voice.

'Hear what?' comes the reply from further away, barely audible.

'A noise, I thought I heard a noise.'

Zag is evidently returning, his voice is getting louder again.

'But you said there was no one in the place, didn't you?'

'There isn't. Fatman? Fatman, you all right?'

'Aye, I'm all right,' I whisper back, harshly. 'I tripped up, that's all.'

'Well be more fucking careful. Go on, Zag, back you go. Get a bloody move on.'

I feel in my pocket, there's a twist of wire in there. I use it to fasten Fatman's hands behind his back, though I've hit him so hard I suspect he won't wake up until morning. My first thought, that I should try to scare the three vandals away, has been replaced by an idea that I might just be able to capture them. There are no real grounds for this optimism save a ridiculous excess of self-confidence, but it makes me move again to the corner and peer round. The petrol can's upside down on the ground, the un-named leader of the group standing well away from the wall holding a lit cigarette. I consider whether I might be able to rush him, but he'd see me. I realise I don't know whether they're carrying guns. Discretion bullies valour into submission; where the hell are Kim Bryden's mobiles? I can't see any details of the intruder, but judging by the movements of his cigarette and his muttering to himself he's nervous, impatient or both. I decide action's called for and I lean forward.

'Hello, Charlie Foxtrot to Tango leader,' I say in a whisper, but loud enough to make sure I'm heard, 'suspected burglary at Winner Profile Systems. Three intruders spotted, assistance required.'

The head villain's away, he doesn't even pause to warn his friends. But he does flick the cigarette from his hand. I watch it describe a lazy arc, before it hits the ground there's a low, soft explosion of flame. I'm there straight away with my extinguisher. A lot of the petrol has vapourised, that's why the ball of flame is so large. After it disappears into an oily smoke the fire remaining is small, I can cope with it easily with only one extinguisher. Then I hear Zag.

'Jocky, what the fuck's going one, I haven't ...'

He's already round the corner, I'm clearly visible in the dying light. I can see him considering flight, but there's only one of me, unarmed. He drops his petrol can, I'm pleased to hear it hit the ground full. Then he pulls a knife from his pocket, heads towards me. He's bigger than me; most men are. His hair is cropped short, I can see the glint of gold-capped teeth in his smile. I can probably run faster than him, but then he might find time to set fire to the building.

'The police are on their way, Zag, put down the knife.'

'I can't see no police,' he says, 'I'll hear them coming anyway. So I've got time for you and for the building.'

'That's not what Fatman thinks, he's tied up round the corner. And Jocky, he's already run away. We've got you on video as well, you might as well give up now.'

He lurches towards me; I back off, watching his knife hand. That's my mistake. Jocky may have run off, but when he stops, when he realises he's not being pursued, when he sees no sign of police cars, he comes back. He circles round behind me. And he kicks me on the back of the legs.

The pain is excruciating, but it's dulled as they inflict similar punishment on the rest of my body. I curl up but can't avoid their boots and fists, I pray Zag's knife won't be brought into action. I think I remain conscious throughout, but I can't be sure. I know I'm awake as they pour the can of petrol over me.

'You made a mistake,' hisses Jocky, 'you should remember you're just an old man, a little old man.'

'Soon be a hot little old man,' laughs Zag. I can taste the petrol fumes in my mouth. Where the hell are those police?

'Who gets to torch him?' asks Zag.

'You can have him,' says Jocky.

'You won't get away with it' I say through cracked lips. I think my jaw's broken and one of my teeth is loose, and I regret the cliché as soon as I've spoken. 'You're on video.'

'Thank you Jeremy Beadle,' says Zag, 'but I don't believe you.' He looks up at the nearest camera and grimaces, lifts his fingers in a V. Then he turns round, drops his trousers and moons, wiggling a large expanse of buttock. That's when, on the periphery of my clouded vision, I sense rather than see a flashing blue light.

'Cops,' says Jocky, 'go on, torch him.'

Zag reaches into his pocket, brings out a lighter and holds it up.

'Bye, little bald man,' he says.

'Hold it!' cries a voice, Carrie's voice. She appears at the corner, no more dressed than she was when I left her. Cradled in her arm is what looks like a sub-machine gun. She walks toward us.

'This is a Hilti gun,' she says, 'it's used to fire nails and rivets into metal and PVC. It's not very accurate over this distance. If I pull the trigger I might miss. But on the other hand, I could send a nail into your leg. Or your eye. Or your balls. Now what's it to be? Do you want to gamble? Or perhaps you should just piss off.'

Zag and Jocky look at Carrie, then at each other. Then they're away to the fence, through a break and into the distant hides of the Parkside Estate.

'Thank you,' I mutter, 'thank you, thank you.' I rise to a sitting position, Carrie bends down beside me.

'Are you all right?' she asks.

'No,' I reply, 'but I know their names, we've got them on video . . .'

'Billy, the machine isn't connected yet, remember? The cameras are working on live, but they're not recording.'

'Shit! Well at least we've got one of them, I tied him up round the corner.'

Carrie shakes her head. 'He's gone. I saw you hit him, I saw you tie him up. I also saw him wake up, he's got away as well.'

'Damn! Why the hell didn't you try to shoot one of them with that bloody gun thing? I doubt it would have killed them.'

Carrie holds up the gun. 'With this? It's not loaded, Billy. And even it if was, it works with compressed air in the factory. It's not connected.' She shrugs. 'Still, it looks good.'

That's when the police cars skid into the compound. I can see the lights of the fire tender entering the estate, the ambulance close behind. 'Too fucking late, boys,' I say, 'too fucking late.'

I hear the sound of footsteps, their approach is leisurely, and look up to see a familiar face.

'What the hell are you up to, Billy?' asks Inspector Kim Bryden. She glances at Carrie, notices her lack of clothing. She sniffs. 'And your aftershave smells like petrol. I don't think it'll catch on.'

106

Chapter Fourteen

The paramedic tells me I don't appear to be concussed. I've a few cuts which hurt like hell where the petrol's found them, my bruises are beginning to form and I can barely walk unaided. But I refuse to go into hospital. The ambulance leaves, the firemen check to make sure there's no further damage, Carrie helps me back into the building. I lean on her; Kim Bryden walks alongside.

'So you're setting up a security system here, Billy?' she asks.

'No, Inspector Bryden, I'm considering buying double glazing.'

'And working late, as you naturally do, you see three villains with petrol cans on your screens. So you go to investigate.'

'That's right.'

'That's what Mrs Ratcliffe here told me.' She turns to Carrie. 'Why were you still in the building, Mrs Ratcliffe?'

'I have the keys,' says Carrie, 'and I had work to do.'

'Do you normally work in such a state of undress?'

'I'd finished *my* work, but Mr Oliphant hadn't finished his. There's a sofa in my office, I decided I'd have a sleep there. It was hot, I took off some clothes.'

Kim nods. I recognised the gesture, it's a sign she doesn't believe what she's hearing.

'Look, Kim,' I say, 'I need . . .'

'Inspector Bryden, if you don't mind,' she replies. I used to know her, if not as a friend then certainly as a colleague of equal rank. We called each other by our first names. But this is the first time I've seen her since I left the force. I'd thought she might understand, but her face shows no sign of any desire for comprehension. It's an old-timer's face, it shows the weariness of someone who's seen too much. It's the face of a woman who wants the shift to end, the night to end, then she'll be a few hours closer to retirement.

'I need a shower, Inspector Bryden. Then I want to sit down. Once I've done those two things then I'll tell you exactly what happened. And *then* you can do your job and try to catch the bastards who tried to set this building, and me, on fire.' We reach the door and Kim Bryden has, at least, the courtesy to hold it open while Carrie helps me through.

'I'm sure Mrs Ratcliffe will offer you some tea or coffee while you're waiting,' I add, 'though she might want to get dressed first.'

'I think I'll need to change my clothes completely,' says Carrie, 'these have got petrol on them. I've some spare here, I often work over. And I can get you some overalls, Billy, we might as well burn your old clothes.'

'Not before you take my wallet out of my pocket,' I say, remembering the cheques inside it.

We stumble on, Carrie and I doing our three-legged hobble, Kim dragging behind, further behind still a young uniformed constable. We manage the painful stairs one at a time, I bring us to a halt outside the door.

'This is my office,' explains Carrie. 'There's a shower inside but I don't really want the place to smell like a filling station for a week. If you'd like to hold Billy up, Inspector, I'll get him a towel. Then he can undress out here. Would you mind?'

Kim always was a smart dresser. She tried to claim a tax allowance for her outfits when she went plain-clothes, but the Inland Revenue weren't having it. That doesn't stop her splashing out. Even now, on nights, she doesn't sink to chain-store produce. Carrie can see that, hence her suggestion. Kim doesn't hesitate.

'Constable, help Mr Oliphant,' she says. 'You can start getting him undressed while Mrs Ratcliffe fetches a towel.'

'Thank you,' says Carrie. 'There's a storeroom just across the corridor where we keep the overalls and T-shirts for our employees, would you mind picking one out for Billy? I'll put the kettle on.'

The young constable takes Carrie's place. By the time Kim returns my T-shirt has been removed. The trousers follow as Carrie arrives with a towel.

'I think I can manage the rest myself,' I say, wrapping the towel around me and pushing the constable away.

The shower's jet of water is powerful. I switch from hot to cold and back again, it brings a little life back to my body, soothes a few of my aches. I've been beaten up before, I know that tomorrow I'll feel worse. My face is cut at the side of my right eye, my left is beginning to puff up. I managed to take most of the kicks on my arms, but they also made contact with my ribs a few times. Not hard enough to break them, though they're tender. My inspection is halted by a knock on the door.

'Mr Oliphant, I don't have all night. Would you mind hurrying?'

'Thank you, I'm still alive,' I reply, but turn off the shower and dry myself as quickly as possible. I don't want to antagonise Kim too much, I want her to find the thugs who attacked me. I also want her to find out who put them up to it. How I get her to pass that information to me is something I'll worry about when the time comes.

Dried, dressed in overalls and a T-shirt too large for me (I suspect Kim chose them that way deliberately) I describe my attackers, give Kim their names.

'Not a lot to go on, is it? Fatman, Zag and Jocky. Local lads, thick as shite – or so you'd have me believe – out for a bit of excitement. You play superhero, bite off too much, and they decide to take advantage. Do you really expect me to devote man-hours to this?'

She's testing me, waiting for me to lose my temper. I don't have the strength.

'Local lads, Inspector, yes. Out for excitement? They came equipped. They had a job to do. Someone was paying them. If you look through the local station's day book you'll find regular complaints of vandalism against this property, statistically more than there ought to be. WPS is being targeted and last night was just another move in what'll be a long game.'

'I can't spare . . .'

'And then,' I go on, determined to finish before I fall over, 'there's the matter of attempted murder. If it hadn't been for Carrie I would have been fried. What was your response time, Inspector? You'll get your citizens' charter taken away from you.'

'The matter will be investigated with the due resources available,' says Kim Bryden. In her anger she's reverting to police-speak.

'I'll be down tomorrow, then,' I say, 'to look through the mugshots. Just in case I recognise them. And what about the petrol cans, are there any prints on them?'

'Forensic are already there, Mr Oliphant,' says the constable.

'David, shut up,' snaps Bryden. 'And Billy, stop interfering. I've already got cars on the estate looking for your runners. Like the constable said, they're taking prints, from the cans and from the fence post where we think they got in. Yes, come down tomorrow, you can look at the faces, you can play with the photofit. But stop trying to run the case for me.'

She stands up, the constable copies her.

'I'll have both your statements typed up. I'll get someone to bring yours round for signing, Mrs Ratcliffe. Mr Oliphant, you can sign yours at the station. Thank you for the tea. Now I must be going.'

Carrie follows her downstairs and locks up. When she comes back I'm still on the sofa. She looks at me, kneels on the floor in front of me. All her make-up has gone. She hasn't had time for a shower yet, her hair is a cacophony of knots. She looks her age.

'Thank you,' she says, 'you saved the factory.'

'And you saved me.'

'I suppose we're even then.' She reaches out her hand to my head and leans forward. She kisses me.

I break away. 'Carrie, I don't even think I could raise a smile.'

'I know,' she says, 'that was just another thank you. There'll be another time. Lie down, sleep.'

'What about you?' I protest as she pushes me sideways.

'I need to shower, then I'll watch the screens. I won't be able to sleep anyway.'

I wake at six to find Carrie's head on my chest, her arms draped over me. I manage to move without waking her, head for the shower-room to have a drink and find pain-killers. When I return Carrie's climbed on to the sofa. Muscular pain, so I've been told, is best dealt with by mild exercise. I decide to test that theory and manage to walk round the room. Feeling adventurous I go out into the corridor, explore various offices. When I come back it's after seven, I ring Norm and ask him to call at my flat, collect some clothes. Then I make coffee for Carrie, wake her. While she showers I look through the drawers of her desk, more for something to do than from any real purpose. There's little of interest: some stationery, remnants of make-up, a pair of briefs, a box of tampons; a locked box of computer disks. A perfunctory glance at the contents of her handbag reveals only that her hair's darker than it appears in her well-worn passport photograph, and that she's collected a large amount of Dutch small change. It's habit makes me do this, and I'm pleased when I hear the shower being switched off. There are other things I should be more concerned with, and there's another long day ahead.

Thursday

Chapter Fifteen

I leave Sly and Norm to continue with the installation. Carrie drives me into town before going home (a rented apartment overlooking the park, she tells me) to sleep. She drops me not far from my office and informs me she'll be back later in the day, extracts a promise that I'll rest, a promise we both know I'll break.

The bank isn't far away and having the cheques cleared is easy, it requires only a phone call from the assistant. I feel guilty, accepting Carrie's money while betraying her by hiding Charlie Harkness's conversation from her. I try to persuade myself otherwise. All I'm doing, I tell myself, is getting my priorities right: they are, firstly, me, Kirsty and Sara; then my employees; then WPS, the company, not Carrie as an individual. Getting involved with Carrie – emotionally, sexually – confuses these priorities. It confuses me. We're both married (though her relationship with her husband seems unusual); the fact that I'm living apart from my wife makes that both more and less of a difficulty. I am, I suppose, free to find a new partner if I wish. I'm just not sure that's what I want; I'm frightened to admit that I might still love Sara when it's clear she doesn't love me.

I walk delicately to the police station. I don't want to hurry, it's too hot and it's too painful. It's my old patch, it'll be the first time back for me since I was dismissed.

And I'm nervous as I push through the doors and into the lobby.

Terry Gascoigne's on desk duty, greyer and wider than I remember him, scrawling in a ledger.

'Morning, Gazza, thought they would have retired you by now.'

'No, Billy,' he says without looking up, 'they can't get rid of me. They keep me here as a stud, to make sure there's quality police genes for years to come.' Then he looks up and smiles, but the smile turns into a wince. 'Bloody hell, lad, you been stopping buses with your face?'

'No, couple of thugs were using me as a football. I'm here to look through the mugshots. Kim Bryden said she'd set it up.'

'Yes, they warned us. I'll tell them you've arrived.' He picks up the phone. 'Hello, desk here, Mr Oliphant's arrived. No, there's no need to come down, he knows his way.' He hands me a visitor's lapel badge bearing my name.

'Billy, me and some of the lads, we didn't get the chance to say goodbye, to say what we really felt. So it's nice to have you back. Hope you find what you want.'

The phone rings, he answers it. I make 'see you later' signs at him, he presses the entry button and I pass into the heart of the building. I could have asked him why he didn't call me. I could have asked why none of the people I once considered friends bothered to contact me. But I don't care any more.

I wander the corridors. I see an occasional familiar face but no one recognises me because they're not expecting to see me. It doesn't take long for someone to escape from the consciousness of an organisation like this. I climb the stairs slowly.

WPC Anderson is probably the most junior constable Kim Bryden could find, that's how important my case is. She's fresh-faced, worried when I eventually arrive because it's taken me so long to get to the office. The room we're to

116

use is windowless, supposedly air-conditioned. It smells of stale sweat. Anderson's uncomfortable in my presence, she knows the procedure but hasn't really had the opportunity to apply it. Most of the time I'm guiding her. But at least she's polite, and when she asks if I want tea I succumb, I need something to keep me awake.

There are faces I remember from my days with the force and I can't resist naming them, acting surprised that they haven't been put behind bars yet. Then I recognise Jocky. I don't say anything, but I memorise his number. There are no names on the photographs, this would give innocents looking through them the opportunity to seek revenge if they knew who a villain was, where he lived. The file of names, addresses and past convictions, all in numerical order, is separate. But it's in a side office behind a locked door, on a computer.

'I don't suppose,' I ask Anderson, 'I could ask you for a glass of water and a couple of paracetamol?'

'Don't you feel well, Mr Oliphant?' She knows about my attack, my face certainly makes me look as if I should be suffering.

'I just feel a bit faint. It's so stuffy in here, is there anywhere I could get some fresh air?'

I know the building better than she does. The only room with a window is the one with the mugshot-name computer. She takes me in there, sits me down, hurries away for water and pain-killers. I switch on the computer, curse as it takes an age to get to the main menu. They've been too lazy to change the password, by the time I hear Anderson's footsteps I know Jocky's address and his past convictions, they're written down and locked away in my jacket pocket. I take the water and the paracetamol, realising I need them both.

'Thank you,' I say, 'I think I'll call it a day if you don't mind. I don't think I'm up to looking through that book any more.'

'Would you like me to get you a taxi?'

'No, it's okay. But you can tell Inspector Bryden I didn't find anything.'

'Yes, of course. Do you need a hand to get back downstairs?'

I could get used to this if it didn't make me feel so old and infirm. 'No, I'm okay. But thank you very much.'

I use the lift on the way back, going downstairs is more painful than going up. Gazza's busy at the desk, I wave at him but he doesn't see me.

Chapter Sixteen

My muscles seem easier if I use them more so I decide to walk down to the riverside. The world changes as I get closer to the river, becomes less civilised. The railway viaduct rumbles above me, the stairs and alleys are dark shadows. The Bridge is high overhead, its green metal and pale grey supports streaked white by pigeons and gulls. The streets and pavements here are mostly empty during the day. It's at night they come alive.

When the police clear the city centre of drunks, tramps and the homeless, usually about three in the morning, they tend to drift down here. They set up home in doorways, wrapped in cardboard and dirty clothes, but most return to their regular begging haunts in time for the morning rush-hour. So I'm surprised to see a figure I recognise still squatting in the old pump-house doorway. He's wearing a red woollen hat pulled down almost to his nose, and he's rocking slowly backwards and forwards.

'Joe?' I say. 'I Joe Steadman?'

There's no reply, just a monotonous groaning. I reach for his hat and roll it back to reveal a face whose blotches and bruises are livid beneath the dirt-encrusted skin.

'Joe? It's Billy Oliphant. I used to . . .' What can I say? I used to blackmail you for information when I was a police officer. I used to buy information for the price of a fix of alcohol or drugs, whatever you needed most. But the need

119

to explain myself further doesn't arise. He stops groaning, looks at me.

'Billy? Billy Oliphant?' He grabs my sleeve, giggles harshly. 'Kicked you out, I heard. 'S that right?'

'What happened to you?'

'Kicked me in. Kicked you out, kicked me in. You out, me in. T'other night.'

'Who kicked you in?'

'Big lads. Told me, don't shoot up near ... near ... I forget where. Kicked me in. Took it away, broke bloody syringe. Bastards!'

I'm tempted to leave him, but he used to help me out. He's gone down a lot since then. 'Look,' I say, reach into my pocket and pull out a ten pound note. 'I've got to go and see someone, but I'll be back soon. I'll get you something to eat. Here.' I rip the note in two, give him half.

'Ta,' he says, makes as if to rise. I push him back down.

'You can't spend it, Joe. I've got the other half. You wait here. When I come back you can have the rest. Okay?'

'Yeah. Yeah, thanks, thanks to God, Jesus Christ, Holy Mary, mother of God.' He's shaking now.

'Don't go away. Understand?'

'Understand. Holy mother, understand. Thank you mother, thank you.'

He climbs to his feet as I walk away.

'Mother,' he calls after me, 'mother, mother mother!'

I turn the corner. These are two or three restaurants, a pub, but the reason people come here is straight ahead of me. *Ladders*. The entrance isn't much to look at, a pair of stout double-doors with no external handles. But inside there's an aircraft hangar of a dance area, a smarter, quieter nightclub, and a casino. None of these are open now, there's only the familiar side entrance. The back lane is tidy, the door open, and I walk in. There's not a lot to see. A plexiglass screen behind which a young man in a suit pretends he's a bank clerk. A door. The carpet's threadbare, the lighting bright, and the security camera high in the corner catches every movement. On the wall behind the clerk a bird has been painted in blue and red, and below it are the words 'Kingfisher Leisure.'

'I've come to make a payment,' I say, reaching for my cheque book. Inside is a statement showing my debt, I post it through the slot in the glass.

'Mr Oliphant?' asks the clerk.

'The one and only.'

'Mrs Palmer would like a word with you, if you have the time.' I have no option to refuse, the clerk knows that. 'Through the door, Mr Oliphant, someone'll be down to collect you.'

There's a buzz and a click, the door relaxes in its frame and I push it open. The room beyond is small but smart. There are three easy chairs; a coffee table loaded with copies of *National Geographic* and *Hello!*, a stack of cups and saucers, a coffee pot, a basket of UHT cream portions and sugar bags. There's music playing, pan pipes desecrating a Beatles song. I try the only other door; it's locked, the security's better than in the police station. I take a seat and try to relax.

The door's opened by an Olympic hammer-thrower squeezed into an evening suit. He's a caricature of every bouncer, bodyguard and doorman I've ever seen, I could walk between his legs without ducking, but I follow when he gestures to me. He leads me along a well-padded corridor, narrow, and stops in front of an open lift door. I go in, he follows me, presses a button. We rise three floors and get out, go along a corridor to the end door. He knocks politely, then enters. I'm close behind.

I find myself blinking in strong sunlight filtered through long white curtains in a room of ambassadorial proportions. There's little furniture: a table and chairs, television and video recorder and, at the far end of the room, a wide desk.

'Please, *do* take a seat Mr Oliphant.'

I recognise the voice. Alice Palmer is sitting beyond the desk. On the wall behind her are life-size drawings of

121

statues, six of them, each bearing a Latin inscription beneath. As I move forward the hammer-thrower glides ahead of me, takes up a position at the side of the desk. I sit down, still looking at the drawings.

'Early nineteenth-century originals,' she says, 'all illustrating some Latin motto or wise saying. "*Laborare est orare*," that's *very* appropriate these days, eh?'

'I don't know Latin.'

'Really? Such a pity, it really *is* the basis of a *good knowledge* of English. *That* saying means "work is prayer". And what *else* do we have? "*In vino veritas.*" "*Timeo Danaos et dona ferentes.*" "*In die castitatem.*" "*Salus populi suprema est lex.*" "*Haec olim meminisse juvabit.*" All drawn in the classes of *Reynolds*, I believe, though no one knows by whom. Worth a few hundred each, not *quite* in the same league as *that* one.'

She points to the side wall. There's another drawing, about eight foot square, of a man holding up three swords while, before him, three men raise their hands to take the swords.

'An *early* sketch, of course, not *firmly* attributed. But it's clear in *my* mind it's by Jacques-Louis David, a half-size preparatory drawing of "*The Oath of the Horatii*" Neo-classical, romanesque – what more can one desire?'

I have no idea what she's talking about. The drawing is faded, stained with patches of brown, it doesn't appeal to me at all. Still, I nod my head in an attempt to ingratiate myself, pull my seat a little closer to the desk. The gorilla to my right is on his feet straightaway until Mrs Palmer gestures him back down.

'My predecessor was injured by someone who *objected* to being asked to repay a *gambling* debt,' she explains. She's stick-thin, short hair dyed black, face powdered and sallow. Her suit is well cut but doesn't fit her properly. Her jewellery is expensive, the bracelet she's wearing looks heavy enough to snap her wrist.

'Mick is here to prevent *that* happening to *me*. If you

move towards me he'll hurt you in some manner I don't *really* want to know about. Break a limb or two, I'd imagine. Cause some internal damage. I mention this because I have *no* wish to see you hurt.'

'Thank you.'

'Though judging by your face I assume there *are* others who *don't* share my feelings.'

'Not everyone has your morals. Mrs Palmer.'

'Quite.' My sarcasm isn't lost on her, just ignored. 'Now then, *your* debt to Kingfisher Leisure. I take it you're able to meet our request for payment?'

The cheque's already written, I take it from my pocket and slide it – moving gently in case Mick considers it a threat – across the table.

'Five thousand. *Good*. And the cheque won't bounce?'

I shake my head.

'The *last* client whose cheque bounced suffered the same fate. Except *he* didn't bounce very high.' She smiles at me. 'A *joke*,' she explains. '*Now* then, I mentioned *future* payments, I believe. *Fortnightly* rather than *monthly*. *Two* thousand a time.'

'But it was a thousand a month!'

'And *now* it's two thousand a *fortnight*. You *see*, Mr Oliphant, the trouble is, you're something of a reformed *character*. You've *agreed* to pay off your debt and, so far, you've done *exactly* what you've said you'd do. And you *haven't* been back to the casino to raise the debt. You've stopped *gambling*, with us at least.'

'Stopped altogether.'

'*Admirable*. But, you see, you're no longer, in effect, a *client*. We'll make *nothing* from you once this debt is paid off. So we might as well have the money as quickly as possible. *That's* the modern thinking.'

'You mean if I was still gambling you wouldn't be pressing me so hard?'

'We'd *probably* have increased your credit limit to *thirty* thousand.'

'That's madness.'

'No, Mr Oliphant. *That's* called knowing your *client*. We wouldn't go *beyond* that, because you're not *worth* any more. That's about the *limit* of your equity in your *major* asset, your *home*.'

'Half that. My wife and I own it jointly.'

'And so you are both *jointly* and *severally* liable for each other's debts.' She rolls the phrase around her mouth as if it tastes pleasant. 'So *please* keep the payments up to date. Your wife – your *estranged* wife, that is – *wouldn't* be happy if we applied for possession because *you* defaulted on a debt. But I'm *sure* you're busy, *please* don't let me keep you from your work.' She nods at Mick who stands up; it's obviously my cue to do the same. I precede him to the door.

'Don't be a stranger, Mr Oliphant,' she says as I'm leaving. 'And *please* give my regards to your wife and daughter.'

I'm so angry when I leave I almost forget my promise to Joe Steadman, it's only when I'm fishing in my pocket and find the half ten pound note that I remember. I head back up the hill to the pump-room but when I get there Joe's gone. He's left his cardboard and a plastic bag; I peer inside it, there are three used syringes and an empty vodka bottle. I look up and down the road but there's no sign of him, he's obviously gone to try to spend his half note.

'Stupid bugger,' I say softly, then shrug. At least I tried.

Chapter Seventeen

I take a taxi to WPS. Sly and Norm have been working well and there's a message for me to ring Rak at the library. I do so from an empty office, I don't want Charlie Harkness to hear my conversation.

'Boss,' she says, 'sorry I didn't catch you yesterday. I've been chasing Ratcliffes on every database I could think of and come up with nothing.'

'Nothing?'

'They lead blameless lives. No debts, no convictions. Ratcliffe Holdings is ring-fenced with obscure companies trading out of Panama or the Caymans, registered in Liechtenstein, Swiss bank accounts. I can't even get the names of directors. James and Carrie Ratcliffe normally live in Surrey. She's rented a flat . . .'

'Yes, I know about that, she told me. How did you find out?'

'Easy peasy. Library ticket.'

'Obviously.'

'Yeah, she's got a couple of Paretsky novels out, a guide to health and safety at work and a medical dictionary, *The Rough Guide to Holland*, the latest Martin Amis – not well reviewed, I might add – and, let me see, *Polymers and Plastics: Their Manufacture and Properties*. Quite a mixture.'

'And about as interesting as a shopping list. Anything else?'

'On the Ratcliffes, no. But you asked about the council contract. There were six firms on the tender list, only five submitted tenders. The locals are Pearson Plastics, Global Windows, and Design-a-frame PVC. I've got their directors' names, turnover and profit figures. I faxed them through to your office, thought it would save you coming out to get them. That's about it.'

'That's good, Rak. Now, what I want you to do ...'

'There's more?'

'There's more. I want you to phone each of those firms, find out what profile system they use, whether they extrude their own or buy in. Okay?'

'Yeah, profile system and supplier if they don't make their own.'

'Then ask what their delivery time is for supply only and for supply and fit.'

'Okay. Do I need to know why?'

'I don't, why should you? Just call it deep background. You'd better say you might have quite a bit of work for them, you're ringing from ... from a small builder renovating six old terraced houses. That should do. And if you think of anything else on the Ratcliffes, let me know. Fax the office with it, I'll be out from now.'

'Anything you say boss. Happy hunting.'

'You too, Rak.'

Norm and Sly have been listening to half the conversation, their work on the wiring and ducting is complete. The control desk is set up, the video loop installed; we still need to finish the alarms on windows and doors, but they need a break.

'Right,' I say, 'something different now. I'm going to pay a call on a friend, the one who tried to fry me last night. He might be a little dangerous. If you want to come along you're welcome, but I'll understand ...'

'Show me the way, boss,' says Sly eagerly.

'I suppose I'd better come to keep my eye on you both,' adds Norm.

I'm pleased. I don't think I could manage anything adventurous by myself. I limp down to Norm's van, mix some soil and water and smear it on the number plates.

'What do we need?' Sly asks.

'I don't know. Crowbars, I suppose. Bring a drill and a grinder as well.'

'Jesus, boss, you planning on cutting his fucking legs off?' asks Norm.

'In case we need to get into the house. I don't want to hurt him.'

'Really?' Sly's surprise is, I think, genuine.

'No. At least, not until he's told me who's paying him.'

'Where to, then?' says Norm. I can remember the address, but I check my piece of paper anyway.

'We're going to call on James "Jocko" Ewart. He lives out the West End, place called Ladysmith Road.'

Chapter Eighteen

Once, not too long ago, rows of terraced houses slid down from the West Road to the river. They were prevented from descending to the water itself by Bankside Road. Bankside Road separated the houses from the factories, the steel mills and the chemical plants. At the end of every road was a pub, a natural place for the workmen to stop on their way home. Here was the greatest concentration of drinking houses in Britain. Then successive governments destroyed the region's heavy engineering; the factories, the pubs, the houses disappeared. Now there are modern flats, often as bad as the slums they replaced. But higher up the hill, towards the West Road where Big Lamp Aggro Boys still daub their initials on any flat surface, the terraces still stand. And that's where Jocko lives.

Norm knows the street. Half the houses are boarded up, some have been torched. We drive past Jocko's address, the curtains are shut. At the top of the street is a pub, the Green Dragon. Norm points at the holes in the render.

'Bullet holes,' he says, 'sub-machine gun. Not a good place.'

'Looks ideal to me,' I answer. 'Keep going till you find a phone.'

'A phone? Round here? Endangered species they are.'

He's right. We have to go into the General Hospital before we find one that works. I get the paper from my pocket, dial Jocko's number. The man himself answers, I recognise his voice. In the background a dog's barking, a woman's shouting, a baby's crying. It does away with the need to find out if he's alone.

'Jocko?'

'Yeah. Who's that?'

'You don't know me, I hear you're a man I could trust to carry out some work. Some heavy work.'

He's wary, I can tell by the pause before he speaks again.

'What kind of heavy work?'

'The kind it's best not to talk about on the phone. But it's well paid if you can come up with the goods on time and keep quiet about it.'

'I can keep quiet. But I don't know nothing about you, I don't know who the hell you are ...'

'Perhaps we should meet then. Talk things over. Have a drink or two. Yes?'

'Okay. Whereabouts?' He's still suspicious.

The Queen's Head, Elswick Road. I'm near there at the moment.' The Queen's Head is known as a meeting place for thugs, but only those from the lower slopes of the hill. By suggesting it I'm giving him the opportunity to offer an alternative, to develop his own plan. Then, hopefully, he'll be more enthusiastic.

'Nah,' he says, 'the beer's piss awful there. Make it the Green Dragon. Know where that is? West Road?'

'No,' I say, 'but I can find it. When?'

'Half an hour.'

'How will I know you?'

'You won't. Get a paper, a *Sport*. Open it up, put two pints of bitter on it. I'll find you.'

'Half an hour then.'

He doesn't bother replying.

Chapter Nineteen

Norm's the one who sits with the paper, Sly's too big and Jocko might recognise me. The two of us wait at the bar where we can see what's going on in the greasy mirror. Sly's bag's on the floor at his feet, full of heavy tools.

The pub's quiet. Everything smells of smoke. The walls and ceiling are stained as yellow as the barmaid's tan. She chews gum and watches a television whose colours are garish and whose volume can't be turned down. It's loud in all senses of the word.

Jocko's fifteen minutes late, but ten of those are spent walking round the pub and peering in through dusty windows. When he comes in he leers at the barmaid then walks over to Norm and sits down.

Norm's been rehearsed. He's to tell Jocko he wants a hit, he'll pay five hundred, two in advance, three on completion. Norm's to hand over details of the victim (a sealed envelope with a blank piece of paper inside) and the two hundred pounds in a privacy, in the toilet. I watch carefully, I see Norm shake his head, mouth the words 'Not here,' look around; then Jocko points to the toilet, stands up. He's a predictable man. He allows Norm to lead the way, he follows, looking around him. As soon as the door closes, Sly's on his feet, I'm close behind.

We've checked out the toilet. There's one cubicle, one set of stalls divided into four compartments. It's finished with glazed green Victorian tiles, many miraculously intact, and echoes with the smell of disinfectant. Sly's in first, he moves fast despite his size. Norm has positioned himself so Jocko has his back to us; he really is a very silly man. Sly's punch in his kidneys sinks him to the wet floor. Then its easy for Sly to turn him on to his stomach and tie his hands, kneel on his back to prevent him moving. I bend down in front of him. Sly pulls at his ears to make him lift his head, Norm skips past to listen beside the door.

'Remember me, Jocko?' I ask softly. 'You tried to torch me last night. You and your friends used me as a football. It wasn't a pleasant experience. Can you remember?'

'Yes,' he hisses.

'Good. Now, all I want to know is who put you up to it.'

He says nothing. I make a sign to Norm, we swap places.

'Down with his trousers, then,' I say, 'spread his legs.'

'No!' he says, wide eyed. He's worried. Norm continues with his task.

'Don't worry, Jocko, none of us are that way inclined. Even if we were, we'd be very wary of putting anything near *your* arse. Except for this.'

I'm carrying Sly's bag. From it I take a mastic gun.

'This is silicone mastic. Quick drying. I've two or three tubes here. The nozzle's quite smooth, you probably won't even feel me push it in. You certainly won't feel the mastic, there are no nerve endings in your intestines. I wonder if there's enough to backfill to your stomach? It's acid based as well, smell it.' I hold it under his nose. 'Acetic acid, I think. That means it dries even in moist conditions. Like inside you.'

I lay the mastic gun in front of him, bend down to look into his ugly face.

'Then it's a matter of time. Can you evacuate your bowels before it sets? Or do they have to cut you open and take out yards of your guts. Will you live, will you die? It's all new territory, Jacko, so far as I know the *BMJ* has never

131

published anything on the adverse effects of silicone mastic enemas.'

I take a small bottle from my pocket, hold it close to his eyes.

'Of course, it's immaterial if I use this as well. How can you crap when your arse is superglued shut?' I bend down and smile at him. 'And if there's any left I can always use it somewhere else. Your eyelids? Ears? I could even glue your dick to your arse. Now then, Jocko, who put you up to it?'

'Ted Samson,' he croaks. I motion to Sly, he lets Jocko's head go so suddenly it bounces off the floor.

'Ted Samson?' I look at Sly then at Norm. Both shake their heads.

'Who is he? Where does he come from?'

'Don't know ... nothing else. Met him in ... the Strawberry.'

'No address?'

'No.'

'How do you contact him, then? You must be able to contact him.'

Jocko's silence indicates I'm on to something. Sly rifles his pockets, finds his wallet. There's almost five hundred pounds in it, some betting slips, scratch-cards. And an address book. Under Ted Samson's name there's a telephone number.

'It's a pity,' I say, 'but it looks like we won't be able to bung up your works after all. Not because we don't want to, oh no. But it's something we can only do once, Jocko, so we'll let you off this time. But if you open your mouth to anyone, I'll come back and glue it shut. And one nostril. Hope you don't have a cold at the time, you'll drown in your own snot.'

I stand up. My muscles ache, I nod to Sly and Norm. Quickly, efficiently, they tape Jocko's mouth shut. Then they pull his shoes off, debag him, back him into the cubicle and tie him to the pipe leading from the cistern to the pan. I toss his clothes into the urinal.

'It's been nice talking to you, Jocko. I hope I never have to see you again.'

Chapter Twenty

On the way back to WPS Norm can't stop talking.

'Did you see the look on his face when you threatened to glue up his bum? I mean, I was sort of standing to one side, I couldn't really see much of it, but I could tell. He really thought you were going to do it.'

'Perhaps I was.'

'Come on, boss, you wouldn't have done that. You couldn't. But it was a good thing to threaten him with.'

Sly takes over. 'But a threat's only worth it if the person you're threatening believes you when you say you're going to hurt him.'

'Well in that case the boss is a good actor.'

I'm not a good actor, I can never hide my true feelings. I found it easy to threaten Jocko. I kept seeing myself, doused in petrol, the flame in front of me. If it hadn't been for Carrie I'd probably be dead. That's what made me threaten Jocko. And I could have carried it through. That frightens me. I wouldn't have cared if I'd had to hurt him, kill him even. And if I had, I'd probably have got away with it. There would have been nothing to connect me with him. I'm seeing a side of me I don't really like.

At my instructions we stop at another phone and I ring Ted Samson's number. It's answered after a long time.

'Who's that?' asks a voice. I can hear music echoing in the background, the hubbub of work.

'I need to speak to Ted,' I say. There's the whine of a high speed saw, a raucous laugh.

'He's not here. Who is it?'

I want to know exactly where 'here' is, but there are no other clues. 'I've got a delivery for Ted, its come through earlier than expected. I don't want the stuff at my place but Ted hasn't told me where it's to go. I can bring it out now, though.'

It's the best I can do, not very believable, too vague. Without knowing more about this Ted it's all I can come up with. Then I have an idea.

'Look, I'm running out of change. I'll ring back in ten minutes for directions, okay?' I put the phone down, ring Central police station.

'WPC Anderson, please. My name's Oliphant, Billy Oliphant.'

I wait for an age before being connected.

'Mr Oliphant? Anderson here, what can I do for you?'

'I've remembered something. A name, it just came to me. I think the people who attacked me might have mentioned it. I was wondering if you could check your records, see if it's in there at all, because I'm not *really* sure about it.'

'I'll do what I can, Mr Oliphant.'

'Thank you. The name's Dampson, or Rampson. Could be Samson, perhaps that would be the best one to try. His first name's Red, perhaps he's got red hair. Could be Ted, I suppose, the memory isn't very clear. Ted Samson? Yes, that sounds a good bet. Could you look him up?'

'I'll go . . .'

'And if he is there a description might help, he might even be one of the attackers.'

'All right Mr Oliphant. Just hold the line.'

She's away for three minutes, I'm timing her, staring at my watch.

'Mr Oliphant?'

'Yes?'

'Hold on please.'

There's the clicking, muffled sound you hear when a phone's being put down on a desk or handed to someone else. That's when I know something's not right.

'Kim Bryden here,' a new voice says, 'what's all this about Ted Samson, Billy?'

I resist the opportunity to swear.

'Who? I said Dampson, Red Dampson.'

'Bullshit! What have you got on Ted Samson? Why his name all of a sudden?'

'It just came to me, Kim, honest.'

'I don't believe you. I could have you, Billy. Subverting the cause of justice, withholding information, and that's just a start. So come clean. What have you got?'

'Look Kim, I'm in a phone box, I've no more change. Once this goes you've had it. I heard from a source that this bloke, Ted Samson, was behind the attacks on WPS. It's not a name I know, so I thought I'd find out what I could. There's not enough for the police to go on, I thought I'd give you a hand ...'

'We don't need a hand, Billy, certainly not from you.'

'... but since you know now, well, I'll just get back to work. Nice talking to you.'

'Billy! I'm warning you!'

'I know. Thanks. I'll try to – sorry, money's running out! See you, Bye.'

So Kim's in during the day, despite having been on duty the previous night. Interesting. And Ted Samson's noteworthy enough for her to speak direct to me, she could easily have told Anderson just to keep quiet. I've learned a little, but not enough. Still, Kim and I are on first name terms again, even if mine is spoken with hostility. It's a start. I dial Ted Samson's number again.

'Hello, I'd like to speak to Ted Samson,' I explain, 'I was on the phone before, I've a delivery to make. If you can just give me directions?'

'Who is that?'

136

'I'm a friend of Ted's, an acquaintance really, I've got this stuff to deliver . . .'

'What sort of stuff?'

'Well. I don't think I should say, seeing as how I don't know who you are. It's goods, valuable goods, goods he wants straightaway, soonest. And when he finds out I've got them but you wouldn't let me deliver, well, he's not going to be pleased. And you know what Ted's like when he's not pleased.'

'Yeah, Yeah, I know. He can be nasty. But I need a name, what are you called?'

'Harry Harrison,' I say, the first name that comes to mind, 'but you won't know me.'

'True. And I'm not expecting any goods from you. You see, my name's Ted Samson, so why the hell . . .'

I put the phone down quickly. Another path blocked. On a whim I ring directory enquiries and ask for Ted Samson's number. Allowing for the Edward Samsons, the Sampsons as well, there are a dozen numbers. None of them match the one I have.

I limp back out to the van. It's midday, I buy Norm and Sly fish and chips then doze in the front seat while they eat. I seem to be going nowhere.

Chapter Twenty-One

Carrie's at the factory when we get back. Sly and Norm are with me when we go into her office, it stops her being over-demonstrative. But she manages to touch my cheek when she examines my bruised face, her fingers slide over mine as she ushers me into a chair. I tell her of the morning's adventures, since it affects her and her company; she laughs aloud when I recount the details of Jocko's embarrassment.

'So what now?' she asks.

'Sly and Norm finish the window and door alarms. I'm going to visit my office, I need to see if there are any messages, open the post. I'll be back this evening to check everything's working. And that's it. All done. The end of the installation.'

'I'm getting used to having you around,' says Carrie. 'You've done a good job. No, you've done more than that, you've risked your life for my firm, for me. It's not much, but I'd like you to come to my place for dinner tomorrow night. So I can thank you properly.' She giggles like a schoolgirl. 'I'm quite a good cook.'

'I'd like that,' I say, 'but I'll be seeing you anyway. I've still work to do. I need to know why WPS is being targeted, who's behind it all. I want to find out more about this Ted Samson.'

Norm and Sly leave the office, their work in the room

complete. Norm winks at me as he closes the door.

'You don't have to do it for me,' Carrie says. 'You've already been hurt, I don't want anything else to happen to you.'

'I'm not doing it for you, I'm doing it for me. I have to do it.' 'It's true, I can feel the obsession developing but without the desire to hide it, to overcome it.

Carrie shrugs, comes round the desk and bends down, kisses me so hard I think my split lip will start bleeding again.

'I'll give you a lift into town,' she says, 'ten minutes? I've some calls to make, I need to check some schedules.'

'Make it twenty,' I reply, 'I want to speak to Sly and Norm. They should be able to finish without me, I want to make sure they know what they're doing.'

'Dinner okay for tomorrow, then.'

'Yes.'

'And I'd like you to stay the night.'

I feel like I felt with my first proper girlfriend when I was fifteen, when I put my hand on her breast and she didn't take it away. Excitement, mystery. A totally unexpected erection. I get up, walk at least a foot above the floor. I duck as I go through the door, frightened of banging my head. I turn to leave and Carrie's already picking up the phone, but she's looking at me as she dials, smiling. I close the door behind me and float downstairs.

Carrie doesn't have Norm's local road knowledge, she doesn't have his skill in watching other vehicles. So we find ourselves stationary on the Bridge, captured by a serpent of traffic, its head a collision two hundred yards ahead. I want to ask about her husband, her feelings for him. I want to ask about her family. I want to ask about her life. But she beats me to it.

'What happened?' she says. She doesn't look at me, just watches the back of the bus ahead, glances at the traffic flowing south.

139

'With what?' It's the hottest part of the day. The air-conditioning is struggling.

'Your life. The police. Your wife. I was asking Norm . . .'

'He talks a lot but he doesn't really say much. He doesn't know much.'

'He was very loyal. He said you left the police after a row. He said your wife found someone else. He wouldn't say more.'

'And what he said was wrong. I was thrown out of the police, deservedly. I was a drunk, I gambled. I went to a party and insulted the chief superintendent's wife.'

'How? What did you say?'

'I told her she had great tits. She seemed to like that. Then I started feeling them, she even liked that until her husband came into the room. That's when she started screaming rape. It wasn't, of course. Not even assault. But it was enough to get me demoted. Then I shopped a colleague, a sergeant who'd been taking backhanders. If I'd kept quiet they would probably have overlooked my gambling. But they didn't. So I was out.'

'Booze, broads and bets. You went through them all.'

'That's why Sara kicked me out. No, that's not true. She could cope with my failings. But then I stopped drinking, stopped gambling. I couldn't find work, though, and it began to depress me. I tried to top myself, not seriously, an o.d. I saw shrinks, I was in analysis. Still am, once a month, though I'm past the worse. But when I was bad I was really bad, I couldn't stand anything being out of place in the house, everything had to be just so. Sara wasn't working so we were home together. It hit her hard. I used to be strong-willed, a loner really. Then all of a sudden I became dependent on her, and she couldn't manage. I went into hospital, voluntarily. When it was time to come out she didn't want me back.'

'Jesus! She kicked you out when you needed her most?'

'No! She tried hard, very hard. It was my fault, not hers.

She'd forgotten what it was like to be free, and then ... I just hadn't appreciated her.'

'And you do now?'

'We still argue. I've a daughter, Kirsty. It's probably better for her as well, that I'm away from home. We get on well now. It's working out.'

'Shit. What a bloody life.'

The traffic starts moving again. Five minutes of silence and she pulls up outside the office.

'You've been through a lot, Billy. Still suffering too, by the sound of it.'

'I'm okay.'

She leans across, pecks me on the cheek. I feel somehow it's a gesture of sympathy, not of affection. 'You're more than okay,' she says, 'you're very special. And getting tangled up with me might only add to the complications in your life.'

'You don't complicate things.'

'You don't know my story yet.'

'Will I get to hear it tomorrow?'

'You might. Even if you don't want to, you might.'

It sounds like the end of a conversation so I get out. She waves as she drives away but doesn't turn. I walk into the building. When I reach my office door I can hear the tapping of the keyboard down the corridor; the typist girl is always there, always busy.

It's hot in the office, the windows have been closed for too long. I break into a sweat as I open them, then bend to pick up the post which has been reproducing behind my door. I ignore the letters, turn to the fax machine which has curled a roll of paper onto the desk. I tear it off and cut it into pages, start to read. Rak was right, there's little of interest in the accounts of the three companies she's been investigating. I skip the information on directors in favour of Rak's notes on how the companies work. Global Windows and Design-a-frame both buy in their profiles from large manufacturers. Pearson Plastics don't make

141

windows at all, they import them ready made from Europe using German profile. I sit down to figure everything out.

WPS got the contract by meeting the specification and having the lowest price. The other three companies tendered; presumably they were also able to meet the specification, though it might have meant altering their method of manufacture. Global and Design-a-frame could absorb extra costs in their own factories, but Pearson's supplier would have to do that. This would increase Pearson's costs by a greater proportion than the other two since the extra overhead would probably have a profit element added to it. There's always the possibility, however, that the German extrusion already met the specification.

The delivery times don't help. Global and Design-a-frame both quote a week for supply-only, two days for frames without glass; they're hungry for work, their factories probably aren't working to capacity. Pearson Plastics offers a far more leisurely three-week delivery time. Rak, bless her, has also managed to get a quotation on a few standard-sized windows. Global beats Design-a-frame on two styles, it's reversed on another two. There's very little between them and they both beat Pearson hands down.

I make a decision to exclude Pearson. Their price must have been too high, they aren't flexible enough, they aren't fighting for business. Second place in the tender stakes must have been Global or Design-a-frame.

There's a knock on the door.

'Come in,' I call, 'it's open.'

It's the office services girl who appears, mouse-like, in front of me. 'Mr Oliphant, I hope you don't mind me taking up your valuable time,' she apologises, 'but I thought you might be able to give me some advice. I was at the meeting, the one where there was a discussion on leases.'

'I remember it well.' It's true, I remember the meeting, though not the girl. She must have crept in at the back of the room, crept out again without anyone noticing her. She

142

looks the type of person to do that, someone who doesn't like speaking in public, who doesn't like approaching comparative strangers asking for advice. But she's here, talking to me, so it must be important.

'What's the problem?' I ask.

She glances at the pile of envelopes, neatly stacked but unopened on my desk. She brings out from under her arm a piece of paper which she hands to me. 'You'll have one too. It's from the solicitors making a final offer for buying out the leases. It's an increase on the last offer, quite a size-able increase. But they'll only hold it for two days. What should I do?'

'What should you do? That's quite a responsibility you're putting on my shoulders, Miss . . . I'm sorry, I don't know your name.'

'Arnison. Pamela Arnison.'

'Pleased to meet you.' I stand up, we shake hands; her grip is weak, ineffectual.

'According to this,' I say, reading rapidly, 'all the tenants must agree to the offer.'

'Yes, I know. I keep an eye on the entertainments place, they don't come in until the late afternoon. But I rang them this morning to tell them. They don't know what to think of it either. We agreed I should come and ask you.'

'I'm pleased you consider me worth asking.'

'We also agreed you could count on us to support you, whatever it is you're going to do. You've got our votes by proxy.'

'Now hold on! I can't afford the time to start . . .'

'We admired what you said in the meeting, about holding out. If you think it's worth doing that, holding out for more, then we'll do it. If you think we shouldn't sell our leases at all we'll follow you.'

'I'm sorry, Miss Arnison, I don't know if I want that burden on my shoulders.'

'But we trust you, Mr Oliphant.'

She's childlike in her determination to get me to help

143

and, in the end, I acquiesce, there's probably no other way of getting rid of her.

'Okay, I'll see what I can do,' I say, 'I might be able to find some information about potential buyers, what they intend doing. I'll let you know.'

A grin attacks her face. For a moment it looks out of place there, but then it realises it makes an otherwise plain young woman look almost attractive and it decides to stay.

'Thank you so much, Mr Oliphant, if you need letters doing in the course of your investigations please let me know, I'm very fast.' She giggles with horror at what she's said and retreats from the room. I smile a goodbye and return my attention to my fax pages.

I sort them into order, staple them together, then set the Pearson Plastics pages to one side. Only then do I notice, at the bottom of the first page, almost obscured by the over-printed date and time, the name of one of the directors. Ted Samson.

I ring Rak straight away, I have to give my name to the telephonist who says she's in a meeting. I tell her to get Rak out of the meeting, say it's bad news about one of her relatives.

'What the fuck do you want?'

'Marry me, Rak. Think what geniuses our children will be.'

'They'd be impoverished fucking geniuses because I won't have a fucking job. I'm in a *meeting*, for Christ's sake, I'm trying to explain why the job I do is *valuable*, and at the same time I'm trying to cover for all the fucking time I spend doing jobs for *you*! So what do you want?'

'The names of the shareholders in Pearson Plastics.'

'Is that all? Can't it wait?'

'No.'

She sighs loudly enough for me to hear, a deliberate attempt to demonstrate how much I use and abuse our friendship, our working relationship.

'I'll do what I can.'

144

'Ring me. Fax if I'm not in. Soon as possible.'

'Will do.'

'Like I said, I love you and want to have your babies.'

'Fuck off, boss!'

At last it's coming. Ted Samson's a director of Pearson Plastics. They must have tendered the second lowest price. If WPS are thrown off the job then Pearson Plastics take over, despite their high prices. Perhaps they get a better deal if they buy in bulk. And the replacement windows on the council estate will probably be limited to no more than seven or eight sizes and styles, there could be savings there. And Ted Samson's the muscle. All I need to know now is who provides the money, who owns the company. I don't actually rub my hands with glee, but a feeling of triumph does pervade my tired, aching limbs.

There's another knock on the door.

'Welcome to Clapham Junction,' I say. 'Come in, join the party.' I normally have one visitor a week, two in ten minutes defies belief. Perhaps this one will be a client.

He doesn't look like a client. His smile is too broad, too self-assured. The man with him doesn't look like a client either, he's the one holds the door open for the first to enter. Despite the heat he's wearing gloves.

The first man, dark wavy hair well-cut, suit nicely pressed, sits down opposite me; the second – younger and blond, leather bomber jacket, bright shirt, no tie – pulls out a small gun and points it at me.

'My name,' says the first man, 'is Ted Samson. I think you've been trying to get in touch with me.'

Chapter Twenty-Two

He leans back in his seat, hands behind his head, sure of himself. He notices the papers on the desk, leans forward to pick them up and glance at them. I see his eyebrows lift, he wasn't aware I was so close. He nods to himself.

'You're good, for an amateur,' he says.

'You aren't, for a professional,' I reply, more to balance the conversation than to annoy him. He remains calm, as I expected.

'I've come to invite you to a meeting,' he says, 'with my boss. You don't have the option to decline. You can decide whether you come on your own legs or with Dave here carrying you. Of course, if Dave carries you, first of all he'll have to tap you on the head with his little gun. Which would you prefer?'

'I could do with the exercise,' I reply, I'm a little stiff. Some yobs were using me as a dance floor last night.'

'Really? I *do* hope you catch up with them.' He rises to his feet, tall, handsome and confident, I dislike him intensely.

'Follow me, then. Dave'll be right behind you, gun in his pocket. Please don't do anything silly. Dave goes through more suits than anyone I know. Always seems to end up with holes in his pocket.'

Dave searches me efficiently as I pass him. The lift door's wedged open so there's no need to wait, their car's outside, its engine running, the driver grinning.

I'm expecting a longish drive, perhaps a blindfold; I'm rewarded with neither. Instead the car rolls smoothly down to the bottom of the hill and stops outside the main entrance to *Ladders*.

'Here we are, Mr Oliphant,' says Ted Samson. He climbs out first and holds the door, Dave follows close behind me. Despite my earlier jibe I'm prepared to acknowledge that they work well together. I glance at my watch; almost three but the club's open. Samson leads me across an empty bar area to a lift. When we're inside he takes out a key which he inserts in the control panel, turns.

'Override,' he explains, 'the only way we can get to the top floor. A good fast ride as well, Dave here doesn't like enclosed places.' Dave's face shows no sign of any emotion at all. He appears to have this particular phobia under control.

When the doors open again we all step out into a small waiting room complete with sofa and easy chairs, a desk and a long-legged secretary. She knows Ted; he bends to kiss her on the cheek.

'Lo, Angie,' he says, and I think I see his hand touch her on the thigh, 'Mr Oliphant here to see the boss.'

She beams at me like an advert for toothpaste, points at the door.

'He's waiting for you,' she says, 'please go in.'

Ted and Dave settle into their seats. They've done their job, I'm no longer important until it's time for them to take me back. I will be going back, I know that much. The gun was bravado, the summons itself was the important part. Too many people have seen me get into the car, come into the building; they can't afford to hurt me. Everything so far has had a purpose, and that purpose is to demonstrate power and the potential to use it. And I'm impressed. I go through the door.

The suite beyond is filled with natural light from a myriad of windows all at strange angles to one another. There's a faint sound of wind-chimes.

'Billy, come in, come in.' The man walking towards me is tall and thin, his white hair tied back in a pony-tail. He's wearing a flowing white cotton shirt and white pantaloons, his feet are bare, it looks like he's trying to make himself appear a sage, a guru. To me he's an ageing hippy.

'Hello, Sargent. I didn't suspect you until your clowns picked me up. But I would have found out eventually.'

Neither of us offers to shake hands. I take a seat without waiting to be invited, he sits cross-legged on the couch opposite me.

'Why should you have suspected me, Billy? You had no reason. Your supposition that I'm the source of all local evil is paranoid, to say the least.'

'But you do own Pearson Plastics?'

He nods.

'And you are trying to put WPS out of business?'

'Oh no, not out of business. I just want them to default on the pilot scheme for the council's installation. Then Pearson's gets the job.' His voice is low and soft. He should have been a doctor with that voice.

'But WPS are progressing quite nicely,' I say, 'and the new security system is damn good.'

'I never suspected it would be anything but, Billy. You always were thorough to the point of neurosis. And yes, WPS are, only just, on schedule.'

'Despite your efforts.'

'Yes.' He rings his hands, grimaces theatrically. 'I always have been too fond of delegation . . .'

'It's called getting others to do your dirty work, Graeme. It's called covering your tracks. I know you're good at it . . .'

'I've never been convicted of any criminal act, Billy, despite thorough investigation from the local police. And the misplaced enthusiasm of one of its officers. Ex-officers, I should say.'

'Like I said, you're good at hiding behind others. You can do it legally, with offshore companies, and you can do

148

it illegally, by hiring villains. But one day you'll be found out.'

'I think not, Billy. But I was saying, until you interrupted me, that I utilise delegation throughout my organisation. And if, in a moment of weakness, I asked "who will rid me of this turbulent priest?" – the priest being WPS – can I be blamed if Ted misread my feelings and took me literally? He is, alas, not a subtle man. And the people he hired were not blessed with great intelligence.'

'They were going to torch me.'

'So I hear. Would you like a drink, Billy?' He gets up, glides across to the bar. I let my eyes follow him, take in the room.

'Iced water?'

I nod.

'Very wise. I think I'll join you.'

There are doors which I assume lead to a bathroom and bedroom. Part of the room we're in acts as an office, and against one wall is a console with switches and sliding controls. Above it are four television screens. There are paintings on the walls, abstract daubs of colour, sculptures are scattered around on tables, large bronzes curve from floor to ceiling; all are subtly lit. The carpet is plush, I'm surprised I haven't been asked to remove my shoes. Graeme sees me looking around.

'Do have a stroll about, Billy,' he says, 'look, feel, touch. Would you like some music?' He doesn't wait for an answer, interrupts his barman's duties to press some buttons at the console. The music has no obvious source, it's tinkling, almost tuneless. I rise, move over to the windows. They look down on the river. Lower than the Bridge's roadway, high above the streets, I'm surprised at how little noise there is. I don't hear Graeme Sargent pad up behind me with two glasses of water, only the touch of ice on crystal warns me of his presence.

'Strange what drives people from alcohol, eh? For you it was realisation of your dependence. And for me? Lack of effect. I can't get drunk, no matter how hard I try. I drink only for the taste. Russian vodka, for example, the real stuff, seasoned with herbs.'

'Is that why you turned to other substances?'

'If you're implying I take drugs, Billy, then you're wrong. Don't touch them, never have done, never will.' He raises his arms, clenches his fists in strong man pose. 'My body is a temple, Billy.'

'Mine used to be. But last night it was desecrated.'

'Yes, Ted was a little careless in his efforts,' he continues, 'that's why I've decided to intervene. But you aren't the easiest of men to persuade, Billy.'

'Try me.'

'Oh, but I have! You spoke to my sister?'

'Who? I didn't speak to . . .'

'Alice Palmer? The rescheduling of your debt? Surely the blow to your head hasn't affected you that much?'

'She's your sister?'

'You mean you didn't see the family resemblance?' He turns his head sideways. They share height, thinness, aquiline features, but I'd made no connection.

'But all she did was ask me to pay more money more often,' I say.

'Oh dear. Dear dear. Obviously that approach was just *too* subtle for you, Billy. Come let's sit down again.' We take our seats once more.

'My sister's too honest. She deals with – how shall I put it? – the visible earnings. That which can be openly accounted for, like your debt. She can't have emphasised the message I wanted to get across. My hope was that by demanding a large payment, your mind would be more focused on the matter of money. I'd supposed you'd be keen to rid yourself of the WPS job – since it is now finished, unless I'm greatly mistaken – and move on to pastures new. But that doesn't appear to have happened.'

'If those clowns hadn't tried to set fire to the building, if they hadn't attacked me, then I'd probably have been out of

150

it by now. But that's not the way things happened.'

'True, Billy, sadly true.'

'And now it's personal. With Jocko, with Ted Samson. And with you.'

'Exactly! And that's why I asked you to come. Let me explain.' He shuffles a little closer to me.

I disliked Graeme Sargent. I know, the police know, that he's behind a large proportion of the city's organised crime. What makes it worse is that *he* knows the police know that. But he keeps himself clean, everything's at arm's length, he's so far behind he can see every move the police make. Plus he's got his grasses, bent coppers, they tip him the wink when there's anything going on which might affect him. That's why we know each other. I was investigating him and his organisation immediately before I was thrown out of the force.

He was involved in that, I'm sure. I was a gambler, I'll admit that, but I used to spread my bets round the independents, the small casinos, one-man betting shops, on-course bookies. Then Kingfisher became acquisitive, it bought up all these little places. That's when I found I owed all my money to one person. Graeme Sargent. And when I was stopped for drink driving I was on my way home from one of Sargent's clubs, I hadn't had too much to drink. Either the drinks were spiked or the samples I gave were doctored, it didn't really matter. I wasn't exactly popular after my antics with the chief's wife. Drunk driving, owing a large sum of money to the man I was meant to be investigating, they couldn't do anything except kick me out. But it was too neat. That's why I told the appeal panel I thought Graeme Sargent was behind it. They laughed, said I was paranoid. But I know he was in there somewhere.

'I've a proposal for you, Billy.'

'The answer's no.'

'How predictable. Hear me out, though. It may be an offer you can't refuse. You see, I'm prepared to cancel

151

your debt to Kingfisher. Write it off completely. I'll even refund the cheque you gave my sister.'

'And what do I have to do in return?'

'Nothing.'

I must admit to a sort of chortling laugh, it doesn't sound like me at all. But it's genuine, the onset of hysteria, perhaps, but a genuine laugh. Graeme Sargent joins in, hissing like a snake.

'I have to do nothing?'

'Nothing at all. But in a pro-active manner. What I need is for you to be at WPS this evening. When my men gain entry through a door left open by you I want you to do nothing. When they break up the machinery I want you to do nothing. When they leave I want you to do nothing. It couldn't be easier.'

I imagine the look on Carrie Ratcliffe's face when she sees the factory destroyed. I've already betrayed her by taking Charlie Harkness's money, her world might already be collapsing if he's been able to persuade James Ratcliffe to withdraw his backing. But that was done because of my need for cash, and that need was a result purely of Graeme Sargent's pressure.

'Piss off, Sargent!' I don't often swear, but I'm willing to make occasional exceptions.

'Now why did I suspect you'd say that? I ask you to reconsider. You see, the cancellation of your debt is the carrot. Much as I loathe using it, there's also a stick.'

On the low table beside him is a telephone; he presses a button on it and Ted Samson enters carrying a plain brown envelope. He hands it to Sargent, stands behind me.

'Ted will stay for a while,' he says, 'in case I need him.' He opens the envelope. 'Here are some photographs of someone you'll recognise. Your daughter.'

They're mostly long shots. Kirsty outside the house, at school, both of those in her uniform. Walking down the street arm in arm with some girls I don't recognise, she looks happy, grown up in high heels and short skirt.

152

'See the girl on the left, the one with long dark hair? She's one of Kirsty's friends. A few months older than her, though. Let's call her Barbara. Keep going, Billy.'

The next photograph is of the same girls, Kirsty included, sitting outside a pub. They're with some boys, laughing and drinking. I feel sick with apprehension.

'Young girls mature so quickly these days, don't they Billy?'

I keep going. Kirsty looks out of place, rather shy, but her friend, Barbara, in the next shot she's sitting on a boy's knee, arms around his neck, kissing.

'Look, I don't know why you're showing me these ...'

'Keep going, Billy.' Sargent's voice is a growl. I do as he says.

There seems to be a sequence to the next few photographs. The girl is undoubtedly Barbara, but she's made-up, eyes wide, staring directly at the camera. The next is similar but she's in a different pose. In the third she's wearing nothing but a G-string. Then even that disappears as she sits, legs apart for the camera. It gets worse. Two men join her, naked. It's clear they aren't simulating the acts they're performing, oral sex, vaginal and anal intercourse. The last photograph is the most chilling. It shows Barbara leaning back on a bed, she's almost wearing a T-shirt. There's a tourniquet tight around her upper arm, a look of desperation on her face as she searches for a vein to inject.

'I'm gonna be sick,' I say.

'Yeah. I feel that way about injections too, I faint at the sight of a needle. But not on the carpet, Billy, please. The bathroom's through there. Ted?'

I begin to retch as Ted pushes me towards the toilet but I make it in time. I haven't had much to eat but that seems to make no difference. I keep on seeing the photographs. I kneel in front of the bowl and vomit. Ted shows his disgust by closing the door and leaving me alone.

I breathe deeply. Graeme Sargent's veneer of civilisation

hides a person who knows exactly what evil his organisation does, he exults in the inability of any authority to connect him with the crimes his minions commit. His showing me the photographs wasn't just a threat – this could be your daughter unless you do as I say. It was a boast. Look at the power I have over others' lives, he's saying. And there's nothing I can do about it.

I stand up, hoping I won't be sick again. There's some toothpaste at the washbasin, I smear some on my finger and try to get rid of the sourness in my mouth. While I do so I open the mirrored cabinet above the basin. There's a mixture of soaps and shampoos, bottles of aspirin and paracetamol. But there's more. One shelf is filled with boxes and bottles bearing the names of drugs I don't recognise. I take out my pen and write them down. Depixol, Stemetil, Caverject, Diamicron; there are large amounts of some of them, when I pick up some of the boxes I can see they're well out of date. I keep writing, Nardil, Triptafen, Glucophage.

'Are you all right in there, Billy?' Sargeant's voice sounds almost concerned.

'Cleaning my teeth,' I reply through clenched lips.

'Don't be too long, please.' He's like a teacher with a misbehaving child. I put the pen and paper away, open the door. He's waiting for me, Ted Samson at his side.

'You still look pale, Billy.'

'Cut it out, Sargent, you don't care what I look like, how I feel.'

'That's true.'

'You've made your point. Just tell me what you want.'

'You cooperation, Billy, as I said earlier. What's the best way into WPS's factory?'

I don't hesitate. 'there's a small pass-door in the north wall. I'll leave it open.'

'Good. My men will be there in the early hours of the morning, about two. I want you there as well, just in case anything goes wrong. Ted here will be in charge. There'll be some hardware about, don't get ideas about bravery. On the assumption all goes well your debt to Kingfisher Leisure will be cancelled. If all does not go well . . .' He shrugs. 'Do you want to take those photographs with you? As a reminder of the evils which can befall the innocents of this world?'

'Fuck off, Sargent.'

I make my own way out. No one tries to stop me.

Chapter Twenty-Three

When I get back to the office there's another fax waiting. 'Ring me,' it says, 'Rak.' Whatever information she's uncovered has obviously been overtaken by events; I already know who's running Pearson. But I ring her anyway.

'There are two paid up shares in Pearson Plastics,' she tells me, 'one owned by a company called Halcyon Daze Incorporated, the other owned by Leia Holdings, both registered in the Cayman Islands. That's as far as I can get. That's as far as *anyone* can get.'

'One of them will be a Graeme Sargent company,' I tell her, 'he runs . . .'

'I've heard of him, boss, I know what he runs and what he doesn't run, Kingfisher Leisure's the umbrella company. It'll be Halcyon Daze. Halcyon is another name for a kingfisher.'

'You're a smartarse, Rak, you know that? Any ideas on the other, then, Leia Holdings?'

'No, probably owned by another company, then another. But you might be able to find out for yourself, that's why I wanted to talk to you. Both Halcyon and Leia have an agent for the receipt of papers, payment of dividends and so on. If you try the agent you might be able to find out more.'

'And who's the agent?'

'A firm of solicitors. Wolff, Artman and Silverstein. Seem familiar to you?'

'Jesus Christ!'

'No, but my omniscience is becoming well known. I may need to put my prices up.'

'I'll pay, whatever the cost. Thanks, Rak.'

'You're welcome. Any other little requests?'

'No, I think that's ... Yes! Yes, you could do me a favour. One of your tenants, I met her when I was at your place the other day, a young black girl ...'

'Jenny?'

'Yes, Jenny. Did you say she was a medic?'

'That's right. On her post-grad year, I think. She was asking about you when we went to the pub, I told her you only liked boys.'

'Rak!'

'Okay, I'm lying. But she *was* asking about you.'

I ignore her attempts at flattery. 'How can I contact her?'

'At my place, but she's on nights at the moment. Want me to ask her to give you a ring?'

'No, I'm not sure what I'll be doing over the next twenty-four hours. I'll be in touch, though.'

'Professionally?'

'Of course.'

'She'll be disappointed. But I'll warn her. Is that it?'

'That's it. Thanks again, Rak.'

'You're welcome.'

When I moved into this office the first thing I did was change the locks. They were old, two lever, I could have opened the door by breathing heavily on it. It's a habit of mine, looking at locks. That's why I know the lock on the solicitors' door is like my old one. That's why it takes me only two minutes to get in using a piece of bent wire. The room smells of old men and tobacco. No one's been there for at least a week judging by the postmarks on the letters lying behind the door, so I'm not too worried about being disturbed. There's a fine layer of dust everywhere. The telephone is bakelite, there's a fan on the desk, and that's as far as the solicitors have gone in acknowledging modern

157

office appliances. No computer, no fax, no photocopier. And the filing cabinets are made of wood.

The files are ordered, neat, alphabetical, I don't need to spend time searching. I simply take out those folders headed 'Halcyon', 'Leia', and 'Sargent'. Then I go back to my office.

The files are thin, they hold the information I expected to find. I photocopy the registration documents, names of shareholders. Graeme Sargent hasn't bothered to hide himself behind another company, he's listed as the owner of Halcyon. The surprise lies with the Leia file. As Rak suggested, there's another company with a strange name, 'Lemmings and Bank Enterprises.' But I recognise the address, it's something Rak has already turned up. It's where Carrie's husband lives. It's James Ratcliffe's home address.

It becomes clearer. If WPS is a success then James Ratcliffe benefits from the profits in proportion to his holding in the family firm, perhaps a twelfth or less. But if Pearson Plastics does the council job then he gets half the profits. So there's good financial motivation behind this deception. But there's also the relationship between Carrie and James Ratcliffe to consider. It looks as if he's jealous of his wife's achievements, her return to work, her success. He probably forced her to stop working in the first place, didn't want her to come back. This is, of course, supposition. I've never met the man, Carrie doesn't talk about him much. But it fits, it all fits. And to make matters worse I know that Charlie Harkness is helping James Ratcliffe bring Carrie down; and I'm helping him.

When I worked for the police I used the same principles each time I approached a case. What used to happen was that I'd be presented with a jumble of facts, mostly unconnected, about the case I was investigating. I'd have found some information myself, the rest would be from others on the team. I'd study everything, eliminate what I knew was untrue. Hearsay I'd keep, but it wouldn't get as much weight as hard fact. Then I'd treat it like a game. Have you ever played that logic game, Mastermind? It's for two players, one selects four coloured pegs and covers them over; the other has to guess the colours and the correct positions of the colours by suggesting a possible answer. The first player responds by stating how many colours in that suggestion are correct and in the right place, and how many are correct and in the wrong place. You can work at it by logic; I can usually manage to find the answer within four guesses.

That's what I used to do with my cases, apply logic. It wouldn't always give me an answer. But it would usually suggest a line of questioning or give a hint of motivation, or lead me a step or two further along the logic path. Then I'd sit down and work at it again, review what I knew and what I thought I knew, check the possibilities. Eliminate the impossibilities. It was exciting, using my brain like that. So when I figure out James Ratcliffe's part in this I sit down, control myself, review the information again. And just like old times it hits me, I know exactly what I have to do next. It feels good to be back in control. It's just me. Me against the rest.

I check my watch. It's almost seven. I call for a taxi, ride out to WPS. Graeme Sargent's instructions were straightforward; I was to be on site. It's the second night of shift changeover, as I arrive they're about to lock up and leave. It doesn't take much persuasion to be allowed a set of keys. I'm known now, trusted. I sit down in Carrie's office and switch on the cameras and the video loop, wait to make sure everyone has left. Then I go down on to the factory floor. It's quiet. There's a smell of oil, plastic, sweat. The forklift truck is parked behind the door Ted Samson and his men are due to use. I find the keys for the truck and move it, a security man's work is never done. I busy myself with other jobs and I'm off the factory floor by nine.

I've some spare time. I use some of it to go to Charlie Harkness's office and remove the tape in his bugging

159

receiver, I replace it with a blank cassette. Then I go down to the switchboard, punch in a number I know so well.

'Hello, love, it's your dad. Yeah, I'm well, working hard. Listen, I need to speak to your mum, rather urgently, is she in? That's great, put her on.'

There's a pause. I don't like to hurry Kirsty but sometimes there are more important things than chattering with your daughter.

'Sara? I need you to do something for me.'

'What's that?' She sounds suspicious.

'I want you and Kirsty to pack your bags, get away for two or three days. Your sister's caravan, it doesn't matter where. Just go.'

'Billy, what the hell are you talking about?'

'Is there anyone with you? Is, what's his name, John, is John with you?'

'What's that of your business? No, he's not, but he's coming round tomorrow to take me out and I've no intention . . .'

'Sara, shut up!'

For once she does as she's told.

'Listen, I've been threatened. If I don't do something – something illegal – a certain man has threatened to hurt me. He's not going to hurt me by attacking me. He's going to do it by going for Kirsty.'

At first she doesn't say anything. Then, when she does, her voice is small, distant. 'Oh Billy! What are you doing? What have you got into this time?' She's almost in tears.

'I can't say anything more. Everything should work out well, but just in case it doesn't I want you well away. Understand?'

'Yes Billy.'

'Go now. Don't tell anyone where you are. You can get in touch with me by ringing Rak, she can be our contact point. Have you still got her number?'

'Yes.'

160

'Good. Go on then, go and pack now. Tell Kirsty I love her. And Sara?'

'Yes, Billy?'

'Be careful.'

'Me be careful? Billy Oliphant. you're a fool! You're the one who needs to be careful, you're the only . . .'

'Yes?'

Her voice, when it eventually comes, is almost a whisper.

'You're the only husband I've got. Bye.'

Chapter Twenty-Four

I switch off all the lights. The monitor screens show only the quiet outside. I set my alarm for 1.30 and take off my shoes, try to find a comfortable position on the sofa for my aching body. I don't expect to sleep but do, surprising myself as I wake to the beeping of my wristwatch. I'm not refreshed; my muscles warn me as I try to rise that they aren't feeling cooperative. I overrule their complaints, fasten my shoelaces and walk downstairs. It's a little cooler outside than in, but not much. There's still no breeze and the air is heavy with the smell of a summer that's outlived its welcome. I walk round the side of the building, jangling my keys, and unlock the pass-door. Then I go back inside, settle myself in front of the screens.

The approach comes without secrecy, without caution. The four men – I count them carefully – lurch across the brown grass like zombies, They make no attempt to hide themselves. Why should they? They know the way's been prepared for them. I wait for them to come closer, zoom the camera in on them. I recognise Ted Samson and his sidekick, the silent Dave, but not the other two; Jocko certainly isn't one of them. The two strangers are carrying familiar weapons, petrol cans. Samson and Dave have handguns.

As they find the wall I leave the screens, hurry – though I feel I'm moving like Quasimodo – downstairs again and outside. I edge along the wall to the corner of the building.

All the doors are in the same wall. The small pass-door, the huge roller-door allowing entry for anything up to the size of a truck and trailer, they're quite close together. There is, of course, no room inside the factory for a truck and trailer; completed windows are taken outside for loading, sealed units are brought in on wheeled trollies. In winter either of these procedures might have to be carried out in darkness; that's why there are four halogen spotlights on the canopy above the big door. The main power switch for these is inside the building and it's on, I've made sure of that. The external switch in its weather-proof box is just around the corner. I reach round carefully, sure the action won't be seen, feel the rubber beneath my finger. I push.

The sudden glare freezes Ted Samson and his arsonists for a moment. They panic. From the corner, in the safe darkness outside the spotlights, I can see them all. They're beside the door, it's wide open; inside is a safe, secure darkness. They're like vampires, repelled by light. Ted Samson hisses his command.

'Inside, quick!'

As the last of them enters, petrol cans in hand, I hurry from my position, switch off the lights as I pass. I stumble, my own eyes can't cope with the sudden blackness, but my fingers can feel the wall beside me. The open pass-door looms out of the stars and flashes of my vision, I manage to step round it. Inside is another door, a metal door. I grab at its handle and heave it towards me, hearing the protests of those within. A torch beam dazzles me, but only for a moment as I slam the door, bolt it and lock it.

It was easy. It went as planned. Ted Samson and friends are safe, locked inside the metal container I manoeuvred against the door earlier in the evening. And from the sounds I can hear, they aren't pleased.

I lock the pass-door from the outside and walk around the building. My heart's beating fast and I breathe deeply, try to control the sense of elation, to inhibit the adrenalin rush. By the time I'm back in the building I can feel the weariness beginning to fight its way back. I make my way on to the factory floor, switch on the main lights. My eyes feel as if they're coated with grit, my body's doing as I tell it but unwillingly, with a half-second delay, and every movement hurts. I'm not even sure if my brain will function; but I've still work to do.

The container's made of ribbed steel, dented in places where it's been handled roughly, but its shell is intact. I approach it warily. I'm not sure if a bullet would pass through it; if it can, I don't want to be in its path. I crouch down behind the forklift at the rear end of the container. I can hear movement within, muted conversation, tapping and banging.

'Can you hear me, Samson?' I yell.

'Oliphant, you bastard! I'll fucking get you for this! We agreed, the boss agreed ... You're a double-crossing fucking wanker, Oliphant! You're dead! Your wife, your kid, they're both dead!'

'Just in case you're thinking of shooting a hole,' I shout, keeping my words slow, 'I wouldn't recommend it. The metal's too thick. You'll just get a ricochet. Might kill yourself. Might set the petrol alight. Not recommended.'

'So what do you want?'

'Peace. Quiet. A sleep to help me decide what to do next. I'd suggest you do the same.'

Ted Samson's voice is angry, he's almost in tears, but he's trying to control himself. 'Come on, Billy, you've had your little joke. You're tougher than we thought, we respect you for that. But it's not worth it, really, when you think about it. You still there Billy?'

'I'm still here.'

'If you let us out now, let us do the job, the boss won't even hear about this. It'll be private. He won't ever know.'

I stand up, make my way back across the floor towards the door leading to the offices.

'Goodnight, boys,' I yell.

'Let me out!' screams another voice. 'I can't stand it! For Christ's sake let me out!' There's the sound of sobbing. 'Please, I don't like the dark. It's too small in here, too closed in.' It's Dave. The hitman has claustrophobia. 'Please let me out, please, please, please.'

The crying dwindles, though I've no doubt it still continues as I walk away.

'Billy! Open this fucking door!' Ted Samson again regaining his finesse with words.

I make my way back to Carrie's office, pleased that one of the benefits of double glazing is its ability to reduce unwanted noise. Although I can see the container squatting on the factory floor I can hear no sound from it. I stretch out on the sofa again and prepare to enjoy the sleep of the righteous. But before I close my eyes I put the tape from Charlie Harkness's bug into Carrie's dictation machine and press playback. It's not that I want to eavesdrop on her, just that I need to listen to a voice not raised in anger, a gentle voice, a soothing voice.

'Hello, I'd like to speak to Mr Rowlinson, Chief Architect. My name's Carrie Ratcliffe. Hello, John? I just thought I'd let you know we're getting another delivery out on site today, it looks as if we'll make up for lost time by the end of the week. Yes, I think we've overcome our difficulties ...'

Carrie's voice, low and tender, takes me into sleep.

Friday

Chapter Twenty-Five

My alarm is set for six and I wake at five to. I don't normally remember my dreams but this one was vivid and unusual. I was a piece on a chess board, a pawn, a black pawn. The other pieces were people I recognised. The white king was Graeme Sargent; the queen was Sara; the black king was Carrie. Ted Samson was there too, a white knight standing close to me, leering down at me. But I was brave, I faced up to him, I fought him (though I can't remember whether this was with fists or weapons of some type); I must have beaten him because he disappeared and I found myself standing on the square he'd formerly occupied.

I was playing a game myself, that Mastermind game with coloured pegs, and I remember saying, 'Yes, that's it, that's the answer!' But when I looked at the game I was wrong, my answer wasn't correct. I realised I'd have to go back to the start, think things through again. This must have distracted me, because when I looked up the white king was heading towards me, fast, moving square after square. He trampled pieces out of the way to get at me, white and black alike. 'You can't do that,' I shouted, 'it's against the rules!'

'My game,' he shouted back at me, 'my rules!' And all the pawns were gathered round me in a circle chanting, 'Sa-cri-fice! Sa-cri-fice!'

I was pleased to wake up. Perhaps that's why I don't

remember my dreams very often; when I do they frighten the hell out of me.

I ring Norm, get him out of bed, ask him to find a vehicle capable of loading the container on to its back. When he complains about the impossibility of the task I swear at him to make him shut up. Then I explain that I wouldn't be speaking to him unless the need was great, unless I knew I could depend on him. He promises to be at the factory before 7.30.

I'm not very gentle when I use the forklift to push the container out of the factory. I ignore the shouts, yells and threats from within. Norm arrives at twenty-five to eight, climbs out of the cab of a skip lorry.

'Excuse me,' he says, I'm looking for Mr Billy Oliphant. You must be his older brother, his remarkably ill-looking older brother. You haven't seen him, have you? He's short-tempered and rude to his friends in the early hours of the morning.'

'Norm, I knew I could rely on you.'

'Boss, you look like a corpse. We finish this job and I'm taking you home, no arguments. Understood?'

'Yes Norm.'

'So what's in the metal coffin?'

'Four would-be arsonists. They've been in there for almost six hours now, no toilet, no water. They'll be hot, uncomfortable.'

'Good.' He connects up the steel chains to the hooks on the container walls, begins to winch it on to the back of the lorry. The factory manager arrives, his face clouded with curiosity. He walks over despite Norm's glare.

'What's going on?' he asks.

'It's okay,' I lie, 'Mrs Ratcliffe knows all about it. Just an empty container I need to borrow.'

He looks up at it, hears the shouts and pleas from inside.

'Doesn't sound empty to me.'

'Sorry, empty was the wrong word. Let's just say the contents are valueless. But I think your work force is

170

arriving and you haven't opened up yet.'

Two or three of the factory hands are wandering towards us. He moves to head them off, to go into the factory and check whether anything's missing, whether I've done some damage.

'What do you want doing with the cargo, then?' asks Norm. The police?'

'No. They go back where they came from. I'd like you to unload them right outside the front entrance to *Ladders*.'

When we get to the nightclub Norm manages to reverse the lorry across the road so it's at right angles to the traffic. He decants the container skilfully, it lands a foot away from the front door of *Ladders*. There is, of course, no one about to complain, save for the few motorists on their way to work. They seem more interested in the operation than concerned at being delayed for ten minutes; one even applauds the accuracy of Norm's skills.

Norm drives me home, he almost has to carry me into the flat.

'Want me to stay, boss? The people in that container aren't going to be pleased when they get out. And you've blocked up the opening to the club good and proper. Someone might decide to come looking for you.'

I peel off my clothes and head for the shower.

'Thanks, Norm, but no thanks. I'll take them a while to figure out what to do, a while longer to find me, and by then I'll have thought out my own moves.'

The shower's hot like acid, I can feel it peeling away the outer levels of dirt-coated skin, cleansing me.

'If you don't need me,' shouts Norm, 'can I make a phone call? Sort out something for the rest of the day?' I can barely hear him through the hiss of the water.

'Help yourself,' I shout back, 'I've got my own work to do later, I've a few phone calls to make as well.' The soap smells good, I cover myself liberally then rinse. When I finish I wipe round the tray, wipe down the walls, then step back into the room.

171

There's something delicious about the feel of warm air on damp skin, a feeling of renewal. Despite my tiredness I can exult in that sense of higher consciousness. The shower was good. But I know that my emotions are too complex to be swayed by a mere stream of hot water. I feel good because I'm back in control. I'm doing what I want to do, what I *need* to do. I'm not working under instructions, real or implicit, there's no external pressure on me, coaxing me in a specific direction. I can do as I please. And I will.

Norm's sitting at my table, leafing through a week-old Sunday supplement.

'On your way, then,' I tell him. 'Thanks for your help this morning. But I really do need some sleep before I get back to work. I'll lock the door when you go out, don't worry.'

I guide him out, watch him saunter down the steps and climb into his cab. He looks across at a blue Transit, nods. In the driver's seat I notice Sly, summoned by Norm's phone call, trying to look inconspicuous, straw hat jammed down over his head. I feel very safe. This time when sleep comes I'm not bothered by the remembrance of dreams.

Chapter Twenty-Six

Carrie's flat is in a tall block overlooking the park. There's a restaurant at the top of its twenty or so storeys, a uniformed doorman at the bottom. He tells me I'm expected, guides me to the lift, shows me which of the buttons to press. Before I ascend I whisper to him, press a ten pound note into his hand.

'If anyone else comes along asking for Mrs Ratcliffe, just send them up, will you? It's a surprise for her.'

I'm dressed smartly, for me, fawn slacks and brown shoes, a white shirt, though it's still too warm for a tie. I'm wearing my second jacket, lightweight in crumpled linen. Sara bought it for me two years before, I haven't worn it much. I'm bearing gifts; a bottle of obscure white wine and some flowers. When Carrie comes to the door I bow formally and offer her both. She giggles. She has an empty glass in her hand.

'Come in,' she says, 'come in. I've been longing for you to get here. What *have* you been up to?'

She's wearing a tight red sleeveless evening dress cut low over her breasts, it clings to her body. She hasn't bothered with shoes, her nails – finger and toe – are painted blood red. She dances a walk across the room.

The smell of cooking is as tempting as the woman. There's a table set for two in front of open French windows; this high above ground there's a pleasant breeze,

I can see a carpet of rough brown-green grass and ribbons of paths stretching towards the city centre.

'Iced water?' she suggests, pointing me to a chair. 'Or can I tempt you with something a little stronger on this special occasion?'

'Just water, please.'

There's a curl of smoke rising from an ashtray on the bar, she catches me glancing at it. 'No, Billy, I haven't slipped into old habits. It's not tobacco. Care to try one?'

I shake my head. She slides across the room to me, a tall glass of water in one hand, whisky in the other. 'I suppose we'll have to concentrate on the other vice, then. Remember the old song?'

'Which song?'

'"Cigareets and whisky and wild, wild women,"' she sings tunelessly, '"they'll drive you crazy, they'll drive you insane!"'

She puts the glasses down on the table beside my chair and descends onto my lap. Her tongue finds my mouth, she tastes of every temptation ever invented and a few new ones she's added herself. Her fingers are gently furrowing my scalp, she places my hand on the thin fabric sheathing her buttock. Then the doorbell rings.

She's annoyed, I can tell by the lines on her forehead, the way her eyebrows seek each other's company.

'Expecting someone?' I ask. She shakes her head.

'Probably got the wrong flat, then, I'll go and chase them away. Won't be long.' She slides from my lap as I push to my feet, stands before me. Her hair has lost a little of its control, her lipstick is slightly smudged (I wipe the back of my hand over my mouth). She's relaxed, had relaxation forced upon her; her posture has slipped, her belly has resumed its slightly rounded look. It's not unattractive. It's the real her. But it's not the way she wants to be. She wants to remain young and, under my gaze, concentrates again on that desire. Her spine straightens, shoulders go back, breasts jut. Her stomach is sucked in. She's herself again.

174

My tiredness of the morning has gone, my muscles are capable of doing what I ask of them without punishing me. I stride across the room as the bell rings again. I know who'll be there. I fling the door open, flick the catch back so it can be closed but not locked.

'Graeme. Do come in. And Ted. You weren't invited but I'm sure we can find a dog bowl for you.'

Graeme Sargent's mouth drops. I'm not the person he expected to see. Ted Samson reacts more quickly, he's standing behind Graeme, pushes his boss against the door-frame in an attempt to get to me. Sargent's raised hand holds him back.

'What the fuck is going on, Billy?' He seems honestly curious. Behind me another voice joins in.

'Is there anything the matter, Billy?' Carrie appears at my shoulder.

I wish I could work like a movie, view different people's reactions all at the same time. I can't see Carrie's face when she finds Graeme Sargent in her entrance hall, I'm too busy watching Sargent himself. He hardly glances at Carrie. His thoughts are more on me and what I'm doing there, why I appear so calm, why I appear to be in control. And I am in control. I decide to demonstrate it.

'Why not come in?' I suggest. 'The view's magnificent. Carrie, perhaps your guests would like something to drink? Mr Samson will be quite thirsty, I imagine. He's spent a large part of the day cooped up in rather a warm, enclosed space with some, dare I say it, rather unsavoury characters.'

'Oliphant, I said I'd kill you and by Christ . . .'

'Shut up, Ted. I'll have a lemonade, Carrie.' Sargent's voice is stable, but as he takes a seat I can see his fingers shaking, drumming and scratching at the leather arms of the chair. Ted Samson moves into place behind him. Carrie's incapable of movement, her face Pierrot-white.

'Mr Sargent would like a lemonade, Carrie,' I say pleasantly. 'I imagine Mr Samson would appreciate a beer. And perhaps you'd better have another whisky. Then we can all sit down and have a little chat.'

'I don't understand,' she says. 'What's going on? Who are these people?'

'He knows, Carrie,' says Sargent, 'he knows. How much he knows is a different matter. What he'll gain from telling us is something else again. So fix the drinks and then we can hear what Mr Oliphant has to say. And then we can decide what to do.'

That much, then, is as I expected. Ted Samson's hand is in his pocket, playing with what I assume is a gun. Carrie, rescued by the need for physical action, is clicking ice on glass on bottle. And I'm leaning against the dinner table sipping my water.

'I suppose you should start, Billy,' says Sargent as his drink arrives. He pushes Carrie into a seat opposite him. 'I hope it won't be too dramatic, though. I hate those TV movies where Columbo explains to the whole cast why the murderer did the evil deed, then he tells them how he deduced who it would be. I always fall asleep, it's so obvious.'

'What murderer?' asks Carrie, 'there's been no murder.'

'There will be,' says Ted Samson.

'Okay then,' I say, 'I'll start. I assume the two of you,' I lean my head towards Carrie and Sargent, 'first met when Ratcliffe came up to consider buying WPS. Perhaps at *Ladders*? I'm not sure whether there's a personal relationship . . .'

'We fucked the first night we met, Billy. The lady's hot, isn't that right, Carrie?'

Carrie looks down into her glass, drains it.

'So you got to know about WPS and the fact that they'd probably get this large, profitable contract. That's when you decided to intervene.' I move my gaze from Sargent to Carrie. 'Why make a little money as a director – a non-shareholding director, as you kept telling me – of WPS, when you could make a fortune as a fifty per cent shareholder of Pearson?' Then I turn to Sargent. 'And you make millions where before you would have had nothing.'

I take a drink, slowly, deliberately.

'I knew of your involvement, Sargent, when you invited me to your office, but I would have found out anyway when I discovered Pearson's holding companies were called Halcyon and Leia. Halcyon was obviously Kingfisher and therefore you, Graeme. I broke into the solicitors' office you use as a letter box for company mailing, found out that post for Leia went to Carrie's home address. Even then I didn't think it was her; I assumed it was her husband who was the other partner.'

'What made you think otherwise?' Carrie's staring at me, deep eyed, beautiful.

'Charlie Harkness doesn't like you. He said he was going to stop the second payment for the work I did, he was going to tell your husband the way you were running the company. He said he'd make sure I got paid, but only if I bugged your phone. So I did.'

'You bastard!'

'He didn't hear anything. I put the bug in while we were wiring up your office and I took the tape out while I was in your office last night. It was only there for twenty-four hours. But I listened to it. I heard you call Sargent. I heard you tell him the factory would be empty. That was the night Fatman and Zag and Jocky came round. I heard you tell him to do something. So it was thanks to you, Carrie, I was almost torched.'

'I rescued you!' she cries, 'I'm the one who *stopped* them torching you!'

'Why did you do that, Carrie? Out of sympathy? Because you have a conscience?'

Sargent answers for her. 'Well it certainly wasn't because she wanted to fuck you, Billy. Why do you think she tried to screw you when she did? She was trying to distract your attention from the video monitors, she told me. I got quite a kick out of that. Pity it didn't work.'

177

'That's not true, Billy, I was getting attached to you, I really was ...'

I silence her by looking at her. I knew she was using me, I'd guessed that much. But I never imagined she'd tried to have sex with me simply as a diversion. I go on, less sure of myself, trying to regain some of the confidence Sargent's revelation has dispelled.

'I used the tape, managed to splice together a little speech. It was a bit disjointed but it worked. "Graeme, I need to see you. Come round tonight, eight o'clock. Come alone, don't contact me before them." Something like that. I rang up when I knew you'd still be in bed, Graeme, left the message on your answerphone.'

'Rather melodramatic, I thought,' Sargent interrupts, 'not the type of thing Carrie would say. That's why I brought Ted. It didn't seem right. Now if you'd left a message saying "I want your cock inside me, come round and fuck me," that would have been nearer the real Carrie. The same real Carrie who untied one of the stupid fuckers you caught at the factory. The same real Carrie who told me you'd found Jocky and got Ted's name out of him. She was telling me everything. While she was in bed with me, fucking me, well, she was screwing you.' He sniggers, his words are light, almost flippant, but he looks at Carrie as he speaks, dares her to gainsay him. And she says nothing.

'I didn't want to believe Carrie was involved,' I continue, 'but I did some more thinking. The company names. Halcyon was, like I said, Kingfisher. But then I made other connections. Kingfisher – Fisher King – Fisher – Carrie Fisher, who was in Star Wars, played the part of Princess Leia – Leia Holdings.'

'I told you it was stupid to play with the names like that,' Carrie says, but her words rattle easily from Graeme Sargent's armoured self-confidence.

I go on. 'Carrie told me her husband insisted on getting a security firm in, Charlie Harkness confirmed that. If I hadn't been recommended ...'

'Recommended? Billy boy, you weren't recommended. You were chosen. By me!' Sargent is more than excited, he's leaning forward in his seat, eyes wide, hands clutching the arms. 'I *told* Carrie to contact you. We wanted someone incapable of doing the job properly. We wanted an imbecile. We wanted an incompetent. So my thoughts turned naturally to you. Drummed out of the police, a drunk, a gambler, on the verge of divorce, no work, undergoing psychotherapy. Not to mention owing me a lot of money. You, Billy, were the natural, the only choice. And then you had to go and spoil it. You had to try hard. For the first time in your life you started doing things right.'

This is unexpected. It certainly explains why I could get away with charging the ridiculous price I quoted. There was no competition. I was the only horse in the race, the only dog out of the traps. All they had to do was coax me along to the finish line, carrot and stick. And all I want to do now is get out, but I can't, I have to finish. I thought I had the high cards, but Sargent's got a long suit in trumps and he's using them all. I hurry on.

'So the idea is that WPS gets burned to the ground and Pearson gets the contract,' I say. 'Presumably there's an insurance scam as well, so Ratcliffe Plastics isn't out of pocket.'

'You got it, Billy. No one gets hurt. WPS has a security system, expensively installed, which can't prevent the factory and machinery being extensively damaged. No suspicions there from the loss-adjustors. Pearson is offered the job at the price we tendered. Everyone's happy.'

'Except the WPS employees who don't have a job.'

'Little people, Billy, they don't count in the grand scheme of things. A bit like you, really. Except you've proved to be more of a pain than we allowed for. You think you're better than you are, even now you probably think you're ahead, you've got something up your sleeve to hit us with. The truth is, Billy, whatever it is you're thinking, whatever it is you're doing, I'll always be able to beat you.

179

You can't win.' Sargent sits back in his chair. His fingers are folded into his palms, his knuckles clenched into balls of fist. His back is broom-shank straight, he's licking his pale lips. He stares at me with cobra eyes, ready to strike no matter which direction I move.

'He knows too much, boss,' says Ted Samson.

'Thank God for cliché-free English, Ted. What are you going to do now, "blow me away?"'

'I could do that, if Mr Sargent wants me to.' He brings the pistol from one pocket, from the other he produces a silencer and marries the two.

'No,' says Carrie, 'no shooting. No shooting, no fighting, no killing, no nothing! I can't stand this, I've had enough. I'm going to ring the police!' She lurches to her feet but Sargent is quick and strong, he grabs her wrist, hauls her back and onto his lap.

'There's no need for that,' he says, 'no need at all. If the police were required Billy would have summoned them, and he hasn't. So he must be thinking of something else, is that right, Billy? Even with my limited knowledge of the law I don't think there's any criminal case to answer. There's nothing to connect the alleged arson attack on WPS with me, or with you, Carrie, or even with Ted here, since Billy so kindly delivered him to my front door this morning. Even if he'd gone to the police with them they couldn't have been charged with breaking and entering; Billy let them in. So what's next, Billy?'

'Civil action? Attempt to defraud the local council? I'm no lawyer but I'm sure a case could be made.'

'And who's going to make that case, Billy? You?'

'No.'

'Who, then?'

I keep quiet. I listen. And I'm rewarded with the sound of the door opening, footsteps in the hallway. Ted Samson's gun swivels towards the sound.

'For Christ's sake, Ted,' says Sargent, 'put the friggin' toy away!'

He does so reluctantly, his glance moving between the hallway and me.

'Evenin', boss,' says Norm, 'having a good time? We've brought you a visitor.'

Sly's the next to appear, large and black and smiling. He's wearing a set of headphones connected to a tape recorder hung at his waist. A large aerial strains for the ceiling; he looks like a human dodgem car. In his shadow, protected by him, is a wide, round, florid man. His face is like a dumpling, not smooth but pock-marked with suet. He's dressed in a suit and he's sweating. I haven't seen him before but I've spoken to him. He's here at my invitation. He steps forward.

'Oh, Jesus Christ!'

'Hello, Carrie,' says the fat man.

'James Ratcliffe?' asks Sargent, looking at me. I nod. 'I suppose you've been listening in to our conversation, Mr Ratcliffe?' he continues. I reply by unhooking a microphone transmitter from my jacket.

'Good thinking, Billy boy. So where does that get us now?' He releases Carrie's wrist, she rubs it as she rises to her feet.

'You must really hate me,' says James Ratcliffe to his wife, his words as round as his body, 'to try to do this to me. I knew there was something wrong, Harkness . . .'

'That shithead!'

'Yes, but at least he had my interests at heart.'

'You should have trusted me, James. Not now, not here, years ago. But no, you wanted a decoration, not a wife. You wanted someone to fuck, someone to mother your children, someone to be there when you got home. And all the time I was telling you I could do more, but you wouldn't let me. Then when you did give me the chance you surrounded me with warnings, with conditions, with your sycophantic Harkness and his computer print-outs. Why couldn't you just have trusted me?'

'Trust? Do you know what that means, Carrie? When

you've slept with at least one man in this room, excluding me, of course, seduced another. And that's all I know about. What about the rest of them? Want to confess to opening your legs for any of them as well?'

'And I suppose you've been faithful, James? Mistresses, secretaries, whores, you've had them all. You'll screw anyone for your own pleasure. At least I do it for a purpose!'

'And a worthwhile purpose at that,' says Sargent, 'the Bentley Estate contract's worth over ten million.'

'Eight million,' I correct him.

'Ten, Billy. That was Pearson's tender. Give or take a few hundred thousand. So I think, Mr Ratcliffe, you should be proud of your wife's efforts. From the commercial side of things, from the *business* side of things, she's done very well. Her own rewards will be considerable.'

'*Would* have been considerable,' I remind him. 'WPS still has the contract, you and Mrs Ratcliffe have been found out, and Mr Ratcliffe knows exactly what's been going on. The whole thing's over, Sargent. You've lost this time.'

He shakes his head, looks at his watch.

'So naive, Billy, so naive. And my oh my, look at the time. I wonder . . .' He gets to his feet and strolls over to the window.

'Such hot weather we're having. Did you read about the grass fires? Spontaneous combustion, they say. I wonder if the same thing could happen here, I wonder if it could happen in, say, a PVC window factory? Look over there, at that cloud of black smoke! Could it be, I wonder, south of the river? Perhaps . . . Isn't that where the WPS factory is?'

He's pointing across the city, beyond the pale carillon-topped Civic Centre, across the river. A column of oily smoke is rising, untouched by the breeze. Sargent turns to me, his voice little more than a whisper.

'I suppose you think you were invited to dinner for your charm, your good looks, your elegant conversation? Or was

182

it just to keep you out of the way? Like I said, Billy, you're nothing. You *have* nothing.' He speaks more normally. 'Unlike Mr Ratcliffe, here, who has the potential to have a great deal. That is, Mr Ratcliffe, the WPS factory, believe me. Ratcliffe Plastics should make a little from the insurance, your fellow directors won't be disappointed. And I feel your wife would be quite happy to offer you a third of her shares in Pearson Plastics, as would I, in commiseration for the unhappy events of the day. We'd welcome your expertise, your wide knowledge of international business affairs. And the venture should prove highly profitable. I'm sure Carrie won't object to this proposal.'

Carrie, sullen, eyes flaming, looks as if she'll object loudly and strongly.

'After all, with the three of us as shareholders, how can we go wrong? Who can possibly object to the way we've handled this business? Who can accuse us of any wrong-doing?'

All three of them look at each other. Then they look at me.

'There seem to be some loose ends,' says James Ratcliffe. He's walked away from Sly, crossed the room to stand beside his wife. As I watch them he reaches for her hand, links her delicate fingers with his fat ones. Her other hand is on Sargent's shoulder.

'You make a lovely threesome,' I say. 'I hope you enjoy fucking each other.'

'Billy, Billy, is that any way to talk to people who hold your future in their hands? I think a little politeness is called for.'

Ted Samson's feeling in his pocket again; Sly and Norm are close beside me, I push them away. If any shots are fired I want to make Samson's targets as difficult as possible.

'I said, no shooting,' Carrie reminds Sargent.

'I agree entirely,' he replies, 'leaves such a mess on the carpet. And besides, there's going to be no unpleasantness,

183

no *nastiness*. Billy has a vested interest in our well-being. He's an accessory now. He let the arsonists into the factory. His debt has been cancelled – I've let that go through, Billy, even though you didn't keep your part of the bargain. He hasn't informed the police of our alleged misdemeanours. All in all I look on that as being a good sign.'

'I haven't been to the police yet, Sargent, because I didn't know if my suspicions were facts. But now I know the truth. So what's stopping me now?'

'I am a little concerned,' adds James Ratcliffe 'about the somewhat open nature of our conversations. And I would point out that I've agreed to no action on my part regarding the acquisition of shares in Pearson Plastics. If the police were involved I can't see me going ahead in this venture and I would, of course, be forced to cooperate . . .'

'James, don't worry. Billy won't go to the police, it wouldn't be worth his while. It's better for him to be quiet for a number of reasons, isn't that right Billy?'

'So tell me about them.'

'Your wife and daughter, to mention two.'

'You can't get your hands on them. They've gone away, I don't know where they are.'

'Really? You do seem very fond of your wife, even though you're separated. You don't live together, do you? It can be such a hardship when a marriage breaks down despite one of the partners still being in love. A bit like that with you, isn't it Billy?'

'Get on with it, Sargent, say what you have to say then I can go.'

'But where to, Billy? Dock Green? Or home? I think I'd prefer the latter. And to help you make the right decision let me mention your wife – what's her name, Sara? – and her current whereabouts. She's gone away for a while, at short notice? Where could she have gone? Where would I go if I were her, no time to plan, not much money? To stay with a relative? Even better, to stay in a relative's empty house! Or a caravan perhaps, a residential caravan.'

'Bastard!' How can he know?

'I could say more, Billy, but not now. Carrie and Jim and I have some business matters to discuss. It should take, oh, no more than an hour or so. Why not meet me back at my place? What time is it now, 8.30? I've a rather pressing appointment at midnight, let's say you come at 11.30. I'll leave word for the doormen, just come straight up to the fourth floor. Ted, give him a key for the lift.'

Samson hands me a small key. I want to throw it back at him. I want to step forward – I'm that close – and hit Graeme Sargent. If I hit him hard enough I can break his nose. One punch could provide maximum pain and damage. But it wouldn't be worth it. The brief satisfaction it would give me wouldn't be enough compensation for the potential hurt he could do me and my family. I decide to content myself with words. They can't hurt him but they provide me with emotional release.

'So much power, Sargent. You think you've got it all worked out. But it's accident. Luck. The dice just happened to fall right for you. But not by much. You're ahead by *that much.*' I hold up my hand, thumb and forefinger so close together they're touching. 'And whatever you do, whatever you say, I'll be right there behind you every step of the way. Make one mistake and I'll have you, remember that.'

I turn to go, usher Sly and Norm ahead of me.

'Billy.'

I should ignore him, but I don't. I turn back. It's my inherited politeness, when someone calls my name I answer.

'Billy, I like the analogy. Dice. Games, Gambling. But you don't really understand what you're talking about. The margins are small in gambling; being *this much* ahead,' he copies my gesture, 'is winning the whole game. And I'm winning at the moment. Always have been. Always will be. Because, you see, I own the dice and they're weighted in my favour. The house always wins, and you're playing my game. It's pre-determined, Billy. You can't get out, you can't escape, you can't win. I already know the outcome. It's die-cast, Billy. Die-cast, old son. Just remember that.'

I can hear his laugh even as I close the door behind me.

Sly and Norm are quiet as we go down in the lift, step outside into the hot air. The pall of black smoke to the south is larger than it was; PVC burns dirty like that.

'Now what, boss?'

'Home, Norm, I suppose. I need to have shower, get changed, dress smart. They don't let you into *Ladders* without a tie. I've an appointment.'

Chapter Twenty-Seven

The front doors are open. I can feel the heavy, hollow catch of drums and bass through the soles of my feet. Its rhythm matches, then seems to quicken, that of my heart. I'm clothed in the noise of the music, it wants to invade my body, transform it from human to automaton.

Once inside – I don't have to queue, I'm expected, searched then allowed straight in – the effect is compounded. Eyes are scoured by migraine lights, the smell of sweat and perfume clouds the brain. And on the dance floor there's the flow and heave of bodies touching in constant motion, like a flock of starlings over the city's winter lights. The dancers have sacrificed themselves to the music, that's why one track runs into another without pause, that's why the DJ's mumbled introductions don't matter.

The doormen have warned their colleague guarding the lift. He's holding the door open, I walk past brandishing the key given to me so reluctantly by Ted Samson. I insert it, the number 4 lights up on the display panel and we begin to rise, the lift and I.

I've done little but think of Graeme Sargent since I left him. He has a hold on me, a greater hold than he's so far chosen to reveal. That's why I'm here. This is the next golden ring. That's Sly's idea. 'He wants you on his side, boss, he can see you're dangerous. This is his chance to tie you to him. It's like in *Lord of the Rings*. "One ring to rule them all, One ring to find them, One ring to bring them all and in the darkness bind them." He's binding you to him. He wants you with him rather than against him.'

It's a possibility. On the other hand, he might just want me out of the picture altogether. Bribes, blackmail, either, both, he'll have some tool to help him achieve his desire, whatever that desire is. My early evening bravado has been replaced by a pessimistic realism, a feeling that I can't beat someone who's marked the pack, dealt the cards and chosen which hand he'll play. I don't know what I'll say to him, what I'll do. Logic dictates I'll do exactly as he says, I've no choice in the matter. My future's pre-determined.

The office on the fourth floor is empty, the desk unoccupied, no papers to show any work is ever done there. The lighting is low, subdued. The door to Sargent's suite is closed; I knock but there's no answer, so I turn the handle and go in anyway.

The windows are open, the curtains are moving slightly, but there's no sign of Sargent. His video screens are on, paused with different views of the same scene. Despite the blurry grain of the frozen tape I can make out the shape of a woman, dark-haired, naked on a bed. There's insufficient detail for me to see any of her facial features. I examine the control desk, find the button with the single arrow sign that usually means 'play', press it. The screens come to life.

The woman on the bed flicks her hair back; I recognise the motion. She smiles; I know the smile. A man joins her on the bed, they embrace, their hands between each other's legs. Graeme Sargent and Carrie Ratcliffe are making love. There's a murmur of traffic from outside, then another sound, behind me, a rasping, gurgling noise, as if some viscous liquid is being forced down a narrow pipe. I spin round but see no one, hear the sound again. It's coming from the high-backed chair in front of Sargent's desk. I move across the room, warily. First I see a bare leg dangling below the chair, then Graeme Sargent's body.

He's propped up, straight-backed, his towelling gown open to reveal his body. It's soiled where he's emptied his bowels, his chest is streaked with vomit. His eyes are wide open, staring from a red-mottled face.

I step closer. He doesn't react. I move closer still, overcome my nausea, wave my hand in front of his face; still nothing but a low mantra of unintelligible noise. I stretch out my hand, feel his wrist. Through paper skin I find his pulse, weak, irregular. There's a box of tissues on his desk, I wipe his mouth, place my hand over it; he's hardly breathing.

'Shit! Come on, Sargent, stop fucking about!' I ease him from the chair and on to the floor. He's dead weight. I try to remember the recovery position, and as I move him on to his side his breath coalesces into what could be words. I don't recognise them.

'Tell me later,' I say. There's a phone on the desk, I reach for it but find my coat grabbed by one of his hands. This time he's looking at me, his lips drawn back over grey, greasy teeth. He hisses; I bend closer; he tries to speak again.

'Die . . .'

'No, Graeme, people like you don't die, you're not that lucky.'

'Die . . .'

'You won't die if you let me go, let me call an ambulance.'

'. . . Cast.'

'What?'

'Die . . . cast.'

Die-cast. It can't be that he's reminding me how much he considers my life a game, not now. So what's he trying to tell me? That there's no free will, that every step of our lives is pre-determined before we're born? He's lecturing me from his death-bed? As if satisfied that his message is understood his body stiffens, then relaxes. I feel for his pulse at his wrist and at his neck; nothing. I bend my cheek

189

to his mouth, ignore the smell of vomit; he's stopped breathing. There's no movement at his chest, no heartbeat, no lungs.

'You bastard, Sargent!' I kneel beside him, cross my hands over his chest and hit him, hard. One . . . two . . . three . . . four . . . five! Then I pull his head back, put two of my fingers in his mouth and scoop, in case he's choking. There's nothing there. I lower my head to his, left hand pinching his nose, right on his chest. I can feel the movement when I blow, but there's nothing there when I stop. I do it again and again, then move back to his chest.

I can't remember the ratio of breaths to hits, of heart massage to lung inflations. I keep going, then return to breathing for him, not sure if I'm doing any good at all.

'What the hell is going on? What are you doing to Graeme?'

I look up briefly. It's a woman, good looking, late twenties. Her hair's damp from the shower, she's wearing a bathrobe similar to the one now lying beneath Sargent's body.

'I think he's had a heart attack. Ring 999.'

She stares at me but does nothing.

'Now!' She jumps as I return to my work, I can hear her voice, small in the background.

'Ambulance please. I don't know the number, its *Ladders* nightclub, down on the quayside. Yes, I think it's a heart attack.'

'Tell them his heart's stopped!'

'There's a man here giving him mouth-to mouth, he says his heart's stopped.'

'Fourth floor, tell them it's the fourth floor!'

'Come to the fourth floor.'

On the video screen Carrie has her orgasm; the girl in the bathrobe collapses in tears; and I realise Graeme Sargent is dead and there's nothing I can do about it. But I'm still working over him when the paramedics arrive, they have to pull me off him so they can administer electric

190

shocks; when the doctor, a minute behind them, shakes his head, I know for certain. The woman I'm embracing, consoling, is a stranger. I try to tell myself that the tears forming in my eyes are for her, with her. How can they be for the dead man before me, a man I hated, a man who personified all that was evil, a criminal? Yet they are for him. No one should die like that.

I leave the tearful woman and switch off the video. It's been a long night.

Chapter Twenty-Eight

The police aren't far behind the doctor. He confers with them in whispers, they look at the body and at me, at the woman, back to the body. Then they speak into their radios. Ten minutes later Kim Bryden arrives. She doesn't seem surprised to see me.

'What is it with you, Billy? Too shy to tell me how lovely I am, so you keep appearing at the scene of crime just to find an excuse to be close to me?'

'What crime is that, Inspector? I'm just the poor bloke trying to save a man's life.'

'So why were you here? Before you started doing your Good Samaritan act?'

'Are you going to charge me with anything?'

'I don't know yet.'

I gesture at Sargent's body being lifted into a body-bag. 'He had a heart attack.'

'Doctor here says it looks like that, but it's best to wait and see. There'll be a postmorten. So tell me why you're here.'

I tell her what I feel able, which is almost the truth; I say Sargent invited me, didn't tell me why. From there it's blow by blow account. I hang around while Kim questions the tearful woman, listen in while I make them coffee. She met Sargent the previous night, downstairs in the club. He invited her up, started the big seduction but didn't go all the way. He asked her back the next night, when she arrived he gave her a drink, told her to take a shower. He said he had a meeting, it should last no more than twenty minutes. She waited thirty then came out to find me trying to raise Lazarus. The bouncers confirm my story and her story; Kim tells her to get dressed and go.

'Can I go too, please miss?' I ask.

'Of course, Billy. I'll give you a lift. Come on.' She's being too polite, but I don't care why. All I want to do is sleep.

We descend to the flashing, dancing purgatory which is still unaware that its chief devil has slipped further down the circle to hell. I mention the allegory to Kim but she doesn't seem impressed. Her car's outside the front door, protected by a flashing blue and white. Together they occupy precisely the same spot my container of criminals did less than 24 hours before. There's a brown packet on the passenger seat.

'Get in,' she says, 'put the sandwiches in the back.' It's obvious she hasn't been counting on spending her shift in the office. She drives slowly, carefully, as if she wants to make the journey last.

'There was a fire this evening, at Winner Profile Systems.'

'Was there?'

'The place was gutted. Probably arson. Know anything about it?'

'No. I've finished my job there. The security systems were in and working. Their operation was nothing to do with me.'

'Just checking.'

We seem to be going the long way round, north on to the central motorway, then east, heading for the coast road. Past the old bus station. Past the cemetery.

'Why were you after information on Ted Samson?'

'I thought he might have been something to do with the attacks on WPS.'

193

'Thought? Past tense?'

'I can't prove anything.'

'He's a nasty man, Billy. Sargent brought him up from London a few months ago. He's hard. But he's also something to do with Pearson Plastics, a competitor of WPS.'

'I know.'

'So its conceivable you might have a grudge against him. And since you seem to be good friends with Carrie Ratcliffe – I'm not blind, Billy, I saw the way you two were looking at each other that night – I hope you haven't been doing anything you shouldn't.'

'What, with Carrie Ratcliffe?'

'Billy, don't play stupid, because I know you're not. Sargent is – was – the money behind Pearson, there's no way Samson could set himself up like that. And now he's dead.'

'But not in suspicious circumstances, Kim.'

'We'll see about that, Billy.' We're back on first name terms now. Perhaps she feels sorry for me, or guilty because I had to find Samson myself. Perhaps she's trying to get me to lower my guard, she might be after information. I don't trust her. After all, she's the police.

'I only worked for WPS, I didn't have any other attachment. There's no reason for me to start a personal vendetta Kim.'

'Not even for Carrie Ratcliffe?'

'Especially not for Carrie Ratcliffe. After you've dropped me off, just go back to the club. There's a video editing station, look at the tape that's in there. Or get one of your lads to meet you back at the station with it. You might find it interesting.'

We're heading along Chile Road now, brightly lit, decorated with dusty litter and tired prostitutes lounging in shop doorways, nearing the end of their shift.

'Don't be a stranger, Billy. Keep in touch. If you hear anything, I want to be the first to know.'

'You can drop me off here, thanks, by the fruit shop. I'm

still not sure what type of thing you want to know about.'

'Oh, nothing in particular. Things in general. Use your initiative Billy.'

I open the door, climb out, close the door behind me. Then I tap on the window. 'Is this a reciprocal agreement? Do I get anything back from you?'

'Depends on what you want.'

'A copy of the postmortem?'

'Why?'

'Why not?'

'I need to know what direction you're moving, Billy. You're not a police officer any more. I don't want you in the way. So I need to know why you want to see the postmortem. I need to know what you're thinking.'

'It doesn't matter,' I say. 'I didn't really want it. I just needed to know how one-sided this exchange of information might be, and now I know. Don't call me, I won't call you.'

I walk away, down a street whose entrance has been blocked by bollards and paving stones. She can't follow me; not that she wants to. When I look back she's on the radio, probably calling up the video I mentioned. I had the first faint stirrings of an erection when I saw Carrie on those screens, before I was distracted by Graeme Sargent's heart attack. I wonder if Kim Bryden will be aroused. Somehow I doubt it. I can't even imagine her naked. She's the type of person who looks most natural when she's fully clothed.

The first tinges of dawn greet me as I enter the flat. I feel tired, very tired. Not even the early morning sparrow will keep me awake.

195

Saturday

Chapter Twenty-Nine

I fall asleep thinking of the things I should have told Kim Bryden, but didn't. The unused medicines in Sargent's bathroom cupboard, his dying words, what good would that information possibly be to her? They might be important, they might not, but they're more likely to mean something to me than to her. Everything I know is too raw, it's impossible to make a judgement on it. I let the information sift itself while I sleep.

It's past midday when I wake. I decide to miss breakfast and go for a run; my body's recovering from its beating, its aches are bearable and I don't intend going far. I find a clean vest, but have to rescue my shorts from the washbasket. A smear of vaseline on my thighs, water in my bottle, bottle in bumbag and I'm ready to go. Just one piece of paper to take as well.

Sometimes I set off without knowing where I'm going. This time I have a specific route in mind. I head down to Armstrong Park, keeping to the shade wherever possible. Once there I take off my vest, I run into the Valley then up the bank onto Valley Road. I stop there for a drink then on, heading west through terraces of tall, long-gardened houses. Soon I'm standing in front of Rak's house, sweat dripping from me, chest rising and falling, hands on my waist. I ring the bell.

The downstairs curtains are closed, but that's Rak's

room. Her curtains are always closed, even in midsummer, even when she's at work. She likes the darkness, the close atmosphere, the feeling of safety. She tells me it's like living in a cave, blocking in the windows adds to her security. I've been in that front room, she has blankets and carpets hanging on every wall and over the door. Once you're inside it's difficult to find a way out.

I step back into the street, shade my eyes against the glare of the sunlight and look at the upstairs windows. The curtains there are closed as well. I go back to the doorbell, ring again. Still there's no reply. I decide to take out my frustration on the bellpush, I lean on it, hoping to drain the batteries as revenge for no one being in. That's when I hear the noise.

'Okay, okay, stop that bloody ringing! You win, I'll answer the door, just shut up!'

I obey. Having already aggravated whoever's stamping down the hallway it would be best not to make matters worse. The door's flung open. Jenny, the girl I met last time I was here, the one I want to talk to this time, is wrapped in a waxed jacket. Her hair is awry, her eyes pinched against the light.

'I was in bed, I'm on nights! What do you want?'

'I want to talk to you,' I say in what I hope is an apologetic manner, 'I thought you'd be awake by now and . . .'

'I'm sorry, do I know you?' Her expression echoes the statement, she doesn't recognise me.

'We met a few days ago. I told Rak I'd call, it was her said you were on nights . . .'

'Mr Oliphant?'

'Yes.'

Her lips and eyebrows, formerly parallel and getting closer to each other, decide to dart in curves of laughter to the opposite ends of her face.

'Mr Oliphant, I *thought* it was your voice! I'm sorry, I don't have my lenses in, I couldn't find my glasses, it's so bright outside I can hardly see you, and it looks as if you've hardly any clothes on.'

'I haven't. I ran here from my place.'

'Really? Rather you than me. But come in. I'll get dressed, you go through, into the kitchen. Put the kettle on if you want, I'll have coffee, strong, black, no sugar. You might have to wash a few cups.' She lets me go ahead then runs up the stairs, hands cupping her rear in case I'm tempted to look up.

The kitchen is worse than it was two days before, no dishes have been washed and new ones have been added to the piles. I find the kettle and fill it with water, switch it on. Then I empty the sink, gather the dishes to one side and put cups and pans on the table. This in turn involves me clearing the table of newspapers and junk mail, empty envelopes, some history text books, and piling them on a chair stacked with similar detritus.

I find it therapeutic, making order from chaos. By the time Jenny's footsteps precede her down the hall the kettle's boiled, her coffee's waiting for her, and the first batch of dishes has been washed.

'Sorry I took so long,' she says, 'I decided to take a shower and . . . My God! I'm in the wrong house!'

'Your coffee's on the table. Don't interrupt or I might stop.'

'Please, Mr Oliphant, don't let me stop you. I didn't even know there was a sink in the kitchen.'

Her hair's tied up in a towel, she's wearing large, round-rimmed glasses. She's decided not to bother with shoes, risky given the state of the carpets in the house, and her trousers are made of multi-coloured patches. A threadbare long-sleeved T-shirt, too large for her, completes the outfit. She subsides into the one empty chair in the room, hooks one foot up to rest on her thigh and sips her coffee. I wash the last of the dishes and stack them before moving on to the cups and mugs.

'Rak said you wanted a word,' she says, 'but I had no idea this was part of the agreement. Is it a fetish or do you do this every time you go into a stranger's kitchen?'

201

'Rak's not a stranger,' I remind her, 'and yes, it is a bit of a fetish. Well, not a fetish, it doesn't turn me on. Just a mild neurosis. I like tidiness.'

'Do you do house calls as well? I've a bedroom could do with some attention.' I turn to look at her with what is, I hope, an expression of wry amusement. 'Good God, did I really say that? It sounded a bit ... Well, it sounded a bit of a come on, it certainly wasn't intended as such.' She shrugs, her mouth a curve of apology. 'I hope I didn't offend you.'

'I'm not offended. But if you'd like to find me another tea-towel? I can't wash any more, the drainer's full.'

'I'm completely out of my mind, Mr Oliphant! Letting you do all this work is bad enough, but sitting here watching you! You must think me terrible.'

'No, but I can recognise immobilising shock when I see it. And I know I'm old, but please, don't call me "Mr Oliphant". My name's Billy.'

'Okay, Billy. I'll dry if you keep washing.'

'That's fine with me. Then I'd appreciate it if you'd help me with a problem I have.'

'Of course I will.'

'I haven't told you what it is yet. It might be illegal. It might even be immoral.'

'The answer's still yes. Rak told me a little about you. You wouldn't ask me to do anything ridiculously illegal or hugely immoral. She also said it was something to do with me being a medic. So I'll help if I can, ask away. Just don't stop washing!'

I'm surprised Rak's been talking about me so much. I must be worrying her. She feels a need to act as a mother figure, that's why she likes having young people around her. When I first met her, found she was gay, found she had a house full of female students, I was suspicious of her motives. She reassured me. 'The wise bird,' she said, 'never craps in its own nest. I look after my girls like they were sisters, they trust me. I've a good reputation, that's why the place is always full. And if it's a bit untidy some-times, well, that's the way they like it.' As well as being a surrogate mother she acts as confessor, matchmaker, adviser, nurse and, on one occasion, midwife; normally her girls take up a fair proportion of her spare time. If she's been able to talk to Jenny about me and my problems (of her perception of my problems) then the present bunch of tenants must be fairly mature and capable of looking after themselves. Either that or I really have given her cause to worry about me.

'In my bumbag, over there, on the table. Yes, under the newspaper. There's a piece of paper inside, it's got the names of drugs written on it.'

She opens the bag, fishes inside. 'You mean this soggy scrap of cardboard?'

That's it. Can you read my writing?' I pick up the tea-towel she's meant to be using, get to work with it. I don't want to interrupt her while she's doing something useful for me.

'I'm a doctor,' she says, 'illegible writing is part of the course.' She pushes her glasses back on the bridge of her nose. 'Yes, I can read your writing. "Depixol, Stemetil, Caverject, Diamicron, Nardil, Triptafen, Glucophage." And?'

'So if I was a patient, if I had those drugs sitting on my shelf, what would be wrong with me?'

'Right. let me see.' She rolls up the sleeves of her shirt, her arms beneath are slim, the colour of light chocolate. 'From what I can remember Depixol is a trade name, it's a type of drug called a thioxanthene. It's used for schizo-phrenics . . .'

'Schizophrenics?' I stop drying dishes, listen more closely.

'Yes. It helps schizophrenics who are withdrawn, apathetic. Now then, what's next? Stemetil. So far as I remember that's used for schizophrenics as well, for patients who are acutely psychotic. But it wouldn't gener-ally be used at the same time as Depixol.'

'Okay, what about the rest?'

'Look, I'll make sure. I've got a MIMS upstairs, I'll fetch it down . . .'

'What's a Mims?'

'Acronym. M.I.M.S. Monthly Index of Medical Specialities. It's a list of drugs, tells you their uses, contra-indications, interactions and so on. It's published every month, medics get it free. I've an old one somewhere, hang on, I'll go and find it.'

She runs out of the kitchen, I hear her thunder upstairs. Then there's the sound of heavy objects being thrown around, a cupboard door slamming. I return to my work, it's another four or five minutes before she reappears.

'Perhaps I should tidy that room myself, then I'd be able to find things. Got it though, it's a few months old but that won't make any difference. Now then, where were we. Stemetil. Yes, it's a phenothiazine, used for minor mental and emotional disturbances. Next?'

I dry my hands and assume the role of prompter, reading from my crib-sheet. 'Caverject.'

'Caverject it is. That's . . . let me see . . . A prostaglandin. That's an interesting one. For the treatment of erectile dysfunction. It's for men who have problems getting an erection. It has vasoactive properties, it provides an artificial erection by relaxing the corporeal smooth muscle, that's the muscle inside the penis . . .' She puts her hands down between her legs, points the imaginary organ of an index finger at the floor.' And then . . .' She lifts her finger up until it's horizontal. 'I'd need a model or a sketch pad to show you properly.'

'So if someone couldn't get an erection, he just takes this tablet and . . .'

'Oh no. It's not a tablet, Billy. It's an injection. It comes in an ampoule as a powder, add diluent, then inject it.'

'Inject it? Inject it where?'

'Into the base of the penis.'

'No!'

'Yes! Honestly, you men are all the same. I mean, at college we'd get all sorts of presentations about drugs and their effects, but this one ... You should have seen the pained expressions on the men's faces, the way they crossed their legs.'

'I can't imagine injecting ... well, you know.'

She warms to her task. 'The first time it's being used it has to be administered by a consultant, he shows the patient how to do it, tests the reaction. Then it's up to the patient. You can't use it more than once a day, no more than three times a week. But the thing is, some men who use it are prone to occasional priapism.'

'Priapism? Wasn't Priapus a Roman god?'

'He's the fella. God of male procreative powers, and gardens and vineyards. Always depicted with a huge erect phallus. So priapism is a prolonged painful erection. Let's see what it says here ... Ah yes, advise patient to seek medical advice if erection persists more than four hours.'

'Four hours?'

'Yep. And that can include an hour or so of vigorous intercourse and possible ejaculation. It's not life-threatening, just uncomfortable and inconvenient.'

'I don't think I want to know. Can we go on? The next item's Diamicron.'

'I know that one, that might explain the Caverject. Diamicron's a tablet used for non-insulin dependent diabetes. One of the problems with diabetes is that it sometimes gives men problems with getting an erection. There's no contra-indication or interaction listed here, but ... I'd have to check to make sure it could be used at the same time as the other drugs. Are there any more?'

'Nardil.'

'Nardil? That's for depression and phobias. All these drugs, they can't be for the same person. No GP would prescribe all these at the same time, it would be too dangerous. What's next?'

'Two more, Triptafen and Glucophage.'

'Triptafen's a funny one, I'll have to check that. Let's see now . . . Yes, it can be used for anxiety and for depression at the same time. And Glucophage is for non-insulin dependent diabetes again. Quite a mix, eh?'

'Yes, quite a mix.'

'But they can't all be for one person, not all at the same time.'

'I can see that. But . . . suppose one person had been taking all these over a period of years, at different times within that period.'

'He – I'm assuming it's a he, with the Caverject – would have been quite a strange person. A diabetic schizophrenic with depression and phobias. That's a nasty mixture.'

'What if he'd been prescribed them and hadn't been using them?'

'That's fairly common among schizophrenics anyway, they don't recognise they're ill, they lack . . .'

'. . . insight. Yes, I know about that. Insight is one thing I seem to have in abundance.'

'Oh! I see! Your tidiness? Obsessive-compulsive neurosis?'

'There were times when I'd cross the street to pick up a piece of litter. I wanted to know why I had it, I spent a while reading about neuroses, psychoses and so on. I never did understand too much, but I ended up with a very clean kitchen.'

'There doesn't seem too much wrong with you now.'

'I'm over the worst.' I fish the last two plates from the sink and rinse them, stack them carefully. 'What about the man taking these drugs, then? What type of person would he be?'

'Complicated. Mentally ill. Why do you want to know?'

'I knew him.'

'Knew? What happened to him?'

'He died. And that's something else I need from you. The results of his postmortem.'

'Billy! What is this?'

206

'It's called trading favours. I wash your dishes, you get me a copy of the postmortem.'

I hardly know her. I can't tell whether she's annoyed with me or secretly thrilled. That's how my association with Rak began, by me asking for more and more ridiculous information. She looked on it as a challenge. Jenny could be about to tell me I should start my run back home now, I want more from her than information, I want her to break some rules. And she has a great deal to lose.

'I'll need to think about it, Billy. Why not have a shower, I'll do some thinking. Then we can talk.'

It's a start. Its not a dismissal, she'll give the matter some consideration. It's probably the best I can hope for. 'Lead me to running water,' I say.

'Quite cold running water, I'm afraid, the heating system isn't that good when the fires aren't on.'

'As long as it's wet I don't mind.'

The shower's cool, not cold. While I'm lathering and rinsing Jenny puts my running kit into a plastic carrier bag. In some dark corner of her room she finds a pair of boxer shorts, slightly too big, covered with red lips; I don't ask what happened to the previous owner. The only T-shirt she has which will fit me, she apologises, is the one she was wearing; she's changed, put on a plain white shirt, and the faded long-sleeved garment is deposited with a pair of baggy trousers similar to her own outside the bathroom. By the time I'm dressed she's towelled her own hair dry and she's sitting at the top of the stairs reading a medical text book. She looks up as I come out of the bathroom.

'You look good,' she says, grins broadly. 'Not because of the outfit, though it does suit you. You look less tired than you did the other day. Less uptight.'

'Thank you. I do feel more relaxed.'

She slams the book shut. 'Good. Let's go, then, to the Mossmobile!'

'The what?'

'The Mossmobile. My last name's Moss. Come on!'

She grabs me by the hand, pulls me downstairs and out into the street. We both wince as the hot air greets our lips, the sun attacks our eyes. She leads me to an old Metro, its white paint dulled to cream through years of neglect, its bonnet still bearing the spring's cherry-blossoms glued to its paintwork. It has a large red nose fixed to its front. She slides in, leans across to open my door. A blast of hot air thermals up at me, almost lifts me off my feet. As I climb in, the engine splutters into life reluctantly. My seat shudders, the floor beneath my running shoes feels thin, fragile. When I look round. I can see blue smoke behind.

The journey is harrowing. I'd anticipated talking about the type of man Graeme Sargent was – how easily we fall into that past tense – but I decide that Jenny's mind is better directed concentrating on driving. She seems to expect other road users to know that her vehicle lacks certain basic amenities. Not only are the brakes poor but there's virtually no acceleration, the indicators don't work and the car pulls firmly to the left. It takes twenty minutes to get to my flat; I'd have been less sweaty if I'd run.

'I haven't had any breakfast,' she says as she climbs out, 'I don't suppose you have anything to eat in the place?'

I haven't had time to do any shopping for three or four days. 'I've eggs, cheese, tomatoes. Bread, but it might be a little stale.'

She curls up her lip.

'I can get some fruit,' I say, anticipating her complaints, 'there's a grocer's round the corner.'

'It's just before three. Is there a chippy likely to be open?'

'A chippy?'

'Yeah! It's this working nights, my body's going to pieces. I need something *really* bad for me. How about a baker's? A steak pie and a doughnut?'

'Yes, there's a baker's at the end of the road.'

'How about you, then? A cream cake, vanilla slice?'

'I'll come with you. My money's in the house, if you wait . . .'

'My treat. In return for an interesting day.'

I let her buy me a loaf of bread and some fruit teacakes. We stand in front of the small range of wines in the corner supermarket, she tries to persuade me I'd like a glass of wine despite my assuring her I don't drink. She looks at me sideways, as if she doesn't believe me, then chooses a four-pack of lager. A selection of crisps finishes her ideal meal.

While I boil the kettle and make myself a sandwich she walks round the room, eating her pie, leaving a trail of crumbs behind her. Perhaps she's testing me, but I'm not tempted to follow her with a dustpan and brush.

'A little spartan, eh?' She lingers over the photograph of Kirsty and Sara, picks it up, turns it delicately to glance at its back. Is she looking for clues? An inscription? 'There's not much here that's personal. Is it temporary? Rak told me she offered you a room at her place. You should be honoured. She doesn't normally like men.'

So Rak's told her about me splitting up with Sara. Note the emphasis. *Me* splitting up with *Sara*. Not 'Sara and I splitting up.' I still consider it my fault. Damnation, it *is* my fault! Guilt is one of the few things I've been able to call my own recently.

'I needed somewhere I could be tidy,' I reply, 'somewhere with no distractions.'

'Like me and the other girls?'

'Like anyone at all.'

'Ah, the Garbo syndrome.'

'Is that medical terminology?'

'Moss terminology. Psychological terminology. One day, though, when I get my paper published in the *BMJ*, they might remember me as the inventor of the term. Or the first user. Posthumous fame.'

'Posthumous?'

'The only type worth having. Money while you're alive,

fame when you die. That's another Mossism, you can write it down if you want.' She finishes her pie, washes it down with the dregs of the first can of lager. 'Sure I can't tempt you?' she asks, holding a newly opened full can out to me. I decline the offer.

'What do you think about this friend of mine,' I ask, hoping to steer her back to the subject, 'the one with the interesting line in medication?'

She flops down on to the bed, kicks off her shoes, leans back to look at me. Her hair is shoulder-length, a little longer, and she's tied it back. Some wisps have escaped, however, and she tucks them back behind her ears as she talks. 'Definitely diabetic. Erectile dysfunction. That's the easy bit, a problem getting a hard-on is a physical manifestation of a specific illness. But then? Schizophrenic, I'd say. Tell me what you know about schizophrenia.'

I'm eating my sandwich, hoping she'll do all the talking. I don't really enjoy answering questions. 'Just what I've read. Mental illnesses are broadly divided into neuroses, such as anxiety, hysteria, obsessional behaviour . . .'

'Where the sufferer has insight, like you.'

'. . . and psychoses, where there's a lack of insight. Schizophrenia is a psychosis.'

'A functional psychosis, together with affective disorders such as mania and depression.' She's enjoying the opportunity to demonstrate her knowledge to a comparatively uneducated audience. 'There was a time when I thought, being the cynical person I am, that schizophrenia was a useful term for describing people who were mentally ill when you couldn't think what might be wrong with them. I don't think that now, not since becoming a member of the establishment, but it's still an area where even specialists can misdiagnose. It's such a broad term. Schizophrenia can cover personality defects or deterioration, withdrawal from reality, hallucinations, delusions, social apathy, emotional instability. Some schizophrenics become catatonic.' She swallows again, points at me with the can. 'Schizophrenia provides the classic generalist view of madness, the poor sod who thinks he's Christ or Napoleon. But the schizophrenic could just as easily be someone who's unhappy in company, who withdraws into a private world where he or she can cope.'

'So there's no such thing as a typical schizophrenic?'

'I don't think so. There are some things most schizophrenics have in common, like an inability to cope with society. They often have problems fitting in, getting work, forming stable relationships. And if schizophrenia strikes in middle age, after a person has been relatively normal, then the schizophrenics' family and friends can often suffer because they can't understand why this person they love has changed so much.'

'Not nice.'

'It's the old story. Mental illness always was the Cinderella of the NHS because the sane couldn't comprehend an illness without physical symptoms. Even now it's suffering. Look at "Care in the Community", a contradiction in terms if there ever was one. And it's as bad in geriatrics, except we don't call it that now, it's "Care for the Elderly". Starved of funds, resources, beds, it's not surprising there's a crisis in the Health Service.'

'Do you always get so talkative on two cans of lager?'

'Yes. Four quieten me down. Then I go on to vodka.'

'And what does that do for you?'

'One day you might be privileged to find out.' Her smirk is childlike and childish at the same time.

'I'll remember that. But getting back to my schizophrenic friend, you said he probably wouldn't be able to function in society.'

'He might be able to function, but I wouldn't expect to find him coping with a high-powered job.'

'He wouldn't be able to run a business then?'

'I doubt it. Not run it well, not for any length of time.' She finishes the second can and looks at the third.

'Interesting.' I reach out and move the two remaining

211

cans away from her. 'Unless your alcohol tolerance is exceptional, two's probably enough if you're driving.'

'You sound just like my father.'

'No doubt he's a wise, intelligent and handsome man. And anyway, you should always think of the safety of your passengers.'

'What passengers?'

'Me. I'm coming back with you, you can take me into the hospital tonight so I can steal the postmortem results. I didn't wash all those dishes for nothing.'

'Billy, you're impossible, I never said . . .'

'But you will help me, won't you?'

She breathes in deeply, shakes her head in mock reprobation. 'You'll need to wear a shirt and tie, I think I can find a white coat to fit you. You can pretend to be a clinical assistant, first day on. And if you're discovered, I've never met you before.' She sniggers and becomes a girl again. 'This could be fun!'

Chapter Thirty

I dress smartly, we drive back to Rak's house where Jenny gets changed, then we set off for the hospital. Jenny explains her position in the medical hierarchy – she's a junior doctor, a registrar, qualified the previous year and trying various disciplines before deciding on a specific area in which to concentrate her career. Or, as she more succinctly puts it, 'dossing about till I find something exciting.'

'Dossing about at present is spending time on casualty,' she explains. 'It's okay during the week except when there's a Wednesday football match. Weekends are horrendous, they're actually putting me off hospital medicine.'

'So what would you do instead? General practice?'

'Possibly. Or travel. VSO. I'm young, I might as well enjoy myself while I have the chance.'

I once felt like that. Self-confident. In the days when doing something was dependent more on the willingness to try it than any aptitude for the task itself. Those were the days I had potential, when I was destined – so they said – for Oxbridge. But with some ridiculous sense of inverted snobbery I went to Sheffield, left after a term saying I'd change my course but didn't go back. Joined the police. Got married. Had a kid. It seems ridiculous, but I was actually at the peak of my abilities at the age of eleven. Wonder boy of the primary school, captain of the school football team, a whole rosy vista of success ahead of me. But after that I couldn't seem to make my mark. I was almost there, lots of times, but something inside kept pulling me back. Fear of success? A deliberate destruction from within? If so, then it worked on many occasions at many levels. Education, employment, marriage, all failures.

'Is my driving that bad?'

Jenny's words drag me back from my mud-pool of self pity. 'Sorry?'

'You had your eyes closed, you were shaking your head. I thought it was because of my driving.'

'No, nothing like that. Just thinking.'

'Dangerous. Wouldn't advise it. As a doctor.'

The Infirmary is a maze of wards and clinics, offices and canteens, laundries and operating theatres. Its oldest, most venerable face is turned towards the university; its lawns and statue of Victoria herself look over the city. But, behind and within, one hundred years of building have taken their toll. There are, Jenny tells me, grassed courtyards with no means of access for gardener and lawn-mower save through windows in the wards. There are subterranean heating ducts whose extent is known only to engineers and cockroaches. By utilising fully the stairs and corridors it's possible to run six miles without covering the same ground twice, though this does involve negotiating an operating suite in almost constant use. She has a fondly cynical knowledge of the place, hardly surprising since she's spent the last six years of her young life working and studying there.

'I've been thinking,' she says as we pull safely into the car-park.

'Dangerous.'

'Seriously. You're certain the body will have been brought here?'

'Yes.' I know that much from my days on the force. 'Last night, or early this morning.'

'In that case the pathologist will have done the PM some

214

time today, they like to get things done quickly. His report will be in his office. His office will be locked.'

'So I'll break in.'

'You'll need me with you, to show you where the office is and then to find the file. And to interpret it for you. I don't think I can do that.'

I wait. She hasn't finished yet.

'Breaking and entering, it's too criminal. If I get caught ...'

'So what do we do? Look at the body ourselves?'

'No, I'm not a pathologist, I wouldn't know what to look for.'

'So what do you suggest?'

'The post room. There'll be a copy of the report to the dead man's GP and also to the police. I can make a reasonable excuse for being there. I think I'd rather do that than ...'

'Let's do it then.'

'Now?'

'You've got time before you start your shift. Like you said, I need you to show me the way and to interpret.'

She's still nervous, but she shrugs, gets out of the car. She doesn't bother locking it. She slips herself into her white coat, hangs a stethoscope out of her pocket, makes sure her identification badge is easily recognisable.

'Follow me, Mr Oliphant,' she says.

'Certainly, Miss ... Sorry, *Doctor* Moss.'

'Quite right. Give me the respect my authority deserves.'

She leads me at a brisk pace down a labyrinth of corridors. We pass cleaners riding polishing machines, porters heaving trolleys up indoor hills. She smiles at some people, nods at others, greets some by name. One man seems eager to talk to her but she tells him she'll catch him later and leaves him doe-eyed in her wake.

'Typing pool,' she says as we pass a cavern of an office, empty now, desks cluttered with word processors and dictaphones. The post room's next door.' She bustles straight in.

The lights are on but no one's there.

'Early evening's a good time to be in a hospital,' she says. 'At night, in the corridors, you're noticeable. But there are visitors around at the moment, staff going on and off duty. It's easy to get yourself deliberately lost.'

The room is small, tables are set against the walls, there are racks with envelopes and wrapping paper, Sellotape and reels of brown parcel tape, bubble wrap and balls of string. In one corner is an assortment of cardboard boxes. There's a wooden rack fixed to one wall, each opening labelled.

'Internal post,' Jenny explains, 'other hospitals, clinics, local health centres. We're looking for external to the police.'

I look closely, in the bottom corner the largest pile of letters is in a box headed 'waiting for franking'.

'Probably these,' I say, 'you take half.'

We look through about sixty letters each, without success. Then we check again.

'Perhaps he hasn't done the postmortem yet,' I suggest.

'Mr Hardman's the pathologist here, Billy. He'll have done it all right. He'd do autopsies on patients before they die if he had the chance.'

'Perhaps he did it earlier today, then, and the report's already been posted.'

'Possible.'

'So we're going to have to raid his office after all.'

'No, I already told you, I won't do that.'

'You don't have to! Just tell me where it is, I'll do it myself.'

'Hold on. There's one more possibility. He might have dictated the letter but not signed it yet. Come on.'

She pushes her letters back into the appropriate pigeon hole and I follow suit, then chase after her. She's trying the door to the typing pool.

'Damn! Locked!'

'Move aside, Doctor Moss. Surgery is called for here.' Three-lever locks aren't quite as easy as two-lever, but this

216

is an old door in an old part of the building. A close look confirms that the lock is barely touching the keep plate. I go back into the post room for a pair of scissors, insert them at the lock between the door and the frame. A little pressure disengages the lock and the door swings open.

'Jesus,' says Jenny, 'remind me not to let you near my chastity belt.' She hurries in. There are too many desks for me to even think about where to start looking.

'Typing pool is for general administrative work,' she explains, 'most of the consultants have their own secretaries who deal with letters and appointments. But Hardman doesn't have to worry about making appointments for his stiffs, so *his* letters are dealt with by one of the *medical* secretaries here in the pool. And . . .' She heads for a small stack of papers on one of the desks, rustles through them.

'What's the man's name, the body?'

'Graeme Sargent.'

'Got him!' She flutters a piece of paper at me. I look around, there's a photocopier in one corner of the room. I go to switch it on while Jenny reads the report. She's nodding, she flicks the end of her nose with her finger as she reads.

'So? I ask.

'Heart attack,' she says, 'caused by a massive overdose of heroin.'

'Heroin? No, it can't be.'

'That's what it says here. He suspected it but could find no obvious needle signs at first. It would have to be taken intravenously to have such an effect. But then he did find some repeated injection sites. At the base of the penis.'

'But . . .'

'Yes, Billy, I know. The impotence drug, the Caverject injections. They're made into the base of the penis. So he's been injecting himself with heroin in the same place. Jesus Christ!'

'No, Jenny, no! He wasn't into drugs. He told me – and I believed him – he didn't take drugs.'

217

'Well he certainly did this time. A huge amount, straight into the bloodstream. And he was a diabetic as well, that wouldn't have helped.'

'What if he didn't know it was heroin?'

'You mean he injected himself thinking it was something else?'

'What if he thought it was that Caverject stuff?'

'Someone switched it?'

'Yes. Could it be done?'

'I don't know. I suppose so, but ... Injections like Caverject come with a diluent, you have to mix it up, then you transfer it to a syringe. There are too many different steps, it would be impossible to confuse heroin in powder form with the base powder of Caverject, it would be labelled properly. No, I don't think so.'

The photocopier clicks to let me know it's warm. I take the paper from Jenny, there's no more than a page and a half of writing. I made two copies, switch off the machine and return the papers to the pile on the desk.

'Come on,' I say, 'I need to think and you need to get to work. Thank you for your help.'

'You're welcome. Any time.' She acts as my guide back to the main exit. 'What's the forecast for tomorrow?' she asks, looking up at blue skies decked with house martins. A rook tumbles in pursuit of a seagull.

'I don't know. I've stopped believing that anyone can predict anything.'

'Well I know I've a few days off. And it looks as if the weather's going to be fine. Could you drag yourself away from your investigations to take a poor girl out in the country for the day?' The white coat makes her skin look smoother, darker. She's looking straight at me, smiling slightly, politely.

'Can this poor girl drive?'

'Not very well.'

'Can I close my eyes in the car?'

Her smile broadens. 'Ring me,' she commands.

I feel an impulse to kiss her, on the cheek, but I'm not sure if that would embarrass both of us. It would be presumptuous of me to assume that, because she's asked me to share a day with her, it might mean more than the need for company. But she *is* standing there, waiting, looking ... well, expectant. I step towards her; there's a shrill piping noise from her pocket.

'Shit! Bleep! Must go!' She turns and runs.

'I'll ring you,' I call after her.

In my pocket are two copies of the postmortem on Graeme Sargent. I need to think about them. I need to consider what, if anything, I should do next. Because I'm beginning to suspect that someone murdered him.

Chapter Thirty-One

I call Kim Bryden from a coinbox.

'Yes, Billy,' she says impatiently, as if she has too much to think of, though she can only have been on shift for an hour, 'what can I do for you?'

'Other way round, Kim. It's what I can do for you.'

'Tell me then.'

'Do you fancy a walk?

'No, I hate walking. If God had meant us to walk he wouldn't have let us invent the wheel. Or the telephone, a handy machine, it lets people talk without them having to meet.'

'Forget it, then. See you sometime, Kim.'

'Billy, you're an arsehole. Why not come down to the station, I can get you something to eat, we can talk in peace.'

'The bandstand in the Exhibition Park. Ten minutes?'

'It had better be good, Billy!'

We're on better terms now, Kim and I, she's beginning to treat me as semi-human. I just hope she'll take the information I'm going to give her in the right way. If Graeme Sargent was murdered then it's more than I can handle, I don't want anything else to do with it. It can be a police matter, I'll be happy to get back to the security business. But I'll have to tell her about my having a copy of the post-mortem, I'll have to mention why I was at *Ladders* when

Sargent died, and that in turn means letting her know about the window scam. She'll be angry that I've hidden so much from her for so long, but I'll have to risk that.

It's a short walk on a warm evening. The park has its share of people enjoying its threadbare lawns and thirsty flowers. Lovers search for cover or disport themselves immodestly on the grass; toddlers stagger with cowboy legs from parent to parent; young men of all shapes play football (defying the bye-laws) encouraged by giggling girlfriends. I can hear laughter from the swings, the distant clap of wood on wood as two boats on the lake bounce off one another. Two long-legged girls on rollerblades circle the bandstand with slow-motioned ease, then speed carelessly away. Summer paints a gloss over the noise and smell of the traffic, the overflowing litter bins, the green paint peeling from vandalised benches. Sunshine draws the eye away from flowers uprooted and thrown to die in copses of thorn, it offers an invitation to ignore the dog shit, the bumbling drunk of a tramp, the broken bottles, the line of regimented beer cans. The warmth descends, settles on my shoulders like a familiar pair of hands, tells me not to worry, everything will be all right.

'Damn!' I've remembered the problem with the office leases. I said I'd do something but I can't even remember what it was. Then it comes back to me, I'm to examine the landlord's latest offer, draft a reply. It can wait until tomorrow.

Through the ornate iron scrolls of the bandstand I can see Kim Bryden approaching, eyes screwed up against the sunlight. I stand up, wave to her. She comes across to join me.

'Why here, Billy? It's a pig of a place. Look at it, the only people who come here this time of day are trouble-makers.' Kim's acidic gaze can't change my viewpoint. I used to be brought here when I was a child, as a special treat. I learned to walk here. Perhaps the magic of my memories hides me from reality. Or perhaps it lets me see reality.

221

'Come on, then, I don't have much time. What do you want to tell me?'

This time I tell her everything, from Carrie Ratcliffe's first phone call to Graeme Sargent's death. Well, not quite everything; I tell her about the Caverject but not the other medicines in Sargent's bathroom; and I don't mention the words he spoke as he was dying. I give her a copy of the postmortem. She doesn't ask where I got it, how I got it.

'So you think Graeme Sargent was murdered. Someone switches his wonderdrug for heroin, he injects himself and snuffs it. From a stiffy to a stiff in one go.'

'Except he didn't like injections, Kim. Someone else must have done it.'

'Oh, yes, I'll fall for that. Billy, would you let anyone approach your dick with the intention of sticking a dirty big needle in it? Would you hell!'

'It depends. If I was wanting to make it with someone badly enough, yes. I might even ask my intended partner to do it. You never know, it might turn someone on.'

'Would that someone have the expertise to use a needle? But leave that aside for the moment. Let's just say it was administered by another; or the stiffener, what's it called?'

'Caverject.'

'Right, let's say it was replaced by someone. Motive?'

'Sargent must have had lots of enemies.'

'Including you, if your story's true. Jesus Christ, Billy, you get into some deep shit! I can't even nail the Ratcliffes and Samson for arson, you're their alibi. They'll probably get away with the insurance scam as well.'

'Did you get the tape of Carrie Ratcliffe and Sargent?'

'Yes. And a dozen others in a similar vein, different women, always with Sargent. We're trying to identify the women at the moment.'

'Why's that?'

'There were quite a few copies of some of them, all edited differently. We think Sargent was sending them out to Dutch porn merchants, in a few months they'd be back

222

here in their thousands advertised as hot continental hard-core. False names for the participants, of course. I doubt they'd ever find out how many dirty old men had enjoyed their talents. Quite an adventurous woman, your friend Carrie Ratcliffe.'

'No friend of mine. Not now.'

'But she was. And if your suggestion is true, if Sargent was killed by an overdose administered by others, then she might be a suspect. Judging by the video she's got a good motive. Publication of that could ruin her.'

'If she was recognised. But in that case any of the other women would have an equally good motive.'

'Which is why we're trying to identify them. Check on their movements just before Sargent died. How about you, Billy? Where were you before the bouncers checked you in? There are other means of access to Sargent's suite.'

She's testing me, not entirely seriously, wondering how I'll react. It's a means of gaining control, putting me on the defensive, trying to get me off guard.

'No alibi between leaving Carrie Ratcliffe's apartment and arriving to see Sargent, I'm afraid. But we both know that if I was planning to kill Sargent I would have chosen a more subtle way of doing it, one that didn't involve me trying to resuscitate him.'

'Allegedly trying to resuscitate him.' Kim's looking around her as she talks and listens. 'This place really is a bit of a hole, Billy. Come on, if you've anything else to say you can tell me on the walk back to the car. It's getting dark. The zombies'll be clawing their way out of the ground before long.' She stands up, begins to walk away, not caring if I follow or not. When I do she continues her lecture.

'Of course, it could be a double blind. If he *was* murdered then you're so obvious a suspect you'd be discounted straight away. But you could be acting clever. Letting us think you would have chosen a better, more complicated method of doing away with Sargent when in fact this was so easy and straightforward it becomes a devious way of diverting suspicion from yourself.'

'If you really thought that, Kim, you'd have arrested me by now. Yes, I've got the motive. But it's not a strong motive. And there's no proof to show he was murdered. It's just a feeling. My feeling.'

'And mine, Billy, I've had the postmortem results since lunchtime. Sargent wasn't a drug user as far as we know, if he had been his body might have been able to tolerate the heroin overdose more easily. If he'd been doing drugs he wouldn't have injected himself directly into the vena cava anyway. So if someone injected him, or swapped his stiffener for heroin – and by the way, there's nothing about this injection in his medical records, he must have been getting supplies illegally, I can't imagine you can buy it at the chemist's – then murder's a possibility. You've filled in some gaps. Billy, but you've also given me a problem. You're the only one who knows about this wonderful willy-injection. And you're one of the people who has both the motivation and the opportunity to have changed the drugs.' She sniggers, a strange sound I've never heard her make before, it sounds as if she's trying to blow her nose. 'I've always wanted to say this to someone, but this is the first opportunity I've ever had.' She turns to face me and glowers artificially, her voice assumes an American accent. 'Don't leave the country, Billy.' She laughs again. Perhaps she's under pressure at work. At least her voice returns to normal. 'And I'll need you to come in tomorrow and make a statement.'

I can understand her feelings, if not her sense of humour. She's right, I could have killed Sargent, I had the motivation and the opportunity. She probably realises I wouldn't have baulked at the task if I'd wanted to do it. The reason she's not arresting me straightaway is that I've provided her with a line of questioning she wouldn't otherwise have had and, at the same time, openly cast suspicion on myself. Plus, and this is only supposition on my part, I think she trusts me. We're heading for the gates. I can see her car parked on the double yellow lines across the road, there's someone in the driver's seat.

'I don't suppose Sargent's records mentioned any other medication?' I ask as we reach the car.

'Such as?'

'Well, sometimes drugs interact with one another. The effect of the heroin might have been made worse by an interaction.'

'No. I've seen copies of his GP's notes, they're as thin as he was. Every six months he had his blood pressure taken, every three months he had a prescription for something to help his diabetes. Did you know he was a diabetic? Under good control, though. And that's it. Nothing else. Not even a headache. He was a fit man.'

He was a fit man who had access to anti-schizoid drugs. He was a fit man who stocked his shelves with them but didn't take them. But I push these thoughts from my mind, they're no longer my business. Why should I worry if Sargent was murdered, why should I care about who did it?

'What happens now?' I ask. The question is innocent; I'm curious to know how Kim will approach the case. But she takes it as a suggestion that there's still work for me to do, that I'm keen to continue with the investigation in some way. She stars at me with her Inspector's eyes, her police-woman's eyes, authoritative eyes.

'For me, questions, investigations, thoughts. I put the jigsaw together. For you? How about an early night, Billy. Then you can start tomorrow by seeing if there's any business out there for you. I'll have a word with crime prevention, ask them to put your name about.'

She's told me, very gently for her, to get lost. She doesn't want me sniffing round the case any more. Don't interfere, she's saying, let the big boys take over. And for once I'm happy to do as she asks. I don't have the resources to chase a murderer. And besides, anyone who can consider killing a man by letting him inject his dick with a lethal dose of heroin is not the type of person I want to cross.

'Good hunting,' I say. She doesn't offer me a lift. I can hear the small voice of the radio operator, it makes me feel jobsick. For just a little while I was doing something special, something useful, something that made me feel worthwhile. I belonged. Now I'm alone again.

'Let me know . . .' I say as the car drives away, but she doesn't hear me. Or she ignores me.

Sunday

Chapter Thirty-Two

I read at home until midnight, drop into a dreamless sleep. Then the phone drags me back into unwelcome consciousness.

'Who is it?' I mumble into the mouthpiece. I look at the bedside clock. 'Christ, it's two in the morning!'

'Billy, I'm sending a car for you, it'll be there in two minutes. Get yourself dressed and down here.' It's Kim's voice, and there's a flash of blue lights beyond the curtains.

'It's here now. The neighbours'll think I'm being arrested. What's going on, Kim?'

'Don't make jokes about being arrested, Billy, I might have to do that yet. I need to talk to you.'

'And if I decide not to come?'

'Then I'll have a warrant to arrest you, Billy, and even if nothing comes of my questions I'll charge you with subverting the cause of justice and anything else I can dream up. Now shift your arse. At the moment this is informal questioning, but it might not be if you don't get a move on.'

There's an impolite knocking at the front door. The other tenants are allergic to the police, they won't answer it.

'I'm not moving till . . .'

'Christ, Billy, shut up! If you won't listen to me, listen to someone else.' She hands the phone on, I can hear her voice in the distance, 'You tell him, go on.'

229

'Billy. It's Sara.' It's her little voice, the one she uses when she's done something wrong, when she wants forgiveness.

'Sara? What's the matter? Is Kirsty all right?'

'Kirsty's okay, she's at my sister's. But they're asking me questions here, I've got a problem ... They brought me down an hour or so ago ... They say ...' She begins to cry.

I can hear Kim's voice as she takes the phone. 'It's okay, we're not arresting you, Sara, we're just asking questions.' Then it harshens, grows stronger. 'Billy, I'd rather have told you this to your face, but since you're so bloody pig-headed you can hear it on the phone. Your wife is one of the women on Sargent's videos. That's why I want you down here. Your motive for murder has just increased in size, it's so big now it's like a barrage balloon in my office and I want to hear you go through the things you told me earlier today again, but taped this time. Okay? It goes without saying that I'm under a lot of pressure and I'm sure you'd rather have me on the case than some smart-arse who doesn't know you and who'd be pleased to think you're being awkward and lock you up for a week while he finds the right questions to ask!'

'I'm on my way.'

'Good.'

Chapter Thirty-Three

I tell my story to a tape recorder, just as I told Kim in the park. Once again, I don't mention Sargent's schizophrenia. I don't mention the drugs he had in his bathroom. And I don't mention the words he whispered to me as he was dying. The last omission is accidental, I simply forget it, that's how important I consider it. It was his dying joke, telling me the future was already set in stone, predestined. The die had been cast; I was what I was and nothing could change me; and we both knew how low his opinion was of my achievements. The schizophrenia and the drugs I keep to myself because I'd have to involve Jenny and I don't want to do that. It wouldn't be fair. And I don't actually think my deductions – because that's all they are, not facts – are important enough to warrant me mentioning them.

It takes no more than thirty minutes for me to tell my story. It's concise, mostly accurate, and there are few follow-up questions for Kim to ask me. When I finish she takes me into her office where Sara's waiting.

'I think you two had better go home,' she says. 'It looks to me like you were both being set up in different ways. I don't know if there was any connection . . . Perhaps Sargent got involved with you, Mrs Oliphant, to provide him with a lever to work Billy. I don't know if he was that clever. I've got Mrs Ratcliffe here. I'm going to talk to her now, she might be able to help. She's got her solicitor with her . . .'

'What name?' I ask.

'Artmann, Daniel Artmann. Why?'

'Old man?'

'No, about the same age as you. Snappy dresser. He's good. If the two of you stop for a cup of tea in the canteen he'll have his client out of here before your feet hit the front street. But I've a feeling she'll corroborate your story, Billy. And we'll check yours with your workmates, Sara. You can go home.'

'Just a thought, Kim.'

She raises her head from her papers, her look tells me it had better be good.

'I don't suppose your men found a syringe in Sargent's room? If he injected himself he probably left it lying around, but if someone else did it they would have taken it away.' My thoughts are ahead of me. 'But he might have had time to dispose of the syringe himself anyway. In the rubbish? Have they searched the rubbish?'

'Billy, I've been a police officer for twenty years. The bags from Sargent's suite were taken away shortly after his body was removed, there was no reason at the time to search them. By the time there was any suspicion of real foul play they'd been taken down to the bins they use for the club's rubbish. I've had men looking through. They've found a syringe.'

My triumphant smile is short-lived.

'They've found almost forty syringes, most of which appear to have been used for some type of illegal drug. We're still looking at them, analysing them, but I don't expect much. Even if we find one with Sargent's prints on them and discover it contained heroin, it doesn't get us anywhere. We already know he was injected with the stuff.'

'But if you don't find a syringe with his prints on . . .'

'. . . It just means that someone else *might* have injected him. But it doesn't let us know who. Don't worry about it, Billy, we can handle it. And you should be thinking about Sara rather than Sargent.'

She's right, Sara's shivering despite the heat. I put my arm round her, usher her to the entrance where Kim's arranged a taxi. I decide to go with her, on the way she tells me her story.

'It was about two months ago, Billy, the practice nurses had got some tickets for *Ladders*. They have these nights when they let nurses in free, it attracts the men who pay to get in.'

'Yeah, I know the thing you mean.'

'They asked me if I wanted to go. Kirsty was staying at a friend's, I would have been in alone, so I said yes. I was quite excited, it was the first time I'd been out since ... You know.'

I nod, trying to encourage her to keep talking.

'I thought I'd feel too old, but I didn't, it wasn't like that. I kept on getting asked to dance, I'd borrowed an outfit from Kirsty, actually, but I didn't look too bad. A couple of young lads kept on buying me drinks, I suppose I had too much. Then they weren't there.'

'What, the drinks?'

'No, the lads, the men who'd been buying drinks. They just disappeared. Then *he* came over.'

'Graeme Sargent?'

'Yes, except I didn't know who he was then. He asked me to dance. He's ... he was a good dancer. And he said nice things about me. Then he offered to show me around. I made some joke about him owning the place, he just nodded and said yes. He took me into the casino and let me bet, I even won on the blackjack. He bought me some more to drink. Then he took me upstairs to show me his flat. It was ... it was beautiful. And he was so much the gentleman. We talked a lot, mostly about me, I think.'

'Did you tell him about Kirsty?'

'I can't remember. Yes, I probably did, I must have.'

'And your sister's caravan?'

'My sister's ...? Yes, I did, we'd just been up there for the weekend. Why?'

'He knew where you'd be. It explains . . . But it doesn't matter now. Go on, if you want, that is.'

'Yes. Yes, I think I do need to tell you. We were . . . We were alone in his apartment. He kissed me, not nastily, he didn't grope me or anything. And then he said he wanted to make love to me.' She huddles down into my chest, shelters under my arm. Her voice becomes a whisper. 'I said yes. He told me to get undressed in the bathroom, he gave me a dressing gown. When I came out he was there, on the bed. I . . . I didn't know about the cameras. I'd had too much to drink, I didn't realise what I was doing.' She's sobbing now. We're heading north, out of the city, there's little traffic.

'It's all right, Sara, you don't have to tell me. I understand. He was a very clever man, a cunning man. A very persuasive man.'

'And in the morning, Billy, when I woke up, he said thank you. He arranged for a car to take me home. And he gave me a present, a gift-wrapped box. When I opened it I found two hundred pounds inside. He paid me for sex like I was a prostitute. I felt so dirty! But I didn't give the money back.'

'Good.'

'I couldn't tell anyone about it. Then, when the police came, I had to go through it all with them. They showed me the video, I couldn't believe it was me, I couldn't believe the things I was doing. But it was me.'

We pull up to the door of Sara's house.

'Please will you stay, Billy, I don't want to be by myself.'

I pay for the taxi as Sara opens the door.

'And I need to know how you're involved, you never told me your part in the story. I still don't know how you're mixed up in things.'

So I tell her. I busy myself making tea and Sara and I stand in the kitchen. For the third time in six hours I explain that Carrie Ratcliffe hired me to do a job because

Graeme Sargent had told her I was no good at it. And then, when I surprised them both by doing what I'd been asked to do, Sargent turned the screws. First the money I owed. Then the threat against Kirsty. And the night he died, the video of Sara was undoubtedly the last screw. He had me exactly where he wanted me. I was the pawn, he was the king. But someone got to him first.

Sara listens patiently. Then she starts to cry, huge, wet tears that drop from her chin onto her blouse. Her eyes are filmed with water and her nose is red, she's sniffing and mumbling. 'And you were trying to help me, you were thinking of me and Kirsty and I was being so selfish.'

'Sara,' I say, 'stop it. You're making a hell of a mess. If you keep on crying I'll have to wash the whole kitchen floor.'

Her eyes open wider still, but her crying stops.

'I can make jokes about it now, Sara.'

She smiles back at me, launches herself across the room and into my arms. I can feel the surge of passion, so strong that Sara pulls away from me. She smiles again.

'It wouldn't be right,' she says. 'You can sleep in Kirsty's room if you want.'

235

Chapter Thirty-Four

It's almost midday when I wake up. I find a towel in the bathroom and wrap it round myself as I pad downstairs. Kirsty walks in as the kettle's boiling.

'Dad! What are you doing here?'

'Making tea. Want some?'

'Where's Mum?'

'I've cut her into pieces and minced her. She's neatly packed into one pound bags in the freezer. Spaghetti Bolognese for dinner?'

'Dad! Be serious!'

'She's upstairs, asleep.'

It's offputting, my daughter's taller than me. She looks older than she ought, but her physical maturity is countered by an inelegant gaucheness which makes her seem vulnerable. I warm the teapot.

'Have you been here all night?' she asks.

'Yes.'

'Did you sleep together?'

'Kirsty! No. I was in your room.'

'So why . . .?'

'Your mum needed some help last night, I was there to help her. That's all.'

Kirsty raises her eyebrows, she isn't sure whether I'm telling her the truth. Then she decided it doesn't matter. She smiles, grins, opens her arms and hugs me.

'It's good to have you around, Dad. I've missed you. Do you think . . .?'

'I try not to, it hurts too much. Do I think what?'

'Do you think there's any chance that you and Mum might get back together again?'

I kiss her on the nose, pull away from her then sit her down. I put teabags into the pot, pour boiling water over them.

'I don't know, love. I don't know if either of us wants that. It looks as if we can stand being in the same house together. But ... It's something that takes a long time, deciding on whether a relationship is going to be sustainable. And she's found someone else, this John person, he's an extra unknown quantity in the equation.'

'You make it sound so cold, so scientific.'

'It's not, love, believe me, it's not. But your mum and I used to love each other a lot. Then things went wrong, you know that. We need to find out whether we can rebuild the feelings we had for each other. Me coming back isn't a decision I can make alone. It's not something your mum and I can decide straightaway. We need to talk. We need to think about what's best for both of us, and for you.'

I put out my hand, touch her cheek. Her skin is so soft. She looks so like her mother.

'What's best for me would be to have you back home again, Dad.'

'In the short term, yes, I'm sure it would be. In the long term? That depends on your mum and me, on how well we can get on with each other. On whether we can talk to each other. So I'm going to go back upstairs with this tea and we're going to talk. Help yourself if you want some. If you hear me screaming come and rescue me.'

She nods her head.

'And I love you.'

'I love you too, Dad.'

Sara's awake when I pad into the room. I put her tea down beside her, part the curtains a little; she winces at the

237

brightness of the day. She sits up and the sheet falls away from her. She's naked. I try not to look at her but I do, and it's noticed. She pulls the sheet back up, covers herself.

'Was that Kirsty I heard?'

'Yes.'

'What did she say?'

'She was surprised to see me. She asked if I'd spent the night. She asked if we'd slept together. She wanted to know if I was coming back.'

'And are you?'

'That's a loaded question. You're the one who asked me to leave. I told her we had to talk about it, think about it. I told her it might not be a decision we could make straight-away.'

'And what do *you* want, Billy?'

What do I want? Do I know what I want? Did I ever, will I ever know what I want? Or am I, like Graeme Sargent said, at the mercy of a future already mapped out for me? In which case my needs, Sara's needs, Kirsty's needs are irrelevant.

'*Que sera, sera,*' I say, 'my Gran used to sing that to me. The Doris Day song. "Whatever will be, will be." That was a long time ago.'

'You haven't answered my question.'

'Was it fair to ask? Is what I want the most important thing to consider? What about what you want, and what Kirsty wants? I mean, the implication is that if I say "I want to come home," you'll say that's okay. But I don't know if that's what you *will* say. I don't know if the way you're thinking is coloured by what we've both been through recently. Perhaps It'll change. Perhaps I'll change.' While I'm speaking I'm looking out of the window, seeing nothing. The houses and streets, the lawns and cars and mother-walked pushchairs, the blue skies and distant jets and tall office blocks mean nothing. The world is me, Sara and Kirsty. I turn round, sit on the bed.

'What do you want, Sara?'

'I don't know, Billy. Really, I don't know. I've been lying here, thinking about when we were young. I used to love you so much. I can't remember stopping loving you, it was more like a gradual wearing away till there was nothing left. There were even times when I hated you. Last night the old feeling was almost back again. If you'd pushed, if you'd insisted, if you'd kissed me when I was in your arms, if I hadn't backed away ... But this morning ...'

'The cold grey light of day. Except it's not cold and it's not grey.'

'It is, Billy, it has to be. It's no good looking at things in colour. Last night was colour, but it won't always be like that. We have to remember the greys. We can cope with the colour. It's the greys that kill us.'

'I'm sorry, Sara, I can't see what you're getting at.'

'I'm saying I can't make a decision at the moment. I'm confused. Now isn't the time to ask me if I want you back in my life on a permanent basis.'

'You made a decision last night. You rang me, not John. Or is he out of the picture now?'

'No, he's still around. But you were the one already involved, I knew you were the one I needed. I knew I could depend on you.'

'So what do we do now?'

'You've already told Kirsty the right answer. We talk, we think, we talk again. It might take a while, but ...'

The phone interrupts her.

'It's okay, Kirsty'll take it. We need to think about her as well. I'm not saying her needs are more important than ours ...'

'Dad!' Kirsty's shout stamps up the stairs. 'It's for you.'

I go to the door, open it. 'Who is it?' There can't be many people know I'm here.

'It's a woman, she didn't say who she was.'

'I'll take it up here, love. Just put the phone down.' I pick up the receiver, cover it with my hand. 'It must be

239

Kim Bryden,' I say to Sara, 'I can't imagine who else might ring here looking for me.' I take my hand away. 'Hello? Is that you, Kim.'

'No, Billy, it's me. It's Carrie.' Her voice is low, controlled. That's what makes me so angry, there's no feeling of contrition, no apology. Just a stark introduction, as if calling me was the most natural thing in the world.

'What the hell do you want? And how did you know I was here?'

'I rang your flat. I rang your office. Where else was there?'

'What do you want?'

'That's what I like about you, Billy, always brief, always to the point. I just wanted to say goodbye, that's all. I'm leaving. Going back down to London with James. We've agreed to start a business together.'

'Don't tell me, you're the whore, he's the pimp.'

'You really are bitter, aren't you! It surprises me, I look on the whole thing as educational. I've learned a lot in the past week or so. But I think it's time to get out now. Poor Graeme, he couldn't get out, even if he wanted to. There was only one way out for him.'

'Did you do it? Did you kill him?'

'Oh, Billy! I was going to ask you the same question! And since both of us are that curious, I think it's fair to say we're both equally innocent. Although your need for revenge seems far greater than mine. I quite enjoyed the association with him.'

'Personal or professional?'

'Both. He was good in bed, Billy. But perhaps you know that already from talking to your wife. Sargent showed me the video. She's a nice-looking girl, your wife.'

'You're sick, Carrie, you're really sick.'

'No, Billy. I don't think so. I'm quite calm, level-headed. I'm taking things as they come, you're the one who's over-reacting. Neither of us can change what's happened, there's no point in us being enemies.'

'It's too late for that.'

'No it's not, Billy. I've spent an uncomfortable night at the police station, from the questions I was asked I assume you told them everything. That's not a problem. I've a good solicitor, there's not much they can hang on me, not criminally. I may have to face up to a civil case, but I can stand that. I don't bear a grudge. It might have worked damn well, but it didn't. Better luck next time. So that's what I wanted to say, no hard feelings on my part. And take care.'

'Take care?'

'Yes, Billy. Watch out. Somebody killed Graeme. I'm getting out. They might come after you.'

'Me? Why me?'

'Perhaps you know more than you think you know. Be careful. In a funny sort of a way, Billy, I'm still fond of you. 'Bye.' The phone goes down.

'Who was that?' Sara asks.

'The woman I was working for, Carrie Ratcliffe.'

'What did she want?'

'She's going back to London. I think she wanted to warn me.'

'About what?'

'I don't know. I don't think she knew. It was just a warning. I don't think this is over yet.'

Sara's never been able to disguise her feelings. When she's depressed she can't hide her unhappiness. When she's feeling good her smile enters rooms before she does. And now she's worried.

'What do you mean, "it's not over yet"? What's not over?'

'This business with Graeme Sargent.'

Her face clouds even further. 'So what happens now?'

'I'll have to leave, Sara. They might try to get to me through you and Kirsty.'

'Who might try to get to you?'

'I don't know. Whoever murdered Graeme Sargent. I need to think.'

'What about you and me? We were going to talk. Isn't that important? It seemed important to you a few minutes ago.'

'Of course it's important, you're important, Kirsty's important, you're the most important things in my life. But there's a chance you might get hurt. I don't know how big that chance is but I can't afford to take any risks. I know ... something, some information, about the way Sargent died. About the way he was killed, because I'm pretty damn sure he *was* killed. So the murderer could decide I'm a risk, he could decide to come after me. And if he does, I don't want you and Kirsty around.'

'Billy! Come on, this isn't New York or Los Angeles. Just because some peculiar woman tells you someone's out to get you, you off and leave? God God, Billy, is her influence on you that strong?'

'Sara, I don't gamble any more, that's why I'm going. Will you give me a lift into town?'

She stamps out of bed, in her anger she no longer worries about me seeing her naked. She hunts in drawers for briefs and bra.

'This is worse than when you were with the police. At least then you had the law on your side. Now I don't know what you're getting up to. I don't know if I can stand this, Billy, I really don't. Just when I thought there might be a chance for us, when I was imagining you settling down to a proper job, when I was thinking how good it might be, then this happens. It's like I said, you should always look at things in greys, never in colour. I mean, you were working for criminals like that Ratcliffe woman and Graeme Sargent. God knows what might happen to us.'

'At least I didn't go to bed with him.' It's a mistake, I regret the words as I speak them, but it's too late.

'Billy, that's not fair!'

I've hurt her. 'I'm sorry, I shouldn't have said it.'

'But you did! Is that what you were thinking all the time?' She throws a flowery dress over her head, talking as she does so. 'Are you going to bring that up every time we talk?'

242

'I said I was sorry.'

The door's still ajar, it's suddenly flung open.

'Will you two stop it?' It's Kirsty, in tears. 'You're supposed to be talking about the future, not arguing about the past! Why not just admit you'll never get on? It's better when you're not living here, Dad! Just go!' She rushes to her bedroom, throws my clothes out then slams the door behind her. I turn to Sara, I don't need to say anything, my face tells her how I feel. Kirsty's taken the heat from our argument. Sara reaches out a hand, touches me on the arm.

'I'll talk to her,' she says, 'I'll try to explain. Come on, I'll take you into town.'

'I don't want to leave her like that.'

'You can't do anything, Billy. *She* needs time and space to think as well. Come on.' She takes my hand and guides me downstairs. We say nothing as she drives me into town. As I get out of the car she looks at me.

'She may be right, you know. It might be better if we do stay apart. I'm sorry, Billy. Call me when you think it's safe. Perhaps we might be able to talk then.'

Chapter Thirty-Five

I buy a sandwich from Barney's pub. In the bottom of my filing cabinet there's a six-pack of lemonade. I feel suitably provisioned for my labours.

I spread my work over all the available desk space. Immediately in front of me is a sheet of double width accountancy paper; I write on it in pencil. In the middle, at the top, I print 'Graeme Sargent – dead.' From there it's like a flow diagram. There are two options – he was or he wasn't murdered. If he wasn't murdered, if he took the heroin voluntarily, then there's no point in looking further. If he was murdered – by injecting himself with what he thought was Caverject but which was actually heroin, or by someone else injecting him – then there are further possibilities. Why did the murderer do it? It could have been for personal reasons and any of the women he'd videoed would have had a good motive. A competitor could have killed him for professional reasons. It could even have been accidental, a friend tempting him to drugs and giving him too much. I don't, at this stage, discount any possibility.

Opportunity is the next point I consider. Sargent was killed by an overdose of heroin injected directly into the deep vein of his penis. Presumably one of his lovers, his *ex*-lovers, might be able to administer such an injection. A competitor, either commercial or criminal? Unlikely, unless that person was about to have sex with him. A female competitor, then? Someone like Carrie Ratcliffe? It's possible, so I write it down.

Off to one side I write down the phrase 'DIE-CAST' in capitals. I look at it, then I scribble a few question marks behind it. I assumed when Sargent was dying in my arms that he was mocking me, reminding me how little he thought of me; the die was cast, he was telling me, I was and always would be, in all things, a small man. Small in stature. Small in ambition. Small in achievement. But it could be that he knew he was dying, that he was trying to give me a clue about his murderer. I look up the word in my dictionary.

'Die' has too many different meanings, too many definitions. Those to do with dying are depressing. 'To cease all biological activity permanently' is as chilling a description of death as I ever hope to see. I leave 'die [Old English *diegan*, probably of Scandinavian origin; compare Old Norse *deyja*, Old High German *touwen*]' and move on to 'die [C13 *dee*, from Old French *de*, perhaps from Vulgar Latin *datum* (unattested) a piece in games, use of past participle of Latin *dare* to play].' This has greater possibilities, given that Sargent knew my gambling habits. But there are other meanings here too, dies are made of metal and used to mould other more malleable materials. Did he mean that personally? That I was capable of being shaped by someone stronger than me? I write it down.

'Die-cast' has its own definition. 'To shape or form a metal or plastic object by introducing molten metal or plastic into a reusable mould, especially under pressure.' That too is a possibility. The plastic profiles used to make windows are manufactured by that method. I write the definition down and underline it.

The idea behind this method of working is that there's no such thing as useless information; all information has value; the difficulty lies in determining that value, in weighting the information. I realise I've been repeating the words 'die' and 'cast' to myself, they're beginning to assume a life of their own. I play with them. 'Die-cast,' I say, 'die-cast, die-cast, die-cast.' Each hyphened word links with the rest, the phrase moves around itself, becomes 'cast-die, cast-die, cast-die.' I say the words faster, 'cast-die, cast-die, cast-die,' discover they've changed, evolved completely.

'Cassidy? Do I know anyone called Cassidy?' I write it down at the side of the paper, underneath I add 'dyke-cast,' 'dyke Cass,' then 'Di Cass.' I need to find the names of the women on the videos. It's a long shot, but if one of them's called Diana Cass (or Cass, Cassie perhaps, a lesbian) then she could have some questions to answer. It's a possibility. At the moment anything's a possibility.

I decide to leave the crime (aware that I haven't, on paper at least, decided whether a crime has been committed) and turn instead to the background. I still have copies of the accounts of WPS and Pearson Plastics; I also have each company's price-list. I need to move from the general to the specific, so I imagine the windows and doors at home (Sara's home – ownership counts less than occupation) and draw them out with their rough sizes. Then I work out the cost of having new windows supplied and fitted by each company. I'm working on the principle that the two prices should be in proportion to the tenders submitted for the Bentley Estate. Those figures were about eight million for WPS, ten for Pearson Plastics. But the figures for a single house aren't even close; they come in at just over £3,000 for WPS, the proportionate figure for Pearson's should be about £3,800. But it's not; it's almost £4,500, fifty per cent more expensive than the WPS price. If the same margin was applied to the Bentley contract then the tender price should be nearer twelve million. So it would appear that Pearson Plastics is about to carry out a fixed price contract for ten million pounds when it should cost in the region of twelve. This needs thinking about.

I believe in passive thinking. Active thinking, concentrating on finding an answer to a problem or set of problems, sometimes doesn't work. That's when passive thinking takes over. The mind knows about the problem to the extent that it can't let go. So even when the active mind is considering something entirely different, the passive mind goes on worrying away at the original problem. It works well at night: you go to sleep thinking you'll never make sense of a jumble of unconnected pieces of information, then you wake up in the morning to find the solution written in bold letters on the bedroom wall. And it's signed with your own name at the bottom. So I decide to go to something else.

I take from my desk drawer the envelope Pamela Arnison, the typing girl, left me. Then I open my own mail, find a similar letter addressed to me. The message is the same (the landlord doesn't know about dividing and conquering); a marginally improved offer to buy out the lease; a condition that all tenants must accept the offer; and a warning that failure to do so will lead to the breakdown of the sale and huge increases in rent.

At school, when I was about sixteen, I was bullied because of my size, because I enjoyed working and because the teachers seemed to like me. When I hinted to my father how much I was suffering he offered to pay for me to have judo lessons. I found out how much the lessons would cost and told my father. He gave me cash to pay for a course of six, about thirty pounds. I didn't have any lessons. Instead I chose the fiercest looking villain I could find in the dirtiest pub on the High Street, told him my predicament, and said I'd pay him to threaten extreme violence against those who were bullying me. He did so. They didn't bully me again. It was dangerous, of course. The gorilla could have turned against me, though I hadn't told him my name and he seemed quite amused that a sixteen year old should want to hire him to flex his muscles. It was possible that the bullies would let things slip for a while then come after me again, but they behaved like real bullies usually do. They backed down when I stood up to them, albeit by proxy.

The letter I'm reading is a bullying tactic, and my

247

response is written to show I recognise that. I tell them that, after discussion, the tenants have decided their offer is risible; that they should consider market forces before making another offer; that rent increases can't be applied *en masse* but only according to the commencement dates of individual leases; and that any application to increase rent will be met with multiple referrals to a rent tribunal. I write this down in longhand then pad along the corridor to Pamela Arnison's office. I can tell she's in because of the noise of her printer, I open the door without knocking.

I'd assumed her frown was a semi-permanent feature on her face, just as she owned a nose, a mouth and two eyes. When she looks up the frown is indeed firmly fixed in place, but it dissolves when she sees me, turns into a blush of a smile.

'Mr Oliphant,' she says, 'fancy you being in on a Sunday.'

'Pressures of work, like you, I suspect. And please, my name's Billy.' I wave the sheet of paper at her. 'I've drafted a letter, I thought you could type it up and get it signed by each of the tenants, if it's any good, that is. If you can read my writing.'

She takes the paper from me, glances at it, then smiles again. That's to show me my writing's no problem to her. Then she reads the letter, she nods once or twice.

'Will it work?' she asks.

'That all depends on what you want to happen. We should get a response. But what exactly do you want?'

'I want to stay here, paying the rent I do.'

'We might get that. But the property's worth more empty than with sitting tenants. They might come up with a good offer to buy out our leases.' They, either the landlord or the prospective purchaser, might also resort to stronger tactics. I decide not to mention that.

'How old are you, Pamela?' I ask. The question and my use of her first name make her blush even more.

'Nineteen,' she says.

'And this is your own business?'

'Yes. I work hard, long hours, and I'm good at my job. My rates are low, I'm kept busy.' She seems a little defensive.

'Aren't you a little young to be running a successful business? Usually at your age a young girl would be working for someone else, getting experience . . .'

'I couldn't get a job. I was top of my class at college, word-processing, copy and audio-typing, the lot. But I couldn't get a job.'

'Why's that?'

'I live on Bentley Estate. With my mam and dad. But once people hear that name they don't want to know you, no matter how good you might be. So I got some sponsorship through the college, a grant, it paid for the first six months' rent. I've been going a year now, I can afford to pay myself and there's money left over. I'll be getting a laser printer next month.' There's no bitterness at her predicament, only pride that she's achieved so much.

'A client of mine was working at Bentley,' I say, 'installing windows. But their factory burned down.'

'Were they yours? I read about that, they were talking about it in our close. We were the first ones to get new windows put in.'

'Yes, Winner Profile Systems, I put some security cameras in there, not that it did them any good.'

'Yeah, they were doing the contract. But our windows were put in by a different firm. What were they called, now?'

'Pearson Plastics? Global Windows?'

'That's it. Global Windows did our house and our neighbours', it was good work, a good job. What was it you said, Winner Profiles? They did the three at the top of the close. There was another firm did the three opposite and a fourth did the three at the bottom. This was before they awarded the contract. The council wanted to make sure the installations were all right, the windows were all right.'

249

'Were the other firms called Pearson Plastics and Design-a-frame?'

'I don't know about the last one, but definitely Pearson Plastics. They put the windows in at my ...' She stops briefly, chooses the right word, then continues,' At my *fiancé's* house. Well, his mother's really, he lives there at the moment. We're going to get a flat together, next year sometime, when I can afford it. Sooner if he can get a job.'

I wasn't aware there'd been a trial installation before WPS's pilot. Obviously the council were keen to see everything progress smoothly.

'So everything was all right with the installations?'

'To finish with, yes. But the Pearson Plastics windows all came the wrong size.'

'The wrong size?'

'Yes, Duane – that's my boyf ... I mean my *fiancé* – he was in when they took the old windows out, and when they put the new ones in place they were all too small! They looked as if they'd fit, but they went straight through the opening. Duane did this course at the tech, he knows about these things, he's even done a bit of moonlighting, putting windows in with a mate who's a joiner. He said the windows were meant to fit behind the check but they didn't.' She shrugs. 'It doesn't mean anything to me.'

It does to me, I once helped build an extension where the walls were constructed with checks. It means that the window openings were built with the outer course of bricks projecting beyond the inner course. The windows were meant to be fitted from the inside of the house, up against the outer course, between the inner course. But Pearson's windows were too small, they went straight through the outer course.

'So what did they do?' I ask.

'They took measurements, went away and came back a few hours later with windows that fitted.'

'A few hours?'

'Yes. Later on the same day. They woke Duane up when

250

they came back. It wasn't difficult, there were no windows in the whole of the downstairs.'

That doesn't fit. Pearsons import their windows. How could they get new ones in the space of a few hours? I search for a meaning. What's the value of this information? Will it help me?

'Well,' I say, 'I'll have to go now. Let me know what everyone thinks about the letter.'

'I will, Mr Billy,' she says, giggles at the mistake. 'I'm sorry, Mr Oliphant . . .'

'If you can't bring yourself to call me Billy then "Mr Billy" is a reasonable second best. Can you manage that?'

She thinks. She nods.

'Thank God for that. Right, I'll go and get some work done.'

'Thank you very much, Mr Billy.'

'You're welcome, Pamela.'

Even before I close the door she's back at her seat, fingers playing flamenco at the keyboard. But she's still smiling.

Back in my own office I eat my sandwich, drink my first lemonade. My next step is now obvious. Pearson Plastics' factory needs closer investigation. They have the capability to make windows there but prefer to import them at greater expense. Why? I need to find out. There are some small difficulties, however. Ted Samson is the managing director, and the last time I saw him he seemed quite eager to shoot me. How can I find out more without risking injury? I reach for the phone.

'Hello, can I speak to Jenny Moss please? It's you? I didn't recognise your voice, it's Billy here.'

She sounds pleased to hear from me. She tells me how nervous she was when we were looking for the autopsy report on Graeme Sargent, how she kept on thinking about it while she was at work, the rush of excitement it brought. She asks what I've been up to. Life, I assure her, is mundane.

251

'You said you had a few days off,' I remind her. 'Have you anything planned?' It's my turn to feel nervous in case she's already made arrangements. Perhaps a doctor at the hospital has asked her out, perhaps friends are coming to visit. There are too many possibilities, why should she want to spend time with me?

'I'm free Monday and Tuesday,' she replies.

'I was wondering if you'd like to come out with me,' I say, 'we could go out on Tuesday, the weather's bound to be fine . . .'

'That's a bit arse-about-face, isn't it? What happened to Monday?'

'Monday? Well, I thought – if you didn't mind – you might help me with a problem I have.'

'Personal or professional?'

I have to think about that. The latter, I tell myself, but my conscience objects. This is more personal than professional now, any further investigation into Pearson will bring no financial reward. No one's paying me to do this work. 'Both,' I say eventually.

'So what do I have to do?'

'You don't *have* to do anything. But what I'd like you to do is visit a factory owned by a firm called Pearson Plastics. I'd like you to pretend you're buying windows. I'd like you to look around the place and tell me what you see there. That's all.'

'It's not something you can do?'

'No. I'm . . . known to some of the people who work there. I wouldn't be made welcome.'

'Sounds exciting! Of course I'll help you.'

'Thanks, Jenny, I appreciate that. I'll call for you about ten, if that's okay.'

'Why not come round now? Or I can pick you up at your place, take you out for a meal? I've just woken up, working nights plays hell with your metabolism.'

The offer's tempting in more ways than I'm willing to admit. I was steeling myself for the disappointment of finding that Jenny was busy; I caught my reflection in the door glass when she said she'd help me, my grin was as loud as a marching band and no less subtle. But I have work to do. I've spent my day thinking about Graeme Sargent's death and the events surrounding it. Now I have to devote some time to my own life. I have to consider what to do about Sara, what to do about Kirsty, how to deal with the problems we have. I have to deal with my own conflicting emotions.

'Billy? Are you still there?'

'Yes, yes, I'm still here. But I think I'll have to say no, Jenny. I've had a difficult day and I really need to work at some problems I've got.'

'Are you sure? You're not just making an excuse so you can go home and hoover your flat? Fold your towels? Make bars of soap from all the cast-off bits you've collected over the years?'

'No, Jenny, I'm not going to do any of that.'

'Good. Because if you were, you can come and do it here where there's *far* greater need of your services. I'll pick you up at ten.'

'I'll see you then.' As the phone descends I realise how much I really do want to see her.

Monday

Chapter Thirty-Six

I'm waiting on the step when Jenny's Metro lurches along the street, smoke trailing like a tiger's tail. She climbs out and runs round to the passenger door, swings it open and bows.

'Your carriage awaits, sir,' she says. She's wearing a cropped T-shirt and a tennis skirt, discoloured training shoes, no socks. Her hair's loose, kept in place only by sunglasses perched on top her head. She looks wonderful.

'Thank you,' I reply, climb to my feet and take my seat.

'You've got nice legs,' she says as she makes herself comfortable behind the wheel. I'm wearing cut-off jeans.

'My best feature,' I reply, trying to disguise my pride.

'Oh, I don't know. You've a nice bottom as well. Now then, where to Mr Holmes?'

I give up wondering whether she's seen my bottom – could she have been looking when I showered at her flat? – and give her directions, taking her, for the sake of my own sanity and safety, through the quieter roads of the western suburbs, down by the river as it nears the sea. We pass through gaunt townships with faint memories of distant glories. Their communities have seen the industries which formed them die at the hands of politicians and businessmen who care only for profits, not for people. It shows in the dirty streets and boarded shopfronts, the weeds growing in cobbled roads, the dowdy, dismal pubs where people go not to drink, but to get drunk. It shows in the girls pushing second-hand prams filled with babies, boys swaggering with self-confidence because that's all they have, unemployed men absorbed in allotments and pigeons and whippets, anything but non-existent work. It shows in the joy they take in small things; a prize on the lottery; a win at bingo. And it shows in their faces, they know there's no such word as paranoia, they know everyone's against them. It's a world beloved of modern travel writers who look, photograph (in black-and-white, so appropriate for the bare bones of the dockyards; and in colour, to show the blood-rust of the riverside hulking cranes), write condescendingly and move on. But no one visits, except by accident.

I describe these things to Jenny as she drives, because talking takes my mind off her driving. She nods and says yes in the right places, but I'm not sure she's listening. It doesn't really matter. I'm speaking for myself, to myself, out of selfishness. Sometimes I need to remind myself that I belong.

When I'm finally quiet for a minute, as we take the slip road and avoid the Tunnel traffic, Jenny asks her first question.

'What do you want me to do in this place?'

'Drive past,' I say, I've seen her do it in my thoughts already, 'drive past so I can have a look. Then drive back the other way, so I can look again. Then go in. Pretend to be looking for a houseful of windows. Ask for prices. Then ask to see how the windows are made. I want to know what machinery they have, how big the operation is, whether they have lengths of plastic profile in the factory or just ready-made windows.'

'Why?'

It's a good question which is difficult to answer. 'Because I'm suspicious.'

'By nature or in particular?'

'Both. They're meant to be importing windows from Europe, Germany I think, but they also have, according to what I've heard, the facility to make windows here. It's cheaper, once you've invested in plant, to make your own windows. So why continue to buy them in?'

'Perhaps they don't. Perhaps they used to import them, but now they make them.'

'It could be that. That's why I need you to look round, let me know what you see. Like I said on the phone, someone might recognise me if I go in.'

She turns right, down a steep slope towards the river. It's a new estate, high-tech with a mix of factories and small clumps of offices. They all have green lawns and dwarf shrubs, red polyester windows and grey curved panels; the car-parks have pristine white lines.

'Over there, Pearson Plastics,' I say. Jenny nods, slows down. The factory itself is within a tall fence, sheltering close to its walls are several different styles of conservatories. There's no one about, though the main gate is open and there are cars parked. There's a breeze blowing off the river, ruffling the flags outside the main building, I can hear the snap of cord against wooden flagpole.

'Just go back up the hill,' I say, 'drop me off. I'll scribble some sizes and styles down on a piece of paper, you can say your boyfriend did them. He can be at work today.'

She nods, no jokes this time. Perhaps she's nervous. There's nothing to be nervous about, I tell myself, but I'm nervous too. I don't like involving others in my problems.

'Just ask for a price, then ask if you can see how the windows are made. Be natural. Smile. You can't fail.'

'Okay.'

'If there's a problem just leave.'

'There won't be a problem.'

She stops the car at the top of the hill, I have to haul on the handbrake to hold it. I climb out, she needs to use both hands to release the brake. Then she turns the car round and heads back down to Pearson Plastics.

It's over an hour before she comes back. I'm in a garden of weeds by the side of the road, trying to keep myself

259

hidden in case Ted Samson should appear, trying to hide my anxiety when Jenny drives up. She swings the door open from the inside. I run to join her.

'They're very persuasive, these salesmen,' she says as she pulls away. 'There was one, just a little bit older than me, he had a contract filled in ready for me to sign! And I was considering buying a conservatory and I don't even have a house to build it on to!'

'Did you get into the factory?'

'Yes, he let me have a look round.'

'And?'

'Hang on, Billy, please. I think I need a drink.'

We're heading along the riverside road, I point at a newsagent's. 'I can get a bottle of lemonade there if you pull over.'

'No, Billy, a *drink*!' She keeps driving, past the Metro station, until she sees a pub. She bounces the tyres off the kerb as she stops, I decide I'll ask Norm to have a look at her car, see how much of her driving problems are due to the vehicle and how much to her.

'I'll have a pint of lager,' she says as I hold the pub door open for her, 'you're buying. And a packet of salt-and-vinegar crisps.'

The pub's cool, quiet. The barman's chatting to the only other customer, he serves me quickly in his haste to return to his conversation. Jenny's already chosen a seat in the window. I take the drinks back to her. She opens the crisps and devours them (I refuse her offer to share), drinks the beer quickly, eagerly, asks for another.

'You're driving,' I remind her.

'We can walk it off,' she replies.

Halfway through the second pint she begins to talk. 'There were two salesmen, both friendly, the young one did the pitch but the older one kept on chipping in with comments. Then he kept me talking while the young one worked out a price for the windows. They had some windows on display, I looked at them and felt them, then I asked how they were made. They told me they used German profile made into windows in Holland and imported, but they kept machinery in the factory to do repairs and alterations. I pretended I didn't really understand, I asked what sort of machines they used, what they looked like. The young one asked the old one to check the price, said he'd show me round the factory if I wanted. I said yes.

'It's a big building, divided up into sections inside. One part was mostly window and door frames, another had lots of double-glazed units stacked in it. There were machines as well, I asked what they did.' She closes her eyes as she recalls what she's seen. 'There was a double-headed saw, two welders, one with four heads and another with two. There was a corner cleaner, a metal saw – oh, and lengths of reinforcement, aluminium and steel – and work tables.' She opens her eyes again, shines them at me. She's asking for approval, she wants me to tell her she's got the names right, the terminology.

'You sound like an expert already,' I say. She nods, pleased she's done well.

'I didn't see any long lengths of PVC profile, just the metal they use for reinforcement. But the place looked as if it had been used, there were bits of metal on the ground, plastic dust around the saw. There were drills and other hand-tools on the benches.'

'Anything else?'

'That's all I saw. There was a part of the factory I didn't go into, the salesman didn't even take me near it. But there was a door marked "private", I asked him what was in there. He said he didn't know, it was a part of the factory they didn't use, it was let out to someone else.'

I reach into my back pocket for my wallet, take out a piece of paper and a small pen, the type they use in those catalogue shops. 'Could you draw the layout for me?'

The drawing's rough but adequate. 'It's a big square, really. The showroom's at the front, offices as well, I assume. The factory bit's behind, L-shaped. So the part I couldn't get into must take up about a quarter of the area. There's a big door leads into it here,' she marks the piece of paper, 'and a normal-sized door here, that's from the inside. I had a look round the outside as well, they've got conservatories set up, that was what I pretended to be doing, looking at them. There are two big doors in one wall, one must be for the part of the factory I was in, the other for the locked part.'

'You've done well,' I say, reach across the table and pat her on the arm. She turns her arm, slides it back so her fingers link with mine.

'There's a security system,' she says, still looking at me, 'no cameras I could see, but the doors and windows'll be alarmed.'

'I didn't ask you to check that. Why bother to tell me about an alarm system?'

'I thought you'd want to know. For when you go back to find out what's in the other part of the factory.' Her grip tightens. 'I can come with you, if you want.'

'No, Jenny, I don't want.' I don't bother denying that I intend breaking into the factory, there's no point in that, she'd read the lie too easily.'

'You'll need someone to drive you here, later on tonight. When it's dark. And nobody thinks a couple in a car's suspicious, we could be looking for a private place to neck. Anyway, I'm volunteering.'

'Why are you doing that?'

'Because I'm mad? Because I find it exciting? Because I find *you* exciting? A mixture of those and other reasons I don't want to analyse, I'm frightened what I might find. So say yes quickly, I might change my mind.'

Despite her warning I take my time making a decision. It would be easier if she wasn't sitting opposite me, looking at me, smiling at me. It would be easier if she wasn't holding my hand. It would be easier if the blood in my veins would slow its passage just a little. I have to fight my feelings, struggle to see reason. I can't let her come with me, it would put both of us at risk. Yes, I need someone to get me to the factory, but Norm or Sly will help out.'

'I'll just be driving, keeping an eye out. You'll be doing the dangerous work.'

I have to say no. I have no choice, I've already involved her more than I should. No, the answer has to be no, and that's what I intend saying. But somehow the instruction to my voice goes awry. 'Okay then, you can drive me to the factory.' I didn't want to say that. Did I say that? How can I have said that?'

Jenny finishes her pint in triumph. 'Good. Let's walk now. I'm just a little woozy. It could be the excitement, but it's probably the lager. Come on.' She rises to her feet and, as I do the same, hurries round the table to link her arm with mine. We step out into the sun like lovers.

We walk and we talk. The walking takes us down to the river, to the Fish Quay and then along the riverside walk to the sea. The talking takes us much further. Jenny asks questions, about Sara and Kirsty, about my childhood, my parents, my past. She doesn't wait for me to ask her anything specific but offers parallels and comparisons from her own life. As we walk her arm detaches itself from mine, sneaks around my waist at first, then into the back pocket of my shorts; my own arm rests across her shoulders. She says how well we fit together.

I buy us ice-creams, we look down from the cliffs on to sands crowded with swimmers and sunbathers. Striped windbreaks shelter their owners from the sun, optimistic surfers venture out without wetsuits. From our vantage point we can see the sheltered, secluded platforms of rock where girls have decided to go topless; a middle-aged man next to us is salivating, watching them through binoculars. Jenny points out the family trudging up the steep path towards the road: a railing-thin tattooed man laden with buckets and spades and a pushchair; a woman, round as a beach ball, face like a doughnut, clutching a hot, screaming baby and two plastic bags; and another child, sexless in swimming trunks and brown skin, bringing up the rear, crying because it doesn't want to go home.

'We can come back tomorrow, love,' says the woman to her child.

'Over my fuckin' dead body,' grumbles the man, lighting a cigarette. He waits for the child to reach the top of the slope. 'For Christ's sake fuckin' shut up!' he yells. His hand like a paddle catches the child's rear, causes further, louder crying.

'I don't think I want any kids,' says Jenny.

'I used to think that too. But . . .'

'Yes?'

'They're the only thing you can love, unconditionally.'

'That bloke didn't seem to think so.'

'No, you don't *have* to. You have to *want* to. But once you do it, once you commit yourself, there's no holding back. You can't half love a child. You can't switch that love on and off. You have to go all the way.'

Jenny turns us as one, we head down Front Street, on the opposite side of the road from the dawdling, crying, over-heated family we've just seen.

'What about other people, Billy? Can't you love them in the same way?'

'I don't think so. You can love them, but it's different. There's too much choice, too much free will. There's no choice in loving a child, your own child. But with another adult . . .'

'Yes?'

'There are other factors. Sex, money, property, work, for each of those there are at least two sides, sometimes more. A relationship between two adults is more compli-cated.'

'You mean you have to work at it?' She seems interested, not cynical.

'Yes, you have to work at it. Not that you don't have to work at a parent-child relationship, but with two adults

264

there's ... there's somehow less of a motive to succeed. It's sometimes easier to give up than to keep going.'

'And have you given up? With you and Sara?'

'I don't know. More important is whether she's given up with me.'

We reach the end of the row of shops. There's a break in the conversation as we try to cross the road. When there's a small gap in the traffic we hurry across (my arm still around her, her hand still in my pocket) with a crazy, asynchronous crab-like run that jars my legs and Jenny's shoulders. We have to disconnect to avoid a fast-moving motorcyclist, and when we reach the other side we're no longer touching. There's a long, narrow, grassy bank dividing the road in two. Jenny sits down; I join her.

'It's amazing the difference perspective makes,' she says. 'Have you ever seen photographs of the Ames chairs?'

'No.' I'm nervous, I can't see the direction she's taking me. And I haven't heard of Ames chairs. But I owe it to her to listen.

'Adelbert Ames was an artist, he devised quite a few examples of *trompe l'oeil* in the fifties.' She pauses, making sure I know what she's talking about.

'"Deceiving the eye", isn't that what it means? Like painting a door on a flat wall.'

'Yes, but with the intent not to depict a door, but to deceive the viewer. To make the viewer think there really was a door there. Ames did the same with three chairs. He rigged up three large boxes with a peephole in each, when the viewer looked through the peepholes he saw three identical chairs. But when the front of each box was taken away only one of the chairs was what we'd consider to be a chair. The second was a deformed structure, like a chair pulled out of shape, but it still looked like a chair when viewed from a particular angle. And the third chair was a diamond painted on a backdrop and a collection of wires suspended, all disjointed, in front of it. But it still looked like a chair from the peephole.'

She pauses, but she won't look at me and I won't look at her. We're sitting side by side, staring at the grass between our legs. But she knows I'm listening.

'You said, when you were talking about you and Sara, that her feelings about you were more important than yours were about her. That's an opinion. I don't know whether it's your opinion or not, it might be hers. But you're implying that you agree with it. You're saying it's your viewpoint. But my view of the relationship is different, I've never met Sara, I've only heard about her second-hand, from you. What's important to *me* is what *you* feel about your relationship with her. You, me, Sara, we're all looking from different perspectives. We can each describe what we see, a relationship. But the truth differs when we're allowed a closer look. Billy, I like you, I wouldn't be saying this if I didn't. Look at you and Sara with honest eyes. Then look at you and me. There could be something between us, if you give it a chance. If you feel it's worth going on.'

I'm surprised at her forthrightness, surprised and frightened by the way she feels. It's taken courage for her to speak like that, and I can't contemplate being as honest as her, my emotions are never that open to me, let alone to anyone else. But I decide to try.

'Jenny, I could lie to you. I could say that Sara and I are finished. But I don't know if that's true. If she said she'd have me back I don't know if I'd go. But I do know I enjoy being with you, I feel attracted to you. I think you're kind and gentle, and I think you're mad because I can't see what you see in me, and that's not fishing for compliments, that's the truth. And that's all I can say. That's all I can offer at the moment.'

We sit in common silence. I realise I'm plucking blades of yellow grass, balding an area larger than my head.

'So what happens now?' I ask. Jenny says nothing. I turn to look at her, find her looking at me. 'Say something, quick, before I kill off the grass for yards around.'

'You're still running, Billy,' she says, 'away from something, towards something, I'm not sure which, I don't think *you* know exactly where you're going. All I can offer you is some company along the way. For a little while. Until our paths separate.'

'I think I'd like that.'

She shuffles towards me like a bad Lautrec impersonator, kneels between my legs and kisses me. She's gentle, her lips taste of chocolate and ice-cream, and the kiss lasts an hour. During that hour we don't breathe; each second is spent exploring the infinite folds and creases of each other's tongues, the crags and ridges and smooth glacier fields of slab-like teeth, the slick saliva secretions of secret open-mouthed flesh. I can feel the kiss even when we part, when she stands up and drags me to my feet.

'I'd like to go home now,' she says.

I put my arm round her again; her hand finds my rear pocket, holds me back as I almost take a step forward.

'Billy, when we get back to my flat, I'd like to go to bed with you.'

'I was hoping you'd say that.'

'There's just one thing.'

'What's that?'

'Don't tell me you love me. Not unless you really mean it. Not unless you want me to believe you.'

267

Chapter Thirty-Seven

On the journey back her hand rests on my thigh, strokes and scratches the skin. I return the compliment; it seems to improve her driving. There's no hurry, no rush. When we get to Rak's house Jenny takes my hand and leads me upstairs. Her room is at the back, the window's small and wide open, it feels cool inside. The place in untidy, not dirty. There are clothes on the floor, the shelves are filled with books and ornaments. There are posters on most of the walls – Schiele and Spencer, Freud and Klimt, Jenny tells me – and paintings, pencil sketches and oils, her own work. There's the usual furniture I associate with student rooms: a desk and chair, both covered with newspapers and magazines; a stereo system; a mongrel sofa and armchair; and a three-quarters bed, its quilt escaping shapelessly onto the floor.

'Sorry about the mess,' she says, 'if I'd thought you were coming back I'd have tidied up a little.'

'It's all right,' I reply, 'it's your room. It's you.'

'And how am I?'

'Untidy. Chaotic. Charming, unpredictable. Deep.' I smile at her. 'But most of all, untidy.'

She smiles back. We're like two virgins, wanting each other but not sure how to start. I don't want to rush, I don't want to hurry because I'm frightened that this first time with Jenny might be the last time. I don't know enough about the way I feel to promise myself anything else. She seems similarly nervous, for reasons I can't recognise.

'I'm not used to being so forward,' she says, 'I'm scared you might change your mind.'

'I won't change my mind,' I assure her.

'We could take a shower together if you want?' she suggests.

'Is that what you want?'

'No. No, not really.'

'In that case I'd like to start by undressing you. Then perhaps you'd do the same for me. And we can take it from there.'

'I'd like that.'

Undressing each other takes little time. She raises her arms to let me pull her shirt over her head, at the same time she levers her feet out of her shoes. She smells of the morning's soap and the day's heat, an earthy, musky smell of autumn leaves. I kneel before her and rest my head against her stomach, she parts her legs slightly to let me lower her briefs. I could wait there a lifetime, I can hear her body moving around me, but she pulls me to my feet.

'My turn,' she says, performs the same manoeuvres in the same order until I too am naked. Then she moves to the bed, lies down. I don't follow her.

'What are you doing?' she asks.

'Remembering you,' I reply. She's lying on her back, her arms raised to touch the pillows. The hair on her head, between her legs, under her arms, is a uniform blue-black. Her skin is smooth and dark except on the soles of her feet and the palms of her hands.

'You're beautiful,' I say.

'So are you,' she counters, 'and I really do want you to come over here and lie down beside me.'

I'm not allowed to say we made love, the word 'love' is proscribed. But that's the word I feel. Jenny's excitement, her adventurous enthusiasm, her humour, her eagerness to please and, just as important, to be pleased, they raise similar emotions and aspirations in my own, slightly older flesh. She rolls me onto my back and delights in the multiple orgasms she experiences; when I come she lies in my arms and teases me back into life. And then we sleep, we wake and begin again, sleep once more. In a moment of wakefulness – by the light coming in through the window and the evening sounds from the street I judge it's about nine – I feel her close beside me. We're touching from toe to head, our bodies unable to separate. We smell, not of lust, but of passion; and her warm breath on my chest is reassuring, metronomic. But when I close my eyes I can't sleep again. I'm in that perpetual dusk where dreams can be dispelled by an act of will, but where my own thoughts are subject to the whims of my subconscious. I try to plan the night's work, but on entering Pearson's factory I find Ted Samson waiting for me, his arm round Sara. She's pointing a gun at me, she laughs as she squeezes the trigger. I force myself back to reality, stroke Jenny's long, smooth back; but then she wakes and looks up at me, and it's Kirsty's face I see. I decide there's no point in letting these visions torment me, not when the opportunity to defeat them is in my own hands. I roll sideways; Jenny and I separate like velcro, she groans but doesn't wake. I find my shorts and pull them on, put my clothes and Jenny's on the end of the bed. Then I begin to tidy her room.

Chapter Thirty-Eight

When she wakes we shower together, go back to bed. An hour later she gets up and makes sandwiches, I pick some dark clothes for her to wear. We eat, then we go to my flat and I dress in my own burglar's outfit. It's almost two in the morning when we park down by the river and peer anxiously at Pearson Plastics' factory.

'There doesn't seem to be anyone there. No cars, no lights.' Jenny's hair's tied back, hidden inside a dark knitted hat, she's a shadow in the dim light.

'We'll see. Come on, let's go.' I've decided to let her accompany me to the factory, but I'll be the one to break in. It's good camouflage, having her beside me, and we don't have to pretend to be a couple. But we're both nervous, and I suspect she's holding on to me for comfort, for support, not from any remnant of passion. I'm wearing a jacket with deep pockets, they hold my skeleton keys, a torch and an electric screwdriver. In Jenny's handbag are glasscutters and a suction pad, a small hammer and a second torch, a pair of binoculars and some wirecutters. I've warned her to ditch everything if we're stopped for any reason; going equipped to enter is as bad as being caught in the act.

We bypass the main gate, keep the fence on our left and head for the back where there's less chance of being seen should anyone pass by. I use the binoculars to scan the eaves of the building. Jenny said there were no cameras but I'm making sure. Even in the dim light I can see no telltale boxes, no glint of infra-red light. I cut the wire fence parallel to the ground, immediately to one side of a stanchion. Then I fasten a large piece of black plastic to the upright.

'If you have to come out in a hurry it's something to head for,' I explain. Then I slide through the cut, hold it open for Jenny to follow.

'I don't know why the hell I'm doing this,' she says. I can't answer, I have to agree with her. We run, bent double, to the factory's nearest wall; then I lead Jenny round to the front of the building.'

'Wouldn't a side door be less obvious,' she says.

'The alarm panel will be close to the front door. I'll need to switch that off.'

'But you don't know the code.'

'I'll worry about that when I'm inside.'

The front door has a good lock, at first I can't find any skeleton which seems to resemble it. I'm sweating, Jenny's crouched over me with the torch beam so pencil-thin it looks like it could cut metal. I consider using the screwdriver with a drill bit, cutting away the lock completely, but it would take too long. That's when I find a key that almost fits. I play with it, talk to it nicely, offer it gifts, gold-plating. After ten minutes the lock succumbs. I sit back on the ground.

'Is that it?' Jenny asks.

'That's the first part, yes.'

'There's still the alarm, the code to switch it off.'

'I know. You wait here. If the alarm goes off, head straight for the fence, straight for the car. I'll be right behind you.'

'What are you going to do?'

'I'm going to use some special tools to find out the code.'

'What are they?'

'Experience and guesswork.'

Before she can say anything else I push the door open and hurry across to the alarm panel. It was glowing green when I looked at it through the door, now it's flashing red. Most systems offer three opportunities to enter the correct code. If all are wrong then the alarm sounds or, if the system has a direct line to the system installer's offices, the installer rings the premises and asks for a pre-arranged code word. If the word is correct, the installer overrides the alarm. This system doesn't look like it links to a remote office. That's good. It means they rely on the police to investigate if the alarm goes off. And most police call-outs are false alarms.

Alarm systems rely on the memories of those using them. The first person at work can often be the foreman, the last to leave a chargehand. At weekends one of a rota of sales-people will need to know the code. It must be something simple. A four digit figure. I look at the control pad, above each digit from 0 to 9 it has letters of the alphabet grouped in twos and threes. I decide to concentrate on the numbers, they're easiest to recall. Most employees know the tele-phone number of the company they work for. That's what I try. Pearsons' number is 2867443 so I punch in 2867; the lights keep flashing red. Next is 8674; still red lights. I decide to pass on 6744, go instead for 7443; still wrong, but the alarm doesn't go off. I notice for the first time a clock counting down in seconds, I'm allowed as many guesses as I can fit into thirty seconds. There are six seconds left, I rush at 6744 with no effect. My legs are getting ready to run but I have time for one more entry, one more guess. I punch in 8227 and the lights flick to green. I turn round and motion to Jenny to enter. My skin's wearing a sheen of sweat.

'What happened?' she askes, 'I saw you enter three or four different numbers. What was it?'

'I was working on logic to start with,' I say, 'thinking about ease of use. I should have realised vanity was more important. The right number was 8227, but it wasn't the number I was entering, it was the letters.' I shine the torch

273

at the control panel. '8–2–2–7, T–E–D–S. Ted's. Ted Samson's. Like I said, vanity. Something else to reinforce the impression that he's the boss, the answer, the password, the key, the code.'

'And what made you think of that?'

'If I was in his position I'd probably do the same. Come on.'

At no time did I consider having Jenny accompany me this far, into the building itself. When I was planning the break-in, thinking the whole thing through, I had her stop by the fence, or at the door, perhaps just inside the door. In my mind I was always alone when I entered the shopfloor. But now I don't feel I want to leave her. It's not because I don't trust her. It's because, if anything should go wrong, I want her where I can see her, where I can protect her. I realise this makes her something of a liability, and I'm sure she knows this. But I want her close by me and she doesn't object to following.

I tell her to point her torch at the ground and we head for the door she indicates. It isn't locked; when I open it I can sense larger, higher space beyond. I widen my torch's beam, shine it into the blackness. The ellipse of light dances crookedly across the floor, is distracted by benches and machines, but manages to rearrange itself into a neat, dim circle on the far wall. I can recognise the layout of the building and the machinery, they're both similar to the set-up at WMS's factory; I can even picture the windows and doors being constructed on this production line. There's only one problem. At WMS there were large racks full of six metre lengths of profile waiting to be cut to size and made into windows. Here there's nothing.

'There's something wrong,' I explain to Jenny, tell her why.

'Perhaps they keep the profile in the other part of the factory, the part I couldn't get into.'

'But why? The profile itself is of little value until it's made into windows.'

274

'They could have run out of profile. Or they might not have started yet. They've got the machinery in place, ready to start, and the first profile delivery comes next week. Is that possible?'

I examine the saw. There are marks on it where it's been used, a snowdrift of plastic dust and flakes is gathered on the floor behind it. There are pieces of swarf below the saw used to cut reinforcement and, here at least, the racks are stacked with steel and aluminium. The welder, used to join the pieces of profile into squares, has pieces of brown paper on the floor below it. I pick one up, show it to Jenny.

'Teflon. It's used on the welder heads to stop them sticking to the profile.'

'So what does that prove?'

'Everything here has been used to make windows. But there's no raw material to make windows with.'

I decide the answer may lie in that part of the factory to which Jenny couldn't get access. I weave my way between the machines, Jenny close behind. When we reach the door she leans close to me, whispers 'Switch your light off, Billy.' I do so, concerned that she may have seen something or someone I've missed. After a minute I find I don't need the torch, I can see in the dull gloom pervading the factory, the grey light struggling to enter through high skylights.

'It's almost dawn,' she says, 'we'd better hurry up.'

'I know,' I say, leaning against the door. It's strong, thick, probably reinforced. It has a mortice lock I don't recognise and a padlock. I shine my torch into the rebate between the door and frame, push hard at the door. It gives slightly.

'I don't think it's let out to someone else,' I say, 'it's part of the set-up here. There's a padlock on the other side as well, it needs someone with access to both parts of the building to get in.'

'Why?'

'Someone has something to hide. Come on, let's have a look.'

I lead the way to the entrance door. It's getting rapidly

275

lighter outside; when Jenny opens the door I can hear bird-song. I reset the alarm and hurry to join her. It takes a long, frustrating time to re-lock the front door, at least twenty minutes. I could leave it unlocked, hope that the first person to arrive assumes it was carelessness on the part of the last to leave. But that's unprofessional, so I struggle on. When the duty's done we cling to the wall as we move around the side of the building. There are, as Jenny said, two large doors, one leading into the main part of the factory, the other into the locked part. There are also two smaller pass doors; all are secure.

'An industrial can-opener would be best for this job,' I say, 'there's no way . . .'

Jenny's hand is on my shoulder, it squeezes and I shut up. There's the sound of a motor, a large motor, and we both look to the brow of the hill where a black truck and trailer combination is turning into the road leading down to the estate. Its headlights catch and freeze us momentarily; I know how a road-bound rabbit feels.

'It's probably not coming in here,' I say, but I'm proved wrong as it turns again, slides to a halt in front of the locked gates. Although we can't be seen, our path to the fence is in full view of the cab. I scuttle to the corner of the factory and peer round, see the gates swing open, hear their grumbling squeal for oil. There are at least two men, one in the cab, one opening the gates. The truck has Dutch number plates. I hurry back to Jenny.

'Round the back,' I say, 'they might leave the gates open after they come in.' I suspect they won't. Whatever's in the trailer, if it's to be stored in the secure conditions of the locked room then those unloading it are unlikely to want passers-by to see inside. We round another corner, I push Jenny to the ground and lie beside her.

'Now what?' she asks.

'This is good,' I tell her, 'we'll be able to see what they need to keep hidden away. We might be able to see why they need to hide it as well.'

We can hear the truck approaching, it performs a lazy curve of a turn, then reverses towards the large doors. The passenger, the one who opened the gates, strolls round the corner and unlocks the small door. He's tall, he walks with an easy, confident lope. Ted Samson. A brief rectangle of light floods the tarmac as he switches on the lights inside, then the small door closes. Less than a minute later the large door opens to release more light and the driver backs his truck partway into the opening. He climbs from the cab and goes into the factory.

'Shit!'

'What's the matter, Billy?'

'We can't see what's happening because the truck's in the building, but if we make a run for it *they* might be able to see *us*. And the man, the tall one, I know him. The last time we met he was very keen to turn me into a teabag.'

'A teabag?'

'Yeah. Make lots of small perforations in my skin. I think he'd settle for one large one between the eyes, though.' I'm trying to think, but my need – to find out more – is in direct conflict with my wish to be as far away as possible. 'Listen carefully,' I hiss at Jenny, 'this is what we'll do. You wait here, I'll see how much they can see. They might be so busy they won't notice us. If it's clear I'll raise my arm, that's the signal for you to head for the fence and I'll be right behind you.'

'And it'll also give you the chance to see what it is they're unloading.'

'Well, yes, I did think of that.'

'All right. Let's get on with it. And if it's not clear?'

'I'll come back. We can wait.'

I Groucho-run to the edge of the door. The light inside is bright, it hurts my eyes, but it allows me to see what's happening. I'm expecting something dramatic, crates of guns, boxes marked 'Semtex, this way up,' plastic bags packed with white powder. I'm disappointed. The two men are carrying windows down the trailer's ramp and loading them into a wheeled bogie. I look back at Jenny, raise my arm, and see her scamper across the open ground to the fence. I retreat a little way then do the same. Once through the fence I hide the opening with a bank of earth and gravel. Then I move along the fence, use the binoculars to see into the factory. They're still unloading windows.

'It doesn't make sense,' I say.

Jenny's fingers tug at my coat. I turn to face her, she looks tired. 'Nothing ever makes sense,' she says, 'at least nothing much. We can't do anything else here, come home with me, come to bed. Does that make sense?'

'To sleep?'

'We need to sleep, it's four in the morning. But then we can wake up and do other things. And you promised me a day out tomorrow.'

'A day? A whole day?'

'I'll settle for half a day. We can talk. We can think. You can pick the subjects.'

'You can choose the venue.'

We head back to the car, torch and pliers clanking in my pockets, Jenny's tools providing the counterpoint in her handbag. She's right. I need to sleep.

Tuesday

Chapter Thirty-Nine

Jenny wakes me with tea and toast. She's wearing a short dressing gown with no buttons, no belt. For some reason she's trying to clutch it round her, an action made difficult because she's carrying a full tray containing our breakfast.

'I know what you look like naked,' I say, 'and I approve. Why so shy now?'

My words catch her pulling the gown around her once more, but she stops, lets the material fall again. She puts her hands on her hips and looks at me with her royal gaze. Then she shrugs herself out of the gown.

'Move over,' she says, doesn't wait for me to obey, nudges me across the bed. 'I'll explain. One, this house is occupied by five young women, oh, and Rak. And it sometimes happens, the morning after a night . . .'

'That's the usual order of things.'

'Don't interrupt, peasant. On any morning it's possible, probable even, that one of the other girls may have brought home a stranger. And I don't relish exposing myself to any peculiar individual who may be wandering the corridors. Hence my modesty. Okay?'

'Okay. And number two?'

'Two?'

'That was one. That implies a two, possibly even a series of consecutive integers.'

'Oh, yes. Two. Two is that the toast is quite well done –

that's a euphemism for burnt – and I didn't want to get crumbs in my pubic hair, so I was going to wear the gown in bed. But that isn't really a problem now.'

'Why not?'

'Because I'm going to let you eat them out.'

An hour later, fed, sated and showered, I'm sitting on the stone step at the front door waiting for Jenny. I hear Rak's asthmatic puff first, feel the tremor of her steps. She runs her hand across the top of my head.

'Lo, boss. I assume this visit isn't professional. I also assume it's not me you've come to see.'

'Right on both counts, Rak.'

'Good. She'll be good for you. You'll be good for her as well. You'd better be or I'll break every fuckin' bone in your body.'

'You do get over-protective sometimes.'

'I've said the same to her. I like you both.'

I turn round. She's leaning against the doorpost, dressed in the same outfit (or something similar) she was wearing last time I saw her. I think she makes her own clothes but she's not very good at it, and she only has one pattern.

'I like you too, Rak.'

'Yeah,' she says dismissively, 'well just be careful.'

'I'll look after her, Rak.'

'And who'll look after you? Listen, she told me what you've been up to – professionally, that is, I can guess the rest – so watch out. Sounds like you're into something you don't really know about. Be careful.'

'I didn't realise you liked me that much.'

'Like you? It's not that I fuckin' like you, boss, I only posted my bloody invoices to you yesterday! Don't get hurt before you pay them!'

She turns and lurches back into the cavern of the hallway, into the warm darkness of her room. A few minutes later Jenny thunders down the stairs. She's wearing a long sleeveless cotton dress and sandals.

'Sorry I took so long,' she says, 'I decided to shave my

282

legs in case we go swimming, then I thought I'd better do my pits.' She lifts up her arms to show me.

'Very nice,' I say, 'but I don't really mind hair on the female body.'

'You're just kinky that way. And I do, on mine at least, when it's on public display. Come on.'

We get into the car and roll our windows down to try to disperse some of the heat, but we don't cool down until the car's on the open road.

'Where are we going?' I ask.

'I'm taking you to one of my favourite places, but it's a secret till we get there. I said last night I'd choose the destination. You can choose the topic of conversation.'

'All right. You. I'd like to hear about you. Miss Jenny Moss is the official topic of conversation for the whole day.'

'That won't occupy ten minutes. But it's your choice, so here we go.' We've turned west onto the dual carriageway which bypasses the city, we're travelling in the inside lane at a constant fifty miles an hour, though we slow down when we come to any hills. There's not much traffic about, and what there is seems keen on overtaking us and leaving us behind. I feel I can trust Jenny not to drive into a bridge, I turn the handle to let my seat recline and lean back to listen to her.

'My name is Jenny Moss. I'm twenty-three years old, I've just finished my medical training, I'm spending time at the Infirmary until I can think of something better to do. That's about it.'

'Come on! I already know that. Where are you from? What's your family like? What are *you* like? Seriously, I'd like to know. Everything.'

'Everything?'

'Yes, why not?'

She says nothing as she negotiates a roundabout, we're still heading west.

'I'm from London. Lewisham originally, though we

283

moved about a bit. My dad left home when I was eleven, it was awkward for a while, but I managed. We all managed, I still see him. I still love him. I've got two brothers, both older than me. One's in the army, he's a lance-corporal, the other's into computers. Every time I ask him he seems to be working for someone else, always for more money. He's in the States at the moment.

'I wanted to be a pilot when I was young, I even applied to join the RAF but they wouldn't have me because I used to get migraines. So I decided to become a doctor. God knows why. My mum's proud of me. So's my dad, he's a civil servant, a higher executive officer. My mum works in a shop.'

She slows to exit the dual carriageway, we're on a minor road heading for the hills.

'I was good at school. I was good at sport to start with, I was a sprinter, but I didn't really grow fast enough. If I'd been three inches taller I might have made it. I enjoyed netball but not tennis and hockey, I don't like rackets and sticks and clubs. I had lots of friends at school, I enjoyed being there. I wasn't bullied, I seemed to fit into lots of different social groups. I must have been quite boring.'

While she's talking her hand finds my knee again. I put my arm across the back of her seat, rub the nape of her neck gently.

'Mmm, that's nice. Where was I?'

'Being popular at school.'

'Oh yes. I sat my A levels, got the grades I needed. I had a boyfriend at school, he was coming here to do an engineering course. We thought we'd find a place together. It didn't work out. There's not much more to tell. I enjoyed the course, qualified, but I don't know what to do next. Go abroad, perhaps? I haven't really had time to think about it. It's the best time to go, when you're young, when there's nothing to tie you . . . I'm sorry, Billy, I didn't mean it to sound like that.'

'Sound like what?'

'Well, it was a bit thoughtless, wasn't it? To say there's nothing to keep me here when we've just ... well, when we've just spent the night together.'

'A night together, Jenny. One. And no promises, no ties, we agreed.'

'You're right.' She changes the subject quickly. 'Look, here we go, over the river past the George. They do nice afternoon teas in there, do you fancy a cuppa?'

'No, let's keep going. I'm curious to see where you're taking me.'

'You mean you can't guess.'

'No, I don't know the area well. It happens a lot, doesn't it, people never really appreciate the things they're closest to. I mean, you've been here five years and you've obviously been out this way quite a few times. You've probably done the coastal route, seen the castles?'

'Yes.'

'I've only done that once, when I was at school. But how often have you been to the National Gallery? The National Portrait Gallery? The Science Museum, that's my favourite.'

'I've never been to the Science Museum. The other two, I've been once.' She giggles. 'With my school.'

'It's true! People don't appreciate the things around them because they *are* around them, no matter where they live, no matter what they do. I mean, how many people who go out walking in the Cuillins are actually from Skye? They're all tourists, incomers.' I realise I've been lecturing, my finger's wagging. 'I rest my case, m'lud.'

'Yes, Billy, you're right. Don't take the things around you for granted.' She looks across at me, and I wonder if she wants her words to mean more than they do. I could ask her, but I don't think I want her to tell me the truth. So I stay quiet.

The road twists and turns over sunlit moorland, I hear the call of the curlew and lapwing. Farmers are busy in rough pastures cutting silage, cattle shelter from the heat

285

under heavy leaved trees. And then Jenny's turning off the road into a car park.

Ahead of us, on a hill of green grass, lie the remains of a Roman fort. The ramparts are never more than a metre or two above ground level, but the shape and size of the buildings are easily seen. There are many people about, most of them families. Children are hurling themselves around the site, shooting make-believe arrows at each other. Parents clutching bags and surplus sweaters, half-empty bottles and rucksacks, are attempting to control and order their offspring without success. As we pass through the gate Jenny turns and grins. 'Race you to the top!' she says, doesn't wait for a reply and dashes along the track. I follow her, she may have been a sprinter when she was younger but I still run, I run distances, and I can see she'll slow down on the hill. I overtake her halfway up, pull gently past her. She spurs herself to a further effort, moves alongside and barges me in the shoulder. I stumble and she's past again, screaming and laughing as she looks over her shoulder to find me pursuing her with the intent not of beating her but of catching her. She's still a few yards short of the crest of the hill when I manage to curl my arm round her waist. As we fall to the turf I make sure I'm below her, protecting her.

'Billy!' she puffs, 'be careful! People will see!'

'See what? That I'm enjoying rolling on the ground with you? Most of them, well, the men, would enjoy being in the same position.'

'No, not that! You're pulling at my dress and I'm not wearing anything underneath.'

We spend an hour or so exploring the fort. The museum, a green-painted wooden hut, is a little dry for me. There's a selection of stones carved with pictures and inscriptions. Jenny seems interested so I buy her entry and a guide book then sit outside in the sun and wait. I can't avoid thinking about what's happening at Pearson's factory; there's no sense, no logic in the set-up. That means I don't have the

286

right information, I've made an assumption somewhere that's flawed. But what assumption? And where? I need something to put me back on track. I start to go back over what I know in an attempt to separate fact from conjecture, I close my eyes to help me concentrate and don't even notice when Jenny comes out from the museum.

'You got constipation?' she asks.

I open my eyes and try to smile. 'Yeah, I can't seem to move with this Pearson business, I can't figure it out.'

'Don't try, then.' She offers me her hand, pulls me to my feet. 'Forget it. Let it sort itself out while you do something else. Come on, let's walk.'

'So why do you like this place so much?' I ask. 'I didn't think you and crowds went together.'

She glances around her. We're heading away from the fort, away from the noise. 'What crowds?' she says. 'Even back there, surrounded by people, I can be alone. I think back to what the place must have been like, I use my imagination. I lose myself.' She reaches for my hand. 'And silence, solitude, they're only a short distance away from noise and crowds.'

She stops. We've descended into a small valley, there's a stream cutting through the lush grass and we're alone.

'No one comes here,' she says, turns to look at me.

If anyone does pass by and notices us, naked on the grass or locked in each other's desire, then they're discreet enough to remain unseen. We wash in cold peat water, let the sun dry us, our damp arms draped over each other. We're lying on our stomachs, Jenny's reading the guide-book.

'Some of these inscriptions, the ones on the stones in the museum, they're quite sad. One man had to leave his wife at home, he's saying how much he misses her. Another's complaining about the weather, he's offering a prayer to Mithras to stop it raining. It's nice, I can actually understand some of what they're saying without having to read the translation.' I can feel her roll to one side, I'm sure she's looking at me. 'Did you do Latin at school?' she asks. I grunt a reply which I hope she'll understand means no.

'Me neither. I had to do a crash course before I started doing medicine, they said it would be helpful.'

'And was it?' I open my eyes to see a bright blue neon flame of dragonfly hovering over another firmly attached to a stalk of grass.

'Yes, it was helpful, but I enjoyed doing it as well.' She puts down the guidebook and scratches a furrow down my back. I press against her hand, cat-like.

'I feel guilty,' I say, 'there's so much I should be doing, figuring out, instead of lying here enjoying myself.'

She straddles my back, brings both hands into play.

'Forget it,' she says, '*carpe diem*.'

'What?'

'It's Latin. *Carpe diem*. Literally translates it means "seize the day". Liberally translated it's something like "enjoy the pleasures of the moment without concern for the future".'

I rotate beneath her, look up at her. The dragonflies dart away. 'I'm all for that,' I reply. '*Carpe diem*. Definitely *carpe diem*.'

Chapter Forty

'*Carpe diem*,' I say to myself, to the night, to the mottled ceiling of Jenny's room. Don't concern yourself with the future, worry about the present. Jenny's lying beside me. When I think of the future I think also of her. She sleeps like a child, flat on her back with arms spread wide, elbows forming right angles, fists closed. Her hair's like night on the pillow, her skin varnished deep and dark. She looks as if she'd welcome my hand on her breast, my lips touching hers; she looks as if she'd wake with a smile. My hand reaches out, ready to test this theory, but I will it back to my side. Jenny's the future, but my first concern is with the present. I have to return to Pearson's factory. There's a secret, some hidden information, and it may be behind those locked doors. If it's not, then I'll have to look elsewhere.

I dress quickly, quietly. I find a piece of paper and scribble a note. 'Couldn't sleep. I need to sort something out. Have borrowed the car, hope you don't mind. Back soon. Billy.' I put the pen down, then pick it up again, 'Love you,' I add at the bottom of the paper.

I drive to my flat, find my dark clothes again and assemble my burglary equipment. Torch, skeleton keys, crowbar and electric screwdriver, if they can't get me through the triple-locked door then I'll turn to the machinery in the factory, there'll be something I can use.

My disqualification for drunk-driving may or may not have been part of a conspiracy, but I was – and still am – a good driver. So I don't speed. I don't rush traffic lights, I take things easy. I can't risk being stopped. I've no licence, no insurance, and I'm carrying equipment which could, even in the eyes of the newest rookie on the force, be used for burglary. I drive carefully.

The Metro's a beast. It pulls to the left, but not uniformly; driving it is more akin to sailing than motoring, it feels as if I'm fighting a strong sidewind. The temperature gauge doesn't work, but this is balanced by the hyperactivity of the oil pressure warning light; it has ambitions to grow up, turn green and indicate direction, so urgent are its flashings. But I checked the oil level before setting off that morning, there's no lack of oil. A leaking gasket?

I survive the journey, park the car at the top of the hill. I head for the factory, but as I round the corner I see I might not have to break in after all. The outer gates are open and a bright red truck and dirty grey trailer are sitting in the open door like a hermit crab in a new shell. I hurry down the hill, straight through the gates and up to the side wall of the factory. I peer round the corner. It's a different set of doors open this time, the ones leading into the main part of the factory. The driver and, I assume, Ted Samson – if the arrangements are the same as they were the previous night – must be inside, unloading. I run, bent double, to the side of the door, the way they do in the movies; if I'm seen I want to present as small a target as possible.

I don't know which side to approach from. Where will there be most cover? How vigilant will the two men unloading windows be? Are they carrying weapons? I decide that Ted will have a handgun, but not the driver; if it comes to fighting then Ted's the one I should aim to disable first. I don't like fighting, I start with a disadvantage because of my lack of height and reach, and I'm not very good at it. I know it's something of a circuitous argument – I'm bad at it

because I don't like it, I don't like it because I'm bad at it –
but there's no way out of that circle. I avoid physical antag-
onism at all times, but if necessary I can retaliate before
I'm attacked. I decide to enter the factory by crawling
under the body of the trailer.

I run to the front of the truck and duck down, scrabble on
elbows and knees along the ground towards the back and
wait between the double rear wheels. The two men aren't
saying much. The windows are sitting in wheeled bogies
which one man pushes to the rear of the trailer and onto a
pneumatic loading platform. When he lowers this to the
ground the second pushes it to one side. I notice that the
majority of windows are left on one side of the room; there
are only two bogies – both with large, wide windows – on
the side of the room nearest the locked door. This is joined
by a third as I watch.

'Is that the lot, then?' It's Ted Samson's voice, he's
wearing jeans and training shoes rather than his suit and
polished brogues.

'Sorry?' comes the accented reply. 'I not understand.'

'I said is that the lot? No more? Jesus Christ, I can see
for myself there are no more, it's a way of making conversation you ignorant Dutch wanker.'

'Sorry, I not understand.'

'Just as bleeding well. Just give me the delivery notes to
sign then you can be on your bleeding way. Papers? Pen?
Signy-signy?'

Although I can't see any of him above the waist I can
imagine his gestures, the look on his face. By what he's
saying it's clear he wants the driver to leave. I make a decision; I'll head for the place where the most windows are
stored, I should be able to hide there more easily than
anywhere else. I wait for the driver's feet to head for the
cab, Ted's go forward as well to see him away. As the
engine starts I roll out from under the trailer then scuttle
across the concrete floor, hoping the driver won't choose
that moment to check his rear-view mirror. Then I'm

amongst the windows and the benches beyond, I choose a
bench that's well-screened and wait. There's a roar of
engine and a plume of diesel smoke as the truck pulls away.
I expect Ted Samson to close the door quickly, but instead I
hear the distant rattle of the other door rotating on its metal
axle, armadillo plates curling over each other. There's a
wait, a short wait which finds me changing position so I can
see the door through white plastic frames. Ted's pushing
another trolley full of windows, windows he's bringing
from the locked part of the factory. He leaves this trolley
with the other three across the factory, goes back out again.
I hear the unseen revolving door closing, the trundle of
uneasy wheels. The fifth trolley is left with its companions;
Ted pulls down the metal door behind him.

He's practised in his next actions. First he switches on
the welder, then he moves to the double-headed saw and
switches it on. He presses a button to set the blades turning
and, satisfied at their action, allows them to slow again.
Then it's the cassette player's turn to feel the surge of electricity, a tape of anodyne country and western. Steel guitars
and wailing fiddles conjure tales of steely cowboys and
wholesome ladies. Ted sings along. He moves a trolley
close to the saw then takes the nearest window and hefts it
into the air, lowers it neatly onto the saw bench. He moves
the clamps to position the saw blades directly over the
welds at two adjacent corners of the window. Then he
presses the red button. The blades, locked back like scor-
pion tails, spin and sing then descend, cut into the soft
plastic. There's no harsh scream as there would be if they
were cutting metal, no bite and tear into wood; the plastic
protests a little but gives way quickly in a snowspray of
swarf. The blades separate the side of the window from its
three companions, then ascend to rest, still spinning. They
have no time to halt as Samson picks up the severed piece
of plastic and moves it to one side, turns the remaining U-
shape through 180 degrees and repeats the operation to end
up with four single pieces of PVC profile. He picks them

up and takes them to the nearest bench, one between me and the saw, lays them out. He reaches down the side of the bench like a snooker player might search for a rest and his hand falls easily on a hooked length of a metal about a metre long. He places this on the bench beside the pieces of profile.

The heat is oppressive. There's no ventilation in the factory and I'm bent double, sweat escaping my body as if it was being chased out from within. Ted Samson must be feeling the heat as well, he takes off his shirt. He's well-muscled, T-shaped, his shoulders wide and waist small. He picks up a small knife and cuts away at the angled end of the first piece of profile. I can't quite see what he's doing, his body shields the action from me, but I assume he's probably removing excess plastic. Soon he puts down the knife and picks up the hook, thrusts it a little way into the length of profile. He brings out a long, thin plastic bag, there's a string attached to it and using this he pulls out another bag and another. He puts the bag to one side and repeats the process with the other three lengths of profile; from each he extracts three bags.

The evacuation process complete, he takes the four pieces of profile to the welder. This has four working heads, he places the four lengths of plastic one in each side then stands back. The heated plates descend and pneumatic rams press the four pieces of plastic against them. Once the correct temperature is reached, the plates ascend and the rams press the angled corners of the rectangle together. They retreat and four more heads cut and trim the excess sprue away. Ted Samson puts the completed frame to one side, no different to the way it was a few minutes before except for the loss of about ten millimetres in width and height. He repeats the action on four other frames. The smallest offers up six plastic bags; Ted Samson removes eighteen bags from the largest. When he stops after forty minutes he has sixty plastic bags before him, each shaped like a large sausage.

He glances at the clock and wipes his hand across his forehead, his body's shining with the sheen of his work. I've been able to move a little, I've been relaxing and tensing muscles in turn, but I still feel stiff.

'I could sink a bloody pint,' he says and I find myself nodding in agreement. He picks up his shirt and threads his way through the benches, away from me, towards the door to the offices. He's gone for a drink or to the toilet, I should have about two minutes before he gets back. I crawl to the bench with the plastic sausages, reach up and feel for the knife Ted was using. I find it and cut the string holding two of the bags together, take a single bag and scuttle back to my place. Safely hunched back where I began I press my finger through the plastic. It encounters a white powder; I lick my finger and poke it back through, bring some of the powder out. I touch it delicately on my tongue, feel a familiar tingle and dryness of the mouth. Heroin.

So Graeme Sargent wasn't only selling drugs, he was importing them. That's why it was so important for Pearson Plastics to win the contract for installing windows in the Bentley Estate, they needed to increase the number of windows coming into the factory. That's why Pearson's pilot windows were too small, they'd made no allowance for shrinkage when they cut the windows open and rewelded them. That's why Pearson's could afford to do the work at a loss. The drugs make the installation and Pearson's financially viable, and probably launder a small part of Graeme Sargent's illegal income. Given the size of the contract, the number of windows involved, the value of drugs imported, Kingfisher could probably pay for the installation in its entirety and still make a profit on the drugs. The heroin in the packs is pure. Cut and adulterated, its street value will increase a hundredfold. The discovery brings too many questions. How many deliveries have there been, how much Heroin? Who's running the show? Was it Sargent? And now Ted Samson? I hear footsteps, Samson on his way back. I still have the drugs; I have to hope he doesn't notice they're missing.

He brings with him two cardboard boxes, packs the drugs into them and carries them away to the locked door. Then he switches on the saw again. The tape in the cassette player has finished but he begins to sing without any backing, if the words weren't intelligible I wouldn't be able to recognise the song by the tune.

'"Where have you been all day, Billy Boy, Billy Boy?"'

He moves from one bench to another, as if looking for something – his knife perhaps? And he keeps on singing.

'"Where have you been all the day, my Billy Boy?"'

He's getting closer to my bench now. I'm so drenched with sweat I'm sure he'll be able to smell me. That's when he changes songs. I don't recognise it, it's as tuneless as the first, but there's something about someone called Billy not being a hero. He's almost alongside now, and two songs with my name in them are more than coincidence. I roll away just as two steel rods pierce the bench top where my head was. I stumble to my feet. He's staring at me, pin-pricked pupils above flaring nostrils and a grin as wide as a fisherman's lie.

'Billy?' he mutters. 'Is that you? Don't want to be a hero?' The rods are firmly embedded in the table but there are more weapons at hand. He darts at a knife in the shape of a crescent moon, a wickedly sharp scythe, he grabs it and swings at me in one action. There's no hope of him making contact across the bench but still I leap away. The movement encourages him, he can see how awkward I am. I still have his knife, I hold it before me and he sniggers.

'Billy, oh Billy boy, where've you been all the day, Billy boy? You've been where you shouldn't be, you've been doing naughty things, haven't you.'

I back away from him, try to keep benches and trollies between us.

'Billy the Oliphant should have packed his trunk, shouldn't he? He should have said goodbye to the whole fucking circus. But he didn't, and now look where it's got him.'

295

He's not blinking, his eyes are wide. As he circles towards me his spare hand finds and discards a screwdriver, settles on a length of aluminium over a metre long. I glance to one side, find another piece, but mine's shorter and made of steel. I heft the piece of metal, feel its weight. Samson snorts at me.

'Not much good, is it?' he says. 'Mine's bigger than yours.'

'Yeah, Samson, just remember size doesn't count for everything. It's not size that counts, it's what you do with it.'

, 'The person who made that up, Billy, little Billy, was a short-arsed bastard with a small dick. Just like you.'

I don't lose my temper. It's something I learned at school, if you lose your temper you get hurt. Usually you get hurt if you don't lose your temper as well, but at least there's a sense of moral superiority when your wounds are being dressed. That's why I don't lose my temper, I just decide to attack him while his guard is down. I drop the knife (there was no chance I'd be able to get close enough to use it) and aim a blow at Samson's head. He sees it coming, lets his knife fall and lifts his metal bar above his head. The aluminium shatters with the force of my attack but the blow's diverted from his head and onto his shoulder. The end of my bar skids across his chest, draws a red welt of blood from his shoulder almost to his navel. He jumps back but there's a bench in his way, I follow up with a swing to his ribs. He manages to roll back onto the bench, the swing passes over him, and he continues his roll onto the floor. I run round after him, determined to press my advantage, but he's not there. I spin round, he must have rolled back again, under the bench. Sure enough he's behind me, backing away from me. He's picked up the scythe, he's brandishing it before him.

'Whose idea was it, Samson?' I ask, surprised at how breathless my voice is. 'It couldn't have been yours, you don't have the brains. Was it Sargent's?'

He's looking from side to side, I see his glance fall on a rack of reinforcement, both steel and aluminium. I lunge forward to hit it, his fingers retreat, but my blow upsets the rack and the lengths of metal fall to the floor. Samson stoops to pick one up in his left hand, as he rises he throws the scythe with his right. I can't avoid it, I'm too close. It hits me on the shoulder, the blunt handle, and as it spins away past my head the blade nicks my ear.

'Equal blood,' Samson mutters, then advances towards me. I've lost the element of surprise. He's taller than me with a longer reach, stronger and probably fitter. He's confident.

'Was it you killed Sargent, Ted?' I'm looking for a way out, I'm at too much of a disadvantage. 'You're on the stuff, aren't you? Did you persuade him to share your habit? He had diabetes, you know, did you have difficulty finding a vein? Is that why you injected him in the cock? Perhaps you were used to handling him like that.' I'm breathing deeply, I can smell Samson's deodorant or after-shave, sweet and cloying.

'You smell like a queer, Ted. Were you jealous of his other women?'

His grin becomes a snarl, then he's on me. I'm like Ben Kenobi fighting Darth Vader, I've a certain amount of skill but I can't counter his brute force. No, forget that, I've no skill at all, just a desperate desire to survive. He's using the piece of metal like a flail, it's coming at me from all directions. I'm using my own rod to ward off the blows and each time he makes contact I can feel his anger resonating down my arms. I'm backing away at the same time, hoping he'll tire, frightened to counter-attack in case it should provide an opening for him. Then I realise what he's doing. I'm moving inexorably towards the saw bench. I try to move to one side but there are frames in the way; I feint in the other direction and Samson's blows double and redouble. Then I feel the ridge of the bench in the small of my back. I have no choice now but to attack him, I aim at his head and he

wards off the challenge easily, I go for his knees and his
metal turns mine aside. I duck a blow which would have
opened the top of my skull and he throws his body towards
me, his rod held two-handed before him. His weight pushes
me backwards onto the table, his metal rod across my
chest. My arms are pinned as well.

'You're not so fucking clever now, are you?' he spits at
me. His face is inches from mine, sweat drips down his
nose and onto my forehead. The whole weight of his body
is on me.

'Arse-bandit!' I hiss back, trying to make him lose his
temper, 'you really had it in for Sargent, didn't you!'

'You don't know how wrong you are, boyo!' His head-
butt hits like a piledriver, too high to break my nose, but
the pain makes me think my brain's been curdled; my
vision blurs.

'You can't get away,' he growls, 'and I'm gonna make
sure you suffer. I know all about you, Oliphant. You're an
alkie, you're seeing a shrink, you've sunk so low you're
even shafting a wog. Well, I've got an idea for some brain
surgery which might help.'

He moves one hand, quickly, jabs at the saw button, then
returns his hand to hold me down. The blades begin to
revolve; one is poised above my head.

'You'll make a terrible mess all over your nice clean
skin,' I whisper, trying at the same time to slide away from
the table. He's not letting me move. He's pressing the
metal rod down across my chest and over my wrists, his
body's still covering mine. I can bend my fingers and move
my toes, but nothing else.

'It'll be worth the price of a shower to get rid of you,'
Samson says, moves his head back slightly to make sure
he's in no danger of being cut. The blade edges towards
me. I'm still holding my own piece of steel, I could flick
it at him but it would hit him with the force of a gnat.
He knows that, he even smiles at me as my fingers move
the steel around. But I'm not trying to hit him, I steer

298

the bar carefully, let it fall directly into the path of the
second saw blade. Its teeth wrest the steel from my hand
and hurl it at Samson, it catches him across the forehead,
he falls back and I'm up. If I had any hair on top of
my head it would have been parted by the blade which
even now is retreating, slowing. I don't enjoy being that
close to a painful death.

Samson could be concussed. He's sitting on the floor,
hands raised to his head, blood flowing between his fingers.
There's a dirty rag on the bench beside me, I throw it at
him but he doesn't see it.

'Did you kill Sargent?' I ask. He shakes his head.

'So who did it?' He shakes his head again. Then he looks
up, sees the rag and uses it to wipe the blood from his face.
I pick up my steel bar, there's a notch in it where the
sawblade cut into it.

'Stay where you are,' I say, 'on the floor.'

'What you gonna do,' he says slowly, 'hit me? You
won't do that, Oliphant, you're too much the good guy.' He
climbs slowly to his feet, sways for a moment, then takes a
step towards me. He's within striking distance, but I can't
hit him. I don't even want to hit him. It would be like
stamping on a spider once you've pulled off its legs.

'Sargent should've let me kill you when I wanted,' he
mumbles, 'but he was too soft. He told me he liked you.'
His laugh is mocking, condescending. 'And me, I got you
wrong as well. I really wanted to hurt you, to make you
suffer. What I should've done is use this.'

He steps away from me and at the same time pulls a
pistol from his pocket. He could have shot me. Instead he
chose to torment me.

'Give up, Samson,' I say, 'do you really think I came
here without telling anyone what I was doing? If you kill
me they'll know it was you. You'll be put away for life.' So
it's a lie. I told no one I was coming here. But Samson
doesn't know that.

'They'll have to find your body first,' he counters, 'and I

know some good hiding places.' He raises the gun. He's unsteady, even when he moves to a two-handed grip the pistol waves about in front of me. But from a distance of two metres he can't miss.

'Goodbye, Mr smart-arse Billy Oliphant.'

I can't think of a way out, I can't even think of anything to say. I close my eyes. I realise I haven't made a will, though it doesn't really matter since I don't have anything to leave to anyone. At least the insurance will let Sara keep the house.

'Come on then,' I say, 'get on with it.'

There's nothing. No reply, no shot. I open my eyes. Samson's still standing in front of me, I'm still staring at the pistol's single, unforgiving eye. His finger's wavering over the trigger.

'Drop the gun!' The shout comes from behind me, loud, fierce. It's echoed by another away to my right.

'Drop the fucking gun, Samson!' From above my head, the open office window. My eyes flick to one side, I glimpse black uniforms, rifles, bullet-proof vests and helmets.

'Oliphant! Lie down on the floor!' Whoever it is clearly knows me. I begin to do as I'm told.

'Stay where you are,' hisses Samson, 'don't move a muscle!'

I freeze again. 'Don't be a bloody idiot, Ted, they've got you!'

'And I've got you.'

He lunges for me, he must think I could be useful as a hostage. I dive to the right and his pistol hand follows me. The police marksmen have no choice. They open fire. Two bullets open his chest, a third hits him in the shoulder and spins him round. I see no more, I'm on the ground, eyes closed, waiting to be told I'm safe. I hear footsteps approach, four or five people, but even then I don't move.

'Billy Oliphant, you're a stupid bastard! You're an

interfering shithead! Why the hell can't you just keep out of things that don't concern you?'

I open my eyes and look up. Kim Bryden's standing over me. A few metres away two black-clad policemen are kneeling over Ted Samson's body. The window frames around him are streaked red.

'I'm really pleased to see you . . .' I begin.

'Stay down!' bellows the policeman I haven't seen but whose voice allows no discussion of the matter, 'on the floor!' He strides over to me, searches me roughly.

'He's clean, Ma'am,' he says.

'He can stay there a little longer, Sergeant, while I decide what to charge him with.' Kim sighs, even from my position on the floor I can hear her.

'Billy, how do you manage it? We've been watching Ted Samson for a while now, and I've a feeling you've just ruined a very expensive investigation.'

I lie down, arms and legs outstretched. 'But who . . .?'

'Shut up, Billy. Sergeant, would you mind helping Billy up?'

I'm hauled to my feet. My hands are shaking. I can't remember ever being so scared before.

'Let me tell you something, Billy. You're an amateur. And you're the worst type of fucking amateur there is, because you think you're good. Why couldn't you leave it to the professionals? Why do you think you've been let off so lightly over your . . . your adventures in this case? Because we've been after bigger fish. Over the past few months there's been a three hundred per cent increase in the amount of smack being sold on the streets. We knew it was coming from Amsterdam but we couldn't tell how it was getting here. But we worked hard, the Dutch police were helpful. They traced a load going into a window factory in Holland but there was nothing to say where it was being sent. The drugs could have been in any of a dozen different lorries, they all had to be followed. This one came here. We were ready and waiting. And then up pops Billy

Oliphant who proceeds to ruin the whole . . . fucking . . . show!'

With each of the last three words she taps me on the chest, each tap harder than the previous one.

'I didn't know . . .'

'Of course you didn't fucking know! Why should we tell you? You're an ex-cop, drummed out of the force and a pain in the arse! Do you really think Samson was the brains behind this set-up? Do you?'

'No, he's as thick . . .'

'*Was* as thick, Billy. We've saved you. He was going to put a bullet through whatever you have instead of a brain. We knew he wasn't running the operation but we could have watched him, taken him in if necessary, applied a little pressure. But instead we ended up shooting him to save your life. Jesus Christ, Billy!'

'I'm sorry.' My apology's sincere. There seems little else I can say or do. 'It could have been Sargent's idea. Someone else could have found out, decided to muscle in. There must be big money involved.'

'Yes, Billy, I *have* thought this through and come to a similar conclusion. The vacuum of Sargent's death will soon be filled, I've no doubt.'

'And whoever fills it is probably the one who killed Sargent.'

Kim shakes her head. 'How long will it take us to find that out, Billy? Even if we do find out, will we be able to do anything about it? And meanwhile the stuff keeps coming in, kids keep pumping it into themselves. What a fucking mess!'

When she looks at me I can see concern, but it's being eclipsed by overwhelming tiredness. She'll be taking early retirement, she can't keep ahead of her emotions. I've seen that look before, always in the eyes of the good men and women, the ones who care.

'Do you want me to make a statement, Kim?'

She looks at her watch. 'No, it's late. Tomorrow'll do.'

'Procedure says you should do it now.'

'Fuck procedure, Billy. Fuck procedure, and drugs, and the whole fucking city. Fuck the police. And fuck you too. Go home, Billy, Go home.'

Wednesday

Chapter Forty-One

There's a key on Jenny's ring to let me into Rak's house. I check my watch as I climb the stairs, it's almost six in the morning. I stumble into the bathroom, shower, then crawl into bed. I don't mean to wake Jenny but do so, she turns and wraps herself around me and I find myself breaking into tears. I'm not weeping, I'm actually crying, soaking the pillow and Jenny's shoulder. I can't control my body, I'm wracked by spasms of shuddering, juddering fits. For the first time in many years I'm desperately aware of my own mortality.

Jenny holds me tight, she soothes me, strokes me, calms me. And when I begin to talk she stops me, makes me wait until I can speak without sudden inhalations of air. Then I tell her where I've been, what I've done. I tell her what Kim Bryden said. She listens throughout. And then she talks, in her slow, reasoned, soothing voice . . .

'I'm not surprised this Kim woman said what she said, I'd do the same if I wanted you out of my hair. How do you know she was telling you the truth?'

'I don't.'

'So forget what she said. Look at what you've achieved, working by yourself . . .'

'With you, and Rak, Sly and Norm . . .'

'By yourself, Billy, stop dodging the issue. You've achieved more than the whole police force. Call that failure?'

307

She sits up, puts her hands either side of my head.

'Billy Oliphant, look at me.'

I shift my eyes to drown in hers.

'Thanks to you a huge quantity of heroin won't hit the streets. Oh, there'll be more, there always is, there always will be while pushing it's so profitable. The addicts'll still be able to get their fixes. But the pushers won't be able to hook hundreds of young kids, thanks to you. There'll be a few more youngsters alive, thanks to you. Call that failure?'

'But the police might have been able to find the person behind it all if I'd kept myself out of it. But I knew best, the great Billy Oliphant stuck his nose in and . . .'

'Billy! Stop feeling sorry for yourself, or go and do it somewhere else.' She hauls herself out of bed, finds my shirt and throws it at me. My socks hit me in the face, then my trousers.

'I'm sorry!' I say, 'Jenny, please!'

She stops her madness. She comes back and kneels on the floor at my side. Her hand rests on my chest, ties the hairs there into whorls and knots.

'If you want to do more work on the case, do it. You've been successful so far, see what else you can do. Or if you think you've had enough, stop. I don't mind. Either way's all right with me. The choice is yours, yours alone, and I'll love you whatever decision you make.'

This time it's my eyes which draw hers.

'D'you realise what you've just said?'

Her spare hand finds the note I left here. 'You said it first.'

She climbs into bed, fits herself to me, face to face. 'You need to sleep, Billy. I don't start until one tomorrow, I'll stay with you. But you should sleep.'

'I don't think I'll be able to sleep.'

She kisses me on the eyes. 'Yes you will,' she whispers. 'Yes you will.'

Chapter Forty-Two

'It's midday,' she says. 'How are you feeling? I've brought you a cup of tea and some toast.'

I can hear her. I'm hungry, thirsty as well, but my mind's still busy chasing dreams of ghosts. They drifted through forests of breeze-tossed birches muttering 'seize the day', but each time I managed to get close enough to ask what they meant, they faded to nothing. If only I'd had longer with them, if only they'd answered my questions, perhaps I could solve my problems.

'Billy? Are you all right?'

Am I all right? Will I ever be all right? Not while I feel responsibility for finding the person who murdered Graeme Sargent, the one who's trying to flood the city with heroin. But are the two one? Am I hunting one person, two, perhaps a gang? At least one answer's been provided for me. I am still hunting. I haven't given up on the case, despite Kim Bryden's dismissal of my efforts so far.

'Billy!' I feel Jenny's hand at my shoulder, shaking me, and open my eyes.

'Thank goodness! I was beginning to think you were unconscious. Are you okay?'

I pull myself upright and discover aches and pains which weren't with me when I lay down.

'What? Yes, yes I'm fine. I'm sorry, Jen, I was deep, it took me a long time to get to the surface.' I rotate my neck until it clicks, reach for the mug of tea steaming by the bed.

'I like that,' Jenny says, 'being called Jen.' She runs her hand through my hair above my ear. 'You were snoring when I came in.'

'Yeah, I do that when I'm really tired, in a deep sleep.'

'It's all right. I'll get used to it.'

The implication behind her words is too much for me to consider so soon after waking. I feel she's waiting for a response, but there's nothing I can say. She looks away to hide her embarrassment, she's said too much, but when she turns back her confident smile is back.

'I have to go shortly, I'm at work until ten tonight,' she says.

'Thanks for the tea and toast,' I reply. 'Do you mind if I have a shower?'

'Make yourself at home. You can go back to sleep if you want, I just didn't want to go without saying goodbye.'

'I'm glad you woke me. I've got things to do. Work.'

'To do with . . .?'

'Yes. I need to keep going on this, I might as well start straight away. "Never put off until tomorrow what you can do today," my grandmother always used to tell me that.'

'An alternative translation of *Carpe diem* I suppose.'

'Mm.'

There's an awkwardness between us. I suspect she wants to ask me if I'll be waiting for her when she gets back, but I could be wrong. Understanding each other, something that was so easy yesterday, seems to have deserted us.

'If you want me to . . .'

'Why don't we . . .' Our words tumble over each other.

'After you,' she says.

'I was just going to offer to meet you when you finish, we could go for a late meal.'

'I'd love to. I was thinking the same thing myself.'

'That's a good sign.' It's the nearest I can get to commitment.

'Ten o'clock at the main entrance?'

'Okay.'

She comes to the side of the bed, bends to kiss me. 'I've left the morning paper out for you,' she says, 'there's something in it about Graeme Sargent. It's his funeral this afternoon.'

'I'll look at it later. And can I read your drugs book, what's it called . . .?'

'MIMS?'

'That's it.'

'On the floor by the bed. I think.' She looks at her watch.

'I'll find it,' I say. 'Go on, get yourself ready.'

There are books and magazines scattered on the bedside table and on the floor. I choose one, a medical dictionary, flick it open.

'I can see why they made you study Latin. It's a conspiracy really, so the only people who can talk to doctors are other doctors.'

'Yes, you're right. Are my car keys over there? No, it's okay, they're on the dressing table. Now then, handbag, where are you?' She talks as she searches. 'Lots of medical terms are in or derived from Latin, doctors even use Latin when they write out prescriptions. For instance, "t.d.s." means the patient has to take the medicine three times a day. And "b.d." means twice a day.'

'How does "b.d." mean twice a day?' I ask.

'Abbreviation. Latin, it's short for *bis in die*.'

'Say that again.'

'*Bis in die*.' She's looking at me, worried, she can hear the tension in my voice.

'The last word, you pronounced it "dee-ay". How's it spelt?'

'It's the same root as *diem* in *carpe diem*, the Latin for "day". It's spelt d–i–e.'

Lightning strikes, it hits the back of my head and jolts my brain into clear thought.

'Billy, what is it?' Jenny's looking at me with curiosity, perhaps even a little worry.

311

'It's the answer, Jenny, it's the whole fucking answer! And I knew it all along, I just didn't recognise it. Graeme Sargent didn't know any Latin. When he was dying, when he *knew* he was dying, he muttered something to me two or three times. I thought he was saying "*die-cast*," but he wasn't, he was saying part of something else. He didn't know how to pronounce Latin. He wasn't saying "*die-cast*", he should have pronounced it "*dee-ay cast*." The "*cast*" is part of a larger word, a Latin word. And I should know it, I should know it, I've seen it somewhere before! Quick, Jenny, what Latin words do you know beginning with "*cast*"?'

'Cast? I don't know, let me see ... *Castra*, it means camp? That's all I can think of, but it might be part of a verb or a noun with a different stem. Something to do with castration? I don't know ...'

'Could it be *castitatem*? *In die castitatem*, does that mean anything to you?'

'It means something like "in the day of ..." whatever *Castitas* means, it's the genitive of the noun. I've a proper Latin dictionary somewhere, not just medical terms, but ...' She shrugs, looks helplessly around the room. 'It's somewhere about.'

I'm already out of bed. 'I'll find it,' I say, 'it's okay, if you need to get away, just go. I can remember the phrase, I just can't remember where I saw it. If I knew what it meant it might help.'

'I wish I could stay.'

I stop my searching. 'Well you can't, you've got your job just as I've got mine. I'll see you later, main entrance.' I kiss her wetly on the lips.

'Make sure you get dressed first,' she says, but I'm already on the floor examining the spines of a tower of books.

'Yeah, I'll get dressed.'

'Take care.'

'I will.'

'I love you, Billy.'

'I love you too.'

By the time I realise what I've said, by the time I turn to look at her, she's gone. The insistent tugging of dead words eclipses the need for rational thought over what's just passed between Jenny and me. I can't manage the two at once, I can't even consider how to cope with Jenny, with Sara and Kirsty, while there's other unfinished business. And it's easier now, as it always was in the past, to put relationships into second place behind the less abstract difficulties of work.

There's no Latin dictionary in the tower I'm looking through. I turn to a mess of volumes shoved haphazardly into the space between Jenny's dressing table and the alcove in which it stands. I turn my head to left and right, examining book spines. *Gray's Anatomy*, *Pharmacologia*, these are expected. Tourist guides to Paris, Iceland and the USSR (the title of the last indicates the age of the books), a thesaurus, two or three foreign language dictionaries. I'm not even tempted to linger over *The Joy of Sex* and *Women on Top*, the Latin dictionary beneath proves more of an attraction. I pull it out, allow the other books to tumble into the gap released.

I put the book on the bed, kneel before it, fumble through the 'C's. Jenny said the word was *castitas*. I find it easily, it means 'chastity'. But there's a footnote, *Castitas*, with a capital, was some sort of minor Roman goddess responsible for chastity. *In die castitatem* would mean something like 'in the day of purity of morals'. I snap the book shut. Then I laugh, not out loud, not raucously, just an internal gesture at the irony of the meaning. Because I've remembered where I've seen the phrase before. It was on a drawing, a stilted, faded drawing of a Roman statue, no doubt of Chastity herself. And the drawing was hung on a wall in the office of Alice Palmer. Graeme Sargent's sister.

Chapter Forty-Three

I have to hurry. A glance at the newspaper shows Sargent's funeral's at 1.30, that leaves no time to go home and dress appropriately. I have to make do with yesterday's clothes, the housebreaking outfit; at least it's suitably dark. I ring Norm, hoping to be able to use him as a driver, but there's no answer. I leave a message for him and call a taxi.

The service has already started by the time I arrive at the cemetery. Its huge Victorian gates lead to the curved walk-ways and random scatterings of old, ornate gravestones, several topped with statues or spires. Further on, past the twin chapels, lie the more regimented lines of the modern dead's resting places. I slide into the chapel, take my place at the rear. There are several heads I recognise, even from behind. Most belong to criminals, confirmed or suspected. There are others who might be innocents; if I was Kim Bryden I'd have a photographer hidden outside, the city's mafiosi rarely gather together and the order of leaving the chapel would, in itself, provide valuable clues to the hierarchy of local criminals.

I've come in halfway through the eulogy. It's fairly meaningless stuff. If I didn't know it was Sargent's funeral I wouldn't recognise him from the picture the clergyman's painting. Reputable businessman, self-made man, philanthropist – even the devil would get a good press in this place. I don't know the hymn, don't have a crib-sheet to

314

follow the service. It's a relief when the singing ends, when heads are bowed in mumbled prayer, when the pall-bearers (*Ladders* doormen all, black coats bulging, foreheads glistening with the heat) begin their slow march down the aisle.

When the doors are flung open there's a welcome breeze, a searing blaze of white light. I stand as Alice Palmer passes, make sure I look at her, make sure she's looking at me. Beneath her wide-brimmed, black-plumed hat her eyes catch mine. I smile at her, she nods back. She doesn't break her step. Her husband (I assume the man with her is her husband, their arms locked at the elbow) on the opposite side of the aisle won't even have noticed me. But Alice Palmer has. And in her momentarily widened eyes I swear I catch a glimpse of fear.

I wait for everyone to follow the coffin, then take my place at the rear. The burial plot is near enough for the pall-bearers to march there, I join the crocodile, make sure I'm between the plot and the waiting mourners' cars. I'm not interested in what's said as Sargent's coffin is lowered into the ground. Of more concern to me is Alice Palmer's behaviour. I consider it a triumph when, in the guise of wiping away a tear, she looks round to see if she can find me. It's not too hard for her, I'm leaning against a pale white gravestone, separated from the rest of the company.

While I'm waiting I take a piece of paper from my pocket. I've already written a message on it in block capitals. 'IN DIE CASTITATEM – WHAT'S BEHIND IT?'

'Ashes to ashes,' I hear, 'dust to dust.' I move away towards the cars, shelter from the sun beneath a yew tree sustained, no doubt, by the copious nitrogen in the soil. In my dark outfit, with the sun bleaching the paths, reflecting from the polished marbles and granites, I'm as good as invisible. I want it that way.

When Alice Palmer moves along the viscous tarmac I step in front of her at the last moment. Her surprise is evident, she starts, moves quickly to one side to protect herself behind her husband's black-suited body.

315

'I'm really sorry Graeme died,' I say, 'I knew him quite well in his last days. We met quite frequently.'

'Yes,' she replies, 'he told me. But I *didn't* expect to see you here.'

'I couldn't let the opportunity to pay my last respects go by.'

'*Thank* you Mr Oliphant.'

'You're welcome.'

She's eager to be off but I'm still blocking her way. 'If you don't mind,' she says, 'I *must* be going. There are *so* many things to do.'

'Yes, I can imagine. Your brother was quite a business-man, he controlled a big organisation. It'll be difficult, almost impossible, to replace him.'

'We'll try.' I still won't let her pass. 'If you're worried about an *arrangement* you had with him regarding your *debt*, Mr Oliphant, I can assure you he *spoke* to me about it. So far as I'm concerned you *now* owe the company *nothing*.'

'Why, thank you Mrs Palmer. That is a relief.' I hold out my hand, she extends her glove, I pass the note to her.

'I'm so glad I came. It's been a pleasure to talk to you, Mrs Palmer. And you Mr Palmer.'

'*Doctor* Palmer, Mr Oliphant,' she says proudly, 'my husband's a GP.'

'Alice,' her husband butts in, 'I'm sure Mr Oliphant isn't interested in my profession. But thank you for coming, Mr Oliphant. Will you be joining us for some refreshments? We're meeting at my late brother-in-law's nightclub . . .'

'I'm sure Mr Oliphant will be *far* too busy, dear.' She's read it! I can tell by the tone in her voice, the anger scowl-ing her face.

'Yes,' I say, 'I have so many other things to do. Have a pleasant wake.'

I walk away. If Alice Palmer called me back I'd still keep walking; if I looked at her I'd be turned to stone.

Chapter Forty-Four

I leave the cemetery then slip back as soon as I see the Palmers climb into their car. Then I head for the back of the queue, avoid the official black limousines and wait for the driver of a dark blue BMW to appear. He's large, fat and perspiring, and his blowsy wife totters beside him on heels too high for her age.

'Excuse me,' I say, 'I've just been speaking to Mr and Mrs Palmer, they invited me to join them for refreshments but I came by taxi. I don't suppose . . .?'

He looks me up and down. She does the same. I'm not properly dressed, but Graeme Sargent knew some strange people.

'Okay,' he says, 'get in the back.'

We're quickly on our way. He lights a cigar, winds down the window, drives with one elbow outside. He says nothing but his wife makes up for this with her chatter.

'It was such a beautiful service, don't you think so? Sammy and I were so upset when we heard what had happened. A heart attack for Christ's sake, and Graeme so damn healthy, I mean, I just didn't believe it.'

I let her talk on, I grunt and nod at appropriate intervals. Her husband looks at me in the rear-view mirror. When his wife pauses for breath he interrupts smartly.

'So how did you know Graeme Sargent?'

'Security. I advised him on security matters. That's my

317

business. But I knew him socially as well.'

'Socially? I didn't know Graeme had much of a social life.' He's sharp, probably as a result of trying to insert syllables in his wife's monologues.

'In the club. I'd go up and see him in his suite. We'd play chess. He was fond of games.'

'He was fond of cunt, that's all I know.'

'Sammy! I'm sorry, Sammy isn't normally so crude . . .'

'Dinah, shut it! Graeme Sargent was a bastard in business and in pleasure. A few years back – quite a while really, when we was both setting up, when we was both young – I lent him some girls. Good girls they was, but they come back ruined. He was a madman. I wouldn't have dealt with him if I'd had the choice, but these days who has the choice? I just hope whoever takes over is half as mad and twice as intelligent. I don't know how he managed to keep things together.'

'Well,' says Sammy's wife, 'I only met him a few times but I liked him.'

'He probably fucked you when you weren't looking, that's why.'

We're down by the river now. Sammy's BMW glides into that large section of the public car-park which has been roped off for those visiting *Ladders*. I get out with them, walk across the road with them, enter with them. There's a queue waiting to be welcomed by Alice Palmer and her husband.

'I need to go to the loo,' I explain to Mr and Mrs Sammy. 'If you get to the head of the line before I get back please tell Mrs Palmer I was pleased she invited me back. We share an interest in art, you see. She said she'd show me some of her drawings. Tell her Billy Oliphant sends his regards.'

I leave before they can say anything, head for the toilets but swerve to one side and end up beside the lift doors. There are no bouncers on guard this time. In my pocket I have the lift key which will take me up to Sargent's fourth-floor apartment. From there I can use the stairs to find my way down to his sister's office. I press the button and the lift's already there, waiting. I go in, turn the key.

It's quiet, nothing but the hiss of air-conditioning. My shirt's sticking to my back, not through heat or exertion but through nervousness.

The lift opens onto the outer office of Sargent's suite. I take out the key and press the button to return it to the ground floor, as the doors close I realise there's only the dull red glow of an emergency light. There's a pen-torch in my pocket but I leave it there, allow my eyes to become accustomed to the darkness. Ahead of me is the door leading to Sargent's rooms, but I don't want those. Instead, I move to the other door, turn the handle slowly, squeeze it open. The corridor ahead is empty, it too is filled with red-tinged darkness. I pass through it, walking on the balls of my feet even though the carpet's thick-piled, able to eat the noise of far louder visitors than me. There's another door and I'm in the stairwell. I head down, hug the outer wall, pause at each bend to peer round the next corner. One floor down, that's where Alice Palmer's office should be. The stairs are at the rear of the building, her office was at the front, there must be a corridor. That's where things could get awkward, there might be people at work.

I creep to the door on the landing, open it slightly, light forces itself through. That's bad, it means people might be there. I open the door far enough to see what lies beyond. It's similar to the floor above, a long corridor, but this one has doors running off. I don't recognise it as the passage I was led along when I visited Alice Palmer, but I enter anyway. I adopt a purposeful look, if anyone appears I can pretend I'm lost, separated from the funeral party and looking for a way back down. I move to the end, find two more corridors, and realise where I am. Alice Palmer's room should be along the second of these. I find the door, open it. The room's filled with afternoon sunlight, it catches the drawings on the wall behind her desk. I hurry to the middle one, the inscription's as I remembered, *In die Castitatem*. 'In the day of purity of morals.' Die-cast. I look again at the drawing. It's of a Roman goddess, one breast bare. In her left hand she's carrying a sword, an owl is perched on her right shoulder, and a serpent is entwined around her feet. I run my fingers around the frame, pull slightly. It's hinged at the left, it moves away from the wall and I can see a small safe.

It doesn't work with tumblers, nor is there a hole for a key. It's a modern safe, electronically operated with a five-digit key pad. That means that each digit can be filled with any of the 26 letters of the alphabet or ten whole integers. That's 36 possibilities for each entry. Five entries. 36 to the power of five is . . . a lot. I've seen the recommendations for entering the code on safes like this. They advise mixing letters and numbers, not using recognisable words. I can't believe that Alice Palmer would allow herself a lapse of security, that she's programmed the safe with, say her own name. I try it, just to prove to myself that she's more intelligent than that; it doesn't work. In quick succession I try variations on telephone numbers, company names; I even try my own name. None work. I leave the safe, keep the drawing unhinged to show someone's visited. I'm close, but there's no way in. I'd expected his, it doesn't really matter. By now Sammy and his wife will have reached Alice Palmer. They'll have mentioned the strange man they gave a lift to, they'll have passed on my message. The only question in my mind is what excuse Alice will have made for leaving. Illness? Distress at the death of her brother? The latter probably. And then, concerned at what I might know, what I might do, she'll come up to her office.

I open the window wide, a narrow ledge leads round the side of an attic window. I've searched the room thoroughly, there's no good place to hide so I'll have to find a bad one. There's a conference table with ten chairs around it, four to each side, one each at foot and head. I push the side chairs in as far as they'll go then crawl under the table, sandwich myself onto the seats of the chairs, keeping as close to the underside of the desk, the middle of the desk, as possible. With a little luck, when Alice Palmer comes into the room she'll assume I've left through the window, disturbed by her approach. A minute's wait brings the sound of footsteps. The door bursts open.

'There's no one here, Mrs Palmer.'

'I can *see* that, idiot. Check the *window*.'

Black, shining shoes topped with black creased trousers hurry across the room.

'No one there either. No one on the ledge, no rope, no one running in the street. Nothing.'

'But someone *has* been here! He's been trying to get into the *safe*, Jesus Christ, I knew I should have . . .' She stops. 'Wait outside. I'm going to lock the door. *No one's* to come in. If anyone asks, even my husband, I said I *wasn't* to be disturbed. Understand?'

'Yes, Mrs Palmer.'

'Go on then! Out!'

I hear the door close, the turn of the lock. Alice Palmer strides past, heading for her safe. She taps in some numbers, I squirm to the head of the table but she's too far away for me to see them. She swings the door open, reaches inside. I hear her sigh, she brings out a video tape. 'Not so clever as you *think* you are, eh Mr Oliphant?' She can't know I'm there, she must be talking to herself, releasing tension. I can see her, she has her back to me. I lower myself to the floor, squirm out from under the table.

'Home videos, Alice?' I say as I'm standing up.

She pirouettes gracefully, takes me in at a glance and then dives for her desk drawer. The gun she points at me is small, her hand's shaking, but I've no doubt she's capable of aiming well enough and pulling the trigger.

'You're proving *tiresome*, Mr Oliphant. I'm beginning to lose *patience*.'

'With me? Why's that, Alice? Something to hide? What's on the video, then?'

'Nothing to interest you, Oliphant.'

'Really? That's a pity. I somehow had the impression it might interest a lot of people. The police, for example. I mean, why would you keep a video in your safe unless it contained something important?'

'Do the police know you're here?' Her voice is worried, but then she smiles, brings her worries under control. 'No, of course they don't. You're not on good *terms* with the police, are you? Not after your role in Ted Samson's death.'

'Lost a lot of merchandise, did you? You are involved, aren't you, bringing the drugs into the country inside window frames? Ted couldn't have thought of that. The police think it was Graeme.'

'And you don't?'

'It would have been an easy solution, too easy. I worry about things when they're too easy, I can't sleep. When I can't sleep, I think. I got round to thinking about what Graeme said as he was dying. "Die-cast." He was giving me a clue. He was talking about your picture, *In die casti-tatem*, and I assumed there was something hidden behind it. That's why I came to the funeral, because I wanted you to show me what was behind the picture, what was in the safe. Thank you for that. And you've helped in other ways as well, filled in small gaps. You told me your husband was a doctor. With or without his knowledge, it doesn't matter which, you obtained supplies of drugs in an attempt to combat Graeme's schizophrenia.'

'Clever, Oliphant, *very* clever.' She looks at the door.

'Let him in,' I say, 'let him hear as well.'

She shakes her head. 'I'll *shoot* you,' she says. 'I'll say you *attacked* me. You've got a *history* of mental illness, you were *paranoid* about Graeme and, when he died, you transferred your paranoia to *me*. Self defence. There are *plenty* of witnesses who saw you at the funeral, others who saw you arriving here.'

'You might get away with it.'

'Oh, I would. Like I've got away with so *much* else.'

322

'Yes, Graeme could never have run a set-up like this. But he was a useful front, wasn't he? Difficult for the police to pin anything on him because he wasn't actually doing anything. But he looked as if he was in charge, he acted as if he was in charge. He probably thought he was in charge. But all the time it was you pulling the strings.'

'Well done. You can't know the *fine* details, of course, but that's a *reasonable* effort at the broad sweep of things.'

'Did you provide him with the Caverject as well?'

'I'm *impressed*, Mr Oliphant, you really are very thorough. Yes, I supplied the Caverject.'

'Administered it as well?'

She says nothing and her silence prompts me to go further.

'He didn't like injections, he told me himself. So someone did it for him. You?'

'I studied medicine, that's where I met my husband. I didn't finish the course, Graeme was ill, I *had* to look after him, sort out his *problems*. He was involved in all *sorts* of petty crime. I just took over, found I was good at it. Graeme was a good front. And now, once you're out of the way, I'll keep on running things the same way I *always* have. The shipment you delivered to the police last night, it was *nothing*. Sizeable, yes, but a shortage for a few weeks will just keep prices high. There'll be more coming in. My supplier is *very* good, *very* efficient.'

'And the lives you're destroying?'

'My goodness me, *In die castitatem* indeed, Mr Oliphant. The people who use drugs are like *you*, small, insignificant even, losers from the day they're born. When Graeme told me you were proving *troublesome*, when he told me *all* about you, I reassured him, I said your work, your investigations, would in the end come to nothing. And I *will* be proved right.'

'Did you kill your brother?'

She inhales, lets out her breath slowly. Then slides the video cassette across the table towards me.

'I *do* hate exposition, Mr Oliphant. Perhaps this will suffice instead. *Please* be so good as to switch on the television and video.'

I eject the tape already in the machine and insert the tape she's given me, press the *play* button then sit down to watch. The scene is Graeme Sargent's bedroom.

'I felt sorry for Graeme, Mr Oliphant. His life was so restricted. In the early days his schizophrenia dominated his life, he was extremely violent to everyone except me. I cared for him, found him medication he could use.'

'He didn't take it.'

'Not always, he was comparatively stable of late. But it was there if he *needed* it, there was never a problem getting more. My husband, you see, is a partner in a *dispensing* practice. I simply dispensed the drugs I needed to a *wide* range of patients, no-one would ever know *I'd* been taking them.'

There's movement on the screen. Graeme Sargent, dressed in his white dressing gown, takes his place on the bed.

'I think I've solved the problem with this bloody Oliphant,' he says, 'I've got him by the balls and he knows it. He's coming round tonight, I'll sort him then.'

'Is that *wise*, Graeme?' It's Alice's voice, fainter, from off screen.

'Wise? Of course it's bloody wise, I want to get this bloody sorted for once and for all. I've got other problems as well, you know, far closer to home than Billy bleeding Oliphant.'

Alice enters. She sits down beside Graeme, puts her arm round him.

'What's the *matter*, Graeme? Are you worried about tonight? There won't be a problem, there's *never* been a problem with it so far, has there?' She's carrying a cardboard box. 'It won't hurt, I've *never* hurt you in the past.'

He turns to her, pats her knee.

'I know it won't hurt, Ally, it's just that . . . It's frustrating, you having to do this. And embarrassing. But you know I don't like needles, and . . .'

'It's not a *problem*, then, is it?'

'No. But that's not the problem anyway. It's that bastard Ted Samson.'

'Ted? I thought he was your right hand *man*, I thought you *trusted* . . .'

'He's a two-faced fucking bastard, that's what Ted Samson is!' Sargent hurls himself from the bed, the changes in his mood are swift. He marches across the room and back, disappearing from the screen then returning, a blur of white.

'I've heard – I've got contacts, Ally, I know these things – that he's started a scam of his own! This contract, this window contract, it was meant to be clean, nothing shady about it.' He stops, back to the camera, arms outstreched. 'Christ, Ally, you worked on pricing that contract, you know it's legit. But Samson's screwed it up, he's well and truly fucked it this time. Do you know what he's doing?'

'Tell me, Graeme.'

'He's bringing fucking heroin in, inside the fucking windows! He cuts them open, takes the smack out, sticks them back together. And not a word to me! Jesus Christ, Ally, I swear I'll tear his balls off and stick them in his fucking mouth!' He begins his marching again.

'Graeme, calm *down*, please. All this excitement isn't *good* for you. Look, Ted's been with you for quite a while. Who *told* you about this?'

'Someone I can trust, he didn't tell me because he thought I needed to know, he told me because he thought I already knew. So I checked tonight with some of Samson's lads, some of my lads, damn it. He's doing it all right, he's double-crossing me!'

'Graeme. Come here. Sit *down*.'

Sargent stops his peripatetics, throws himself face down on the bed.

'I'll sort it out for you, Graeme. If Ted Samson really is doing this then I'll ask for a piece of the action. Don't you worry about it. I'll see we don't suffer.'

'It's not enough, Ally.' Sargent's voice is muffled. 'It's not enough, I need more. So I'm going to play smart, I'm going to ring the police, tell them what he's up to. It'll work both ways, I'll get on the right side of the law for once, that should bank me a few favours. And it'll show everybody else in the organisation that they shouldn't fuck me about. The pigs'll sort Samson out for me. They'll go round, they'll put him away for twenty. That's what I'm going to do.'

'Is that *wise*, Graeme? *How* will you manage without him? And what if he decides to tell them about *you*?'

Sargent spins round, sits up quickly, grips his sister by the shoulders. 'He won't say anything, he wouldn't dare! I could get to him, even in prison I could get to him. And I don't need him, Ally! I don't need him, I don't need anyone.' He grins, wide-eyed. 'The only one I need is you.'

He moves his hands to her face, still staring at her. Then his hands move down to her breasts. When there's no reaction one hand moves lower, it slides under her skirt and raises the hem, cups her groin. Then he leans forward and kisses her. It's not the kiss of a brother to his sister, it's the kiss of a lover. She doesn't move, either to push him away or to encourage him, but accepts his kiss. When he separates from her she looks at the cardboard box.

'I'd better make this up *now*, Graeme, we want to make sure . . . Damn!'

'What is it, Ally?'

'It's out of *date*. It must be old *stock*. It's all right, I've some more in my office, I'll go and get it. When I come back we can talk about *Ted*, I think you're right, it would be a good example to *others* if we told the police. But we'd have to think of the best way of doing it so they don't suspect *us*.' She stands up. 'I'll be back in two mins.'

Sargent watches her go, there's a sound of a door closing, then he lies back on the bed. I half turn to look at Alice Palmer.

'You all the time? Your idea, your set up, your organisation? Your profits?'

She nods.

'And he was going to ruin it. So you decided to stop him. You decided to kill him.'

She nods again. 'At *first* I thought I'd give him enough to knock him *out*. but then I realised it was a good chance to get rid of him altogether. He'd outlived his *usefulness*. He was going mad again. He could have spoiled *everything*.'

'But he was your brother!'

'Yes.'

'Did he screw you?'

If the question surprises her she shows no sign of it. 'Yes. A long time ago. But if you're thinking that was part of the motivation for me *killing* him, you'd be wrong. I was a willing participant. That's one of the reasons he was happy for me to give him the *injections*. It was familiar territory.'

Sargent isn't moving, not even to the sound of the door reopening.

'I saw your girl,' says the screen Alice, 'she looks *very* pretty. I'm sure you'll *both* have a good time. Come on, let me see.'

Sargent twitches aside his gown to reveal his genitals. Alice sits down on the bed beside him. She's brought with her a small hand towel, rolled up as if she's carrying something fragile.

'I suppose you'd already done the switch,' I say.

'Yes. Pure heroin.'

'So you knew it would kill him?'

'I was pretty sure.'

'You're so bloody cold.'

She waves the gun at my head. 'If that means I can contemplate killing someone, decide *how* to do it, then carry it out, yes. I'm cold. Is that so much worse than killing in the *heat* of the moment? Did Ted Samson die any easier because no one had *planned* his death?'

327

We're both watching the screen. Alice reaches out, strokes her brother's penis gently. He raises himself to his elbows, looks at her face, then lowers his gaze to her hand. He isn't reacting to her ministrations.

'Now?' she asks. He nods his reply, lowers himself back down to the bed, turns his face away. Alice unrolls the towel beside her to reveal the syringe. With her left hand she pulls at her brother's penis to tighten the skin, searches for an entry point at its base. Then, gently, she eases the needle into the flesh, depresses the plunger, and removes the needle. She wraps it again in the towel then, looking completely relaxed, begins to stroke her brother's thigh.

'It's all right now,' she says, 'don't you worry, *everything'll* be all right.'

'I need to get Samson,' says Sargent, 'I need to fix him.'

'We can talk about that *later*, Graeme. Just relax.'

'Relax. Yeah. Relax.' He giggles, seems surprised at the sound, holds his hand to his mouth. 'Ally, what's happening? It doesn't feel right. The room's spinning. It's all . . . it's all bright, coloured!' He giggles again, it turns into a snort of laughter. He's behaving as if he's had too much to drink, he's tossing his head from side to side, his arms and legs are beginning to move as if he's fitting.

'Ally? Ally, what's . . . What's happening?'

His movements are subsiding into a tremor. His pale skin's becoming flushed with pink, his face more red. He tries to sit up, with an obvious effort manages to do so. He needs his hands to keep him there, spread wide on the bed, and he's trying desperately to focus on his sister. She stands up, steps away from the bed, out of the camera's view.

'Ally, where are you? I can't see you.' The tremors are becoming worse.

'It's all right, baby, I'm *here*, watching you.' Her voice is still sweet, kind. 'And I'm going to watch you till you pass out, because I've just injected you with pure *heroin*. You'll be *dead* in a few minutes, Graeme. Unconscious first, then you'll just stop breathing. They'll do an *autopsy*, cut you open to find out why you died. They'll find it was a heroin o.d., they won't be suspicious. No one will be able to connect *me* with it.'

'Why?' His voice is a cracked whisper.

'Why? I don't *need* you any more. In fact, you're becoming a liability. You're getting in the way too often. Ted Samson's working for *me*, little one, he's *my* man. So, really, is everyone else in this place. Now seems as good a time as *any* to get rid of you. So goodbye, dear brother.'

Sargent mutters something, some unintelligible, harsh word. Then he looks at me. He isn't looking at *me*, of course, but at the camera. Perhaps it's a deliberate act, perhaps the camera, though hidden, has some warning light indicating that it's working and he wants to know that that's the case. Or it could be that the movement's involuntary, that he can't *not* look at the camera, that he wants the lens to catch the full drama of his death. Either way, his action's noticed.

'Graeme! You're *not* making another one of your *movies*, are you? Preserving your final moments for posterity? And you weren't going to *tell* me, even though I have something of a starring role.' She moves back into view, stares up at the lens. Graeme Sargent can be seen behind her, his breathing's becoming more ragged, he's collapsed once again to the bed. His face is swollen now, his skin tinged with blue. Ignoring him, Alice Palmer smiles at the camera.

'I'll have to remove it, of course,' she says, 'Though I will get a large amount of pleasure from looking at it. In private, of course.' She returns to the bed, kneels on it and places her fingers on her brother's neck, feels for a pulse. His eyes are closed, his gown's almost off and I can see no sign that he's still alive. The screen Alice smiles and walks away; a few seconds later a migraine of black and white replaces Sargent's bedroom, a high pitched hiss of noise attacks the ears.

'*Do* switch it off, Billy.'

329

I turn off the television, press the eject button. I put the tape on top of the video recorder then return to my seat, turn it to face Alice Palmer. She's more at ease now, sitting down with the handle of the gun resting on the desk. The barrel's still pointing at my chest.

'Are you impressed, Mr Oliphant?'

'No. I used to think your brother was unpleasant. Some villains have a way with them, even though they're doing wrong you can't help liking them. But Graeme always was a nasty man, and finding that you were the one turning kids into addicts and hookers, threatening shopkeepers who wouldn't pay for protection, knee-capping, murdering, that doesn't change the fact that he was a bastard. But watching that video made me feel sorry for him. He didn't have much of a start in life, not if he was mentally ill, but having you as a sister sure made it worse.'

My words seem to wash over her, I'm not even sure she's listening. But when I stop she's in there quickly, in case I start again.

'I'm looking *forward* to this, Mr Oliphant. I was considering *other* means of persuading you to behave. Since threats to your wife seem to have little effect on you, I was going to move my attention to your *girlfriend*, Jenny, isn't that her name? A young *doctor*? At the *infirmary*? You're moving up in the world. But then, I forgot, she's black. That moves you a few squares back again. It's not that I'm prejudiced, oh no, I quite like black people. I believe *every* white should have one.' She snorts a laugh. I suspect she's trying to make me angry and she's succeeding, but I grip the arms of the chair, try not to show it.

'But *now* it looks as if I won't have to resort to damaging her *pretty* little face. Instead I'll damage yours.' She raises her gun, sights down the barrel and pulls the trigger. It clicks. She pulls it again. Another click.

'You should always make sure your gun's loaded,' I say, rising slowly to my feet. 'Perhaps these might help.' I take the clip of ammunition from my pocket, scatter the shells

330

on the floor. 'I may be inexperienced in these matters, but I don't think it's right to leave a loaded gun in someone's drawer when you're going to accuse her of murder.'

She screams. I know the door's locked, but her body-guard isn't going to let a small thing like that get in his way. He enters like a rhinoceros, still upright despite the door lying on the ground at his feet. I dive for the video recorder, the only evidence that Alice Palmer murdered her brother is that tape. The black plastic feels comfortable in my hand, I tuck it into my shirt.

'Get that tape!' Alice says. She backs away, round the room, sheltering behind her man. He's big, but not so big that he won't be mobile. He's obviously strong. He's not grinning like the over-confident hardmen in Hollywood films, the ones who die with their smiles newly wiped from their ugly faces. He's weighing me up, wondering what my strengths are, considering how to attack me with the least possible damage to himself. In short, he seems reasonably intelligent. I've sunk without thinking into an ape-like semi-shuffle, keeping furniture between me and my adversary. I decide to stop this. I stand upright.

'She killed her brother,' I explain. 'The evidence is on the video. If you do as she says you'll be an accomplice. You'll go to prison for a long time. But if you help me, if you let me go, then there won't be a problem. What do you say?'

He's obviously not a man of words, he replies by leaping over the desk at me. So much for reasoned argument. I scuttle to one side but he's after me, he manages to grab my arm and throws me against the wall. I'm trapped now, in the corner. Alice is beside the door.

'Get him,' she says wildly, 'get the fucking *tape*!'

The hardman closes in. I feint to the left but he has me covered, to the right and he's there before me.

'Okay,' I say, 'okay, you win. Here, take it.' I remove the tape from my shirt, hold it out to him. As he stretches out his own hand I aim a huge, violent kick to his groin. He manages to lean back and twist, my kick glances against his thigh, but I use my momentum to squeeze past him. At least I would if he wasn't so quick. He shoulders me to one side, I bounce off the wall and into his arms. He's holding me from behind, my arms pinned to my sides, crushing me.

'Just keep him there,' says Alice. She scuttles across the room, I try to kick at her but the breath is squeezed from me and she manages to extract the video from my torn shirt.

'You can *kill* him now,' she says triumphantly.

I can feel the increase in pressure. I'm not sure if the hardman can actually kill me like this, or whether I'll pass out, thus allowing him to strangle me. I think he's already broken one of my ribs, I felt a crack and heard a scream which sounded like my own voice. I decide to play dead, let my chin go forward, hang limp from his arms. I feel the pressure release then tighten again as he tests me. The pain from my ribs is agonising but I remain quiet. He drops me to the floor but, like a wrestler, he's on top of me straight-away, hands at my throat. I can't breathe at all, there was a little air left in my lungs to begin with. I try kicking but my blows have no effect, arching my back does nothing, he's too heavy. My arms are pinioned between my legs, I find that thrashing about I can release them enough to move my right hand a little. I flick my eyes open. The hardman's staring at me. I have only one chance. I turn my hand into a claw and grab at his trousers, at the sacs of flesh beneath, I grab hard and twist.

The effect is better than I'd hoped. He drops away from me, lies at my side bent double, groaning. I climb to my feet and pick up a chair. With the little strength I have, in between choking intakes of breath, I break it over his head.

Alice Palmer has already made her escape. I head for the door, pausing only to grab the unloaded gun she dropped. I see her turning the corner at the end of the corridor. She's ignoring the lift, making for the stairs. I'm hampered by my lungs' insistence that I give them some air, by the pain in my ribs, but she's older than me and I'm gaining.

When we reach the ground floor she's no more than ten metres ahead. There are more people in the club than when I arrived, she seems to find passage through them easy. I, on the other hand, am taking care not to barge into any of the hoodlums who might have hardware with them. I smile graciously, all the time marking Alice Palmer's passage towards the main entrance. As she goes through she says something to the doormen, by the time I arrive they're shoulder to shoulder blocking my way. I turn my hasty walk into a run, take Alice Palmer's unloaded gun from my pocket and level it at them.

'Out of the way!' I yell. 'Or you get your fucking balls blown off!'

They move quickly for men with such bulk, I'm straight through and blinking in the harsh sunlight. I look around but can see no sign of my quarry. I lurch towards the road, there's the sharp, insistent bleating of a car horn and a distant cry.

'Over here, boss, over here!'

As my eyes become accustomed to the brightness I see Norm's Volvo, his straw-hatted head grinning from the driver's window. He's parked on double yellow lines, oblivious to his effect on the traffic in the narrow street.

'Where did she go?' I gasp.

'I got your message, thought you might need me down here, so . . .'

'Tell me later, Norm. The woman who came out of the club ahead of me, where did she go?'

'Grey-haired, black trouser suit? She ran straight across, headed for the river. Want a lift?'

The road snakes round a one-way system here. If she's on foot it might be better to follow her in the same way.

'No, you drive round to the quayside. See if we can catch her between us.'

Norm guns his car into the road and I'm off again, round the corner and under the stone and steel bridge supports. That's when I see her. She's standing by the open door of a

333

car, something low and red. She sees me coming and, even from a distance, I can tell she's laughing. She hurls the video tape into the river. I don't see it fall, I don't hear the sound as it hits the water, but I know it's lost. I don't slow down. If I can get to her before she starts the engine I might be able to drag her out of the car.

The car-park is long and narrow, two rows of herring-bone parking slots and a central driveway down which I'm running at full speed. Alice Palmer's car starts first time, screeches backwards into the driveway to face me. She accelerates; the squat rear of her car twitches from side to side, tyres kick up a black rubber smoke. I veer to one side and she aims for me, misses but glances off a blue Escort, rebounds onto the other rank of cars then she's away. I leap over the metal barrier to watch her roar up the hill towards the city centre. That's when Norm arrives, passenger door opening as he slows.

'Follow that car?' he grins.

'Yeah.'

'Yess! I've always wanted to do this. Hold on!'

My ribs hurt as I fold myself into the Volvo, they hurt more as Norm's foot hits the floor.

'We'll have to move to keep up with that,' he says, 'Mazda sports job, it'll go.'

'I have faith in you,' I groan, fastening the seat belt but holding it away from my chest.

We're charging up Dean Street, Norm's leaning on the horn, driving up the middle of the road.

'Use the mobile if you want,' he says, gesturing at the phone hooked beside the radio.

'Who for?'

'Police? Not that they'll be long in coming after us if we both keep driving like this. She's not interested in the Highway Code, is she? Let them know what's happening anyway. And there's Sly, he's on standby in case you need him.'

'Sly as well?'

334

'We've got to look after you, boss. You can't do it very well yourself, can you?'

Alice Palmer seems to be driving at random. I'd expected her to head north, out of the city, she lives somewhere up there, but instead she's crossing her tracks, going to and fro with no apparent reason. I leave the driving to Norm, pick up the phone and dial Central Police, ask for Kim Bryden. She's there straightaway, just as the first police car snakes in behind us.

'Billy, what the fuck are you doing?'

'Listen, Kim, I'm following . . .'

'I know, I fucking know! You're chasing Alice Palmer, she's already been screaming blue murder down the phone saying you'd tried to kill her in her office and now you're trying to blow her off the road . . . just a minute . . .' Her voice disappears for a moment, then returns. 'You'll be able to see we're following you, Billy. Just pull over, the sooner the better. Christ, Billy, you're in deep shit!'

'Kim, she did it. Alice Palmer killed Graeme Sargent. Look, it's a long story but she confessed she did it. To me.'

'Witnesses?'

'No, but . . .'

'It won't stand up Billy, there's proof you've been harassing her just like you did her brother, hundreds of witnesses in the club saw you chasing her, you pulled a gun on the doormen. We've already got men down there taking statements. Now pull over!'

'There's proof, Kim, a video tape. Sargent had his camera switched on when she injected him with heroin. She had it hidden in her safe, that's why I was at *Ladders*. She showed it to me, tried to kill me.'

'Is this the tape she threw in the river?'

'How did you know . . .?'

'CCTV monitoring the car-park, Billy.'

I take a deep breath, as deep as I can manage given the pain I'm in and the jostling I'm receiving from Norm's driving.

'No. She thinks it's the tape but I switched them. The real tape's in her office, in the video player. Get one of your men to find it. For God's sake tell him to be careful not to wipe it, it's prime evidence.'

'It sounds like the only evidence. Okay, Billy, let's assume you're right. Let us take over now, just slow down and stop.'

'Her first, Kim. Get her to stop and I'll do the same.'

'Billy! Stop giving me orders!'

'Okay. *Please* ask her to stop.'

'What the hell did I do to deserve you? Just hold on, don't disconnect.'

The reception's poor, we're in the canyons of high Georgian offices, then past the railway station and heading for the river again. The hissing vanishes until we hit the other side. Alice Palmer's car's three or four vehicles ahead of us, travelling fast but under better control than when she first set off. Police One, remarkably restrained, no flashing lights or screaming sirens, is tucked in hard behind us. Further behind we've been joined by Police Two, and the helicopter dogging us above is probably also striped.

We manage to move closer, now we're right behind but Alice Palmer's making no attempt to outrun us. I can see her talking on her mobile. Then she puts it down, and suddenly she's away, jinking in and out of traffic, heading west towards the bypass. Norm sets off after her; Police Two, lit up like Christmas, overtakes us; Police One keeps us company.

'Billy? Are you still there?'

I hold the phone closer. 'Yes, She didn't want to stop, I take it.'

'She's hung up. I told her about the video. She said you were lying. I told her I believed you, she said you were bluffing. By that time my boys were watching the video, they confirmed she and Sargent were on it together. I told her. She said you were a bastard. She said she'd get you where it hurt. Then she hung up. We've a dozen cars out, Billy, you've probably seen the chopper as well, she can't get away. But she might just be mad enough to try to crash into you, so please, I'm asking nicely, turn back. You've done well, but having you around now will make things rather more difficult.'

She's right. There's nothing more I can do. Norm's gamely trying to keep up with the red sportscar but it's beyond the Volvo's capabilities. I tap him on the shoulder.

'Next exit,' I say, 'head for home.' I turn my attention to the phone. 'We're coming in, Kim. Make sure you get her.'

'We'll try. Come down here, sit in. See how things are going.'

'Yeah, I'll do that. Might as well be in at the death.'

'The finish, Billy, the finish. I don't like words like "death".'

Chapter Forty-Five

'What the hell is she doing?'

Kim Bryden's staring at a single television screen showing the view from the helicopter. Behind her a bank of other screens shows different roadways throughout the city and beyond. She also has reports from the cars following Alice Palmer. Norm and I are in the background, we've been told to sit still and keep out of the way.

'Where is she now?' I ask, too far from the screen to make out any detail.

'Heading north again on the bypass.'

Since Norm and I gave up the chase she's crossed and recrossed the river, sticking to major roads which the police would have difficulty blocking. She's ignored loud-speakered demands that she stop. But there's been no direction in her meanderings, nothing to say she's heading for somewhere specific.

'Perhaps she's waiting for night,' I suggest, 'if she's got enough petrol to keep her going that long.'

'Could be thinking of picking up a hostage,' proposes a uniformed sergeant beside me. 'Has she got a gun?'

I shake my head. 'Not unless there was one hidden in the car.'

'So what's she doing?' asks Kim.

'Perhaps,' I say, 'she's thinking of what to do next.

Considering options. Not that she has many. But if I was her . . .'

'Yes?' Kim turns to look at me.

'How long before the helicopter has to refuel?'

'An hour, hour and a half?'

'Got a second one? Or a light aircraft?'

'You think she might be waiting for that?'

'Her car can get away from anything you can put on the road, she won't care about injuring any other road users. She's travelling at random, there's no way you can set up road blocks. Once the chopper's down she might go for a sprint. And remember, she's been the brains behind Sargent's operation for years, she'll have contacts, places to hide.'

Kim's on the phone asking for a second helicopter to be made ready, but she's interrupted by one of her radio operators.

'She seems to be making a move,' she says, 'off the bypass on to the West Road.'

'Got her on the screen,' says Kim.

'Traffic's bad on the West Road,' says another voice, 'jams heading out of town.'

'But she's heading in,' I say, 'and the housing estates off the West Road are laid out like grids, you can't block her if she heads in there.'

'She's done just that. Car One's with her but she's not paying any attention to . . . Shit!'

'What?' Kim's demand is urgent.

'Car One's gone off the air. Hello, four three six, have you visual? You have? Take over pursuit, you are now Car One.' The operator looks at Kim. 'Car One's crashed, into a bus. Four three six has already requested ambulance assistance, they say it looks bad but there's another car close behind them can take control. They had visual but . . .'

Kim's instructions are spare, swift. 'Patch chopper audio direct to Car One plus my interpretation, red Mazda now heading east onto Moor Road, possibly aiming for Central Motorway east.'

'One one six and zero nine seven at Central Motorway exits one and two southbound.'

'Three nine nine at southbound carriageway Cowhill roundabout.'

Kim makes her decision. 'Three nine nine to halt traffic at the roundabout, I want that carriageway empty! Get two more cars there to assist. All southbound entrances to be closed.'

'Northbound too,' I say, 'if she sees southbound's no go she might decide to go on the wrong side.'

Kim looks at me warily but gives the instruction. 'Close northbound at the bridge, take traffic through the city.'

'She'd better get on to that road now,' someone says.

'She's got no choice,' says Kim, 'she's on Moor Road, there are no other turn-offs.'

'Chopper's lost visual, Ma'am.'

'What?' Kim whirls again to the screen. The helicopter's hovering above a tree-lined avenue, the branches forming a tunnel of green hiding the road from view.

'Where's Car One?' Kim asks.

'Just turning on to Moor Road now,' says an operator, 'proceeding eastward and .. They have visual. But the red Mazda's stopped. No sign of occupant. No witnesses, they say. Nothing. Instructions, Ma'am?'

'What's at the side of Moor Road? Anyone?'

'The moor, allotments, a park, playground.'

'Damn, too many places to hide. Okay, listen people. I want the blocks lifted, I want officers on site. Tell Car One I want them standing on the roof to see if they can see her. Sergeant, you're in charge here, I'm heading for the scene.'

She doesn't run, but her walk is surprisingly quick. Her driver and two constables are ahead of us, racing down the corridor, but I can barely keep up with her without breaking into a trot and Norm's left trailing.

'Billy,' she says wearily, 'where do you think you're going?'

340

'With you. You invited me, said I could be in at the kill.'

'The finish, I said. You'll know more about what's going on if you stay here.'

'Why are you going, then?'

'Because I want to be there when we find her. But you've got too much at stake, I don't want you hurting her. I don't want her hurting you.'

'Oh, come on Kim! What do you think I'm going to do?'

'I don't know, which is why you're staying here. Understood?'

I stop without warning, Norm bumps into me. 'And thank you for your invaluable help!' I shout after her.

'Now what?' asks Norm, breathing heavily. I say nothing, tramp back along the corridor to the control room. He follows me wearily, resignedly.

The sergeant looks up as I go back into the room, but his gaze soon returns to his monitors. A glance shows traffic jams on most roads.

'Any news?' I ask.

He shakes his head. 'She's disappeared. No trace. Thing is, the allotments there back straight onto Felton Road, and that has dozens of other roads and lanes leading off it. Could be she's slipped into someone's backyard. She might be hiding in a garden shed, an outhouse, a coal-house.'

'She could have nicked another car,' says Norm, 'she could be across the river by now and no one knows.'

'I don't think so,' I say. 'She's stooged around for ages, then she seemed to be going somewhere specific. She abandoned the car exactly where she couldn't be seen. So why?'

'Perhaps she phoned someone, had a car waiting.'

The sergeant shakes his head. 'We were monitoring her calls, she didn't do anything like that. I think she panicked. Took opportunities when they arose, no planning, no thinking ahead.' He looks at me, waits for my comment.

'Perhaps. But if anyone's cold blooded enough to think clearly in the middle of chaos, she's the person. I don't know the answer, I just don't know.'

After ten minutes I've had enough of waiting. I can't find a comfortable way to ease the pain in my ribs, sitting or standing, and there's very little happening. I nod to Norm, he seems as pleased as I do to be leaving.

'To tell the truth, boss, all these uniforms make me nervous. They're all right in ones and twos, but being stuck in a room full of them is too much. They're so young, so . . .'

'Sincere?' I suggest.

'Shiny,' he counters. 'I get dazzled by their boots and their buttons. Feel as if they might bring on a migraine. You all right?

'No, Norm, I think I'll have to see a doctor. The pain's getting worse.' We're in the car-park, I find I have to lean against a wall for relief.

'How 'bout casualty at the Infirmary? They could x-ray you there . . .'

I don't hear the rest of Norm's wisdom. I feel as if I'm going to faint, but it's not because of any pain I'm suffering. It's a sudden awareness of something I've missed, something I should have known, something triggered by a single word. It's a mistake I've made, a mistake which could cost a life. I've made mistakes before; lives may have been lost because of them. But if so – and there's no way of knowing for certain, no way of winding back time to alter an action or a decision to see what changes might arise – then the lives have belonged to ciphers, nameless people unknown to me as individuals. But this time, if I'm right, I certainly know who's going to be hurt, and why.

'Norm?'

'Yes, boss?' He looks worried. 'Shit, boss, you look ill. Do you want me to find you a seat? What should I do?'

'Is the Infirmary close to Moor Road, where Alice Palmer left her car?'

'It's not close to the main entrance, not by road. The one-way system's hectic round there, you have to go all the way round the houses. But I think there's a back gate, for pedestrians, quite close to . . . You don't think . . .?'

'I know. Alice Palmer's in the Infirmary. Come on, let's get to the car, we can use the car-phone to warn them, to contact Kim as well.'

We run for the car, for once Norm makes it before me. By the time I'm in the passenger seat the engine's on and the Volvo's crawling forwards. I grab for the phone, dial the police station number.

'Front gate?' asks Norm.

'Accident and Emergency. That's where Jenny'll be. That's where Alice Palmer'll be heading. Why the fuck won't they answer this bloody phone? Hello? Hello, I need the operations room, sergeant in charge. My name's Oliphant, Billy Oliphant.' There's a pause, the music I'm forced to listen to fades in and out as Norm weaves through the traffic.

'Reception in town's never good,' he says. I hear a faint voice on the other end of the line.

'Shut up and listen!' I say, as clearly as I can. 'Alice Palmer's last words were that she was going to hurt me as much as she could. She abandoned her car near the back door of the Infirmary. My . . . my girlfriend, Doctor Jenny Moss, is working there in Accident and Emergency. I believe Alice Palmer intends injuring her, perhaps even killing her. Please send armed officers to assist. Do you copy?'

There's a crackling hiss but no voice at all.

'Norm, how do I find the Infirmary number?'

'Enquiries, but if you've lost the police you won't be able to get anyone, they all go through the same network.'

'Fuck!'

'We'll be there in a minute, boss, don't worry. Hold on!'

He avoids a queue of traffic by sliding round a small roundabout the wrong way, heaves the car over a central kerb and screeches round a corner.

'Glad it's a bleedin' Volvo,' he says.

We're running parallel with the Infirmary now, Casualty's inside the main gate. I don't know how the

Volvo makes the final turn, but Norm's still in control as we skid to a halt in a space reserved for ambulances.

'Try the phone again,' I yell as I race into the building, 'if you can't get through come inside and use one.'

The automatic doors open too slowly for me, I have to break my step before I can squeeze through. A male nurse bristles towards me, he's obviously seen the mode of my arrival.

'I'm Detective Inspector Oliphant,' I say, I flash him an illegal photocopy of my old warrant card, 'I'm looking for Doctor Jenny Moss, I suspect someone is in the premises with the intention of causing her harm. Where is she?'

I'm leaning forward because of the pain in my side, in my chest, I feel sick, my clothes are dishevelled, I look more like a patient than a policeman. But the desperation in my voice gets through to him.

'Consulting room twelve,' he says. 'She's seeing a suspected heroin overdose. Straight down the corridor on the right, I'd better come with you.'

A patient with a suspected overdose? It can only be her, it can only be Alice Palmer.

'No,' I hiss at him, 'it might be dangerous. Ring the police, tell them what's happening. Make sure no one else comes down the corridor until the police get here. Okay?'

'Okay.' He's frightened, that's good, he'll do as he's told. I'm frightened too. I lurch down the long passageway to room 12, trying to think of what to do next. Should I look for a disguise, search for a weapon, burst in and hope that the element of surprise will carry me through. What if it's not Alice Palmer? It has to be! I pause outside the door. Alice had no gun. The only weapon she'll have been able to find in a hospital is a knife, a blade of some kind. If she's in there, if she's holding Jenny captive, then the blade will probably be at Jenny's neck. Me bursting in might just cause the injury I want to prevent. I step forward, knock on the door.

'Doctor Moss,' I call, trying to disguise my voice,' I need to show you some x-rays.'

'I'm busy,' she answers, it's definitely her voice, 'I'll see them later.'

'But they're urgent,' I say, 'we need your opinion straightaway.'

There's a slight pause but no noise from within. Then Jenny speaks again. 'Come in.'

I open the door slowly. I see Jenny sitting behind a desk, its wooden front preventing me seeing any of her below the waist, I lift my fingers to my lips when she recognises me. She gestures downwards with her eyes. Someone's hiding at her feet. I look around the rest of the room, there's an examination couch and on it a figure I recognise, seemingly unconscious, dirty red hat still crammed on his head.

'I didn't know we had Joe Steadman back with us,' I say. 'Is he all right?'

'Unconscious,' Jenny answers, 'life signs seem okay. He's been lucky this time. Now then, what about these x-rays?'

I place my hand on the desk. Jenny slides her own across, trying to mimic the necessary sounds, touches my hand and squeezes. While she's doing so I do my own miming act. I point an imaginary knife at her.

'Yes,' she says, 'surgery looks imminent.'

'They'll want you to give a hand,' I say. 'How long will you be?' While I'm talking I point at the curtains gathered at one end of Joe's couch, then at myself.

'I'll be as quick as I can,' she replies, nods.

'I'll take the x-rays, then.' I make suitable shuffling, scratching noises. 'Poor Joe, he doesn't look very comfortable. He gets acute photophobia when he odees, I'll just close these curtains, shut off a little of the light.' I draw the curtains around the couch, at the same time shove Joe's feet away from the edge.

'Must go,' I say, 'don't worry about the surgery, I'll sort things out for you.' I open the door. It's self-closing, I slide on to the couch so my feet won't show below the curtain, by the time the catch clicks I'm in position. I hear Jenny's chair being pushed back.

'About *time*, my dear, I was getting a little *stiff* down there.' It's Alice Palmer's voice. 'Now stand up slowly, *very* slowly. I'm a little nervous, I'd *hate* to hurt you by accident.'

'But you wouldn't mind doing it by design?'

'Yes, that's about it. *All* actions should be deliberate. Carefully thought out. Premeditated. Not that these are all *synonyms*, of course, I point that out to you, an intelligent person, in the expectation that you'll realise how *serious* I am in my intention to kill you. But it *must* be in my own way. In my own time.'

'And how do you intend doing this?'

'Ah, calmness in the face of adversity, I *do* admire that. Such a *pity* you had to become involved with that Oliphant fellow. I'm afraid I said some rather unpleasant things about you – to him, that is – regarding the colour of your skin. That was before I met you, of course. Now I feel I know you, I realise how fortunate he was to have associated with you. But he has done me a *great* wrong, and in his absence I'm afraid your death is the *only* thing which will compensate me for my mental, physical and financial suffering.'

'You'll be caught.'

'Probably. I'd put my chances of escape at less than ten per cent. But killing you won't *alter* those chances, and I've already murdered my *brother*. What's an extra dead body? *Now* then, stand please. Put your hands on your head. I want you to go to the cupboard where the *bandages* are kept and bring me several of various sizes. I'll be *right* behind you, this rather unpleasant little scalpel will be resting snug at your side. *Don't* do anything silly. Very well, off we go.'

I hear two sets of footsteps, a cupboard door opening and closing. The cupboard's on the far side of the room, if it had been closer I would have made my move. But I daren't even consider it while the knife is poised over Jenny's flesh. The footsteps go back to the desk.

'Please, sit down again. Now then, I want you to tie your *ankles* to the *legs* of the chair with the *bandages*. Nice and tight, please. *That's* right, keep going.'

'Billy will come after you.' Jenny's voice doesn't show any fear.

'He may try. He'll fail. You see, my dear, he doesn't have the *intellect*. He's a *struggler*, he's had a little luck of late, but more than his fair share. And while I'll admit the odds are *against* me, his part in bringing me to justice will be negligible, I assure you. All done? Good, now see if you can do the same to your *left* arm using only your *right* hand. Just wind the bandage round, I'll tie the knots.'

'You're mad.'

'Mad? Is that your clinical opinion? Would you care to be more precise?'

Jenny's playing for time. I ease myself backwards, press my back against the wall, bring my legs up and climb painfully to my feet. I need to see what's happening, and the place I'm least likely to be seen is at the top of the curtain.

'Do *you* think you're mad?' Jenny asks.

'I've never felt more sane in my life. But the question is certainly interesting. You ask me, whom you suspect of being *psychotic*, if I consider myself *mad*. If I say yes, then I'm mad but at least I'm not psychotic because I have *insight* into my madness. But if I say no then I have no insight and am therefore psychotic. *Either* way your diagnosis of insanity is self-fulfilling. Congratulations, Doctor. You would have had a good career in psychiatry ahead of you. Now keep still while I fasten your *other* arm.'

'You're suffering from a psychosis. Does schizophrenia run in your family?'

'Not any more. Now a gag I think, keep your head still.'

I peer over the top of the curtain. From that viewpoint I watch Alice Palmer wind a bandage round Jenny's head at

347

the level of her mouth. Jenny's trying not to look at the curtain, but her eyes can't help themselves. I catch them in mine, smile to reassure her. Then I wait again. From below me Joe Steadman begins to snore.

'It *sounds* as if your patient won't drown in his own vomit after all,' Alice Palmer says. 'But I fear we may be *interrupted* if I don't begin shortly. Would you like me to tell you what I intend doing? You have no *choice* in the matter, of course, part of this whole spectacle is informing you how you'll die. I *did* consider evisceration, but it would have been *entirely* too messy. A bilateral mastectomy would have been interesting had I been able to see your lover's reaction when he saw your body, but this poor little knife isn't really suitable for *that* type of job. That leaves only one option. I shall cut your throat. Death will come quickly, I believe that you will suffer little pain. That is good, the *real* pain will be borne by Mr Oliphant.'

She moves from behind Jenny's chair, stands in front of her. If I'd been taller, stronger, fitter, if my ribs hadn't hurt so much, then I might have been able to leap the space between us, pin her to the floor. I might even, with a little luck, have managed to break her neck as we fell. But I know the distance is too great, and the moment is gone anyway, she moves back again to stand behind Jenny's chair.

'It *has* been pleasant meeting you, Miss Moss. I'm *so* sorry it had to end this way.' Her knife is poised at Jenny's neck. I can't risk delaying any longer.

'Excuse me,' I say, 'don't you think we should talk this matter through first?' Alice Palmer starts, looks up. My arms are already raised to show I'm not carrying a weapon. She crouches down behind Jenny, I'm sure I can see a small gash of blood where her blade has nicked Jenny's skin. Neither of us says a word. I suspect that if I move the scalpel will move faster, but I don't know how long I can remain balanced on the couch, hands above my head. Jenny's eyes are tightly closed.

'I'm here if you want me,' I say, 'let Jenny go. You've

no quarrel with her.' I keep my voice low and slow, conciliatory. 'I won't fight, I won't argue. Just say what you want, Alice, tell me what you want.'

Fear leaves her as she realises she's still controlling matters. Her right hand, her scalpel hand, relaxes a little. Jenny opens her eyes.

'If I don't get down soon I'm going to fall down,' I say. I'm giving her back responsibility, authority. I'm stretching time.

'Keep *one* hand above your head,' orders Alice Palmer, 'open the curtain.'

I do as she says, I can feel my thighs trembling with the effort of standing in a permanent crouch.

'Now get down, *slowly*. Lie on the floor, face down.'

I continue my descent, spreadeagle myself on the floor. I have no plan of action, all I want is for the door to burst open and a wonderful, blue-suited policeman with a very large gun to kill Alice Palmer. But for that to happen I have to keep Alice talking, stop her from acting.

'I knew you'd be here,' I say. 'Not bad guessing for someone who has no intellect, eh? But you aren't a very difficult person to outguess, Alice. It's one thing to pick on your brother, someone who depended on you, and then kill him. But I don't roll over and die quite so easily.'

'You will if I *tell* you to, Oliphant.' Her voice is confident again, taunting. There's a snuffling noise from the couch, Joe groans in his sleep. 'Holy, Mary, mother of God,' he intones, but they're words spoken in his own world, not ours. Alice Palmer ignores him.

'You'll do just as I *say*, Oliphant, because if you don't . . .' She smiles at me, for the first time I notice how smooth and even her teeth are. She raises the scalpel to Jenny's neck, then takes it higher. She cuts along her cheek, three times in quick succession. Jenny flinches, whimpers through the bandage.

'Tribal marks, Oliphant.' Blood oozes from the wounds. Alice Palmer bends and laps at the sticky redness.

'Jenny was right when she said you were mad,' I say. 'Everything you've done points to that. It's a slow madness that's been building up over the years, and killing your brother finally tipped the balance. You're over the top now, Alice, you're well and truly on the other side. Bring on the straitjacket and the padded cell, tie the ropes tighter at full moon, you've just qualified to join the ranks of the loonies.'

'Shut up, Oliphant!'

'It's true, you know it, I know it. Where's it to be? Broadmoor? Rampton? Life will be life for you, Alice. And do you think you'll die easily in your cosy bed? Oh no, someone will take a dislike to you. Someone stronger than you, cleverer than you, more devious than you.'

'I told you to shut up!'

'They'll come for you in the night, Alice. They'll find a way to get you. And you'll suffer!' I watch her as well as I can from my prone position, she's taken the scalpel away from Jenny altogether, she's changed her grip, she's holding it like a knife and she's taken a step towards me.

'What's your worst fear, Alice? They'll find it. And they'll boil it up, get rid of the excess till there's nothing left but concentrated fear, and that's when they'll come.' I'm not sure how well I'm getting through to Alice, but Joe seems to be reacting.

'Dear Lord,' he mumbles, 'forgive this sinner, this poor foolish sinner. Forgive me, Lord, forgive me.'

'They won't just make you face your fear, Alice, that won't be enough.'

'Be quiet! I swear I'll kill you!'

'Save me, Lord, save me holy Mary, mother of God!'

'They'll pour your fear into your soul, they'll make you eat it and drink it, they'll make you wash in it, they'll hold you down and inject it into your veins until you become your fear, until it becomes you!' I don't know how long I can keep this litany going, my own grip on sanity, on consciousness, is sliding into grey. But Alice's feet stride

350

towards me. I roll on to my back to see her looming over me, scalpel high above her head. She's staring at my throat.

'Mother of God, mother of God, mother of God . . .'

'I'm going to enjoy this,' she says.

'Mother!' Joe's suddenly awake and sitting up in one movement. From the front I can see his eyes fix on Alice Palmer, his arms stretch wide like a crucifix. 'Mother!' he cries again. She turns to face him, scalpel held in front of her, and I reach up, grab her ankles and pull. I need to knock her to the ground, I have to jack-knife my body to do so and the agony makes me scream. I fight against the pain.

'Mother. Mother, I want my mother!'

Alice Palmer's fallen on to her back, fallen heavily, but she's still holding the scalpel. She waves it at me as I kneel over her but I ignore it; it cuts into my arms as I punch her face for the first time; it drops from her fingers as I hit her again, then despite my strength ebbing from my body I hit her again and again.

'Mummy! You're hurting my mummy!'

Joe pulls me away from Alice Palmer. Her nose is broken, she's unconscious. I sense rather than hear or see the door open.

'Bloody hell, Billy, you taking up surgery as a hobby?'

'Trust the police to be like the cavalry, Kim. Always too late.'

Afterwards

The weather's broken. Thunderstorms and heavy rain have dissipated the heat, washed the dirt and dust away. It's cool, I can feel the clean freshness on my skin as I stand by the window and watch the streetlights reflected in pools of night-black water. Dawn will be here soon, a grey, damp dawn promising Autumn. I'm tired but I can't sleep. My sides hurt where my ribs are slowly repairing themselves, but that's not the problem. There are matters unresolved.

Two weeks' bed-rest and a voluntary news embargo allow me to catch up on my reading. Then Rak's surprise party brings several conclusions but no answers. Norm and Sly (they both lose no opportunity to tell me) have spent the day tidying the house. Rak's tenants have prepared a meal, the guests are waiting as Jenny tows me into the kitchen. Kim Bryden's there, not in the least apologetic, but certainly friendly.

'Unofficially, Billy, the force is pleased with you. Officially you're still a reject and a bloody meddler and you'd better not come within a mile of anything like this again. But off the record . . .' She pecks me on the cheek. 'Off the record, thank you.'

Pamela Arnison's there with her boyfriend, I have to hold her away from me when she tries to envelop me in a hug. She backs down, blushes.

355

'You did it, Mr Billy, the offices aren't going to be sold!'

My face must show how puzzled I am.

'At first I thought it was your letter that did it, but then I didn't see you in the office for a day or two and this strange man came in to collect your post.' She points at Norm. 'I told him what you'd been doing, he told me about the other things you'd been doing. Then he came back later with that lady, the large lady over there.'

'Rak?'

'Yes. She asked me some questions, then she went away. She phoned me the next day. The firm that was going to buy the building was owned by Kingfisher Holdings, and the whole Kingfisher empire's gone down thanks to you.'

Rak divines my puzzlement, waddles over to join us.

'Kingfisher was being propped up by illegal activities. Take away Alice Palmer and the whole thing disintegrated. The police are mopping things up now. *Ladders* is closed, up for sale. You've got a lot to answer for.'

I feel like the hub of a wheel, people keep drifting across to talk to me before drifting away again. Halfway through the evening Sara and Kirsty arrive. They've visited me in hospital, telephoned me at home. I took the opportunity to ask Kirsty about her friend Barbara, the girl in the photographs Graeme Sargent showed me; she denied knowing anyone of that name, that description. I asked Kim Bryden to investigate, she came up with copies of the photographs, identified the girl as a porn actress. The photographs were fakes, set-ups. Sargent really wanted me off his back.

'I'm pleased you came,' I tell Sara.

'Rak persuaded us,' Sara explains, 'I didn't really want to come, I thought it wouldn't be appropriate, but . . .'

'But I said we ought to at least put in an appearance to show how proud we were of you. Well done Dad!' Kirsty's kiss is wet and loud.

Kirsty circles the room, reacquainting herself with old

friends, meeting new. Sara and I exchange stilted small talk until she asks me what I'm doing next.

'I'm thinking of starting up as an investigator,' I explain. 'I've done quite well out of this, made contacts, got publicity. I've a good team to call on when I need them. I might be able to make a go of it.'

'I don't like that idea, Billy. It's just like you being back in the police, but even more dangerous. You were nearly killed this time, you were injured. What happens next time?'

'But I'm good at it, Sara. It's probably the one thing I *am* good at. And, most of the time, I enjoy it. It's not always dangerous. The pay, if I can get the business in, is good. I'd be able to give you and Kirsty some money fairly frequently.'

'She's still hoping we might get back together.'

That's when I notice Jenny watching us from the shadows. She's watching in the same way a zoologist might look at two animals' courting rituals, with interest but divorced from whatever's happening, unable to interfere.

'I haven't been able to give it much further thought,' I admit, 'but . . .'

'I have,' Sara says, 'and I'm not sure . . .'

That's when the doorbell sounds and Kirsty, quick off the mark, runs to answer it. She hurries back.

'It's John come to pick us up,' she says. 'I'm sorry we have to go, Dad, but I'm going to a stopover at a friend's and John's taking Mum out.' They both wait for my reaction.

'I hope you both have a good time,' I say eventually. 'Take care. I'll give a ring.'

'Thank you, Billy.' Sara kisses me gently as she leaves.

I have to find Jenny, she's in the kitchen. The three gashes on her cheek are almost healed but, according to the plastic surgeon who examined them, there'll always be scars. She chooses not to hide them with make-up.

'Made any good decisions tonight?' she asks.

357

'I'll see how it works out, this private investigating business. Otherwise? Decisions seem to come to me ready made up. If you mean Sara, she's just left with her man.'

'And how do you feel about that?'

'Relieved.'

'Because you don't have to decide?'

I reach out and lose my hand in her hair. 'I could lie and say no.'

She puts her own hand on the back of my neck. 'I'd know if you lied.'

I can relive the night in deeds and conversations. I can listen to Jenny's gentle breathing and wonder how long she'll stay, when she'll want to move on. I can watch the rain, hear its movement down slick roofs and resonant gutters, see its staccato dance on pavement and puddle. I can see what I'd once thought of as conclusions are actually no more than the end of beginnings, that there's always more to follow. And I can't sleep. I said it was because there was a matter unresolved, but it's more because I know what resolution is required but can't do anything about it.

Kim triggers the insomnia as she leaves, with words which pre-empt my own.

'There's always someone else willing to break the law,' she says. 'Behind each criminal there's another and another, a new one perhaps, or a cleverer one who's managed to hide his traces. There was Jocko trying to burn the factory, beyond him Ted Samson, beyond him Graeme Sargent who was a front for Alice Palmer. And who was her supplier? Who contacted her in the first place? We'll probably never know. But we'll keep on trying to find out.'

I know.

I can't sleep because I know and I can do nothing about it. I have no proof. But amongst the library books Carrie

Ratcliffe borrowed was a medical encyclopaedia; did it help her diagnose Graeme Sargent's illnesses, Alice Palmer's inherent madness? The Dutch guidebook showed a need for specific knowledge, the Dutch coins in her handbag confirmed regular visits to Holland. Were they to arrange the loading of drugs into windows? There was no doubting Carrie's ambition, what had she once said to me? 'I want to obliterate every bastard who's ever tried to hold me back. I want them dead by the side of the road.' I can recall her voice that last time she called me, not to warn me, but to hint at her triumph. She was getting out. She'd survive.

There's no case to be made against her, nothing definite to show Kim Bryden. All I have is a handful of coincidences. For instance, when Samson and I were fighting, when I suggested he was a homosexual who'd had sex with Graeme Sargent, he told me how wrong I was. The aftershave which had triggered my remark, its feminine smell which had seemed familiar – it was the same perfume Carrie used. Was Ted Samson another of her lovers? Is that why he sneered at the implication that he was gay?

The only person who might be able to incriminate Carrie is Alice Palmer, and she's talking to no one, not to the police, to her husband, to her lawyer or to her psychiatrist. That's why I haven't mentioned my suspicions to anyone. There's no evidence.

My clothes are folded neatly over the back of the chair. I pick them up and place them on the dressing table. I take my shirt and fold it arm to arm, lie it down; I hang my trousers so the creases are just so; I rearrange my shoes so they're central on the floor beneath the chair; then I stand back. There's something wrong, I'm not sure what.

I pick them up again . . .

Dirty Money
Barry Troy

High finance, low morals...

When Paddy Brett is found murdered in Bullock Harbour, Dublin, he leaves behind a widow, two children and a sizeable fortune. If they can find it... For Paddy was one of the slickest financial operators in Ireland, with an outstanding – if not wholly legal – ability to hide money where the taxman wouldn't know about it.

Dublin inventor Johnny Constantine can't believe his childhood friend is dead or that he has been left in charge of Paddy's complex finances. He soon learns that the boy he once knew had become corrupt and amoral, had an unhealthy interest in teenage girls and that even the inheritance he left his family is far from above board, hidden in an illegal tax shelter.

He also realises several others are aware of Paddy's financial activities: his desperate family, his crooked colleagues, and members of Dublin's underworld plus their East-European affiliates. All of whom had a reason for wanting him dead...

Body of a Girl
Leah Stewart

In Memphis, where the heat clings like a second skin, Olivia Dale's job as a crime reporter is at once surreal – stepping in and out of strangers' lives with her notebook – and all too real. But her latest murder investigation has struck a little too close to home.

As she looks down on the twisted body of a young woman who has been kidnapped and gruesomely killed, she realises how easily it could have been her. Olivia even looks a little like Allison Avery. Chasing a lead story, she finds herself drawn deep in to the secrets of Allison's life – and tempted by her own dark side...

Hypnotic and chillingly realistic, Leah Stewart's psychological thriller marks a taut and compelling crime debut.

'It's hard to believe that this is a first novel; harder still to believe that Leah Stewart is only twenty-five-years old. A smart sexy literary page-turner...The secret at its heart will astonish you'

A. Manette Ansay,
author of *Midnight Champagne* and *Vinegar Hill*

A SELECTION OF NOVELS AVAILABLE
FROM JUDY PIATKUS (PUBLISHERS) LIMITEI

THE PRICES SHOWN BELOW WERE CORRECT AT THE TIME OF GOING T₀
PRESS. HOWEVER JUDY PIATKUS (PUBLISHERS) LIMITED RESERVE TH
RIGHT TO SHOW NEW RETAIL PRICES ON COVERS WHICH MAY DIFFE
FROM THOSE PREVIOUSLY ADVERTISED IN THE TEXT OR ELSEWHERE.

☐ 0 7499 3230 9	**Dirty Money**	*Barry Troy*	£5.9
☐ 0 7499 3223 6	**Body of a Girl**	*Leah Stewart*	£6.9
☐ 0 7499 3225 2	**Special Circumstances**	*Sheldon Siegel*	£5.9
☐ 0 7499 3211 2	**A Study in Death**	*Iain McDowall*	£5.9
☐ 0 7499 3210 4	**Moscow Nights**	*Ellen Crosby*	£5.9
☐ 0 7499 3106 X	**The Merchant's House**	*Kate Ellis*	£5.9
☐ 0 7499 3234 1	**The Confession**	*Janet Bettle*	£5.9
☐ 0 7499 3231 7	**Grave Concerns**	*Rebecca Tope*	£5.9

All Piatkus titles are available by post from:

Bookpost PLC, P.O. Box 29, Douglas, Isle of Man IM99 1BQ

Credit cards accepted. Please telephone 01624 836000,
fax 01624 837033, Internet http://www.bookpost.co.uk
Or e-mail: bookshop@enterprise.net for details.

Free postage and packing in the UK. Overseas customers: allow
£1 per book (paperbacks) and £3 per book (hardbacks).